PRAISE FOR

"One of the genre's finest talents..."
—Melinda Helfer, *Romantic Times Magazine*

"Ms. Potter has the unique gift of homing into our
deepest emotions, bringing reality, hope and the
belief that love can heal all wounds in our lives.
You will believe good always triumphs..."
—*Romantic Times Magazine*

PRAISE FOR
CHASE THE THUNDER:

"Patricia Potter uses every skill to
transport readers not only into the era,
but also into the hearts and minds of her complex
characters.... Even stronger, however, are
Ms. Potter's messages about how love can give the
most hardened man a new lease on life, and that
trust and honor are important to any relationship."
—*Romantic Times Magazine*

PATRICIA POTTER

has become one of the most highly praised writers of historical romance since her impressive debut in 1988, when she won the Georgia Romance Writers of America's Maggie Award, and a Reviewers' Choice Award from *Romantic Times Magazine* for her first novel. She has received the *Romantic Times Magazine* Career Achievement Award for Storyteller of the Year for 1992, and its Career Achievement Award for Western Historical Romance in 1995. In 1996, she was nominated for a Reviewers' Choice Award for best British Isles Romance. Ms. Potter has been a Romance Writers of America RITA finalist three times, and has received a total of three Maggie Awards. Prior to writing full-time, she worked as a newspaper reporter in Atlanta. She has served as president of Georgia Romance Writers, and currently is a member of the national board of Romance Writers of America.

PATRICIA POTTER

Chase the Wind

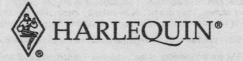

HARLEQUIN®

TORONTO • NEW YORK • LONDON
AMSTERDAM • PARIS • SYDNEY • HAMBURG
STOCKHOLM • ATHENS • TOKYO • MILAN • MADRID
PRAGUE • WARSAW • BUDAPEST • AUCKLAND

HARLEQUIN BOOKS

by Request—CHASE THE WIND

Copyright © 2000 by Harlequin Books S.A.

ISBN 0-373-21705-6

The publisher acknowledges the copyright holder
of the individual works as follows:

CHASE THE THUNDER
Copyright © 1989 by Patricia Potter

AGAINST THE WIND
Copyright © 1993 by Patricia Potter

CONTENTS

WANTED:

The conclusion to an unforgettable family saga,
created by unforgettable author
Patricia Potter.

You first met Sean Mallory in
Between the Thunder,
part of the two-in-one collection
THE SOLDIER AND THE REBEL,
on sale in November 1999.
In that story,
Ryan tried to teach her brother Sean to trust...
and forgive.

In *Chase the Thunder*,
another woman, Casey Saunders,
tries to teach the Rebel to love....

Chase the Thunder

To Tracy,
A wonderful editor and a great friend.

Prologue

South Texas, 1867

Sean Mallory stood on a bluff far away from the other mourners and looked down on the burying ground. The amber in his brown eyes burned like golden fire.

It was his fault!

All of it.

As he watched, six men gently lowered the wooden casket into the ground with ropes. When they were done, his sister approached the grave and threw one of her carefully nurtured roses onto the pine lid. He met her look as she searched him out. It begged him to join her, but he could not.

His guilt and pain were too deep to share.

There had been three other burials today. And he felt responsible for them all. While he regretted the deaths of the other men, none racked his soul as that of Jimmy Carne. Friend and comrade through four years of war and partner for two long trail drives. Now dead by the hand of a maddened butcher whom Sean had once had the chance to kill. And hadn't.

It had been a fatal mistake, but one he would remedy. Until he did, everyone he valued was in danger.

The tall, wiry Texan looked up at the pristine blue sky. As his golden bronze hair ruffled in the hot wind, he fingered his gun belt. After the war, he had thought he would never use his gun again...not against another man, but Wilson had forced his hand. He didn't know whether it was vengeance or necessity that drove him. Whatever it was, he would find Bob Wilson. He would find him...and kill him...and heaven help anyone who got in his way.

Chapter One

Central Texas, Summer, 1867

Eavesdropping was not a very honorable thing to do.

Casey Saunders knew that. But she also knew it was the best way to get information no one wanted her to have.

She ran a dusty, impatient hand through her short hair. It had been a long, hot ride, and she had arrived home to find the door to the parlor closed. It was seldom closed unless there was a discussion going on inside that her father didn't want her to overhear.

Which meant that she had better.

Especially when an all too familiar name was being bantered about. Hers.

"I don't care if Casey's the best shot in town," said one of the voices. "Two Springs would be the laughingstock of Texas."

"I won't accept anyone else," came Sheriff Ray Saunders's angry reply. "And you know I need a deputy for the next couple of weeks...at least until my arm is better."

"There're a dozen young men in town eager..."

"None of them have Casey's sense...or talent with a gun."

"Now, Ray, be sensible. Casey's just too damned small to be taken seriously. She'd be more trouble than help."

"What about last week when we took those cattle rustlers? Couldn't have done it without Casey, and you damn well know it. I would be dead if it hadn't been for her shooting. I *trust* Casey, and I need that more than anything else."

"Damn it, I don't care if you did raise her like a boy. She's still just a girl. Whoever heard of a girl deputy?"

"If you don't want her, you don't want me," Ray Saunders replied. "She's as good as any man. I trained her myself."

"It's unnatural, that's what it is," the disembodied voice countered, and Casey's rage started to boil. She had lived with that attitude all her life. Everyone wanted to change her. Even her father had molded her in his own image. As much as possible, anyway.

Casey leaned against the door, feeling all the old frustration that no one would let her be. Every old biddy in town had tried to take her under their wing at one time or another, only to find it a challenge of impossible proportions. Somehow, an afternoon tea always led to a wrestling match with one of the family sons, or a Sunday picnic to a horse race or shooting match. Once, when her father was out chasing an outlaw and she was temporarily imprisoned in the mayor's home, the mayor's wife had taken away her britches and shirt, leaving her with no option but a hand-me-down dress. It had taken Casey only thirty minutes in the stable to soil the garment beyond redemption. The mayor's wife had uttered an unladylike oath, and surrendered. Which had suited Casey just fine. She was used to doing what she wanted, when she wanted and how she wanted.

Casey took great pride in her ability to outride, outshoot and outfight any young buck in town. There had been any number of contests to prove it, but for Casey, there was only one person in the world to please. That was her father, and she knew she pleased him well. He had wanted a boy, and she had done her level best to give him the finest possible substitute. Sometimes they both forgot she was anything else.

It angered her that no one would take her for what she was, but only for what they thought she should be—a prancing, useless female who thought about nothing but silly dresses. Why would anyone want to wear a dress and, even worse, stays when they could have the freedom of baggy trousers? It was certainly beyond her understanding.

She heard her father's roar in answer to the mayor's last comment. "Unnatural, is it? At least Casey has the sense to take care of herself, not like some of the..."

There was a strained silence from inside the parlor. The mayor's daughter had recently been married off at a shotgun wedding to a no-good drifter, after being caught in a compromising embrace in the town stable. It was not considered good manners, or wise, to remind Mayor Abel Caruthers of the catastrophe.

Her father switched to another tack. "If you won't let Casey fill in for me until this damned gun wound is better, I quit."

"Now, Ray, don't be hasty." Casey could hear the sudden caution in the mayor's voice. She knew that despite some personal differences, the mayor held a deep respect for the sheriff's ability to keep the town clean...without infecting it himself as so many lawmen did. There was a fine line between protecting a town and controlling it, and the mayor was smart enough to know the difference. Too many towns had been taken over by lawmen who were no better than the criminals they were hired to eliminate.

"It's settled, then," her father said. "Casey will wear the badge until I'm well, then she becomes my deputy."

"Consider Casey," the mayor pleaded in one last attempt to change Saunders' mind. "She should be thinking about a husband and home...how old is she now...? Nineteen?"

"Near enough," Saunders said, "but she has no interest in such things, and I'm not going to force her."

"Force her, hell. You've done your damnedest to keep her from it. Because of your own bitterness. It isn't fair to her."

"That's none of your business, Abel. You want me for sheriff or not?"

Casey recognized the tension in her father's voice, and her own fists knotted. He had never talked to Casey about her mother, had, in fact, left the room whenever she had asked questions.

But she had learned, by eavesdropping, of the woman who had deserted both of them so many years ago. And she knew how deep her father's hurt had been, and how great his rage. He was determined his daughter would never be a simpering, betraying temptress like her mother.

He had even altered Casey's name. Her mother had insisted upon Cassandra. But after she'd left child and husband to go off with an actor from a traveling troupe, her father had shortened it to Casey.

Casey had not known anything about her mother until she was thirteen and an old friend of her father's showed up one day. Puzzled at her father's cool reception of his guest, Casey had listened at the closed door while the stranger told Ray Saunders his wife was dead.

"Good" had been her father's terse response.

Sometimes eavesdropping hurt.

It hurt now, too, to think she was being rejected simply because she had been born female. It was just so unfair.

And it meant as much to her father as it did to her for the two of them to stand together. Just as a son would.

Sheriff Saunders won the argument. Just as Casey had suspected, Two Springs wouldn't risk losing him.

Casey wore the badge with quiet pride. She had worked hard to develop the skills needed for the job, and she was good at it. And in the week following the confrontation in the parlor, everything had gone smoothly.

The townspeople were not about to test Casey. They considered her somewhat of an oddity, but they respected her abilities and knew she would tolerate nonsense no better than her father. They also knew they would have to answer to him if they openly flouted her, and kept their snickers to themselves.

Two Springs, Texas, had the enviable reputation of being a law-abiding town with a strong sheriff. With so many other towns lacking such refinement, most outlaws just took their business and persons elsewhere. There was no sense asking for trouble. And Casey didn't expect any. There was a rumor that the notorious Wilson gang was heading their way, but she thought Two Springs would be spared the gang's attention. There was little here worth the grief outlaws would find.

Still, she was cautious and, at her father's suggestion, posted guards on both sides of town. Casey knew he was chafing at his own helplessness. His gun arm had been shot during a battle with some unwary rustlers, and it was slow in healing. Even then, he had wanted to continue sheriffing until infection set in and the doctor had ordered him to bed. Only the threat of amputation had convinced the sheriff to rest and take the prescribed laudanum.

Casey rubbed her hand against her denim trousers and held it up to shade her eyes in the bright sunlight. It was hot as hellfire...and dry. Even the slightest breeze was enough to stir the dust in the street into tiny whirlwinds, and it had settled over everything. Devil's chariots, she used to call them when she was a kid.

She looked for signs of life, but the town was quiet. Everyone seemed to be escaping from the late afternoon's burning heat. There were some horses in front of the town's biggest saloon, and a buggy in front of the general store, but that was it. Even the children had disappeared.

Two Springs. The name had always made her laugh. There weren't any springs, only dry gray plains. The founding fathers had had a strange sense of humor or been out in the sun too long. Or were just so dumb they couldn't tell springs from dust.

The town survived on deep wells that also served the ranches stretched out over the surrounding barren country in obstinate challenge to the unwelcoming nature of the land.

Casey knew little else but Two Springs and the outlying area. She had been born in a rip-roaring Kansas town, where her father had been a lawman. But after her mother had disappeared, they had moved to Texas, to a place where the citizens didn't know or care about one another's past.

But Two Springs had grown, and was growing still. It had escaped much of the pain of the war itself and even the reconstruction troubles. Its people minded their own business. And while they cussed the Yankees, they had, for the most part, left the fighting to others. Fighting the land was enough for them.

The town now had a small church, which also served as a school, four stores, a blacksmith shop, a gunsmith, two saloons that catered to the ranchers and their cowboys, a combination land office and bank, a hotel, which housed several ladies of dubious virtue, and a two-cell jail. It was a flourishing little town, being the only trade center in the area, and it suited Casey well enough, although at times she hungered to see more. Perhaps even the oceans she had read about. Now *that* would be something! All that water. It was hard to imagine in her mind. Maybe some day...

She looked in Smith's General Store and saw herself reflected in the glass, dusty that it was. She gave a grunt of dissatisfaction. No wonder no one thought of her as a lawman, even with the gun belt buckled around her slim hips. She was too thin...and too small, even with the boots. A dusty broad hat was clamped down on her short hair, which was much too curly for her taste. Even oil didn't help much. It still swirled around in rebellious curls. Her face was dominated by eyes that she feared often revealed more than she wanted, though she struggled to keep them impassive. She knew how important that was. Especially in a card game or a gunfight.

"You can't let the other man know when you're going to make a move," her father always cautioned. "Don't blink. Don't allow the slightest hint of what you are going to do."

Yet her eyes were her most striking feature. They were a brilliant green and sparkled like emeralds when she laughed or raged. She had been schooling herself to turn her emotions inward since she was a child. Her father had never approved of tears, or displays of temper, or even affection. He had never overtly touched her, though she knew he loved her in his own way, and she tried constantly to live up to his standards.

Only rarely did she wonder if she was missing anything. There had been no cowboy or young man in town, who had turned her "on fire" as they said in the dime novels she was sometimes able to find. Casey had reached the conclusion that it was all make-believe at best, and lies at worst. She had never been kissed, or held, or courted. Men didn't court young ladies who could lay them low or beat them at a turkey shoot.

But she could ride against the sunset, and make as good a camp as any man, better even; unlike most men, she was a good cook. She knew the joy of complete communion with her horse, and the satisfaction of providing for herself in the wilderness. She could join the wind and outrace the thunder. She didn't need anything else.

The thud of racing hoofs against the dry earth brought Casey back from her daydreaming.

"Casey..." the rider managed to get out as he threw himself down from his horse whose sides were heaving from the wild ride. "Wilson...the Wilson gang...just minutes behind me...the sheriff...?"

Casey went completely still. Then she was all action. "Go round up any man you can find, Dan."

"Your pa...?"

"Still real sick..."

"God, Casey, we need him. Ain't nobody going to take on Wilson without him. Nothin' 'gainst you, but..."

"They're going to have to," Casey said, "unless they want to lose everything."

Dan Adams headed to the town's largest saloon while Casey ran to the bank. In seconds, she had the petrified clerk taking money from the safe.

"Leave a little, just enough so they won't suspect anything," Casey said. "Then take the rest to the church and hide it in the cellar. And don't come back," Casey ordered.

"But your pa?"

"Hellfire, do as I say," Casey ordered. By now, her eyes were glittering with anger that anyone would try to attack the town she was charged with guarding.

Danny met her back out on the street. "They won't come, Casey. Not without your pa..."

Casey ran to the small house she shared with her father. She didn't have time to convince anyone. If her father was awake...perhaps he could. She didn't see any other choice. This was no time to stand on pride.

It was as if the senior Saunders had sensed something was wrong. By the time she came running through the front door, he was at the head of the stairs, his gun belt in hand, his face still flushed with fever. "What is it?" he asked, slowly making his way down the steps.

"The Wilson gang. They're heading this way."

"How far away?"

"Dan Adams says minutes."

"Damn, why couldn't they wait a few more weeks?"

Casey had no answer. She felt as if she was failing him, failing her town.

"Help me with this, Casey," the sheriff said, waving the gun belt in his left hand. His right arm was in a sling.

"But, Pa..."

"Help me, Casey." His tone left her no choice.

She twisted it around his thickening waist, trying first one position, then another to figure out the best way for his left hand to reach the gun. He could shoot with his left. Not well, but at least he could fire.

"What about the men in town?"

Her face was ashamed. "They won't come without you."

"Head on out there, and tell them I'm coming. Get as many as possible positioned in the windows."

"And then I'll come back to stand with you."

Ray Saunders hesitated. He had raised her to this, and now he felt a rising guilt. She looked so small, so slight, like a child carrying a stick gun. He had no right to ask this of her, or even permit it. Her life was just beginning.

Without looking her in the eye, he grunted. "No. You're the best shot we've got. Take the rifle up to the stable loft. You'll have the best view there. And keep out of sight as much as possible."

"But…"

"Do as you're told, Casey. I don't have time to argue with you. You go where you're needed most."

"You can't meet them out here alone."

"I have all of you to back me up. Now git!"

"It's not fair…"

"Casey!"

Casey turned toward the saloon. Now that the men saw Ray Saunders in the street, they were coming to offer their guns. Casey pointed out the most strategic windows and saw that the women and children were herded over to the church. She reluctantly fetched a rifle from her father's office, and made her way over to the stable. Climbing quickly up into the hayloft, she positioned herself carefully in the shadows beyond the wide-open doors at the front of the building.

And waited.

Each second seemed to last a minute, and each minute an hour. The town was ghostly still. She hoped that the outlaw gang had not noticed Dan and was riding in unawares. She had heard rumors about the Wilson gang…that it was ten, then twenty, and lately nearly fifty men. There were only about ten men in town capable of hitting anything more than five feet away from them.

Her father remained in front of the jail. Alone. He was so brave. And he valued his reputation for courage more than anything he possessed. Even herself, she realized with a sickening lurch in her stomach. She should be down there with him. And by damn she would. She started to move when she heard the incoming riders. And then she heard their shouts. There were dozens of them, ballyhooing and firing guns and stirring dust until everything was in confusion.

Casey could barely see, but she sighted her rifle on one of the men in front and held her fire; there had been no order. Then she saw her father step out, and crumple to his knees. She saw a rider pointing a gun at him, and she fired, rejoicing in the jerk of the man's body as he was lifted from the saddle and thrown to the ground by the impact of her shot. And then guns were going off everywhere and bodies were twisting and falling...from the buildings... from the horses. Casey saw her father jerk again, as a bulky man in front sent bullet after bullet into her papa's body. She aimed, but the man's horse moved just as she fired, and she saw his eyes searching for the source of the shot. Despite the distance, she memorized his face and his pale blue eyes, which glittered with blood lust as he pointed out her position. She ducked as bullets thudded into the hay around her. When she looked out again, they apparently thought she'd been hit, for all their attention was now on the bank. They were swarming all over it, and she could hear their curses. Through the haze of smoke and dust, she could see her father moving...just barely. He was trying to reach his gun. The bulky man was aiming again, and she was horrified to see that he was deliberately shooting to torment.

She shot again, and this time the bullet found its mark. The outlaw clasped his arm, and glared up at her, and another rain of bullets peppered the hay. There were still shots coming from the townspeople and she watched several of the outlaws below arguing. Bodies were everywhere. Horses were screaming with pain and confusion. Petrified with horror, Casey watched as some of the outlaws galloped out of town. Only a core remained, the bulky man among them. He was still glaring up at the barn. She saw another outlaw motion urgently to him, and he reluctantly turned his horse away.

Casey couldn't wait any longer. She left her gun and went down the ladder with the agility of a monkey, bursting out of the doors toward her father. She did not see the outlaw leader turn back, nor see the gun pointed at her. She raced over to her father, her momentum carrying her to his side even as a bullet ripped into her leg. She fell, her hands reaching for him, her eyes searching his face for life. But there was none. His eyes were open, but empty.

Disregarding her own pain, she took his hand and clutched it.

"I'll get him for you, Papa. No matter what, I'll get him for you," she whispered.

Suddenly Casey was swamped by a gray tide of pain and carried into a deep, empty void.

Chapter Two

Sean Mallory woke in a sweat. He had been doing that often lately. It had started after the raid on Ben Morgan's ranch.

The nights were haunted by the same scenes...the screaming raiders, the deafening noise of gunfire, his sister's terrified look, the crying of the babies. And finally the dying agony on Jimmy's face.

He would always see Wilson astride his horse, out of range, his face twisted in hate. "I'll be back," he would yell. "When you least expect it, I'll be back. And I'll kill you all. Hear me, Mallory?"

And then the man was gone, and Sean couldn't go after him, not with Jimmy dying in his arms, and other men groaning in pain. He would follow later.

Sometimes the images meshed with older ones from the war. But they all concerned death and the pain of loss. It had been his life for such a damned long time.

He rose and walked to the window, looking out the dirt-crusted glass. Two Springs looked like any other small Texas town. It was quiet now, quiet and still in the first light of dawn, but two weeks ago its streets had been covered with blood. He had a fleeting image of the raw violence that had killed so many men in the now peaceful streets.

Would the killing ever stop? He was beginning to think not, and there was a cold place in a heart that had once been open and optimistic. He had seen too much, had watched friends die, had killed good men himself. He had experienced betrayal, and couldn't quite rid himself of the cynicism born of it.

Although Sean had always naturally attracted people to him, he was now reluctant to trust, to befriend. He knew his smile was often empty, and the apparent warmth in his eyes due more to their strange amber lights than any emotion. If you didn't feel, you couldn't hurt. And he was tired of hurting. God, how many of his men had died during those years of combat.

Hell, no sense thinking about it now. But sleep had gone, and would not be back. Sean picked up the guitar he always carried with him and listlessly picked at the strings. It was the only thing left of his father and during hard times had been his one link to sanity. He had always been able to exorcise his devils with music. But it didn't help. Not now.

A wave of deep loneliness washed over him. When was it he had lost hope for a normal life? For a home, and wife and family? It seemed as if he had always been taking care of other people, never himself, and he was weary of it. He was tired of duty and what it cost.

Catching up with Wilson and killing him would finally bring it to an end. But then what? In the few months before Wilson's raid, he had tried to settle down on his ranch. But he had been restless and lonely, and the obvious happiness of his sister, Ryan, had only increased the feeling of emptiness in his own life. He didn't know whether he would go back...even if he did survive Wilson.

His music grew stronger under his thoughts, and he heard a pounding on the thin wall and a fine string of curses.

"Sorry," he replied, and lay down the guitar. Just because he couldn't sleep didn't mean he had to wake everyone else.

There was no sense in rising yet. Nothing would be open. And who in the hell would answer questions at dawn. But he chafed at waiting.

He had been following Wilson for a month, and it seemed he was always just barely missing him. Then he'd heard about the raid at Two Springs, and that two of Wilson's men had been captured. He hoped to question them and find out where Wilson was heading next.

He'd ridden in late last night and had to rouse both the stableman and the woman at the boardinghouse the man had recommended. He was told then that the two prisoners had been taken to Fort Worth because the sheriff had been killed during the raid. He had decided to stay overnight, get some rest, and obtain as much information as possible about the number and description of Wilson's band.

He had set a mad dog loose, and it was his responsibility to kill him.

He wandered back to the window. The first pale shades of pink lit the sky spreading a false aura of peace across the dry, hot plains. There was some movement in the street now.

He shaved cleanly, careful of the crinkling lines around his eyes. His sister called them laugh lines, but Sean thought they came from squinting against the sun. Besides, he seldom felt like laughter anymore. He dressed quickly, indifferently. Brown shirt open at the neck, brown denim trousers and a dark brown bandanna. He combed the hair that had bleached to a bronze color in the sun wincing when the usual unruly shock fell over his forehead.

The boardinghouse had a small dining room, and Sean was served a breakfast of biscuits and ham and eggs. He was the only guest, and Mrs. Ketchum fussed over him like a hen over her chicks. He had been living on jerky and beans for the last month, and the food was excellent. When he was through, he decided to start his questions.

But when he began, the woman's eyes filled with tears. Her son had been one of those killed during the raid. She was already a widow, and now had no one left.

"Someone has to stop them," she said, tears rolling down her face.

"Is there anything you can tell me?" Sean asked gently.

"I was in the church. But Tom Kelly at the hotel saw everything." She looked at him doubtfully. "Are you going after them?"

Sean merely nodded.

"Alone?"

"They killed a friend of mine," Sean said, and Mrs. Ketchum felt somehow comforted by the promise in his voice.

"Please get them," she said. "Please."

Her guest's smile was gentle, but there was nothing gentle in the steely determination in his eyes. "I will, Mrs. Ketchum. I can promise you that."

Kelly, the desk clerk at the hotel, was full of information and eager to impart it.

"Must of been a hundred of them...riding in like a pack of devils, yelling and hollering..."

A nearby man corrected him. "Weren't no hundred, Kelly. More like fifty."

Kelly swelled with indignation. "There be a hundred if there was one...I know. I was shooting at them...not like some I know who went ahiding." He gave the other man a chiding look.

"I had kids to look after," the man said defensively. "And besides, that was the sheriff's job. God save his soul."

Sean broke in before the argument precluded him. "What happened to the sheriff?"

"Stood in the doorway, he did," the desk clerk said. "Bravest thing I ever saw. But he didn't have no chance...no chance at all. The leader gunned him down like a dog, kept firing bullets into him like he enjoyed it."

"Was the man left-handed?"

"Sure was. Strange thing now you mention it. His right hand seemed all twisted."

"Were there any deputies?"

"Just the sheriff's kid. We kept telling him he needed more help, but he insisted Casey was as good as any man."

"As any man?"

"Casey's a girl...a woman, I guess you could say, though you would never know it the way she dresses. I'll say this, though, she sure can shoot. She got at least two of the outlaws before she was hit."

Sean felt a new stab of guilt. He had let Wilson live when he could have killed him. And now a number of people were paying for his mistake. "Bad?"

"It was touch and go for a while. The shot hit a small artery and she almost bled to death. Did some damage to her leg, but she's healing pretty well. Problem is she's all by herself now and this town don't want a woman sheriff."

"Where is she?"

"Staying here at the hotel. Town's paying for it. She says she's going after the Wilson gang for killing her pa. She'll do it, too. Them two were real close."

"A girl would be no match for Wilson."

"Well, she ain't exactly *any* girl, but you're right. Maybe you can talk her out of it."

"Maybe," Sean said. "I feel like I owe her something, anyway. It's partly my fault Wilson's on the loose."

"When I see her, I'll tell her. Where will you be?"

"Checking around. I'll be in the saloon later."
Kelly nodded.

Casey limped across the hotel room. Her leg was still sore, but she was tolerating the pain better. Thankfully the bullet had only ripped into the flesh and chipped a bone.

It had been two weeks since the raid, two lonely, miserable, frustrating weeks. The townspeople had made it clear that she would not take her father's place, and she hadn't even tried to protest their decision. She had failed. Failed her father and her town. The fact that she had saved the bank's money seemed incidental.

She had even lost the small house where she and her father had lived. It went with the sheriff's job, and a new man was due any day, so she had moved into the hotel until she was well enough to go after Wilson. She had been offered a room at Mrs. Ketchum's boardinghouse, but she wasn't up to all the fussing she would have to endure in return for the favor. She wanted only one thing now... Wilson. She hadn't figured out how she'd find him, but she'd catch up with him and put one bullet after another in him. Just as he did her father. He wouldn't die easily.

Casey counted her assets. She had two horses and her father's life savings. The cash amounted to a little less than fifty dollars, which she had already sewed in various places in her trousers. She didn't trust the hotel, not with doors that didn't lock and the constant procession of cowboys visiting some of her less respectable neighbors.

The townspeople had been kind. Many had offered their own homes to her, but she knew it meant they would expect her to act more like their own ideas of what a girl should be.

She figured to light out tomorrow, or perhaps the day after if her leg continued to ache as it did now. Wouldn't do much good to injure it any more; it would just slow her down later.

The knock on her door came as a surprise. After her repeated refusals of help, she had been pretty much left alone the past few days. That suited her fine. She now felt a surge of resentment at the intrusion. Some interfering neighbor trying to change her mind again, she guessed.

"Who is it," she asked, ready to deny entrance.

"Kelly" came the voice of the hotel clerk. "Some gent's been asking about Wilson downstairs. Thought you might like to know."

The door opened so fast that Tom Kelly blinked.

"Who?" Casey asked.

"Ain't never seen him before. Tall fellow."

"What did he want to know about Wilson for?"

"Ain't the kind of person you ask," Kelly said. "He seemed interested in talking to you."

"Couldn't be one of them?" Casey asked suspiciously.

"Nah. I got the idea he's chasing him."

"Lawman?"

"Didn't say so, and they usually do."

"Where's he now?"

"He said he would be in the saloon. Wanted to know everything that happened. Told him 'bout your pa."

Casey frowned. "Did you tell him anything about me?"

"Just said Ray had a kid who had been deputing for him. That you'd been hurt, too."

Casey closed her eyes. Perhaps this was the answer to her prayers. Perhaps she could tail along.

"What'd you think of him?"

"I wouldn't like him for no enemy," Kelly replied. "He's got hard eyes."

"Thanks," Casey said, and closed the door just as abruptly as she had opened it, leaving the clerk with his mouth opening and closing like a fish.

Casey stood there for a moment. So someone else was

tailing Wilson. They would have a better chance if there were two of them.

But she had no illusions, not after the past few weeks. She had been rejected over and over again. It would take time to prove her worth and in the meantime damn few men would saddle themselves with a woman. Even one who could shoot and ride with the best of them. She doubted whether this man would be any different.

She studied her options. She could pretend to be a man, but that would be impossible when everyone in town knew differently. Or she could put on a dress and try to sweet-talk him into taking her. But she quickly discarded that notion, too. She had no idea how to go about it...even if she'd wanted to. Seeing her grimy reflection in the mirror she gave that idea even less chance than the first.

Which led to the third. Don't give him any choice. She would just follow him and reveal herself when the time was right. Perhaps she could help him out in some way that would make him indebted to her.

The first smile in two weeks touched her lips. That was it.

With energy born of hope and determination, she ignored the pain in her leg and went into action. Stuffing her broad-brimmed hat over her short hair she painfully pulled on her boots and strapped on her gun. She needed to take a look at this stranger before making any final commitment.

It was midday, and the saloon was nearly empty. It wasn't hard to identify the man she sought. He stood at the bar, towering over the others, his hair bronze in the stream of light that shone through the window. Although his back was to her, she saw the easy grace of his stance, the lean muscular strength as he shifted slightly from one foot to the other as if too restless to stand still for long. There was something very sure, very competent in every small movement.

Suddenly hesitant, Casey paused, as if something inside was cautioning her. But she threw it aside and limped up to the bar, keeping her eyes away from the mirror that decorated the wall behind the bar.

The barkeep grinned at her. "Good to see you, Casey. Want a beer?"

At Casey's nod, he quickly drew a glass from the large keg behind him and handed it to her. "Feeling better? We've been missing you."

She smiled at the barkeep, and her piquant face was unexpectedly striking as the smile encompassed the brilliant green eyes. "Thank you, Bert," she said, and saw in the mirror the way the stranger was staring at her.

One of Casey's hands clutched the bar as she studied his face in the mirror. Her knees felt weak and threatened to give way, and not from the wound. He was, Casey noted instantly, the most compellingly handsome man she had ever seen—even through a mirror. His face was lean, but his lips were generous. His chin was strong and determined, and his eyes...

They were almost magnetic. Deep set and framed by thick black lashes, they shone with an amber fire that sparked from deep within. And they were regarding her with a great deal of interest...and, she was bitterly afraid, amusement. Their eyes met in the mirror and suddenly she realized it wasn't amusement but a sort of understanding compassion.

Something strange was happening inside her. One hand clutched the bar a little tighter as the other lifted the glass and she downed the beer, coughing a little as she finished. Red-faced, she nodded to the surprised barkeep for another. She winced as she saw his look. She had never had more than one beer at a time, and she usually nursed that one for an hour or two...."

"Miss Saunders...?"

The deep resonant voice spoke beside her, invading the defenses she was desperately trying to erect against the little flashes of heat streaking painfully through her.

Unwillingly, her face turned toward his, and for a moment she wondered how Tom Kelly could have said the stranger had hard eyes. They were the most beautiful eyes she had ever seen, warm and sympathetic with just a trace of humor. The amber flecks gave them an aura of secrecy, and she imagined how they could flare with anger. His eyes were surrounded by little laugh lines, and now his mouth creased into an easy smile that seemed to constrict some part of her heart.

"I heard about your father...I'm sorry." It seemed strange he knew all about her, and she knew nothing about him. His attitude was even stranger. He didn't seem to look at her as an oddity, as so many men did.

Her throat was dry as she started to speak. "Casey," she said, her voice carrying a mortifying trembling note. "Everyone calls me Casey."

"Casey, then," he agreed, and a dimple flashed in his cheek. "I heard you were wounded, too. Are you all right now?"

She could only nod as she stared up at him. He was at least a foot taller than she. Her eyes came to his chest, just where his shirt opened to his neck. His skin was a smooth bronze color....

Casey chided herself silently. This is ridiculous. But her mouth wouldn't make a sound. She nodded again, her eyes moss green with confusion.

"I'm...I'm fine...."

His smile broadened, the corners of his eyes crinkling. "I feel a little responsible. Is there anything I can do?"

The last comment snapped her back to reality. "Responsible? Why?"

"I had a chance to kill Bob Wilson once, and I didn't

do it. I plan to rectify that error." All humor and concern were gone from his face, and Casey suddenly understood Tom Kelly's words. It was as if another man stood there. His eyes were as hard and cold as stone, and his mouth was a tight, grim line. The relaxed grace was also gone, replaced by a barely contained promise of violence. It was like watching day turn abruptly into night without the soft transition of twilight.

The fluttering within her grew stronger; the inherent violence was even more unnerving than his easy friendliness.

"Who are you?" she whispered.

The smile was back, almost immediately, but some of its ease was gone, as if it were forced. He gave her a small courteous bow with no mockery in it. "My name is Mallory. Sean Mallory. And you didn't answer my question. Is there anything I can do for you? Do you need any money?"

"There is no need."

"But there is. I know what sheriffs make." His eyes softened as he saw a haze fill her eyes. He expected tears, but she seemed to hold them back as if by sheer will. "And, as I said, I feel somewhat responsible."

Casey just stood there, her heart beating harder than it ever had before. "Take me with you," she whispered, unable to tear her eyes from his face. She saw the quick refusal, and her heart seemed to stop movement altogether. "You said..."

"You ask the impossible...you're not much more than a child..." He regretted the words immediately. She looked as if he had just plunged a knife into her. The fine lips trembled and the green eyes turned from soft moss wistfulness to a startling glistening bright green.

"I've been my father's deputy...I can shoot as well as anyone, as well as you, probably, maybe better...and I promised him...I promised him." Her chin lifted with wounded indignation. "I'm not a child. I'm nineteen."

Sean looked at her in disbelief. She looked more like fourteen with her smudged cheeks and an old hat pulled down over half her face. A rough shirt and jacket covered any shapeliness that might be there. But she wore that gun belt as if she knew how to use the Colt in its well-oiled leather holster.

His voice softened once more. This…waif…reminded him of his sister, Ryan. She too had dressed in boy's clothes and ventured into one danger after another. And had done well at it, too, he remembered. She had saved his skin more than once. But Wilson was too smart, too vicious, too cunning not to demand his total attention. He simply could not afford to be responsible for someone else.

"No," he said quietly, and Casey knew his answer was final.

She stared at him with a kind of hopelessness and turned away, limping slightly, but her head and shoulders back with a pride that touched him.

Sean turned back to the barkeep. "Is there anyone to take care of her…that I could leave some money with…?

"Casey? Hell, she can take care of herself…always could. But it's a damn shame the way Ray raised her. She could be right pretty with those eyes and that smile…" He sighed, wiping off Casey's glass without washing it and putting it next to the other empty ones. "But she's right…she can shoot and ride as well as any young buck in town.…"

Sean shoved some bills at him. "Just see that she gets this."

"Sure…but like I said, Casey can take care of herself…"

Sean didn't wait to hear the rest. The girl had disturbed him more than he wanted to admit. If only she had asked for something easy. He kept remembering her expressive eyes. Funny how they dominated his thinking. He tried to recall the rest of her face, but it wouldn't come. Just as well. The last thing he needed was a youngster tagging along. For that's what she was...despite her claim to nineteen years. It was damned impossible.

Best thing he could do now was leave town. He looked west; the sun was setting, spreading a golden shade across the sunbaked plains. Damn. He had spent the day talking to everyone who would talk to him, gathering every description possible.

His eyes narrowed as he watched the fading light. He wouldn't get far tonight, not in country full of prairie dog holes. And he had had too little sleep last night. A bed would feel good again, and he knew his horse could use the additional rest and oats. Maybe he would stay. There was damned little chance he would run into the Saunders girl again.

Casey stared out the hotel window, watching compulsively as the tall, lean figure hesitated outside the saloon before walking over to the stable. He reappeared shortly without his horse. So he would be staying the night again. Good. It would give her leg another day to heal. She studied Mallory as he talked to old Mack, the stable owner, then turned toward one of the saloons. The stranger disappeared into the saloon, and she felt a sickening loss.

Later, she would go down to the hotel kitchen and eat a large bowl of stew. She didn't like the attention she usually stirred in the dining room, especially now. She would turn in early and be up before dawn, watching to see which road Mallory took. She wouldn't be far behind him.

She *would* follow him. She knew deep in her bones he would lead her to Wilson. She wouldn't admit to herself there might be another reason. It was too ridiculous a thought. *She* was not like other girls who dreamed and moaned over men who sought to dominate them.

Casey shivered despite the heat. She didn't understand what was happening to her, but it was more than a little frightening.

She limped over to the mirror and looked at herself critically. The result brought an unfamiliar tear to her eye. She did look like a child. She angrily wiped away the hovering tear. Sean Mallory was just another arrogant man. She didn't need him. Except to find Wilson. *She* didn't need anybody.

It was dawn when Sean rose from a bed at the boardinghouse on the main street. A glance out the window showed a bleak cloud-studded sky. He was already wet from the humidity that hung in the air like some malignant presence. He hoped it would not rain, though he knew it would be only too welcome to the surrounding ranchers.

His mood matched the grayness of the day. His only lead was the two men being held in Fort Worth. He suspected Wilson was licking his wounds someplace north in the canyons, but without any more information he could waste weeks, perhaps even months, in fruitless searching.

Damn, but he wished he had arrived before the outlaws were taken away. He could have questioned them. His lips firmed as he made his decision. He would head for Fort Worth. He paid his bill and saddled his horse, leading the black stallion outside. With only a brief, wary look at the sky, he vaulted into the saddle with ease, and turned north.

Fort Worth. Sean Mallory was going to Fort Worth. Mack was a talkative sort, and Casey had no trouble extracting the information from him. The stranger had purchased a supply of oats and asked the length of the journey to Fort Worth.

Casey saddled her own horse and eyed her father's gelding with sadness. "Sell him," she said finally to Mack.

"Get the best price you can and put the money in the bank for me."

The old man nodded. "Where you going, Casey?"

"Fort Worth. I have business in Fort Worth," she said as she swung awkwardly up into the saddle.

"You sure about this, Casey?" the stableman asked. He had always liked the sheriff's daughter. She treated her horse better than most anyone in town, and he respected that.

She nodded. "Just don't forget about Pa's horse." A slight tightening of her legs pushed the horse into a trot.

Her head and shoulders went back with determination. She would reach Fort Worth before the stranger. She would show him how well she rode, how competently she took to the trail. And then he would have to take her. He would just have to.

Chapter Three

Casey kept her face emotionless but inside she smirked. She smirked at the cards she was holding and she smirked at the fact that she had obviously reached Fort Worth before Sean Mallory.

True, she was exhausted, even after several hours' sleep in the cheapest hotel room she could find, but she had inquired earlier at the town's livery stable and no one of Mallory's description had yet appeared.

She had ridden day and night, stopping only for a hour or two to rest the horse and eating only jerky and hardtack. It had been a miserably hot and tiring journey, but it was worth it.

After a short nap, she changed clothes, binding her breasts first, and trimming her hair. She had often passed for a boy, and she knew she could not enter a Fort Worth saloon as a woman. Even one carrying a gun. She was in no mood to take the abuse and ribbing, if not worse, that would be heaped on her at her entrance.

She had discovered which of the saloons in the raucous area called Hell's Half-Acre attracted most of the action. It would be that one, she figured, that would draw Sean Mallory, as well.

Casey avoided looking at the gallows. She had heard that the two outlaws from Wilson's band had been hanged several days before. There was to be another hanging tomorrow—a gunfighter named Ty Donaldson. Casey had heard of him, everyone in Texas had heard of him, but he had nothing to do with the Wilson bunch, so she didn't give it much thought other than an involuntary shudder as she passed the gallows on her way to the saloon. She had never seen a hanging, never wanted to. There had been men in Two Springs sentenced to death, but her father had always taken them to the state prison for hanging. Hard as he was, he had never wanted anything to do with it.

The saloon was noisy with celebrating cowboys, some of them having come some distance to see the hanging on the morrow. They hadn't cared about the two outlaws, but Donaldson was something different. Donaldson had a reputation.

Casey disregarded the talk, lounging around the various card games until she found one she could join. She had watched for several minutes, and it looked honest, and when one of the players left she immediately took the seat, ignoring the disdainful stares.

"Ain't you a little young, kid," said one of them.

"I got money," Casey said impassively. "Anything else you need to know?"

The man shrugged and two other players eyed each other in speculation. The kid should be easy.

Casey noted the looks and felt a certain satisfaction. She had been playing poker with her father since she was six years old, and had beat him since she was sixteen. He had taught her every trick there was. And, as a sheriff, he knew them all. It had been their principal source of entertainment during the quiet evenings together.

She had her fifty dollars minus the cost of the hotel room and stabling her horse. Prior to leaving the hotel room she had taken twenty from the little pockets she had sewn in both sets of clothes, hiding the remainder in the secret folds. Now she put the twenty on the table, half turned her chair so she could see the saloon entrance, and pulled her hat farther down over her face.

"We playin' or not?" she said, and the dealer started passing the cards.

It was five-card stud, and Casey lost steadily. When she had lost half of her small stake, she pushed her chair back as to leave, remaining reluctantly after much loud convincing. She bet five of her last ten dollars, and won twenty, then ten and won thirty. At the end of thirty minutes, she had one hundred dollars stacked up in front of her, and the previously laughing faces were now sweating.

Casey dealt.

Sean rode slowly into Fort Worth, and his eyes immediately went to the center of town.

There was something inherently ugly about a gallows, and Sean had a decided distaste for hanging, having once been close to it himself.

He left his horse at the stable and asked about a hotel and a saloon. He also asked about the two outlaws and was told they had been hanged two days earlier.

A rush of defeat flooded him. Too late again. Always too late. Damn. He needed a drink. Then he would see the sheriff and hope that the two men had said something before they died.

He left his belongings in a room at the Worth Hotel and found the saloon the stabler had recommended. It was a large space, with a long bar running the width of it and more than twenty tables scattered around the floor. It was noisy and he didn't bother to glance around. A drink. That's what he needed now.

He squeezed in between two men standing at the bar,

completely unaware of the small figure hunched over her cards not three feet from him.

"Here for the hanging?" the barkeeper asked as he set a mug down in front of him.

Sean looked up, surprised. "Hanging? I thought it was over?"

"Ah, them. They weren't nothing," the man said. "But tomorrow. Tomorrow, they're hanging Ty Donaldson." There was a note of awe in the man's voice.

Sean felt as if he was strangling on the beer.

Casey heard him choke and all her senses came alive. Despite the two pairs in her hand, she laid her cards down. "I fold," she said, wanting desperately to concentrate on the conversation behind her.

"Donaldson?" she heard him ask with more than casual interest.

"Yeah, the gunfighter. You must have heard of him."

"Guess everyone has," Casey heard Mallory say. The reply would have sounded natural to most, but Casey had heard enough inflections in Mallory's voice during their conversation in Two Springs that she knew something was wrong.

She shoved her chair back, a little closer to the bar.

"He killed the son of one of the biggest ranchers around these parts...Harper Caldwell. Caldwell's old man's ready to hang him himself," the barkeep said.

"Donaldson killed Harper in cold blood?"

There was an immediate silence at the bar.

"That's what the judge said," someone finally replied.

Another voice chimed in. "What's your interest, anyway, mister?"

"No interest," Mallory said. "I just never heard Donaldson was a back shooter. I saw him draw once. He doesn't need to back shoot."

There was another unusual silence. "Well, there's different versions as to what 'xactly happened."

Another new voice entered the conversation. "For God's sake, Jack, shut up."

The tension was palpable now. Casey could feel the fear in the room. She knew Mallory could, too. What in hellfire could be his connection with a notorious gunman?

She bent her head and looked at the cards that were just dealt, but her concentration was elsewhere. Her head turned slowly toward the bar and she saw Sean's back, saw him drink up his beer and turn to leave. Her leg went out.

Mallory stumbled over it, catching his balance against the table as he glared at the offender. He could barely see the face of the cowboy under the hat, but then he saw the bright, glittering eyes and he straightened in surprise and anger.

"You should watch where you're going, mister," Casey said, lowering her voice an octave.

Casey didn't know what she expected, but it wasn't that glint of admiration in his eye. Or the amusement that softened his grim mouth.

"Seems I'm slowing up," he said, the corners of his mouth turning up in a slight smile. "Haven't we met someplace before?"

"Could be," Casey allowed, as her fellow players started to shift impatiently. "Perhaps another game, another town?"

Damn little imp, Sean thought. "Almost certainly," he said. "And where are you heading now?"

"Depends," the little ragamuffin said. "I'll be looking for another game."

"My room," Sean said. "Number 9 at the Worth Hotel. In an hour. And we'll play a real game of skill."

One of Casey's opponents looked up. "I would like to be included."

"Sorry," Sean said. "This is a personal game." He looked at Casey's angelic expression. Damned if he hadn't been outmaneuvered. He looked at the man who had just spoken. "And I would be very careful with him, friend. Very careful."

With that warning, he turned and walked away, leaving Casey with a little half smile on her face and three of a kind in her hand.

Sean leaned his lanky frame against the outside wall of the saloon and grimly eyed the gallows. It was late afternoon and the sun was beginning to cast shadows. It was almost as if a man was hanging there now.

What else could go wrong?

First Casey Saunders, then Donaldson.

Donaldson, Ty Donaldson. Damn it all to hell. It was none of his business, none at all. And he wouldn't have given it a second thought if he hadn't heard something in those voices at the bar, hadn't sensed that something was very wrong.

He had never liked Donaldson, never been able to understand why his brother-in-law did, but there it was. Donaldson had once helped Ben Morgan and consequently Sean felt some sense of responsibility.

It was complete insanity to even think what he was thinking. Breaking someone out of jail. Particularly a dangerous kid whose only talent was the gun. Particularly a former Yank who hated all Rebs, himself included. Donaldson had made that quite clear, over and over again.

Sean looked over at the jail and saw the barred windows. He wondered if Donaldson could see the gallows from where he was jailed. And how he felt. Or if he felt anything at all. If there was one thing Sean remembered about Ty Donaldson it was his empty, blue-violet eyes, glinting like cold amethysts against a lean, hungry face. He was dangerous. Had always been dangerous, and, as a Yank, had killed scores of Sean's fellow countrymen before turning hired gun after the war.

That he was even considering helping him galled Sean Mallory.

But the idea wouldn't leave him.

Sean spent four long, lonely years killing and robbing for his country, for Texas, for the Confederacy. He had, afterward, sought peace. But it wouldn't come. The hate was still too strong, the bitterness too raw.

So why should he give a damn about a Yank and a gunfighter whose life would be short under any circumstances? And whose demise would be mourned by no one. Except possibly Ben.

With a long sigh, Sean walked over to the Worth Hotel. Before he did anything about Donaldson, he had to take care of Casey Saunders. He half smiled thinking about her. Her smile had been triumphant, and he knew she thought she had made her point. She could ride with the best of them and, from the looks of the pile of money in front of her, play poker the same way. She was full of little surprises and obviously not easily discouraged.

And he did not want her to get mixed up in this mess with Donaldson. Somehow he knew she would…if she stayed. He would have to bargain with her. But with what?

When he reached the room, he unlocked the door, thinking as he had an hour earlier that the flimsy lock wouldn't keep a mouse out. But then who would want a spare rough shirt and worn denim trousers, and a battered guitar? He sat on the bed, fingering the guitar, as he waited for Miss Saunders and searched his mind for a proposal that might satisfy her.

Casey paused before room 9. When she found the courage, her knock was loud, more bravado than anything else.

Her knees were shaking.

The door was opened almost immediately, as if he had been waiting impatiently. She faced him defiantly, wishing he wasn't quite so handsome.

His eyes were narrowed and his expression was obviously meant to be intimidating, but for some reason Casey didn't quite believe it. Not completely. Not when there was a tiny, almost imperceptible twitch at the corner of his mouth.

"What in the devil are you doing here?" he asked abruptly.

"You asked me to come," she said innocently.

Again there was an unwilling tug at his mouth, which he quickly controlled. "I mean in Fort Worth?"

"Same as you, I 'xpect," she replied. "*I* was too late, too," she said sympathetically, though the impudent tone of her voice drove home the point that she had reached Fort Worth before he had.

Sean eyed her cautiously. When he had met her two days earlier, he had known she was female. Her clothes then, while hiding much of her body, could not entirely mask a feminine shape, and her hair had been longer. Now she looked all boy. Her slim form had lost its curves and the curls had been cut from around her face. But the smile was the same, tentative as it was. It was half shy, half impish and Sean was shocked by the power it had over him.

He turned away from her, wanting to think. "Did you manage to keep your winnings?"

So he had noticed the pile in front of her. Their exchange in the saloon had been so quick, she wasn't sure he had. Now was the time to convince him.

"Yes," she said simply. "I'm a good poker player. They thought I was a green kid."

"I can see why," Sean answered with a slight smile.

"I'm good at lots of things," she hurried on before he continued that line of thought. "I'm good on the trail. I can hunt and clean any varmint there is. I shot two of those outlaws, one dead. And I'm good at finding out things."

Casey hesitated before continuing. "Like that gunfighter they're hanging tomorrow. I found out all about it."

Sean whirled around. "Why in the devil do you think I care about that?"

"You do," she insisted stubbornly. "I heard it in your voice."

Little witch. She was a bewildering little witch. "You heard nothing," he said harshly.

"It *was* a fair fight," Casey continued as if he hadn't spoken. "There were witnesses. But everyone was either scared to death or bought off. That Caldwell fellow must be awfully important."

Sean didn't say anything, but his lips firmed in a grim line.

"Everybody's afraid to talk about it, but they thought I was just a dumb kid...even after I won all their money." The last was said in a slightly wondering tone, and Sean's expression eased. He almost had to smile. Despite himself, he wanted her to continue.

"They say," Casey added, "that Caldwell's son even started the whole thing...wanted to prove he was the best gun, that he didn't give Donaldson any choice though the gunfighter tried to avoid it. They say Donaldson's shot struck Caldwell's son before his gun cleared leather." There was a note of awe in her voice. She didn't like hired guns, but she appreciated skill when she heard about it.

Sean stared at her in amazement as the information came pouring from her lips and found himself asking questions. "Did 'they' say anything about the sheriff? Where he stood on all this?"

Casey hesitated. She had been raised all her life to respect the badge and those who wore it. If her father had had any passion, it was for the law. No matter what, you didn't break it.

"They say Caldwell owns him," she said reluctantly.

Sean Mallory was so still Casey wondered if he had heard. She looked at him curiously. She couldn't understand how someone like Sean Mallory, someone who was dead set on chasing a bunch of outlaws, could have any connection with a notorious hired gun.

"The gunfighter a friend of yours?" she asked finally.

Sean started pacing the floor, and Casey thought he would ignore her question. She knew it was none of her business, anyway.

But his answer, when it came, was even more puzzling. "A friend? No."

"You have something against him, then?"

Again there was a long silence. Sean's hand combed his thick hair in a gesture that bespoke frustration.

When he looked at her again, his eyes were hard and cold. "You aren't going to quit, are you, Casey?"

"I'm going to go after Wilson if that's what you mean. Be easier if we went together. I know that. But one way or another I'm going." There was steel in her voice, and Sean didn't doubt her words for one second.

"Damn it, you could get us both killed. I can't concentrate if I have to worry about you."

"You don't have to worry about me. Pa never did. He knew I could handle myself."

"That's the damned trouble," Sean said almost to himself. "Your father didn't worry about you. Running around by yourself, playing poker in saloons. God knows what else."

Casey's back straightened, and her chin went up. "My pa loved me. He wanted me to be a lot more useful than some simpering female that can't do anything but sit in a parlor and make sweet talk.''

Sean swore under his breath. And then gave up. He actually didn't have much choice. He was aware now of her tenacity. She would follow him whether he wanted it or not, and she would be safer alongside where he could keep an eye on her. But not immediately.

''I'll make a bargain with you,'' he said, instantly noting the wariness in her eyes.

''What?'' The question was filled with suspicion.

''There's some business I have to take care of here. It has nothing to do with Wilson. Go on to Abilene and wait for me there. I'll be there inside of four days.''

''How do I know I can trust you? Maybe you're just trying to get rid of me?''

For the first time, Sean grinned. ''I somehow don't think that's possible. Besides, if we're going to be partners we have to trust each other.''

''Then tell me why you're going to stay here.''

The grin left. Damn but she was stubborn. ''I told you...it's none of your affair.''

''It has something to do with that gunfighter, doesn't it?''

Sean's eyes narrowed again.

''You're going to stay for the hanging,'' she probed again. ''Then why can't I stay?''

''Because a hanging is nothing for a woman to see, it's nothing for anyone to see.''

Casey knew there was something more, a lot more. Sean Mallory's hands were balled into tight fists, and his body radiated tension.

''There isn't gonna be a hanging tomorrow, is there?'' Casey said with some accusation in her voice.

His silence told her at least some of what she wanted to know.

''You can't break someone out of jail,'' Casey said.

"You could get killed. Then what would I do?" she blurted out awkwardly.

He raised an eyebrow, and Casey wanted to swallow her tongue.

"I mean," she struggled on, "that I don't want anything to happen to you. And besides," she said hopefully, "it's against the law."

"I kind of figured that out," Sean said. "Which is exactly why I want you to leave."

"I could help," she offered suddenly.

The other eyebrow raised. "Break the law, you mean?"

Casey rationalized. "Well, it's...it's a matter of... justice, isn't it?"

"Something like that," Sean replied, "but I'm making an offer, and it's the only one I will make. Either you go to Abilene this afternoon, or you ride alone."

"But I have a room," she protested.

"I'll pay for it," Sean said promptly. "Your promise, Casey? You will leave this afternoon."

"But..."

"Your promise, Casey?" There was no compromise in his voice and Casey knew he would not change his mind.

She put her hands behind her back and crossed her fingers. She tried to cross her toes in her boots. "All right," she said a little sullenly.

Sean was getting to know her. "I want to hear you say it."

"All right, I promise," she said, her mind working feverishly. Her eyes brightened. She *would* leave town. But she hadn't promised she wouldn't come back. "I promise," she said again, this time with more assurance.

"Will he come with us?" she asked. She still didn't understand Sean's connection with the gunfighter. There certainly had been little liking in his voice.

"No," Sean said. "He doesn't like me any more than I like him."

"Then why…?"

"Damn if I know," Sean Mallory said, and the glint in his eye told Casey that she would get nothing else from him.

"Abilene, then," she said.

"Abilene," he confirmed, and opened the door to let her out.

Chapter Four

Sean watched from his hotel room as Casey Saunders left the hotel and disappeared into a less reputable area of Fort Worth. He would have liked going with her, to see that she was safe, but if anything went wrong tonight he didn't want any connection between the two of them.

Drat her, anyway, for choosing such a wretched area of town. She obviously was less willing than him to spend money. He had offered to pay for the room, but she had refused, saying she had won enough at poker to pay for whatever she needed.

He waited until she reappeared, carrying her worn saddlebags, and entered the stable, and even longer until she rode out on a fine-looking chestnut. She *did* ride well, moving easily with the horse like a born horseman. She turned and looked up at his window, but he couldn't see her expression under that hat. When she had disappeared, he took his own saddlebags, locked the door and went to the desk clerk.

Sean asked about a bath and was directed to a barber who had a back room for baths. He wanted to look a little more respectable when he visited the sheriff.

The jail was quiet, he observed. But then, why not? No

one wanted to deprive Caldwell of his pleasure, and no one probably thought the gunman's fate of interest to anyone...except possibly Donaldson himself. There were no extra guards, no added sentries.

The back room of the barbershop was empty except for himself, and he quickly dismissed the young boy who filled one of the two bathtubs with hot water for ten cents. Sean sunk into the tub, feeling the warmth creep into his body. A hand raked his thick copper-tinged hair, and it spilled over his high forehead. His eyes were tired and he closed them as he pondered every aspect of what he planned to do.

It was essential that Ty Donaldson understand immediately what was happening, but he didn't spare worry about that. If nothing else, Donaldson was extremely quick when his own skin was at stake. A survivor. A predator. Both words described the young man Sean Mallory intended to rescue.

When he was finally through, Sean dressed leisurely. He took a small derringer from the saddlebags he had brought with him and strapped it to the inside of his lower left leg. He pulled on his denim trousers, the dark brown cotton shirt and finally the soft, worn boots. Last came his gun belt, and the well-used Colt, which hung from his hip. The leather of the holster was dark with use and sweat, and he bent over and tied the leather thong, binding it to his thigh.

The street was noisy with rowdy cowboys when he walked across the dirt to the sheriff's office. He hesitated for a moment before knocking, then entered at the shouted invitation to do so.

The inside of the building was dark and dingy. A stove stood against one wall, an evil-smelling coffeepot on its top. A rifle case stood in the corner, a chain crossing through each trigger area. One rickety desk sat near the center of the room, a heavyset man behind it.

"Somethin' I can do for you?"

"Looks like you had some excitement around here," Sean commented.

"Some," the sheriff said uncommunicatively.

"I was hoping you would still have the two from the Wilson gang."

"Hanged them two days ago."

"Did they say where Wilson might be going?"

"Nope. What's your interest, anyway?"

"I'm looking for them."

"Why?"

"Wilson killed a friend of mine…I want him."

The sheriff looked at him dubiously. "By yourself?"

"If need be."

"Then you're a damned fool. What's your name, anyway?"

"Mallory."

The sheriff sat upright, his brow suddenly creased. "You wouldn't be that Mallory who captained that guerrilla group up in Colorado…" There was new respect in his voice. "You ran them Yankees almost crazy."

"Not crazy enough," Sean said with some bitterness.

"One of your men, Cal Adams, has a small ranch north of here. He deputies for me sometimes. Told me all about you."

"Did he also tell you Wilson used to ride with us?"

There was a short silence. "No, he didn't."

"I think most of us wanted to forget it. But I can't, not now."

"Well, he's not around here anymore. I personally think he's headed west. He's been too active south of here."

"Those two you held…you sure they didn't say anything?"

The sheriff was getting friendlier by the moment. "Not to me."

"What about the other prisoner back there? Maybe they told him something."

"Donaldson? Doubt it. He's a real loner. Doesn't cotton up to anyone…'cept maybe a rabid coyote. They might have something in common."

"Can I talk to him? He might have overhead something…"

"If he did, he wouldn't tell you anything, you being an ex-Reb and all…"

"Still, I came a long way and I hate to leave empty-handed," Sean said.

"Ah, hell," the sheriff said. "Won't do you any good, but go ahead. Might just cause him some aggravation, and I wouldn't mind that at all." He reached out a beefy hand. "I'll need your gun." It was a protection for Mallory that prompted the lawman's request, not any fear that Sean might aid his prisoner. Donaldson was a former Yankee officer who flaunted his loyalties and was blatant in his contempt for Southerners. That these two men might have anything in common, except hate, was unthinkable.

Sean nodded briefly and handed over his Colt and watched as the lawman fondled it enviously. "Nice pistol."

"Gift of the Yankees," Sean answered with a slight smile.

The sheriff nodded approvingly and rose slowly, taking a ring of keys from his desk drawer. He went to the door in back of the small office and peered through its barred window before unlocking it. He nodded his head. "He's in there. Help yourself, but keep your distance. He's quick as a rattlesnake. And twice as mean."

Sean's eyes didn't reveal his relief at the sheriff's trust, or, apparently, laziness. He watched as the man sat back down before he opened the door and went through it.

The back room held three cells—two small ones with a

single cot, and one large one with several wooden bunks. Thankfully, only one of the small ones was occupied.

A man, lean as whipcord, lay on the bare cot, his head pillowed on hands. He looked up with disinterest at the sound of steps until he saw Sean, and his eyes widened with surprise. But he didn't move.

Sean glanced at the empty doorway he'd just left. The sheriff was out of sight but wasn't more than several yards away. Words would carry easily.

Sean Mallory and Ty Donaldson eyed each other with the old wariness. It didn't help that the young gunfighter was still wearing his blue cavalry trousers or the arrogant half smile that always told the world where it, and everyone in it, could go. It was obviously an attitude undimmed by his present quarters and the close proximity of a noose.

Sean knew Ty was not much more than twenty, and still he had the coldest eyes the Texan had ever seen. And now they were fixed on him without wavering, without curiosity, without any emotion at all. They held only a slight recognition, and that held no warmth. The two men had disliked each other instantly when they met two years earlier, immediately after the war. Ty had been imprisoned in a Texas prison camp with Ben Morgan, and the two men had become as close as Donaldson would allow. The young Yank had tried working for Ben after the war, but Sean suspected Ty had no stomach for the hard ranch work. And he had been trouble from the beginning, baiting and starting fights with the Texas hands.

But Donaldson's hatred of Southerners went deeper than the war. *That* had been evident to Sean from the beginning. So he had merely avoided the man, thinking him a very dangerous youngster.

It hadn't taken long for Ty's restless nature to overrule any loyalty he'd had for Ben. One day Ty just disappeared, but Sean and Ben had no trouble following his new career:

gunfighting. The boy's reputation had spread rapidly, as
had the number of bodies he left in his wake. Sean suspected Donaldson was a natural killer, although Ben had
quietly disagreed.

The object of his thoughts rose slowly from the dirty cot,
and sauntered over to the bars. His dark hair was curly and
fell in mussed waves over his forehead and the collar of
his black shirt. His cheeks were shadowed with black stubble, but the eyes were as clear and watchful as ever. It
seemed strange now to see him without a gun strapped
tightly to his side, but even his belt had been taken, and
his black shirt had come loose from his army trousers and
fell over his lean hips. His every movement appeared lan-
guid, like a stretching tiger, but Sean didn't miss the sup-
pressed violence and tension that lay lurking just under the
surface. Ty Donaldson had not changed in the past months.

When Donaldson finally spoke, his voice was so low
Sean could barely catch his words.

"What the hell are you doing here?"

Sean was also wondering the same. He had done some
questionable things in his life, but this was probably the
most idiotic. But he was committed now, and he merely
looked toward the jail door, warning Donaldson with his
eyes.

Now there was a question in Donaldson's too-old, too-
hard face as he approached closer to the bars, his eyes
weighing Sean carefully. Sean could see Donaldson's puzzlement as he started to understand that some kind of help
was being offered. And Sean could also feel the simmering
resentment that accompanied that understanding. It was obviously as galling to the gunfighter to take his help as it
was for Sean to offer it.

Sean's hesitation disappeared as he heard the scraping
noises of a chair in the next room. In a lightning-fast movement he leaned down and removed the small derringer from

where he had fastened it on his leg, and handed it to Donaldson. With approval he watched it vanish quickly somewhere in the prisoner's trousers, under the loose shirt.

"Your horse?" Sean whispered quickly.

"The stable. They were going to auction him in the morning." Ty's lips barely moved.

"Which one?"

"Bay with a white streak on his face."

"He'll be in back after midnight."

Ty nodded, his eyes empty of any thanks or gratitude. He turned away and took the several steps to the cot before lying back down, his head once more pillowed on his hands as the sheriff entered.

"Any luck?"

"No," Sean said. "But you were right. Arrogant bastard, isn't he?" He didn't even try to lower his voice.

"Won't be much longer," the sheriff said. "Hanging has a way of humbling the bravest of them. He'll be on his knees like the rest."

Sean went out the door without a backward look, grateful that the sheriff couldn't see the slight tug of his mouth. Regardless of his personal feelings, Sean knew the sheriff couldn't have been more wrong about his prisoner. Donaldson would have gone to the gallows with the same uncaring disdain that accompanied him in life. But now, he thought, no one in this town, except himself, would know that.

Ty rolled on his side, cushioning his head with his left hand.

Once more, his right hand touched the gun tucked inside his trousers next to his skin. There would be no hanging. He might well die, but it wouldn't be that way. He tried to smother the resentment he felt toward his benefactor, but he couldn't.

At first he hadn't believed it. After Mallory left, he had checked the gun carefully. The tiny single-shot gun was loaded. For some damn godforsaken reason, the man was giving him a chance. The fact that Sean Mallory had not liked doing it was quite obvious. Ty had not missed Sean's last comment to the sheriff, and he had felt every drip of acid in the words.

Why? That was the question. Why was Mallory doing anything for him?

God, he hated feeling indebted. Particularly to a Texan, an ex-Reb.

But perhaps it wasn't important. Perhaps he would die tonight, anyway. And better by a bullet than being on display. That had been the one thing he dreaded. Being on display. Dying publicly for the curiosity and amusement of a crowd.

If nothing else, Mallory had spared him that. He owed the man a debt and he was damned if he would owe a Texan anything.

If he made it out of here, he would repay it. Quickly. No matter what it took. And wipe out any account between the two of them.

But the question of why continued to plague him. Why in the hell had Mallory lifted a finger to help him?

Ty still didn't have an answer at supper time. When the sheriff brought in his meal, which was little more than slop, Ty tried to probe.

"Why in the hell did you let that fellow in here earlier? Don't I have any right to privacy?" He had more than one reason for asking. He wanted to know exactly what Sean had told the sheriff to gain admittance. And what, if anything, could be traced back to Mallory.

The sheriff grunted. "You ain't got no rights at all, anymore, Donaldson." He looked at his prisoner who was still lying indolently on his cot, paying no attention to the meal being shoved through a small opening at the bottom of his cell. The gunfighter's arrogance never ceased to infuriate him. He decided to goad his prisoner.

"Was a Reb war hero, he was. Killed his share of you Yanks, I hear. Stole a lot of gold and guns. Outsmarted the bunch of you."

"That don't give him any right to bother me now with all those damn fool questions about those other fellows. He's no lawman." Ty's voice turned mocking. "Of course, the law is too damned busy cozying up to the ranchers around here 'stead of risking their hides and going after outlaws."

The sheriff flushed. "Shut your damn mouth, Donaldson."

"Or what, Sheriff?" Ty baited. "Just exactly what will you do to me?"

"How'd you like to wear manacles your last night?"

Ty shrugged. "This damned rat's nest's so miserable already, who cares? You keep a damned poor jail, Sheriff."

"It's good enough for the vermin we keep here," the sheriff retorted, turning to go.

Ty briefly regretted his defiance. He hadn't learned anything before his temper got the best of him. "You didn't say why that fellow was here."

The sheriff turned around and eyed his prisoner. Donaldson was now standing, stretching lazily in the center of the cell, looking all the world as if he dominated it. When their eyes met, the sheriff, for some incomprehensible reason, couldn't tear his away. The pale blue-violet stare was as binding as the chains he had threatened Donaldson with.

"Seems Wilson killed a friend of his," the sheriff said finally. "Damn fool's chasing him on his own."

Ty felt as if he had been kicked in the chest. Ben. Was it Ben who had been killed? Surely Mallory would have said something if it had been. But he kept his voice mild.

"One less Reb if he does," he said, carefully inserting a note of satisfaction in his voice while he was feeling a raw pain unique to him.

"There will be one less of you tomorrow," the sheriff said angrily. "The hangman will be here shortly to look you over, measure your neck for the rope. You won't be so damn cocky then."

"Real sure of that, are you?" A soft laugh followed the sheriff out the door, and Ty heard it slam with no little satisfaction. Annoying the sheriff had been his only pleasure for the past several days. It had taken his mind from the impending execution.

He disregarded the mess on the plate, but drank the black coffee, thinking it tasted like mud more than anything. So Mallory was after the Wilson gang. All alone. It was suicide. And because of a friend. Could it possibly have been Ben? The thought ate away at him. Ben Morgan had been the only friend he had ever had.

Ty thought about the first time he had met Sean Mallory. They had disliked each other on sight, recognizing in the other a certain deadly quality, but sharing little else in common. Sean was everything Ty detested. He was a Texan and a Reb. He had an ease about him, a sense of humor that seldom flagged, and a smile that came so damned easily. Ty had always thought those qualities a part of the privileged lives many Southerners lived...at the expense of others. And he had long hated each and every one of them for it.

The walls of his cell seemed to close in on him. He loathed feeling so penned, like a rat in a trap, though now there was an escape hole. He wondered how Mallory was going to get his horse, but he had no doubt he would. Mallory exuded calm competence, and Ty had heard often enough how the Southerner had eluded Northern troops for nearly two years as a guerrilla in Colorado. He didn't like Mallory but he had to respect his coolness.

He wondered briefly why Mallory hadn't just left the gun. It would have been enough. More than enough. But Sean had planned every move down to the smallest detail. The Reb was not a man to leave loose ends. He would see this damn thing to the end. Ty's mouth crooked in a small sardonic smile. Mallory was a damned noble fool.

The afternoon inched into evening. Warned about the hangman, Ty slid the gun under the bare mattress and messed the blanket to hide the slight bulge. He didn't know what the hangman measured…they certainly hadn't bothered with such formalities with the other two, but then he had been told he was special. Caldwell wanted a spectacle and had even gone to the expense of hiring his own hangman. He hadn't wanted Ty to hang with the other two…that would dilute the effect.

Ty looked to where the pistol barely made a crease in the blanket. It was a damned small gun. And it had only one load. He would have to be careful, very careful, not to bungle his one chance. Once he took the sheriff, or preferably the less cautious deputy, he would locate his own Colt. The gun had been custom-made with a shaved trigger and long barrel for accuracy. It was like a trusted friend, and he felt empty and alone without it.

He set the tin cup on the floor, and the noise seemed to echo in the cell. He could hear the sound of celebrating cowboys outside, and he felt his own isolation. It had never bothered him much before. It had been his life ever since he could remember. He had never needed anyone, never wanted to, not since his mother died.

He didn't now, goddammit. He hadn't asked for help. Especially from a Texan. The old fury frothed inside him as images of his tortured childhood flashed through his mind. He had been born in Kansas, the illegitimate child of a woman deceived and used by a Texas planter. The man had promised marriage and seduced her, then disappeared. Ty's grandfather had grudgingly taken in his ruined daughter and her young son but never let them forget for one moment the circumstances of his birth. When Ty was old enough, his grandfather had worked him like a slave; and his mother, the one person Ty had ever loved, also labored twelve and fourteen hours in the field. When Ty was twelve, his mother fell sick and his grandfather had refused to spend money for a doctor. Emma Donaldson died in agony from a cut that had become rotten with gangrene. Ty, hard and strong from years of work in the fields, had almost killed his grandfather before disappearing, taking only a gun with him.

He had lived by his wits for two years, wandering, making a few pennies cleaning up saloons or stables. And practicing. Always practicing with the gun. No one, he vowed, would ever treat him as his grandfather had, no one would ever control his life again.

Ty was only fourteen when the war started, but his hard face and eyes had aged him and an eager enlistment sergeant readily believed his claim to sixteen years. He was given a field commission two years later after nearly single-handedly wiping out a Reb position in Mississippi. It was his sixteenth birthday. Soon after, he was ambushed on a patrol and spent his seventeenth and eighteenth birthdays in the Reb prison where his hatred for Rebs grew proportionately with his frustration that once more others were controlling him.

In his entire life, Ben Morgan was the only man who had ever become his friend. They had met in the Reb prison. Perhaps it had been Morgan's own quiet bitterness that linked them. Perhaps Morgan's determination to escape, an attempt that had been very nearly successful. After the war, Ben had offered him a job on his ranch, but the long hours reminded him of Kansas, and prison had given rise to a restlessness he could not still. Not knowing how to say goodbye, he had left without a word and turned to earning money with the only skill he had.

Ty had thought to find his father and take revenge for his mother's pain. But the man and his only son had died in the war, and the widow had gone to live with relatives. So Ty had transferred his bitterness to all Texans. He would stay in Texas and make them pay. As many of them as possible. And now he was indebted to Mallory...in the strongest possible way. Although he hadn't asked for help, he hadn't refused it, either. The knowledge settled like a lump in his stomach, and Ty knew he had to return the favor. A life for a life. Sean Mallory would need his help against the Wilson bunch. He would need all the help he could get. Even if he didn't want it. And if the dead "friend" the sheriff mentioned was Ben Morgan, Ty would have his own reasons to destroy Wilson.

The hangman came and went. Unlike Ty's mental picture of a cadaverous-looking man in a drab black suit, the man was fat and cheerful, which did nothing for his black mood.

He felt like a rabbit being eyed by a vulture as the man visually weighed him, clucked about his long hair, and asked him to turn around several times.

"Go to hell."

"You don't understand, young man," the visitor said huffily. "Hanging is an art. It's a craft. I mean, you want to die right off...and these things are important...."

"For the best show, you mean," Ty said. His hands tightened in rage. "How much is Caldwell paying you?"

The hangman turned to the sheriff. "Can't you make him more cooperative?"

Even the sheriff was offended by the man. "How? There doesn't seem to be much more we can do to him."

It was a very evident truth, and the hangman sighed in defeat. "I'll be here at dawn. And I'll get a barber...he should be at his best."

"Damn you will," Ty growled, forgetting for the moment that he should be gone in the morning.

The hangman looked at the sheriff pleadingly.

"You wanna try barbering him?" the sheriff said. "Because I sure as hell don't."

"Mr. Caldwell won't like it."

"I've gone as far as I will for Caldwell," the sheriff replied. "Now if you don't mind, I have rounds."

Ty watched the retreating figures, noting the regretful look the hangman sent him.

He smiled inwardly. It would be more regretful in the morning. His lips pressed in a grim line. He wouldn't see the man's expression but he could imagine it. It was another damn thing he owed Mallory.

Sean drank his beer slowly. The saloon was crowded with boisterous cowboys, all anticipating the next morning. The sight made him sick.

He had never been able to understand the attraction of a hanging. He had seen enough death to last him a lifetime—quick, violent death. But there was something particularly accursed about a ritual execution that drew men and women like a fair.

The way everyone in town was drinking, he shouldn't have any trouble at the stables. It was important that no one see him. When he finished with Wilson, he wanted to return to San Antonio, and his ranch, without wanted posters following him.

He doubted whether he would be suspected unless something went wrong in the next few hours. Anyone could have passed Donaldson the gun and, given Sean's known war record, few would connect him with a hard-nosed Yank. Once they were clear, Ty could contact Ben and have him look into the matter. His brother-in-law was respected within the reconstruction government and had used his connections several times to right wrongs.

Either way, Sean thought, after tonight he could wash his hands of the young gunman. He would be quite happy never to see the arrogant young killer again.

The saloon was still noisy when Sean finally made his way cautiously to the stables. No one remained in the streets, and he made it unseen. A quick glance told him even the stablemen were celebrating. He found his own horse and saddled it quickly, then searched out the bay. He wondered which saddle was Donaldson's but finally selected the poorest-looking one, leaving ten dollars in its place, It would more than cover the cost.

He saddled the bay and checked once more out the stable door before mounting his own horse and leading the bay out. The streets remained empty except for one drunken cowboy who lay spread out on the porch of one of the saloons. He could hear laughter and talk coming from the various saloons up and down the street, and his stomach once more constricted. He nudged his horse into a quick walk and disappeared between two buildings, ending up behind the jail. Sean relaxed in the saddle, not knowing how long it would be, but reluctant to dismount. He thought about leaving Donaldson's horse and going on, but there was something inside him that wouldn't let him leave a job unfinished. Even this one. He hoped Donaldson wouldn't be long.

Casey had circled around town and reentered on the north side where some of the worst saloons and bawdy houses were located. She dismounted and tied her horse in front of one of the more disreputable drinking holes.

She felt fairly sure Sean Mallory wouldn't frequent this sort of establishment. Casey felt a heavy load of guilt at her duplicity, especially after Sean Mallory had been so reasonable. She was terribly afraid he'd take back his offer if he discovered her, but he might just need help. She couldn't bear anything happening to him now.

She slunk into the saloon, trying to be as inconspicuous as possible. She sidled up to the bar and asked for a beer, her ears catching every little piece of nearby conversation. It was all about Donaldson and the hanging next day. Some had been at the hanging two days earlier, and bets were being placed as to whether Donaldson would break down like the others. Casey wondered about the man everyone was talking about, the man for whom Sean Mallory was willing to risk his life and freedom. A killer. A gun for hire. The type of man she had been raised to despise. And *she* was aiming to help...if necessary. Her father would turn over in his grave.

As twilight faded into evening, she left the saloon. She walked, pleased that the leg wasn't hurting quite as much, until she was within sight of the stable and the jail. Both seemed very quiet. She sat outside the corner of one of the saloons, almost out of sight in the shadows, and pushed her hat nearly over her eyes. She leaned back against the wall as if she were just another drunk and watched covertly, her heart pounding with fear.

Chapter Five

Ty had been pacing his cell for the past hour. It should damn well be time for the sheriff to be leaving. If past evenings were any clue, he usually left around midnight, taking one last check around town before returning home. His deputy, Everette Collins, stayed overnight with the prisoners. But the sheriff seemed to be staying later than usual, or perhaps it was Ty's own tension that made it seem later than it actually was.

He finally heard the sheriff warning Collins to be particularly careful of the prisoner. "He'll be desperate," he heard the sheriff say. "Don't get close to the bars where he can reach you, you hear? If he wants water or coffee, you can give it to him, but make him back up against the wall before you put it through the bars."

"Yessir."

"He may be a Yank, and a damned insolent one at that, but I can't say as I like anything about this," the sheriff added. "There'd be hell to pay if anyone really looked into it."

"A gunfighter like that ain't got no friends."

"I suppose not," the sheriff said. "Still I don't like it…but Caldwell…he's the biggest man around these parts.

Didn't have much choice. Anyway, he would have hanged Donaldson himself if we didn't. At least this way it'll be done proper and legal.''

Listening intently in his cell, Ty's sharp ears picked up every word. He wondered wryly whether he should be grateful. Damned hypocrite. The comments only served to deepen his cynicism. He wondered suddenly what Mallory was getting out of this. It had to be something.

Ty waited another thirty minutes or so. He didn't want to take the chance the sheriff might return and make one last check on his prisoner.

He felt damp and sticky, his shirt wet with perspiration. Part of it was the necessity of waiting, of controlling his impatience. Another part was the heat and the suffocating feel of moisture hovering in the air. It was unusual for Texas, this thick, heavy air. Ty looked out the barred window, clenching the iron with his fists. Only a few more minutes and he would be gone from this cage.

His cell was nearly black. The only light came from the barred window between the cell area and the sheriff's office. His eyes were used to the blackness and now he searched for any sign of Mallory. There was none. He could see the building next to the jail and part of the street out front, the part with the gallows. For a moment he wondered if it were all a cruel joke, that Mallory wouldn't be there after all, that Caldwell would be there with more punishment in mind. He laughed, a short bitter sound. Trusting Mallory, for God's sake. What irony. But he had no choice.

The sky was alive with churning clouds, and there was no sign of a moon. It would be a good night to escape, especially if a rain came and wiped out all tracks. But it had been threatening for days now, and still it stayed in the skies, teasing and mocking those who needed it so badly. Rain was scarce in Texas, particularly in late summer. But perhaps he would get lucky—for a change.

Ty slipped the gun from beneath the mattress. Tucking it in his trousers, he approached the front of the cell, and his hands went around the bars. "Collins," he yelled, and soon saw the man's eyes peer at him from the door separating the office from the cells.

"Whatya want?"

"I can't sleep. What about some coffee?"

"That won't help you sleep none."

"Don't expect anything will," Ty replied in an unusually somber tone. "Besides, I don't want to waste any of my last hours sleeping, and coffee would taste mighty good." He couldn't resist a last dangerous jibe. "Even yours."

The deputy's face hardened, and for a regretful second Ty thought he might have talked himself out of his chance. But the man merely nodded slightly. Several seconds later, he heard the key in the lock of the outer door and watched Collins enter with a tin cup in one hand and the keys in another. He let go of the breath he had been holding. That had been the one problem, the keys. He had worried that Collins might leave them in the door lock outside.

"Get back against the wall, Donaldson," the man said, and Ty obeyed. He waited until the man had stooped down and then he took out the derringer.

"Don't straighten up, Collins. Don't move one inch."

At the sound of the icy voice, Collins froze and only his eyes moved upward. At the sight of the gun the tin cup clamored to the floor.

Ty moved forward, his hand very steady and his blue-violet eyes glittering like cold gems. "That's right, Collins. Stay there. I have nothing to lose. And if I don't leave here, you don't, either. Not alive, anyway."

He approached slowly until the pistol was inches away from the deputy's head. "Now hand me your gun, handle first. Carefully." He accepted the gun, then tucked the derringer back in his trousers. "Now you can straighten up and unlock the door."

It took Collins several seconds, his hands were shaking so badly. As Donaldson had pointed out, the prisoner had nothing to lose by killing him. Collins also knew it would be the most practical thing for Donaldson to do now.

When the door swung open, Ty permitted a grim smile. "You are a very wise man. Now give me your bandanna." Ty took the gritty piece of cloth and ordered the deputy to back up to the barred door that had swung half open. He forced the man's hands between the bars and quickly tied them to the metal. He then pushed the door with the deputy attached back in place and locked it, leaving the deputy completely helpless. He took his own bandanna and gagged Collins.

With no additional words, he went out the door that separated the cells from the office, locked it behind him and stuffed the keys in his pocket. He quickly ransacked the desk until he found his gun belt and Colt and buckled it on. His saddlebags were in a corner and he took those.

Ty looked out the jail window. Lights were everywhere. There were even a few drunks lying against the wall of the saloon across the street. He looked around the office until his eyes settled on a long duster in the corner. The coat would cover his Union pants and distinctive black shirt. He quickly pulled it on, then appropriated a dirty-looking hat on a chair. Collins' hat, he supposed. His grim lips turned upward slightly, and he darted out the front door and around the corner to the back.

Sean was there, the bay stamping nervously behind him. Without a word, Ty threw the saddlebags over his shoulder and swung into the worn saddle, and the two men spurred their mounts into an unhurried trot. At the edge of town, they simultaneously pushed the horses into a gallop.

* * *

Minutes had passed unbearably slow for Casey. She watched the swirling clouds above while keeping one eye on the jail.

She finally saw the sheriff leave the jail, and saw the door being closed behind him by a second man. The lawman sauntered down the street toward the rougher part of town, and Casey pressed back in the corners until he passed, indifferent to her presence.

The jail continued to look silent and peaceful. She saw a flash of white against a barred window of the jail but she couldn't make out any features. Could it be the gunfighter? What was happening, anyway? Caught between fear and anticipation, Casey's insides were swishing around like a jug of homemade whiskey on a bucking mule.

The door of the jail opened cautiously, and she saw a tall figure slide out the door and around the side. The man's hat was pushed halfway over his face and his long coat completely covered his body, but there was a certain animal grace to him, and she knew instantly it must be Donaldson. Seconds later, she saw the two horses trot from behind the building and recognized Sean's lean body and the man in the duster. From what Sean had said, she suspected they would separate quickly.

Sighing with a certain relief, Casey started to stand. She would get her horse and make her way quickly to Abilene. She had to get there before Sean did. Just as she started to turn her back to the jail, she saw the sheriff heading back up the street. He was returning to the jail. Casey gulped. It was too soon. With a posse fast on their tracks, Sean and his gunfighter wouldn't have much of a chance. She didn't give a good cold damn about the gunfighter, but Mallory...?

Biting her lip, she looked around, then crossed the hard-packed street to the jail. The door was open and she peered in. The sheriff was cursing, taking keys from his pocket and working the lock in a door. His back was to her, and his cursing was so loud he didn't hear her careful footsteps. Her gun was out of the holster, and just as he sensed someone behind him and started to turn, her hand went up, bringing the butt of the pistol hard against his head.

Casey moved quickly out of the way as the man fell. Stunned by what she had done—striking a man of the law—she stood there motionless for almost a moment until she heard muffled noises from inside the cell area. She stooped down and checked the man. He was breathing, thank God. She started to leave, then hesitated. She didn't know how long he would be unconscious, and she wanted to give Mallory as much time as possible. She closed the jail door and searched the office for handcuffs and leg irons.

When she found what she needed she cuffed the sheriff's hands behind him, then put the leg irons on, fastening one manacle to the right ankle, pulling the chain up and around the handcuffs and finally fastening the other manacle to the left ankle. She looked at her victim with satisfaction. He was completely hog-tied, unable to move at all with his legs pulled up nearly to his hands. She thought about gagging him, but was afraid he might choke. She would take the keys, and even when discovered, the sheriff would not be freed easily. It would be a very humiliating position, and Casey felt a return of guilt as she thought about how her father would feel if someone did this to him. But her father would never have allowed anyone to take him unawares. The sheriff deserved a lesson because of his own incompetence.

Freed from any lingering self-reproach, she quickly blended back into the shadows. Reaching her horse which was patiently waiting two blocks away, she mounted and joined a group of cowboys as they rode out of town.

Sean and Ty rode until the sky lost its inky blackness and turned gray. The clouds were heavy and tinged with a deep purple, but still there was no rain. They were moving along a shallow river, occasionally guiding their horses through its shallows to obscure their tracks. Neither had acknowledged the other's presence during the night, but now Sean reined in his horse. Ty followed suit.

The two men regarded each other levelly for a moment, both without evident emotion.

"This is where we part," Sean said.

"I understand you're going after the Wilson bunch," Ty answered, his face tense. "Because of a friend. It wasn't Ben, was it?"

Sean's face showed his surprise. He should have known Ty would have somehow milked the sheriff of information, but the depth of concern in Donaldson's voice startled him.

"No," Sean said shortly. "It was Jim Carne."

Donaldson had met Carne several times. "What happened?" There was no sympathy in his voice, only a cold interest.

"Wilson raided Ben's ranch. Jim and I happened to hear it was going to happen, and I was barely in time to warn them. Most of Ben's men were out on roundup and there were only a handful of us, but we managed to set up an ambush. We got a number of them, but Wilson killed Jim and three others, and got away.

"Ben and Ryan?"

"They weren't hurt, but Wilson vowed to return. None of them are safe as long as he's alive."

"Where's Ben?"

"We decided he should stay with his family in case Wilson doubled back."

Donaldson's lips twisted. "I bet Ben wasn't happy with that."

For the first time, Sean smiled. "No, but then he has

twins now, and for once he recognized the wisdom of my thinking."

Ty's expression didn't change. "I'm going with you."

"The hell you are." Sean's smile disappeared. "It's none of your concern."

"You can't go after Wilson yourself. You don't have a chance. Especially since Wilson wants you, too."

"What do you know about it?"

"Ben told me what happened…that you saved his life when Wilson tried to kill him, that you crippled Wilson."

Sean's eyes narrowed. "Donaldson, I don't like you. I don't want or need your help. This is between Bobby Wilson and me. And I don't want a trigger-happy kid with me."

"Then why in blazes did you help me back there?"

Sean looked at him in astonishment. "You surely don't think it's because I wanted your help?"

"Then why?"

"Because I don't like hangings, and because that shooting was *one* thing you shouldn't die for."

"Ah, a sense of justice." Ty sneered. "A Reb with a sense of justice."

Sean's eyes were as cold as Donaldson's. "I want only one thing from you now, Donaldson. And that's never to see you again. That's the only thanks I want…if you even understand the word." He turned his horse away from the young gunfighter.

"Damn you." Donaldson's intense words penetrated Sean's weary mind, and he turned back to the gunfighter in anger.

"I'm not going to let you get away with that, Mallory," the kid was saying. "I'm not going to owe you or anyone else. Especially you." The last words had a bitter bite to them.

"Can't you get it through your head. You don't owe me a damn thing. I didn't do it for you. You owe me nothing."

It was like talking to a tree, Sean thought as he looked at the expressionless face. He was fast regretting his rescue effort. But then he had known he probably would.

"I'm going with you," Donaldson was saying, incredibly enough. He lazily dismounted and took off the duster and hat, shaking his thick mane of hair free. He took the brim of the hat and sailed it through the air.

"No." Once again their eyes locked.

Donaldson shrugged and Sean thought he had won. He moved his horse forward, wanting to be on his way. He was convinced, as the Fort Worth sheriff was, that Wilson was moving west, and he had already lost more time than he wanted. There were hundreds of miles of plains ahead of him, and he still had to meet Casey Saunders. He was already regretting his promise to her...and now there was Donaldson. Two very dangerous children. And he didn't want the responsibility for either of them.

The rain started late in the afternoon. Heavy and nasty. Sean covered his guitar with an oilskin and himself with a slicker and pressed on. It was difficult to tell how late it was but he decided it was near time to stop. When he reached a river, he followed it for a while, judging the protection value of one small stand of cottonwoods before continuing on. He finally found a more substantial shelter in a small bend of the river.

Sean unsaddled his horse and hobbled it, then took his pack under the cottonwoods where water dripped through the leaves. It was going to be a miserable night. He laid his slicker on the ground, put a blanket on top, then crawled in and wrapped the slicker around his body. He needed sleep.

But sleep didn't come. He was wet. He was worried

about Casey Saunders, and he wondered what in the hell Donaldson was up to. Finally he fell into an uneasy sleep.

Damn! Casey cursed bitterly to herself as the rain pelted her. She was glad she had slipped a poncho in her bedroll along with one change of clothing, and now she huddled within it, feeling the water drip down inside the collar and cling miserably between her skin and shirt.

Her leg ached painfully and her eyes were strained. She had not traveled this way before and was afraid to leave the main trail. The last thing she needed was to get hopelessly lost.

But she also didn't want to blunder into Mallory. She figured she would keep a sharp eye out and when she saw him circle around and get in front. Sean Mallory must never know she had stayed in Fort Worth. If he found out what she'd done to the sheriff, he'd never trust her again. And his trust was more important than him knowing she might have saved his life.

He wouldn't understand. Just as her father wouldn't have understood. Some men saw things in black and white, and she was fearfully afraid that Sean was one of them.

Suddenly she saw him up ahead, and he was alone. So he had gotten rid of the gunslinger. She dropped behind. The land was too flat here to circle around; she would have to wait until Mallory stopped for the night. Frustrated and wet and tired, she wondered about the cost of duplicity.

Casey knew the White River couldn't be far, and there would be some shelter among the trees from the rain. That's probably where Mallory would stop for the night. She fervently hoped so.

The deep gray of the rainy day was blending into the darker colors of dusk when she saw another rider. It wasn't Mallory. She knew that from the way the newcomer sat on his horse. Somewhere way in the distance, she caught sight of Mallory again, and instinct told her the second man was following him. Why?

Could it be part of a posse from Fort Worth? If so, why just one man and how in hell had he caught up with them? It was not a familiar figure, not the heavy build of the sheriff or the slight one of his deputy. The man wore no hat or slicker, only dark clothes that seemed to blend into the night. The rain seemed not to bother him in the slightest.

Casey urged her horse behind a small gulch where at least part of her and the horse were invisible and the rest of them none too easy to see with the rain. There was something secretive about the rider, and Casey felt a tightness in her chest. He had to be up to no good. Never mind that she was out in this night without evil intent.

She watched as the man followed Mallory's path, intent on his quarry and never looking in her direction. He entered a clump of trees on the riverbank and disappeared.

Casey waited several minutes, then guided her own horse in the same direction. Remembering everything her father had taught her, she very cautiously followed the same path, dismounting when she reached the trees.

She tracked him on foot, by instinct, knowing her movements, made awkward by her limp, were silenced and shielded by the pounding rain. As it had the night before, her heart thumped loudly, louder, she suspected, than her footsteps and those of her horse. She had been on manhunts before, but there had always been someone with her. She was going blind now, and her confidence dipped down to her wet, muddy boots.

Her right hand slipped her gun from its holster and her left hand soothed the neck of her horse, calming its growing nervousness. Spying a thicket through the rain, she tied her horse to a sturdy bush and went on alone, her already small form bent low to evade detection. She would find out exactly why the scoundrel was following Mallory, and she would stop him. She didn't know exactly how at the moment, but she would stop him. She crept silently forward.

Ty Donaldson tied the reins of his horse to a branch. There was no sense going any farther tonight. Mallory would be stopping soon himself, and he would pick up the trail in the morning. The blasted rain had to stop sometime.

He knew Mallory thought he had lost him. Mallory had not worried about a posse and the Texan had done precious little backtracking, and Ty had stayed well out of sight.

The gunman had done some backtracking of his own. Circling several times, he had seen nothing but an itinerant cowboy whose small figure and unhurried pace seemed innocent enough. The rain would erase any tracks and discourage a posse. Besides, they were way outside the Fort Worth jurisdiction now, and it would take Caldwell time to assemble a private army. He didn't doubt for one moment that the rancher would do that. As well as put a heavy price on his head.

A price on his head. He had tried to avoid that this last year. He had carefully selected his jobs and had never drawn unless someone drew first. He had been a bounty hunter, settling scores for those willing to pay someone to do it for them. Every man he had gone after had been a bastard. And through it all he had managed to stay legal, though sometimes just barely. That damned Caldwell kid. He had been determined to fight. Ty had even let him get away with calling him a coward. Knowing Caldwell's influence and knowing it was a situation he couldn't win, Ty had decided to leave, but as he came out of a saloon the kid had accosted him and drawn his gun. Ty had no choice. The next thing he knew he was in jail. Two days later there was a mockery of a trial.

The last man in the world he thought would help was

Sean Mallory. He still had some difficulty accepting it. But deep down in the dark recesses of his soul he was grateful.

Ty took an oilcloth from his saddlebag and rigged it over several low branches to keep the rain off. He wished he had kept the sheriff's duster, but it reminded him of the man, damn his crooked hide, and he had wanted no such recollection. He wrapped himself in two blankets before lying on the cool wetness that seeped through the covering. As always, his gun was inches from his finger.

He sensed rather than heard an approach. His hand took firm hold of the gun, but it was wrapped in several layers of blankets. He was still freeing it when he felt a pistol in his chest. Instinctively, his feet came up, his finger on the trigger of his own gun, and then it was kicked out of his hand and went skittering out of sight. Now free of the blanket, he sought to see his attacker, but there was only a shadow. As his hand whipped out, he felt a knee slam into the most sensitive part of his body, and he doubled over with agonizing pain. Then the gun was in his face, and fury overtook caution and pain. He leaped for the figure and they both went tumbling against the bank and rolled into the muddy shallows of the river, each scratching and kicking the other in a desperate effort to survive.

Casey knew she had lost her chance, and thought now only of staying alive. Her mouth was filled with mud and her leg was an agonizing furnace of pain. But still she bit and scratched, trying once more to hit that one part, which she knew would paralyze him for moments. But it was as if he knew exactly what she intended and foiled her every move. And then his superior strength started to tell, and she felt her head being pushed underwater. Muddy water rushed into her mouth and nose, and everything began to fade away.

Chapter Six

Just as she thought she would lose consciousness, Casey was jerked up by the back of her shirt and dragged onto the bank. The gloom of the night was so deep that she could barely make out the murky form of her opponent. She could, however, feel the cold menace flowing from him.

She sputtered some of the mud out her mouth as her stomach hit the ground. She was roughly turned around and she felt a hard body settle down around her with a squishing sound.

"Who in the hell are you?" The voice was the angriest Casey had ever heard, but she could do nothing more than sputter. It seemed as though a lump of mud had settled in her throat, and when she tried to speak it just went down deeper.

The pressure on her lungs increased, and she struggled to sit up, her hands flailing in a vain attempt to free herself, but they were caught in tight fists, and she did the only thing left to her. She threw up.

The muddy contents of mouth and throat went directly at her attacker, and she heard a long blasphemous curse— low and cold and terrifying. But he released his hold on her hands, and one of them went straight into his stomach while her legs sought to unroot him from his position on top of her. She had just thought she might succeed when another voice penetrated her consciousness.

"Both of you...hold it right there." The voice had a disturbingly familiar quality.

Her enemy stiffened, his hands going slack, and Casey's good knee automatically aimed for his hip, hitting with all her strength. She felt him grunt, then felt his fist hit her face, stunning her.

"Damn it, I said stop." The disembodied voice wavered in her consciousness as she absorbed the pain.

With shock she heard her assailant's words. "He jumped me, Mallory, and I want to know who sent him."

"We'll both find out, then." Somewhere in her mind, Casey wanted to die. They knew each other, then. A small nagging feeling told her she had made a mistake. A very humiliating mistake.

She heard the small scratch of a match, then saw the slight glow through the drizzle. It came down toward her, and she wished she was back in the river, sinking in that horrible mud. Anything would be better than having him see her like this.

There was a silence, and Casey could hear her heart pounding. It grew so great inside her that she thought it must be as loud as the thunder that had just passed.

"Casey?" The voice was hesitant, disbelieving, and she hoped, for a moment, her heart would just go ahead and explode and she would be spared the next few moments. But it was not to be. She felt the body straddling her shift uncomfortably.

"You know him?" her burden said, and Casey couldn't miss the surprise in his voice.

"Her," the voice drawled to Casey's immense embarrassment. "She's a her," Sean continued. There was amusement dancing in his voice, amusement and...

something else, something warning. Casey's wrath drained slowly as she desperately sought an explanation for her immediate whereabouts.

"Her?" The man shifted again and his hands ran along her body. He let out another oath and she was instantly free, at least her body was. One of her wrists was clasped in a tight, firm grip and she was forced to her feet.

She tried to adjust her eyes to the darkness, but there was another match shining directly into them. She knew she was covered head to toe in mud, and the fact that she had failed miserably—and apparently misconstrued everything—did not help her confidence.

But Casey's innate audacity and dignity prevailed. Her shoulders straightened and the brilliant green eyes shot sparks...even in the darkness.

"He was following you," she charged of the man who still held her arm.

There was a long silence as Sean Mallory regarded both of the mud-covered figures in front of him. All he could see of the girl was the shimmering brilliance of the green eyes, yet he sensed a desperate hurt, and it touched him as little else had in the past years. She had thought she was protecting him and had almost been killed for it. It mattered little that there was no need. The act itself spoke of her courage.

"Casey...this is Ty Donaldson. Apparently he was also, ah, trying to protect me." The wry irony in his voice did not entirely escape Casey. She wanted to melt into the ground.

Ty Donaldson. So this was Donaldson. If only he knew she might have saved him from recapture, he would be sorry for the mud still lodged in her throat and the hurt in her leg. But she couldn't say anything, or Sean Mallory would know she had returned to Fort Worth despite her promise. She swallowed her angry words and tried to jerk her arm away, but he held it tight, like an iron band.

"Let her go, Donaldson." Sean's voice was low but its iron-willed command lashed like a whip.

"Not until I know more about her," Ty said defiantly. "It's my skin."

"Mine, too, in case you've forgotten," Sean grated. "Let her go. Now."

Donaldson stared at the hard amber gleam visible in Sean's eyes despite the darkness. He reluctantly released Casey. "Damned wildcat kicked me," he muttered.

There was a deep masculine chuckle in response. "Would you like to tell me where, Donaldson?"

Although Casey had heard profanity often enough, she winced at the unnecessarily long reply.

Mallory's wry voice interrupted the stream of words. "I'm sorry I asked." When the stream of invective continued, his voice sharpened. "That's enough. There's a lady present."

There was a sputtering that had matched Casey's when she was pulled from the water. "Lady? Lady, my ass. She ambushed me, damned near gelded me and tried to drown me."

Mallory's voice now was like the quiet purr of a tiger. "All that by a slip of a girl...and you think I need you?"

Casey stood absolutely still. She couldn't see much, but she sure could feel the hostility reverberating between the two men.

"I know you do" came the harsh grating reply.

"Look, Donaldson," Sean said, his voice icy. "I don't want you following me. You're dangerous for me. I don't think anyone linked me with you, and I damn well don't want them to."

"What about the little hellion? Who is she?"

"The daughter of the sheriff in Two Springs." Again

there was a hint of humor in Sean's voice...along with a warning.

"Sheriff?" The gunslinger seemed to choke on the words.

"She did some deputing for him," Sean continued easily, and Casey knew if she could see his face in the dark there would be that breath-catching grin. It was obvious he enjoyed baiting Donaldson.

"You aren't taking...?"

When Sean answered, the amusement was gone. "Wilson killed her father. She has a right."

A painful silence followed. A match was struck again, and Casey saw Mallory eye her bedraggled, muddy appearance. "Do you have other clothes?"

She nodded miserably.

"I would suggest you change into them before you get pneumonia."

In the flickering light of the match, Casey saw the gunfighter was as covered with mud as she was. Her curiosity rose as she looked from one man to another.

They were as different as could be, she thought. She couldn't make out their facial expressions through the dark mist but their stances told her much about them. Her father had taught her to judge a man by the way he stood and walked and held himself.

There was a confidence and ease in Sean Mallory, in the way he moved, in the way he spoke as if he expected immediate obedience. His gun had been put away, but she still recognized a tempered fire in him, a firmly controlled violence.

The other man was like a tight spring ready to snap into savagery. He was shorter than Mallory, though not much. His body was wiry but Casey could testify, unhappily, to its raw strength. Everything about him spoke of simmering danger. A sidewinder, she thought. He reminded her of nothing as much as a rattlesnake ready to strike.

Donaldson finally spoke again, an edge to his voice. He didn't like her examination. "I still want to know why she was out there sneaking around."

The match went out, but Casey wasn't misled by the deceptive softness in Mallory's next words.

"I think I would like to know that, too...Casey. You promised to go straight to Abilene."

"What's *he* doing here? I thought you said he wasn't coming." Playing for time, Casey nodded her head toward Donaldson disdainfully. She coughed suddenly, still feeling the mud in her throat. The pain in her leg had grown from a whisper to an all-consuming hammering.

Sean eyed the two shadowy figures with both frustration and exasperation until he saw Casey's form start to sway. He remembered her limp and the injury she had sustained just weeks earlier. He had seen only part of the punishment she had taken from Donaldson, and he wondered how she was even standing.

The swaying grew more pronounced, and he was over to her in three strides, his arms catching her just as she started to fall. He lifted her up, wondering at her lightness. She had not looked so light or vulnerable in the saloon, nor in his room. Perhaps because of the gun she had worn with such familiarity and confidence. But now with her head against his chest she seemed incredibly young and defenseless.

His voice was curt when he looked over to Ty. "My camp's just ahead. Bring her horse, then you can clear out. I told you once I don't want you around. You're nothing but trouble. This proves it." He turned around.

Ty's voice grated at him. "Look, she attacked me, damn it. And I still want to know why."

"I can tell you right now it had nothing to do with you.

She apparently had some idea you were a danger to me. I guess you two have something in common. Neither of you seems to understand anything I say.''

"But she's just a girl..."

"From what I saw, the 'wildcat' was doing all right for herself...." There was a softened note in his voice that Casey heard despite the haze that was beginning to engulf her. She felt protected and safe in his arms. She didn't remember ever being this close to another person before. She knew the mud clinging to her must be ruining his clothes, but he seemed indifferent to it. She could feel his warmth through his wet shirt, and hear the soft beat of his heart as she instinctively tried to snuggle closer.

The movement energized Sean. She needed some care. The rain had just about stopped, and perhaps he could get a fire going. His camp, such as it was, was less than a quarter of a mile away. "Bring her horse," he ordered again, not bothering to wait and see whether Ty obeyed him. After four years of commanding his own troop, he was used to being heeded. His long legs covered the distance quickly.

He had found shelter under a cottonwood and an oilcloth still protected his blankets. He looked upward. The rain had stopped, but the sky was an unrelieved inkiness. He looked down at the girl in his arms and was close enough to see long lashes covering her eyes. Sean wondered briefly if she had fainted, but the lashes fluttered open and her large green eyes were incredibly clear and bright.

"Can you stand?" he asked gently, wondering at the unfamiliar tenderness he felt. He had always liked courage, and the girl obviously had more than many men. A smile curled the corners of his lips. She had come close to taking Ty Donaldson, by God, and there wasn't a man living who could claim that.

But now she looked like a child, a small, mud-covered,

hurt child, and a knot formed in his stomach. She nodded, and he flinched inwardly at the complete trust in the gesture...and the way she had clung to him during the short walk. He hadn't wanted the responsibility for her, but he sure as hell had it now. As he carefully set her down she stumbled and only his steadying hands kept her from falling.

He looked over to Ty who stood tensely a few feet away. "Unwrap that oilcloth, and see whether you can start a fire." He felt Ty's hesitation as the young gunslinger remained where he was, resentment radiating from him like a cold chill. It was obvious Donaldson disliked taking any orders from him. Sean's voice hardened.

"Do it, Donaldson, or get out of here."

Stiff with animosity, Ty finally complied, unwrapping the oilcloth and dry blankets. "She better change clothes first," he finally said, then wished he hadn't. It would serve Mallory right if the spitfire smeared mud over everything. He himself felt sticky and miserably uncomfortable encased in his own drying mud. Damn her, anyway.

"He's right," Casey whispered, once more feeling completely mortified. She tried to lean away from Sean, to keep from getting any more mud on him, but his hands were like steel around her shoulders.

Sean nodded to the other man. "Get her saddlebags."

"Get them yourself, Mallory. She tried to kill me. Damn if I'm going to be her maid."

Sean's voice was deadly. "Get them!"

Casey looked from one man to another. Neither was moving. The gunfighter's legs were spread apart...like she had seen her father's just before he went for his gun. She expected that to happen any second. Casey could once again feel the naked dislike between the two men, and she wondered about it.

"No," she said. "I don't want anything from a hired killer."

Ty bowed low. "I see my reputation has preceded me. You have your wish, my fine young lady." Despite the mocking tone in his voice, Casey thought she heard something else, a little hurt, perhaps. But that was impossible. Gunfighters didn't have feelings.

Ty turned and was swallowed by the darkness, leaving Sean and Casey alone.

"Damn his hide," Sean swore.

"I still don't understand why you bothered about him? You obviously don't like each other."

"It's a long story, and I need to see to you first." Without another word Sean set her on the blankets and leaned down, pulling off her boots. He winced at the squashing noise they made as he pulled. After her dripping footwear was dumped upside down and left to dry, Mallory disappeared and reappeared with her bedroll and saddlebags. His eyes had grown accustomed to the darkness now, and he watched as she pulled out a pair of trousers, shirt and vest.

He eyed them speculatively. "That's all you got?"

Casey wished for the first time in her life that she had something else...like a dress. Every touch of his hand had spread little fires up and down her veins, and she didn't want them to stop. She nodded miserably.

"I'll see about getting a fire going while you change," he said abruptly. "I want to look at that leg of yours but I can't do much without light."

"It's all right," she said in a low voice. "Truly it is. It's just still a little sore."

"All that mud won't help." His statement was abrupt, with little of the former sympathy. "What did you think you were doing, anyway?"

"I thought he was following you, that he was planning to kill you."

"And so you decided to save me, is that it?" His voice was rueful with a hint of humor.

"I…I…" It *did* sound ridiculous now. Particularly after what had happened.

And then he asked the question she had been dreading. "And why were you behind me? You should be half a day ahead of me."

Casey hated to lie. She had, in fact, never been good at it for that reason. And she particularly hated to lie to him. She consoled herself with a half truth.

"I did leave town…like I promised. Then…well, I was tired, and I just thought I would get some rest…I rode practically the whole night earlier. And when I started again, I saw you, and there was someone following." She didn't dare say she hadn't recognized the gunfighter because he had discarded the coat and hat. Then Mallory would know she had been in town at the time of the escape. "And you said," she added defensively, "that *he* wouldn't be with you."

There was a silence and Casey was afraid he didn't totally believe her.

"So I did," he said finally. There was a strained note in her voice that made Sean wonder if she wasn't conveniently leaving something out. But it made sense. He thought about the angry Donaldson and started to laugh. He couldn't deny he had enjoyed seeing the arrogant young gunfighter covered in mud and his discomfort at nearly being bested by a girl half his size. He felt, rather than saw, Casey withdraw at his laughter.

He leaned down. "'Twasn't you I was laughing at, wildcat. It was Donaldson. He needed that lesson, and I thank you. But I think it'll be a while before he forgives you for it."

"I don't care if he ever does. If it hadn't been for this leg, he wouldn't have thrown me off."

"I believe you, wildcat."

Funny how the word sounded so different on Mallory's lips. Almost like an endearment. It had been more of a curse when Donaldson had uttered it. "Then you'll still let me come with you?" The question was hopefully posed.

There was another silence. The words came reluctantly. "We'll talk about it tomorrow."

Feeling an emptiness as vast as the dark night, Casey tried desperately to convince him. "I'll do whatever you tell me." She did not think she should push him at this particular moment. He might want to know more about last night.

"Change your clothes," he said abruptly, "while I try to find some wood that's halfway dry.

"Tell me about that gunfighter...why did you help him? Why was he following you?"

"He thinks he owes me."

"Because you helped him break jail?"

"Something like that," Sean said shortly, not wanting to explain his actions.

"But why did you do that?" she insisted. "*You* aren't a gunfighter." Despite the way he wore his gun and that cold light in his eyes when he mentioned Wilson's name, she knew he wasn't a professional. She had seen too many who were.

"No," he said softly. "I'm a rancher."

"You were in the war." Again she spoke with surety, and Sean's eyes measured the girl once more. She was instinctive and bright. He nodded.

"The South?"

"Yes, and before that, with the U.S. army," he added with a strain of bitterness. He had reluctantly resigned his commission when Texas seceded from the Union. It was not a decision easily made, and the next four years had proven to be a hell of conflicting loyalties.

He didn't understand why he was saying so much, particularly to a girl he didn't know well. She hadn't really even asked any questions. She probably *was* a good deputy. She had a unique ability to make people talk.

"Change your clothes," he said again, "and get some sleep."

Sean searched for wood, as much to give her some privacy as any belief that he would find some dry enough to use. As he thought, it was hopeless, and he returned empty-handed. A flash of a match showed the girl had changed and was huddled up in the blanket, asleep. He lit another match and watched her until the flame burned his fingers. The short mud-slicked hair framed a fragile face that seemed achingly vulnerable. Long eyelashes covered the hopeful eyes he recalled all too well, and her lips were curved in a small smile.

Since she was using his blankets and oilcloth, he took her bedroll and unrolled the blankets, wishing she, too, had an oilcloth. She didn't seem to have much of anything. He lay down, feeling the damp earth under him. But he was tired and at least it wasn't cold. He fell into a restless sleep plagued by two shadowy ghosts that flitted in and out of his dreams.

Sean woke to the smell of smoke and coffee. He was startled that he had slept through its preparation. He slept lightly and usually woke at the slightest sound.

The girl must have been extremely quiet. It was dawn, and the sun was just barely peeking over the horizon, shedding a rich pink glow that promised a bright day. The clouds were gone and the pale blue sky was rainwashed. His eyes wandered over to the source of the smell, and he saw the small, lithe form of the girl bending over a struggling fire.

He wondered briefly how she had managed it. The wood

must still be wet, and he doubted if he would have had even her limited success. He kicked off the blanket and rose, stretching to rid his body of the kinks. He felt a soggy wetness in his clothes, but the sun would soon dry them. He could already tell it would be a hot day.

Sean saw the girl's eyes turn on him, then move away quickly as if embarrassed at being caught watching him. His lips twitched with a smile as he studied her.

Although her clothes were clean, her tousled curls were matted with mud. Her face was smeared as though she had made some attempt to wipe it clean but succeeded only in spreading the mud around. It made her look impossibly young, yet when his eyes met hers there was a secretiveness in their green depths that surprised him. They had been so open yesterday, so full of determination and anger and curiosity.

"Coffee," she said in a low, controlled tone with none of the desperation he had sensed during the night.

"Hmm," he answered. The smell was enticing, particularly after the uncomfortable night. "You're a miracle worker. How in the devil did you get a fire going?"

She smiled shyly, and again he was stunned by the way it spread slowly to her eyes and made them sparkle with sudden light. "I told you I'm good at lots of things," she said matter-of-factly.

But then the smile disappeared, and her face seemed to scrunch up with self-condemnation. "Despite last night," she said with chagrin, "I can take care of myself rather well."

"I believe you," Sean said gently, the amber in his eyes turning them a warm golden brown. "And there's nothing to be embarrassed about...Ty Donaldson is one of the best there is. You did damn well against him."

Casey felt her heart squeeze into a tight ball. She had never seen such warmth in a man's eyes. Indeed, she had never met anyone like Sean Mallory. From the first moment they met, he had treated her as a person. He had not sneered, or laughed, or condescended. Her throat constricted and she had a difficult time swallowing. She wished for the first time that she was good at more things than starting a fire and making good coffee and shooting. Good at being a woman, for instance. She knew nothing about that, absolutely nothing. In total confusion, she ducked her head and poured him a cup of coffee.

Aware of her sudden withdrawal, Sean took it without comment. He watched as she unpacked a pan and some bacon from her saddlebags. An unusual contentment settled over him as the smell of sizzling bacon melded with that of the coffee. He knew she was uncomfortable under his gaze, but his eyes kept wandering back to her. She looked older this morning; perhaps it was because the hat was missing, or the mud was not quite so thick. Perhaps it was the competence with which her hands moved as she fed the fire and fixed the meal. Or perhaps it was the touching dignity after the fiasco of the night before. He was reminded of the bartender's words in Two Springs. Without that mud and with different clothes, she would be "right pretty."

Casey divided the bacon between them, giving him a much larger share. He protested, but the smile lit her face again. "I had an unappetizing dinner last night," she explained with a small self-depreciating laugh. Sean found he liked her and was startled to realize how much. But he was not going to let that affect him. He couldn't. It was simply too damn dangerous. He had lost too many friends in the past six years. He didn't want to start caring again.

"Perhaps," he said slowly, "you should return to Two Springs."

Casey's face didn't give any sign of the stab of pain she

felt inside. "I won't be any trouble...I showed you I wouldn't slow you down...and you said..."

"I think that was a mistake. I won't be responsible," Sean said slowly. "I've been responsible for people for years and they keep dying on me. I won't have you on my conscience, too." Like Jim, he thought. Like Jim and so many others.

Casey darted a look at him. This man would always be responsible for others, regardless of how hard he tried to avoid it. So many things in his face, in his eyes, spoke of it. He may not be aware of it, but the very fact he risked his life for someone he didn't like said more about him than any words he might utter. But she didn't want him to feel responsible for her. That wasn't what she wanted, or needed. Not someone to be responsible for her, but someone to partner with. She wouldn't allow herself to think there was anything else, like the sudden rush of blood deep inside her when he spoke, or the way her breath quickened when he looked at her.

Instead, she jumped to another subject. "The gunfighter? You started to tell me about him last night."

"No, I didn't," he said, but his mouth crooked in a slow smile.

"Will you tell me now?"

"You're changing the subject."

She smiled, and he knew he had momentarily lost. There was something very special about that smile, something that stole part of his heart and held on to it.

"We have a mutual friend," he said simply.

Casey's mouth quirked up. "He has Yank trousers on," she observed, and Sean was once more surprised at her quickness. With all that was going on last night, he was surprised she had noted that detail. He wondered when she had observed Donaldson's clothing...on the road or in those brief moments when the matches were lit. He recalled her questions about whether he had been in the war and smiled. She had had a reason for them.

"My friend wore them, too," he replied.

Casey digested that comment for a moment, then probed again.

"I've heard of him. Everyone's heard of Ty Donaldson. But there were never any posters on him."

Like last night, it was a statement rather than a question, and Sean grinned at how effective she was in extracting information. He wondered if it was something she had learned from her father or whether it was instinctive. But he wasn't going to fall into the trap.

"That so?" he said, doing a little prodding of his own.

"None I saw, anyway," she continued as a twinkle appeared in her eyes. She recognized the game between them and challenged him to continue.

"Then there probably weren't any," he observed, not adding that situation had probably changed in the past week.

She saw his eyes change slightly as a certain amount of wariness appeared. "Seems strange he's just following you, 'stead of riding with you."

There it was again. That invitation to speak without a direct question that might offend. No wonder she had learned so much in Fort Worth.

"Not strange at all," Sean said. "He wasn't invited."

"Like me?"

Sean met her eyes and the mischief in them was gone. Instead, there was pain. Sean felt a warm rush of sympathy, but pushed it back. He wasn't going to change his mind.

"Do you have any other family?" he asked, changing the subject.

She shook her head.

"Friends?"

"A sheriff doesn't have many friends, particularly when

his usefulness is gone.'' There was a bitterness in her tone that he hadn't expected.

"There has to be someone in Two Springs."

"No."

The blunt, stark answer caught at him as tears could not have. There was such a casual acceptance of being alone.

"What are you going to do?"

"Go after Wilson. I promised my father." Again, it was a flat, unemotional statement of purpose. "With you or without you."

"And if you find him?"

"I'll kill him." Her voice remained flat, but her chin was set and Sean knew she meant it.

"If he doesn't kill you first...or something worse."

"I saw him shoot bullet after bullet into my father," Casey said in a tight, pinched voice. "He didn't try to kill him, not right away. He wanted to see him beg." Her chin went up. "But he didn't. My father was the bravest man I ever knew."

And you have to live up to him. Sean cursed the man he had never met. He had placed a burden on his daughter no one should bear, particularly a young girl. And he cursed himself because he was finding himself bound to her. He couldn't let her go on alone. Because he knew she would. And alone she would have absolutely no chance against Bob Wilson. But his face revealed nothing as he still sought a way out.

"Then what?" he asked.

There was a tiny shrug. "I'll find someplace...maybe try mining." She added, defiantly, "I could be a good lawman but no one will give me a chance. I know that."

Once more, he felt something invading a part of him that had never before been touched. In some ways Casey reminded him of his sister, Ryan, whom he loved and had tried to protect. But where Ryan had ridden into danger for love, Casey was doing it for vengeance. And where Ryan was as equally at home in a gown as in trousers, he wondered if Casey ever would be.

But both had a rare kind of courage, a quality he respected above all else. And intelligence. It was there in her questions and in her watchful eyes.

But she was a child, damn it…a sometimes beguiling one despite her shapeless clothes…and she shouldn't ride alone with a man, no matter how honorable his intentions. But neither could he allow her to go after Wilson on her own.

"Mr. Mallory…"

His thoughts were jerked back to the moment. "Mr. Mallory." It had been a long time since anyone had called him that. Despite the fact he had been made a major in the last months of the war, he had been "Cap'n" to his men for four years, a title that continued when many of them followed him on the cattle trail. He suddenly realized it was the first time she had addressed him by any name, and it had been awkwardly said. It made him feel old, older even than the thirty-seven hard years he had lived. All the same, a smile tugged at his mouth. His quest was becoming monumentally complicated and his inborn quicksilver humor surfaced. He resisted the temptation to laugh, knowing it would hurt her feelings and he had done enough of that last night.

He eyed her speculatively, and his smile disappeared. "If…and I said if…I agree to let you ride with me you will follow my orders. All of them."

She nodded eagerly.

"If I tell you to stay someplace, you will do it."

She nodded again. At the moment she believed it.

Sean wasn't as sure. "I mean it, Casey."

She sat there, weighing his words, feeling a great burden of shame. She had lied to him once. She decided she wouldn't do it again. Once she gave her word this time, she would keep it, no matter how much it hurt. But then the agreement would only apply as long as she rode with Sean Mallory. When they caught up with Wilson, she could dissolve the agreement with honor.

Sean saw the flicker in her eyes and interpreted it correctly. "No games, Casey. No stretching the rules."

Hellfire, Casey thought. He read her mind like a book. But there would be a way to get around his edict and her promise when the time came. An honorable one. There had to be. In the meantime he would guide her to Wilson. She nodded reluctantly.

"What about the gunslinger?"

"What about him?" Sean said sharply.

"Is he going along?"

"Unless you find a more effective way to dissuade him than I have," Sean replied lazily, hiding the irritation he felt at her interest.

He relaxed at her next words. "I don't like gunfighters."

"Don't worry...he'll keep his distance. He doesn't like me any better than I like him. And I don't think he took much to you, either." The last was said with an engaging smile that sent shivers up and down Casey's spine. There was a certain approval in it.

"I still don't understand..."

"Neither do I, Casey. Not him. Not you. Now let's ride. We've already wasted valuable time."

Casey hesitated. "Can I wash first?" She did not want him to change his mind about taking her along but she knew the mud would become intolerable as the day progressed.

Sean nodded curtly, as if he was already regretting the decision, and Casey felt a painful twist inside. She would be quick, very quick. She grabbed some soap from her saddlebags and walked along the bank of the river out of his sight. The water was muddy along the edges but the center, where there was a current, looked clear. She had to get the mud from her hair. Looking around carefully, she saw no sign of life and quickly undressed before plunging into the river. She was very careful not to go any deeper than her waist. She didn't know how to swim and the current was swift from the heavy rain the day before.

Casey rubbed her face until it hurt and then washed her hair. It took longer than she'd thought, and after two washings it still felt coarse and ugly. For one of the few times in her life, she wanted to look...well, acceptable if not actually pretty. She knew she would never be pretty. She berated herself for thinking of such trivial matters when she should be thinking of her father, of how he looked as the bullets hit him.

Sean waited impatiently, then with a nagging fear. The current in the river was swift from the rain, and he doubted the girl could swim. Few women could. He fought with his worry for a few moments, knowing full well this was exactly why he shouldn't take her with him in the first place. She would slow him down. She would be nothing but trouble. Damn. Why in the hell had he changed his mind again? He was usually decisive.

In combined irritation and worry, he decided to go after her. He was just emerging from some trees when he saw her. Like a water nymph, she stood in the water. The droplets in her hair sparkled in the sun, and small silky curls framed a face that enchanted with its smile. He stepped back, ready to retreat when she started toward the bank, her body slowly taking shape as it emerged from the water.

Sean stood transfixed, unable to move. She was lovely, her body sleek but softly rounded in all the right places. He felt an ache deep within him that became a gentle warmth flooding his body. Balling his hands into fists, he whirled around, cursing himself for a bloody fool. What in the name of God had he done?

But he had given his word. Twice. He would just have to tame himself. His body told him exactly how difficult that would be. He realized that he had just sentenced himself to a very agonizing version of hell.

Chapter Seven

Casey felt better than she had since her father died. The bath seemed to wash away some of the hurts, both in her mind and body, and she felt renewed, purposeful, and more alive, than ever before in her life.

She knew a tingling excitement as she thought about riding with Sean Mallory. She couldn't forget his hard strength last night when he had carried her, or the warmth of his golden eyes. She had seen those moments of smoldering rage when he talked about Wilson and again in the brief confrontation with the gunfighter last night. She had encountered enough dangerous men to recognize the quality in Mallory, and she would not like to be the object of his anger.

Her step was light when she returned to their camp. Mallory was tying a guitar to his saddle and didn't look at her as she approached. She saw from the way he tensed that he noticed her return. When he faced her, his eyes were a cold, hard brown, and her heart dropped. She was sure he regretted his offer.

"I was too long," she said hesitantly. "I'm sorry."

Sean's lips compressed into a grim line. How could he even be thinking what he was thinking with a girl young enough to be his daughter? But the ache in his loins had deepened as he'd turned around and seen the swirl of wet curls framing her face, the sudden fiery defiance in her green eyes a stark contrast to the hopeful smile on her lips.

He wanted to go back on his word and avoid the pain he sensed was coming. But he couldn't do it.

"It's all right," he said abruptly, but his voice held none of its former warmth, and Casey felt a cold chill settle inside her. He *was* regretting his decision but was too honorable to go back on it. She would prove to him he hadn't made a mistake.

His glance went to her leg. She was not limping as badly this morning. "How's your leg?"

"It's better...it's getting better every day... I just...sort of strained it last night."

"Perhaps I should look at it."

"The wound's healed," she said quickly. "The muscles just hurt sometimes."

His gaze was very intense, as if weighing her words. "Tell me when you get tired."

"I won't get tired," she insisted. "I won't slow you down." Her hand went nervously to her hair and she searched the ground for her hat before realizing she hadn't seen it since the scuffle the night before. As much as she hated to strain Mallory's patience any longer, her hat had been one of her few gifts from her father, and she loved the battered, shapeless thing.

"I forgot something," she said self-consciously. "You go on. I'll catch up."

"Why?"

Casey bit her lip, looking even younger than before. "My hat. I must have dropped it last night."

Sean's chilly expression thawed. Donaldson wouldn't be happy to see her. But he merely nodded.

"I won't hold you up, truly I won't," she reassured him.

He surprised her by grinning. "Give Donaldson my best," and the sudden devilish light in his eyes almost blinded her. She wished she didn't continually feel so confused when he was around...or go quite so mute.

In desperation, she moved away and saddled her horse with an efficiency that once more won Sean's approval. She swung up easily into the saddle, and he smiled at the relaxed seat he remembered seeing in Fort Worth. He was beginning to learn she had not exaggerated her skills.

He stepped toward her. "Casey..."

"I won't be long," she repeated.

His grin disappeared. "Don't rile Donaldson too much. He can be unpredictable..."

Casey sniffed. "I can take care of myself, particularly with a gunfighter. He's nothing but a paid killer."

"That's exactly what I mean," Sean said, his amusement gone. Whatever he thought of Ty Donaldson, he didn't think he would hurt a girl, but when goaded...he didn't know. Still he couldn't follow the girl everywhere. He had to trust her judgment, or he had no business allowing her to come along.

Sensing his continuing hesitation and reluctance to take her, Casey turned her horse around and went toward the direction she and the gunfighter had tussled the night before.

Bemused, Sean watched her disappear. Whatever problems he encountered in the next few weeks, he suspected boredom would not be among them. There would be nothing amusing about the odd duo that he had reluctantly acquired. His lips firmed grimly again. They were already presenting him with any number of difficulties, all of which warred with his fierce desire for order and careful planning. Boredom. Had he ever wished it gone? He suspected he would crave its peace before all this ended.

* * *

Filled with a contentiousness born of her own uncertainty and spoiling for a fight, Casey spurred her horse toward Ty Donaldson. Although her goal at the moment was her hat, she was also curious about the gunfighter and his connection to Mallory. She wanted, needed, to understand.

When she reached Donaldson's camp, she was met with a hostility that fed her own.

He was bare chested, having just come from the river where he too had bathed. His blue cavalry trousers were soaked wet and pasted to his well-formed thighs, and his black hair was dripping. His eyes were a piercing blue-violet that chilled straight through to the bone.

"Ah, the little hellion." It seemed to suit her better than "wildcat" this morning, especially with all his bruises. "Want a rematch?"

"I wouldn't soil my hands with a varmint like you," Casey said with an insolence that equaled his.

"Nooo...? Then to what ill wind do I owe this visit?" His manhood was still tender from the blow last night, and he didn't like being reminded that he had been surprised by a female. His eyes narrowed with a threat that usually sent wiser souls on their way.

"You have my hat," Casey said.

Ty looked at a tree and the object under it. "You mean that's a hat? I thought it was a dead animal of some sort."

"You must be smelling yourself, Donaldson. Pure polecat."

"You didn't smell so good yourself last night," he mocked in return.

"Not so bad I didn't surprise you," she retorted. "From your reputation I thought you would be better than that. I'm disappointed."

"Don't be, little girl. I didn't have to try real hard with you. If Mallory hadn't interfered..." He left the sentence dangling.

"If he hadn't, you wouldn't be walking today," Casey retorted, looking with satisfaction at the part of him that still ached with a half smile as if she knew it was still paining him.

Ty fought to hold his temper. He had never fought with a woman until last night, and he wouldn't have then had he known his attacker's sex. Except, perhaps, to give her a good spanking. A really good spanking. His eyes glinted with sheer anticipation at the thought, and he took several steps in her direction.

But Casey quickly read his intention and whirled her horse around. In a quick movement she was off the animal and back on in a fraction of a second, triumphantly holding her hat and spurring her horse beyond his reach. It was all so sudden that Donaldson couldn't get near her. He looked after her with astonishment and a grudging admiration as she disappeared from view, a light laughter lingering in her wake.

Any laughter Casey had quickly disappeared when she caught up with Mallory. His face was as hard as Donaldson's and showed no greeting. She pulled up beside him, wanting to say something but his forbidding look stopped her. Instead, she pulled on her hat, hiding her face underneath its wide brim, and adjusted her horse's gait to his.

From time to time, she stole a glance at his face, only to find it frozen, his eyes dark and hooded with no trace of the golden sparks that made them so magnetic. He wore no hat, and the sun hit his ruffled bronze hair, causing it to glitter with specks of gold. It was thick and curled just a little, giving him a permanent tousled look, which increased throughout the morning as his hand raked it impatiently, pushing the gold-tinged strands from his sun-colored forehead.

By midday his dark brown shirt was plastered to his body

with sweat, outlining the wide shoulders and hard, lean chest laced with muscles. He had rolled the sleeves of his shirt up above his elbows, and Casey's eyes were constantly drawn to the bronzed arms and strong hands that were beautiful in their symmetry. Golden hairs emphasized the deep, rich dark color of his skin. She kept remembering how those same hands had started little wildfires in her body.

Don't, Casey, she scolded herself. Think of Wilson and what you need to do. If Mallory even suspects your mind is wandering up these trails, he will leave you faster than a rabbit in a prairie fire.

But she wished he would talk to her, instead of twisting his mouth in that determined grim line. She still didn't know exactly what to call him. She had started with "Mr. Mallory," and he hadn't invited anything else this morning, but it sounded so formal if they were to be riding together. She decided to dare a question despite his forbidding look.

"Mr. Mallory?"

He looked over at her, squinting in the sun like a lazy golden cougar. He answered with a raised eyebrow.

"What should I call you?"

The eyebrow went higher.

"I mean," she continued awkwardly, "'Mr. Mallory' sounds a little...well...strange." An impish look lit her eyes. "I mean," she struggled on without any assistance from him, "if we run into trouble or something it might take time to say, 'Watch your back, Mr. Mallory.'"

Sean couldn't suppress the beginnings of a smile. She looked so expectant, so hopeful.

"Sean," he said slowly, hoping he wasn't making a grave error. But he'd gone this far, and it was ridiculous to think a name could put any distance between them. He was committed now. "Call me Sean," he added with a crooked twist of his mouth. "Partner."

A small glow started inside Casey and spread rapidly. "Partner." He'd said "partner." She tried his name in her mind. Sean. Sean Mallory. It was an attractive name. Like him. Lean and hard and sure. And yet it had a warm musical quality. She tasted the sound of it on her lips and liked it even more. "Irish," she said.

"To the core," he replied, the lips easing even more. "With all the black moods and tempers. Are you sure you want to brave them?"

Casey turned her eyes away so he couldn't see how very much she wanted to brave them. She would give him no chance to change his mind. Yet she didn't want him to stop talking.

"The guitar. You play?"

"A little."

She wished she didn't have to pry everything out of him. She didn't want to appear too curious. That was another lesson she'd learned from her father. If there's a reason to ask questions, do. Otherwise, a man's business is his own.

But she couldn't resist now she'd started and met with some success, small as it was.

"You said you felt responsible for Wilson?"

Sean's slight smile disappeared, and Casey was afraid she might have lost the ground she'd won.

What to tell her. Sean agonized over the question. He was reluctant to talk about the past, about the year that tested all his loyalties and values. But after several moments of silence, he started talking.

If she was going to go with him, she ought to know what kind of enemy they were chasing, what kind of fanatical hate they were up against. Perhaps then she would follow his instructions more readily.

"Wilson rode with me during the war. He volunteered for a special troop I was forming and, much to my regret, I selected him. He was a crack marksman and didn't know the word fear. But neither did he understand obedience or honor. He was a killer from the start, and he grew worse. God help me, I should have gotten rid of him as soon as I recognized what he really was. But I needed men badly.'' A muscle tensed in his cheek. ''And he was the best there was with a rifle.

''I took a prisoner, a Yank colonel who was once a friend of mine. Wilson tried to kill him in cold blood when he was chained, and I shot Wilson, smashing his right hand. He vowed vengeance against us both and he almost succeeded several months ago. Instead he killed a man who had ridden with me for six years, among others.''

''You and this Yank colonel? You were together again at the time?''

Christ, she was quick. ''He's my brother-in-law now.''

''And he's the 'mutual' friend you and the gunfighter have?''

Sean wondered if she would ever cease to surprise him. She had very accurately pieced together any number of little bits of information. It was unsettling.

''I'm afraid so,'' he said shortly, his tone warning against any additional questions. Much of the past was still painful to him and he wasn't ready to share it.

Casey nodded, pleased at the amount she had learned and not ready to risk endangering the tenuous trust he had extended. She fell quiet, going over what she had heard.

Sean Mallory was becoming more and more intriguing by the moment.

Sean quickened the pace. There weren't many places to hide in this area of Texas, and he had a hunch that Wilson would follow the Santa Fe Trail into New Mexico, along the Pecos River and up into Colorado. With new herds leaving daily for the mining towns, they would offer rich pickings, indeed. And the sooner he found the outlaw, the faster he would get rid of the two millstones around his neck.

At least that's what he told himself.

He didn't have to look at his companion to know she appeared more boy than woman again in those shapeless clothes and ridiculous hat. Yet his mind wouldn't let go of this morning's brief glimpse of her coming out of the water. She's a child, he reminded himself. A child.

He must be crazy. Crazy to take her along. Yet he thought he could protect her better this way. And, damn it, he seemed to have an overwhelming urge to do exactly that.

Sean searched for reasons why. Was it for her? Or for himself?

He could not deny the deep emptiness he had felt for the past several years. Perhaps it had grown even more painful as he'd observed the deep and sensitive love between his sister and his friend. It had been unmistakable and searing from the first moment the two had met and had overcome any number of obstacles. Reluctant at first to give his approval, Sean had come to delight in the union, but the couple's unbridled happiness had made his own loneliness more acute. His parents had had a similar magic before their deaths many years earlier, and he had vowed that he would never settle for anything less. Not that there had been much opportunity in the past years to look. He had been the next thing to a monk during four years of war, and two years on the cattle trails had yielded little more in the way of feminine companionship.

Damn. It was ridiculous to even think of Casey in those terms. There was something he had to do, and something she felt she had to do, and that was all there was between them. Except, perhaps, an easy companionship that had been there almost from the beginning. He liked her. Liked her independence and courage and stubbornness. Liked the way she probed so very gently but skillfully. He thought of her chagrin last night when she was covered with mud and yet there had been a certain touching pride about her. She and Donaldson had been like two beavers fighting over the same small pond, teeth bared and tails up.

Sean rode them into exhaustion that day. They found one ranch where they refilled their canteens, but didn't see anything of Ty Donaldson until Sean finally called a halt at dusk. The ground was covered with prairie dog holes, and he didn't want to risk the horses by traveling at night.

Without being told, Casey immediately started gathering buffalo chips for a fire and then produced flour with which she made biscuits, and bacon, which she fried as Sean looked on with amazement.

"Any more talents I should know about?" he asked with a satisfied smile as he finished dipping the fresh biscuits in the bacon grease and savored the cup of coffee.

Casey merely smiled in return, embarrassed by the compliment and uncertain about the answer. She shrugged and started cleaning the skillet she had brought with her.

A full moon was halfway up the sky, spilling its light across the prairie. The sky was a dark, rich blue, not quite midnight black yet, and beaded with thousands of flickering stars. The evening was quiet and still as if recovering from the fierce, wild storm of the night before. A misleading calm, Sean thought. Nothing was peaceful these days, at least not in Texas. Between the outlaws and Indians and the carpetbag government, no one was safe.

He took out his guitar and fingered the strings. He had covered it with the oilcloth last night, but it was still damp. He crossed his legs and let his hands take over, first with "Lorena," then a Spanish lullaby. He lost himself in the music until he heard Casey's soft voice humming along. It was a rich throaty sound and he glanced over at her. The hat was gone, and the short curly hair seemed to catch light from the moon while the green eyes glowed brightly in the flames of the fire. There was a soft wistfulness in her face that belied the toughness he sometimes saw in her. Now she directed a tentative smile at him and he felt a tenderness different from any he had felt before.

Trying to drive it away, he changed the tempo of his music into a spirited version of "Dixie," but it faltered when he saw a lone horseman approach. From the lean, careless posture, he knew it was Donaldson. His fingers moved again, this time giving "Dixie" an impudent, defiant air as Donaldson drew up to the dying fire.

"You never know when you're beaten, do you, Mallory?" Ty's lazy question was just as insolent as Sean's music was defiant, and Casey could feel the renewed tension in the air.

Sean's voice was frigid when he answered. "A good thing for you, perhaps, that I don't or you might well have been in the ground tonight and Texas would be well rid of you."

Casey hoped with all her might that the gunfighter, or Sean, would continue. She was consumed by curiosity over this antagonism between them.

But Ty's lips merely tightened. "You aren't taking *her* with you, are you?"

Casey stiffened, but Sean merely smiled...if the sardonic twist of his mouth could be called a smile. "I don't think that's any of your business."

"It is if it endangers us all. She's nothing but trouble."

"And you aren't?" The question was posed quietly, but filled with implication.

The young gunfighter tensed. "You have to be crazy. She isn't even pretty. I've never seen a girl dress like that before. It ain't right."

Sean looked over to Casey and saw a flicker of pain dart across her face before it puckered into rage.

"At least I don't murder people for money," she retorted. His comment hurt, because he was right. She had been told that often enough but it never mattered before. Now it did. Terribly.

"No," the young gunfighter sneered. "You just like ambushing people!"

"When they're sidewinders like you," she agreed, her voice suddenly silky. Only Sean detected the steel in her tone and he looked on with interest. She was giving as good as she was getting.

"Go home, little girl," the gunfighter mocked.

"You don't have the right to tell me anything. Fact is you're the danger, you and that poisonous reputation."

The two glared at each other until it was Ty who dropped his eyes. She was, in part, right, though he hated to admit it. It was the reason he had swallowed his pride and caught up with Mallory.

Ty knew Caldwell would not give up easily, not after his son's death. He felt sure the rancher would put a price on his head, and there would be bounty hunters swarming around him like bees to a clover field. As much as he detested Mallory, he didn't want *anyone* caught in the cross fire as a result of helping him. At the same time, he couldn't let go of the notion he had to rid himself of an obligation.

He momentarily ignored the girl and fixed his glittering amethyst eyes on Sean. He sunk into his saddle, his shoulders seeming to fold into artificial ease. His eyes told Sean there was nothing relaxed about him. His sharpened tone fortified that image. "Where are you heading?"

Sean's mouth crooked upward. "You mean you're not going to follow anymore? And to what do I owe this respite?"

Ty's mouth tightened. "I have some business," he said grimly.

"Don't let us keep you."

"Damn you, Mallory. You need me. More than ever with her along." His nod in Casey's direction was pure contempt.

Casey had had all she could take. This arrogant young jackass riled her more than all the detractors she had encountered up to now. He suddenly represented each and every one of them, and she hated him. All the more so for his callous comments in front of Sean Mallory. She wished with all her being she could wipe that scornful smile from his face by telling him she helped him get away. But she bit her lip as she looked at Sean's set face.

"I can shoot as well as you," she challenged. "And I sure as hell can ride better." She winced at the curse word that escaped her lips. She had resolved not to utter any more profanity in front of Sean, but Donaldson brought out the worst in her. Even while she recognized she was probably making a fool out of herself again, she couldn't stop. All gunfighters were lower than a toad's belly and she'd be damned if this one would get the best of her. She noticed Sean's narrowed gaze on her. It was neither approving nor disapproving, merely watchful.

Donaldson's eyes glittered and the grim set of his mouth twisted into a small smile. "Like to test that statement?" he asked.

"Any time," she retorted.

"Tomorrow morning, then," Donaldson answered, his smile spreading to a satisfied grin. "We'll have some target practice."

He nodded to Sean. "We'll get back to this conversation in the morning." He turned his horse around to the direction from which he'd appeared and spurred the animal into an easy canter.

There was silence as both Sean and Casey watched him disappear.

Casey eyed Sean quizzically, wishing she knew what he

was thinking, but his face was like granite as he carefully lay down the guitar. "It's time to get some sleep," he said shortly. "There was precious little of it last night."

Casey flinched, knowing she had been the cause of that. She suspected she had angered him, or disappointed him in some way. She also had a nagging fear she might have made a mistake, but she knew she was very good with a gun. Perhaps not as fast as the gunfighter, not if everything she'd heard was true, but she was deadly accurate. It would give her a chance to prove herself to Sean, to show him she wouldn't be a burden, that she could pull her own weight. She lay down on a blanket, using her saddlebags as a pillow, and looked up at the star-studded sky, listening to the comforting noises of the night. She was vividly aware of Sean Mallory who had doused the fire completely and was now lying some ten yards away. She wished she didn't have this intense longing to feel his touch, but the least tiny thought of him hurried the blood along in her veins. Her body cried out for something she didn't understand but she knew it centered on Sean Mallory.

A tear rolled down her face. His face had shuttered after Ty Donaldson left, and she had felt none of the warmth that had sometimes reached out to her during the long day in the saddle. He probably thought her no better than Donaldson, a nuisance, a stone around his neck. She certainly had ruined any chance that he might look at her as a woman after her foolish heated words with Donaldson and her subsequent challenge. The most she could expect now was his respect, and she would do her damnedest to earn that in the morning.

With an aching loneliness, Casey closed her eyes and tried her best to summon a sleep that would not come.

Sean Mallory eyed the two combatants critically. Ty had appeared, as promised, with the first light of dawn, but Casey had been up for more than an hour. A pot of coffee was half gone, its pungent smell filling the still air. Sean knew she was tense; her shoulders were squared and her mouth unsmiling. Her eyes were moss green with none of the brightness he had seen in them yesterday. Instead they were clouded and secretive. There had been no smile this morning, not even a hint of one, and she had poured his coffee silently.

Sparking with antagonism like two barnyard roosters, Ty and Casey decided on a target, a small, lonely bush. Ty tucked his bandanna among its prickly branches and counted off steps.

The two of them then stood, their feet apart, their eyes intent on the target, waiting for Sean to make the count.

Not for the first time this morning he wondered why he was taking part in it. They looked to his jaded eyes like two children playing with toy guns in the street.

But he needed to know their capabilities if they were to travel with him. He knew Donaldson's reputation, but he had never seen him handle a gun. And there was much you could tell in that split second between drawing and firing.

On the count of three, the shots exploded within a hairbreadth of each other, though Ty unquestioningly was the fastest. Sean walked to the bush. There were two bullet holes, close together, on the piece of cloth.

Casey and Donaldson moved farther back, and once more Sean gave the signal. Both young contestants were lightning fast, their movements clean and graceful, but Ty had the extra speed and confidence. Once more their aim was true.

The contest went on, and the sun climbed higher. As the two moved farther and farther away, Ty continued to excel on speed, but Casey's aim remained in the center of the target, while Ty's accuracy decreased. Sean guessed it was the difference in experience. Ty's need had always been speed, necessary in a face-to-face gunfight in which he excelled, where Casey's skill was acquired on posses where marksmanship was more important.

Sean finally called an end to it. The youngsters had battled quietly and with the deadly dedication of two people who were very good at what they did.

Better than he was, Sean admitted, as he watched. He was a good shot, but he had never been a fast one. In war, you didn't have to be fast. You only had to be accurate and thorough. And he had always been that. As he watched Casey and Ty, he felt his blood chill at their concentration in so deadly a skill. He tried to equate it with the quiet, often-shy Casey with whom he shared the day, and could not.

Ty had gone to fetch the remnants of his bandanna, and he eyed both pieces of cloth with something close to respect. He turned to Casey.

"Not bad...for a girl. Not so fast, though."

"At least I can hit the side of a barn," Casey returned maliciously.

"Doesn't do any good if you're dead."

"Doesn't do any good to be fast if you can't hit your target any better than that." She wouldn't admit that those few inches at such a distance were rather insignificant.

Ty eyed her with frustration. She just didn't know when to quit. Like Mallory. They belonged together, he thought venomously. He turned to Mallory.

"I asked you yesterday. Which way are you heading?"

"Why don't you forget all about this? I told you there was no need."

Ty stared at him with frustration. "I could just follow you, and then someone might link me with you. I don't really think you want that."

"Damned right, I don't." Sean's gaze wandered over to

Casey. Her eyes were darting back and forth, interest hovering deep within their recesses.

"There's no way I can get rid of you?" he asked Donaldson hopefully.

"Not until the Wilson matter is solved."

"It's not your affair."

"Even if I didn't owe you, I would do it for Ben. And from what you say it's his affair, too."

"He would gladly relieve you of it. Besides you showed precious little loyalty to him on the ranch." An unusual dark scowl clouded Sean's features.

Casey didn't think Donaldson's face could harden more than it already had, but she was wrong. A muscle flexed in his cheek and for a moment Casey thought he might attack Sean. When he finally spoke, it was through clenched teeth. "He didn't need me, you know that, Mallory. It just created problems."

"Problems you made," Sean said contemptuously.

The muscle seemed to want to jump out of Donaldson's cheek. Casey's hand went to the handle of the gun she had just loaded and holstered, but after a moment the gunfighter seemed to force himself to relax again.

"Will you tell me where you're going, or do I keep tailing you? And," he added slowly, "I trust you'll keep to your word. You're the honorable type." The last was a sneer.

It was all Sean could do to keep from punching Donaldson, but that would solve nothing, and at least he would get Donaldson off his back for a little while. "The Santa Fe Trail," he said slowly. "Perhaps I'll get lucky and a bounty hunter will get you before you catch up."

"Perhaps," Ty said, as he ambled over to his horse. "But I wouldn't bet on it."

Unfortunately, neither would he, Sean thought grimly to himself.

Chapter Eight

Casey tried. She really tried.

But on the fourth day, she gave up attempting to be anything but what she was.

She had wanted desperately to please Sean in every way she could, even if it meant suppressing her normally fierce desire for independence and equality.

She had let him hunt, and she had done the cooking. She had let him help her mount and dismount. She had kept silent when she wanted to ask millions of questions.

She told herself it was because of Wilson…because Sean was her best chance for revenge, and she didn't want to do anything to anger him. But way down deep she knew she was lying. It was because something new was happening inside her…something terrifying because she didn't understand it…something wonderful because of the new senses it awakened…something mysterious that lay just beyond her reach. But she was afraid to grab for it, afraid it would disappear for-ever.

Thoroughly perplexed, she tried to mold herself into the best possible traveling companion. She did what was expected, even though she chafed under his assumption that she would do the womanly things, like cooking, while he did the male things, like hunting.

Part of her desperately wanted to tell him about the sheriff in Fort Worth, to show him how competent she was, how helpful she could be. But a look at his firm, disciplined mouth always stopped her. She had more than a little suspicion that Sean was not a man who tolerated either disobedience or lying. So she kept her silence, glancing sideways at him from time to time. His smile had not reappeared in the past days, despite her attempts to win his approval. He was grim, keeping her at a distance, speaking only when necessary and touching only while helping her on and off the horse.

Hellfire. As if she needed help! She had been helping herself nigh on to nineteen years, but she allowed it without comment because she was fascinated with the effect of his flesh on hers.

She was ashamed to admit she wanted his touch to linger, but it never did. He usually jerked his hand away as if burned and she could only surmise that it was distasteful to him. So after three days, Casey decided it was hopeless trying to earn anything other than polite formality from him, and she might as well go back to being the person she had always been—a bit mulish, perhaps, but independent.

It had been very dry since the freak storm the night she had attacked Donaldson, more like the Texas weather she had always known, and the land had flattened to an empty waterless grassland. Sean had shot three rabbits, but other than that they had eaten mostly biscuits and jerky. They had seen numerous bone-thin longhorns, descendants of herds brought here years ago by the Mexican ranchers, but Sean had been reluctant to kill one, knowing they could take little of it with them since he wanted to travel fast.

Once more he puzzled her. Most men couldn't care less about whether there would be waste or not. They would just cut a piece of meat and leave the rest for the buzzards and coyotes. When she had looked at him with questioning eyes, Sean merely shrugged, his mouth losing none of its taut control.

"Respect life, Casey," he said. "Never take it lightly, never take more than you need." He increased the pace then, leaving her more mystified than ever about a man who was willing to spend months hunting another, to kill him, when he refused to kill a cow because he couldn't eat all the meat.

But then everything about him baffled her. He was unlike any man she had ever met, a strange combination of gentleness and strength, of compassion and murderous intent. She would never understand him.

And she wanted to. But not at the price of her own independence, of being who she was. After days of trying to be something she was not, she decided to give up. When they stopped at the end of the fourth day, she stretched in the saddle, ignoring his hand.

"Guess I'll go see if I can find us a rabbit," she said.

For the first time in days, he smiled, his eyes crinkling in concert with the eased lips. Her heart bounded at the mischief in them as she realized, only too clearly, that he understood exactly what she was doing. It was scary the way he could read her mind.

But he merely nodded. As she turned her mount, the smile grew to a grin. "I'll make the fire," he said, gentle amusement softening the voice that had been harsh for the past few days.

It didn't take Casey long. The grass harbored hundreds of rabbits and she was as good a shot with a rifle as she was with a pistol. A fire was going when she returned, and Sean said nothing as she took a knife and quickly skinned her kill.

When she looked up, she saw his eyes warm on her, and

she basked under their impact. How strange that she had been trying to please him without succeeding until she pleased herself.

Casey darted a look at him. "How come you know so much about people?" she asked.

The lines around his eyes crinkled again. "I don't," he said, "but I have a sister, and I learned a lot from her." The smile grew wider. "All about stubbornness...and one-minded determination. You remind me a lot of her."

"Your sister?" Casey said in wonder. "Like me?" She could scarcely believe there was someone else like her.

"There are similarities," Sean added dryly. "She was with my troop part of the time during the war...could ride as well as any of them. Like you. She even helped me escape jail once."

"Is that one of the reasons you helped Donaldson?" she asked.

"Partly, I guess. They wanted to hang me, too. It left me with a poor taste for such proceedings." The smile was gone, and Casey felt as if she had lost something important. She remembered his tenseness in the hotel room in Fort Worth when he had said a hanging was nothing for a person to see.

"She married that Union colonel?"

Sean nodded, but his face was expressionless again, and Casey could almost feel him withdrawing from her although he didn't move.

The quick grin returned as he changed the subject. "I'll cook," he said, "since you brought back the food."

Casey could only nod, dazed by the quickly changing currents in his mood, afraid for the moment to test this new one. She fetched her old frying pan from the saddlebags. She had learned years ago that it was well worth the trouble on the trail. You could do anything with it...make bread, stew, biscuits. Anything. She watched him in the twilight as his hands split the meat and piled it in the pan, and slowly her eyes began to close. She hadn't realized how tired she was.

She woke to a curse and the smell of burning meat. When her eyes opened, Sean was trying to rescue the rapidly burning pieces of their dinner from the center of the fire with a knife. He gave her a sheepish look as one poor burned piece emerged from the flames, and his lips turned into a lopsided smile that tugged at her heart. "I'm not used to one of these things," he finally allowed.

It was astonishing to know he wasn't good at everything. It was worth losing the rabbit. A giggle started inside Casey as she watched him hold the piece of blackened meat as if it were about to bite him. "I think there's some jerky in my saddlebags," she said, choking back her laughter.

He gave her a pained expression that set the laughter free.

"I think I'll let you do the hunting if you promise never to cook again," she added, merriment spilling from her like water from a fall. Her eyes sparkled and the tones of her laughter rang as rich as chimes in a church.

Sean was stunned. It was the first time he had seen her so carefree. She was enchanting. Not just pretty, but beautiful, and he felt a peculiar lightness, a wild surge of joy, that was totally new to him. He wanted to take her, and hold her, and make the laughter go on and on. Instead, he steeled himself from touching her. This was not the time nor the place, and nothing could be so damaging to them both or to his goal as falling in love. If, he thought with a touch of disbelief, that was what was happening.

But he could barely tear his eyes from her as he straightened up, or suppress his own smile as he rose and gave her a mock bow. "Jerky, it is," he said, grateful for a reason to turn away from her. "I can, at least, serve..."

Controlling his feelings became more and more difficult

during the next few days, and Sean stepped up their already killing pace. But although Casey often limped at the end of the day, she never complained. She even seemed more relaxed than before, more confident, quicker to smile. Each time she did it was as if a rainbow had emerged after a storm, and Sean felt his heart lurch. He was beginning to realize more each day that he had to leave Casey someplace safe. He could barely think of anything but her, and he simply couldn't afford that. He would get them both killed.

On the tenth day, Sean and Casey stopped at a small ranch for water. They were greeted enthusiastically by a man and woman and two small children, all achingly hungry for company. Their closest neighbors had pulled up and left a year ago after an Indian scare, and the Kelloggs were now the only settlers within a fifty-mile radius.

When they stopped, Sean simply introduced Casey as a younger brother. It made explanations easier, and with her hat brim pulled down over her face, and the rough clothes, she was readily accepted as such. Her husky voice passed well enough for a boy's, and she had a natural reticence that made her comfortable with few words.

"Stay the night with us," the rancher's wife, Susan Kellogg, pleaded. "We have a loft where the boys sleep, but they can use the barn tonight. Please."

The loneliness was evident in her face and Sean's eyes met Casey's. He had driven her mercilessly over the past few days, hoping she might weary of the journey and give up on her own. But now he knew that was a futile wish, and she looked so damned tired, her shoulders slumped and eyes dulled of their usual brightness. A hot meal and a bed would do wonders for both of them.

He nodded, wincing at the guilt he felt when he saw the instant delight in her face. He had been so concerned with keeping his thoughts and mind away from her that he had ignored her exhaustion and pain.

Susan Kellogg gave them a brilliant smile. "I baked some bread this morning, and we have a fine stew."

Sean smiled that warm smile that always made Casey's blood stop flowing. "You don't know what a treat it will be, Mrs. Kellogg."

Casey felt a familiar lump in her throat. He had a way of setting anyone at ease with that slow, easy smile, everyone but her. After the burned dinner he had not given her any hint of his thoughts, nor had he taken out his guitar, much less graced her with a smile. It was as if he were placing as much distance between the two of them as possible. But now the breathtaking smile was back and settling on someone else like a warming sun.

She couldn't deflect a wicked stab of jealousy, even though she knew he was merely being polite. Mrs. Kellogg might, at one time, have been a pretty woman, but now her face was weathered and aged by the sun, and her eyes dulled by constant fear and hard work.

Dinner was a gay affair. Even Calvin Kellogg, who seemed naturally taciturn, was talkative. A lean, thin man whose face was hardened by work and recurring disasters, he asked searching questions about the Indians, outlaws and the reconstruction government.

"Their taxes are driving out hundreds of ranchers," Sean said grimly. "Carpetbaggers are flooding Texas trying to scoop up land for practically nothing, and the government is helping them. The army or state police arrests anyone who complains or tries to do anything about it. And that's the only damn thing they're doing. They're not doing anything about the Comanche or Kiowa raids, or bands like Wilson's."

"I heard tell of him...someone through here a couple of weeks ago said he raided a ranch to the west of me, took all the cattle."

Sean's body tensed. "Did they say what direction he took?"

"A posse followed them until they reached the Territory of New Mexico. They were going due west toward the Pecos."

Sean nodded with satisfaction. His hunch had been right.

"You going after him alone?"

"Hopefully we can find some honest law where he's headed."

Kellogg looked at Sean and Casey dubiously and changed the subject. "You been in the war?" The question, the rancher thought, was unnecessary. His visitor had a lethal quality that seemed to separate those who fought in the recent war from those who hadn't.

Sean nodded.

"The South?"

Again, Sean's short nod. "And you?"

"I stayed out of it. Just couldn't do it. My father fought with Sam Houston, and Houston opposed secession. I did, too...figured it the slaveholders' fight...though this reconstruction business is changing my mind. Ain't right taking people's property like that."

Sean's warm smile flashed. "My father was also with Houston. Perhaps they fought together."

"San Jacinto?"

Sean nodded.

"By God," Kellogg said. "Then by sure damn they did. This calls for a drink."

He rose from the table and disappeared, returning with a large jug. "Some of the best whiskey in these parts," he commented as he poured a portion in two cups, then eyed Casey warily. "He old enough?"

Sean eyed Casey speculatively, amusement dancing in his eyes as he saw her hopeful apprehension. Contradictions. Always contradictions. He nodded. "A little, perhaps."

Casey, who had never had anything but beer, took a large swallow to show she was a match for them. It burned like nothing she had ever experienced, catching in her throat and staying there. To her humiliation, she started to choke, and Sean slapped her back, sending her into agonies of coughing.

Kellogg tried politely not to smile, but the two boys were not as diplomatic and grinned ear to ear, while Mrs. Kellogg rushed for a cup of water. Flushed and mortified, Casey took it and quenched some of the fire that remained in her throat. She looked at the rest of the whiskey as if it were a war-painted Comanche.

"That's why the Indians call it firewater," Sean said. "You drink it slow and carefully." His lips twitched with the effort not to smile, and he saw her green eyes catch fire. Her chin went up with the familiar defiance, and he felt a disturbing mixture of pride and tenderness. She was like a half-wild kitten still feeling its way, full of its own independence and irresistibly curious about everyone and everything around her.

He watched as she tried the cup again, this time a tiny sip. She grimaced but struggled gamely on. He understood. The whiskey was strong, even for him. It somehow matched the unforgiving life on these plains. He thought briefly of his land near San Antonio, in the rich hill country of Texas, with its thousands of wildflowers and winding river, and for a moment he yearned for it with all his being. He wondered why anyone stayed here where the earth baked into layers of clay, and the colors were all dull except for the brilliant, tortuous sun.

After dinner, Sean fetched his guitar and entertained the Kellogg family until late in the evening.

Casey watched as the boys climbed all over him, and he

patiently showed the older one how to play a tune. His face softened in the light of the candles that warmed the barren adobe home. The golden streaks in his eyes were bright as his hands caressed the strings of the guitar. She thought she had never heard anything so lovely as the sounds he created, and they revealed more about him than any word he had uttered. There was a haunting loneliness under that power, a searching, yearning quality that embroidered even the wild flamenco that filled the house with its pounding rhythm.

He ended with a love song, and Casey saw his delighted smile when Kellogg asked his wife to dance and the request brought a sudden blaze of joy to the woman's face. Sean Mallory was the nicest man she had ever met, when he wasn't thinking of Wilson or that young gunfighter, she amended. She could tell how much he enjoyed giving pleasure. He was so handsome with the smile on his face and his eyes alight with enjoyment. He had changed to a clean dark brown shirt, which served to emphasize the bronze color of his skin and the golden brown of his eyes. His face was knitted in concentration as he played, the strong cheekbones leading down to the finely drawn lips. Again, Casey felt paralyzed as a hard knot formed in her chest. She wished he was playing just for her. She shook herself. He must never know she was thinking such things, or she would wind up alone. Trying to swallow the lump in her throat, she dropped her eyes, afraid everything she felt was only too evident. Casey wished intently that she was pretty, and she glanced down at her rough trousers with distaste. They smelled of horse; all of her, in fact, smelled of horse. She thought of the mayor's unfortunate daughter, remembering the sweet smell the girl always wore. Casey had always scorned such fripperies, but now she wished with all her heart she had some.

All too soon the evening ended. Casey and Sean were

given a candle lamp and they climbed the ladder to the loft. Sean had to nearly double over or his head would hit the roof. When he saw the small space had only enough room to hold the rope bed and its corn-shuck mattress, he winced. He had planned to find a place on the floor, but there simply was no room.

His eyes met Casey's in the candlelight, and they held for just a moment, neither able to decipher the other's expression.

"I guess we'll have to share," Sean whispered since their hosts were right beneath them.

Casey couldn't quite interpret the wry expression on his face but immediately assumed it was reluctance. The hurt showed in her face.

She looked impossibly young to Sean. And scared. *She's afraid,* he thought, and felt a stab of pain that she should fear him. She had taken off that damned hat, and her fingers combed her hair, sending tiny curls around an oval face that was vibrant and strong. He was amazed to discover how much he wanted to touch it. Instead, he turned away from her and sat on the bed, removing his boots. He continued to sit there while she did the same, finally taking one part of the bed, keeping as close to the edge as possible.

But when Sean blew out the candle and his hard body reclined on the bed, the entire mattress tipped and Casey rolled right into him. She jerked as though she'd been burned, and scooted back to her own side, only to roll back again, this time into his waiting arms.

Casey heard his soft laughter. "I don't think we can do anything about it...the bed seems to have intentions of its own."

He felt her body tense against his, and wished he could dispel her fear. "Don't worry, wildcat," he comforted. "I'll not harm you." But her body didn't relax, and he realized his was none too relaxed, either. She was softer than he'd imagined, and her curves fit nicely into his, too nicely. It had been a long time since he'd been with a woman.

Sean turned quickly...before Casey realized what was happening. He swore softly to himself and his need grew, rather than dissipated, as her body once more settled comfortably against his. She wriggled, trying to put some space between them but that only made things worse. Sean almost groaned. The more she squirmed to get away, the more she seemed to melt into him. It didn't seem to matter that they were both fully clothed; every movement seemed to ignite new firebrands up and down the length of him.

Casey thought she would die of humiliation. Whatever she did, she rolled back into him. She felt his warmth burn through her, and she longed to have his arms around her again. But they had rested there only briefly, and then he had quickly pulled them away. In distaste, she thought. She was small and bony compared to the mayor's daughter. And she was wearing the same disreputable clothes she had worn for the past five days. But for those few seconds, she had felt safe and protected. And cherished. She had never felt cherished before. But now his back was to her, and his whole body was stiff. A tear started deep in her eye as she tried to climb up the mattress toward the side of the bed, only to crash again and land against his back. The impact caused him to groan slightly, and she was glad the darkness would hide her embarrassment should he turn back and face her again.

She heard a soft rumble, and the mattress shook. The tremors grew greater, and Casey couldn't stop herself from touching him, to discover what was wrong. He was shaking, all of him, and for a split second she was terrified. Then a chuckle escaped the fist in his mouth, and she realized he was laughing. Hurt to the core, she tried to move away once more, but his hands stopped her. ''Best to give up," he whispered between spasms, "and make the best of it."

Casey felt him turn to face her and his arms go around her. Slowly she relaxed against his hard strength, feeling the quivers of laughter that still rocked him. Her mouth widened into a smile as her own sense of the absurd snared her, and her body began to quake with its own laughter. The two of them rocked with a desperate merriment they dared not voice until it gradually disappeared. They were left with the warmth and comfort of each other's bodies and the gentle joy of shared laughter, which at the moment seemed to bind them more than any momentary passion.

Sean's hunger, though not gone, was curbed, and he relished the feel of Casey in his arms, wondering at the contentment it seeded deep within him. His body curved protectively around hers, and he closed his eyes.

Casey stayed awake. She didn't want to lose a second of this feeling to sleep. His arms were so strong. It was as if she had been waiting for this all her life.

Ty tore the poster from the wooden signpost and crumpled it in his fist. He knew Caldwell had long arms, but he'd never thought they'd be this long. Or this fast.

So his hide was worth five thousand dollars. Alive. Caldwell wanted him alive. He was only worth two thousand dead.

At least that evened things up a little. It would eliminate some of the greedy back shooters. But only some. There were others who would be happy with the two thousand.

He pushed back his hat. The description was damned unflattering. Flat, pale eyes, it said. And lank black hair. His hand raked the thick, dark, slightly curling mane as if in reassurance. The poster also had him two inches too short. A small deadly smile played on his firmly etched lips, and his eyes glittered with their own peculiar brightness. Caldwell would pay for that description. But that could wait. Right now his concern was establishing a false trail.

He rode into Dry Gulch, which was nothing more than a tiny scattering of buildings: a general store-saloon, a small stable where horse-trading was the main activity, a land office that also served as a post office, and a few dilapidated shacks. From the last time he'd stopped here, he knew there was no law, no women and no curiosity. The town merely straddled one of the north-south trails and eked out a bare existence from the few travelers.

Ty pulled his hat down over his forehead, almost to his eyes, and dismounted. He quickly tied his horse to a hitching post and strode inside the general store.

It was small, one side so crowded with goods that a customer could barely make his way through the items, which ranged from canned goods to flour to sewing kits to saddles. The other side merely offered a few tables and chairs.

Ty was the only customer. He took one of the chairs, stretching his legs over to rest on another, his spurs adding new designs to the already scarred wood.

He knew the proprietor, Sam Jones, who ambled slowly over to him. Ty had been here previously and had immediately recognized one of his own stripe. Sam Jones was a former Union-leaning Jayhawker in Kansas and later an outlaw until he got tired of running. He'd moved down to this isolated part of West Texas, changed his name and seldom mentioned his Union sympathies. Ty's blue cavalry pants had got him to talking one night, and they had discovered a common past if not a friendship. Neither man knew much about the other, but there was a certain bond between them, and Ty doubted that Sam Jones would try to take the reward. Sam Jones harbored the same distaste for the arrogant Texas ranchers as he did.

"Whiskey?" Jones asked now.

Ty nodded.

"Been traveling far?" Jones asked as he poured a wicked-looking amber liquid into a dirty glass.

"Far enough."

"Seems you been getting famous!"

Ty pushed his hat back and smiled, a hard smile that made even Jones feel a cold shiver. "'Pears that way. How long ago did those posters show up?"

"A cowboy...looked more like a hired gun...was by two days ago." Jones reached under his counter, and Ty's hand automatically went for his gun. Sam gave him a wounded look, and his hand came up with a stack of the posters. He looked at Ty with a certain amusement. "I don't want to die for two thousand dollars, or even five thousand. You can put that away."

Ty's grim expression didn't ease, but the gun slid back into the holster. "Sorry."

"Don't be. With that price on your head, you couldn't trust Jesus Christ."

"But I can trust you?"

Jones shrugged. "Damn if I'll do their dirty work for them."

"Why do you stay here?"

"It's a sight far from Kansas. And it suits me well enough, especially taking their money and watching the army bleed them dry. 'Nother drink?"

Ty nodded, looking at Jones speculatively, wondering exactly how far he could trust him.

Jones poured himself a drink and sat down. "Somethin' I can do for you?"

"I need Caldwell off my back for a while."

"Gonna be hard to do. Those posters are everywhere. What about the army? Can't they help? You bein' an ex-officer in the army and all, and Caldwell and them being Rebs?''

Ty raised a bushy black eyebrow. ''With my reputation?''

''The poster said 'Murder.' Now I don't believe that.''

''I killed him all right, but it was a fair fight, and the Caldwell kid forced it. The damned sheriff was in Caldwell's pocket.''

Jones chuckled. ''Looks like you got even, though. Man who brought those posters said you left the sheriff tied like a hog headed for dinner, his ankles chained to his hands. Would have liked to seen that. Lost his job over it, I heard.''

Ty stared at the man. ''What in the hell? I didn't even see the damned sheriff. You must mean the deputy.''

''Him, too, I hear,'' Jones continued, startled at the raw astonishment in Donaldson's face. ''He was fired, too.''

Ty's mouth closed as he considered the information. Who in the hell…? It couldn't have been Mallory. They had left together. Who else? He certainly had no friends in Fort Worth, no one who would lift a finger for him. It must had been someone with a personal grudge against the sheriff.

He shrugged. No sense telling Jones that. His face settled into its usual hard mask.

Jones only briefly wondered about the exchange. Curiosity was not one of his vices, not when he had so much to hide himself. ''What now? Leaving Texas?''

''I'll be damned if I'll let the likes of Caldwell run me out. But there's something I got to do, and I don't want bounty hunters on my trail.''

Jones grinned. ''Which way you want me to tell them you're headed?''

''Southeast…San Antonio and then Mexico. They'll believe that.''

"I ain't going to ask where you're really heading."

The younger man remained silent.

"Wherever it is, I wish you luck."

Some of the glitter left Ty's eyes, and his expression softened for a fleeting moment. "Thanks, Sam. I won't forget it."

Jones averted his face. "No need. I like seeing those bastards chase their tails. Damned little amusement out here. Besides—" he grinned "—I might ask a small reward for giving them such valuable information."

He poured them both another drink and the two men lifted the glasses in recognition of the conspiracy, then downed them in one swallow.

Ty kept heading south during the day, twice stopping for water at ranches along the way. He wanted his trail to support Sam Jones's report. At the end of the day, he stopped and took out a small mirror. He trimmed the back of his hair and shaved his face, all but an area above his mouth, wondering briefly how he'd look with a mustache.

Not too happily, he changed into a black pair of trousers, which he had purchased at Jones's store, and stuffed his Union ones into his saddlebags. He felt strange without them but they had been included in his description on the poster. He had worn them during two years of war and two years of prison. Though faded and threadbare they were as much a badge of honor as he had ever had, he thought wryly. They had also been his red warning flag. By flaunting them in Texas, he was flaunting his father and his past, telling the whole damned world to go to hell.

When he was through, he found a small creek and rode his horse through its center for ten miles before heading due west. He would avoid every living soul until he reached New Mexico.

Chapter Nine

Casey felt a hollow place inside she had never known existed until now.

She had discovered the warmth of being close to another human being, felt the overwhelming ache created by the nearness of two bodies, come alive with his touch and been comforted by his gentleness; and she knew she would never be the same again. She treasured every moment of last night at the Kelloggs' and believed that Sean could not have been entirely unaffected by it.

She had thought it might lessen the strain between them: the stiffness, the long silences. But if anything, it had made them worse. She realized what they had shared had not changed anything though she didn't understand why. How could he not feel the same things she had during those warm intimate hours of lying together? They were burned into her soul. They seared her flesh and her mind.

Somehow, during the night, revenge had become less important, and Sean the center of Casey's world. Vital to her, to her very being. But when he rose the next morning, his eyes were hooded and his manner cool. And Casey had shivered with a sudden chill.

Breakfast was as noisy as the evening meal had been.

The Kelloggs hated to see their guests leave and continued to ask questions. Their young boys were enthralled with Sean and begged for another quick song before he left, and Sean obliged with a smile and a lively version of "The Yellow Rose of Texas."

After a meal of coffee and bread, and one precious egg apiece, Sean finally rose, thanking the family with a smile, which disappeared quickly as he mounted. Minutes later, Sean and Casey were back on the trail. Only Casey looked back at the small desolate shelter where something sweet and miraculous had happened. To her, anyway, she thought sadly as she glanced at Sean's closed face.

She wished during the day that Sean would say something, but he was silent, pressing their horses, and themselves, as if the devil were after them. Casey lost herself in the memory of his rumbling laughter during the night, the arms that had held her so protectively. She remembered the feel of his hard, lean body and ached to reach over and touch him.

But it was as if he had erected a barrier, one he meant to keep between them. His eyes were hard and filled with intent. He obviously regretted the warmth they had shared during the night.

The hollow place inside her grew deeper and wider. The want was enormous and all-consuming. In complete misery, she rode side by side with Sean, her heart crumbling with every long, silent mile their horses consumed.

Sean wanted to kick himself. It had been incredibly stupid to hold Casey in his arms. It had awakened something in him that was barely leashable. She had felt so right snuggled trustfully against him, and every sense had responded to the feel of her body. They had been like two well-matched spoons. But they weren't well-matched at all. She was young and inexperienced, and he had seen much too much and lived too hard. It was only that he had not had a woman in a long time. Any woman would have wakened the same driving need. Even now, just thinking of the night caused his loins to ache.

He looked over to her, hoping that the sight of her in the shapeless clothes and hat would ease the throbbing inside him, but it only made it worse. He kept seeing her as she had come out of the river. Nothing could hide her natural grace. She was probably one of the most guileless people he had ever encountered and he wondered, somewhat cynically, whether it was a quality that would endure.

She was dangerous for him. Dangerous in many different ways. The most obvious, he knew, was his growing attachment for her. He knew such sentiments could kill them both. He did not need his senses dulled by this child-woman who made him yearn for things he had long since dismissed.

God, it was impossible. He remembered telling his sister that Ben Morgan was too old for her, and now here he was thinking about a girl even further distant in age. And experience. And maturity.

He spurred his horse into a trot, trying to throw such uncomfortable thoughts away to the hot, dry wind that made the tall grass move like waves in a sea. This business would end, and with it the strange attraction he had for Casey Saunders. He wondered momentarily whether her real name was Casey. Perhaps it was better not to know.

They stopped later than usual, a bright full moon providing more than enough light to keep going after dark. Sean found a small creek where some stunted trees struggled against the harsh climate and the area was littered with buffalo chips. He thought they were far enough southwest to avoid any Indian trouble, but still he eyed the bright gold moon with some wariness. This was the favorite time for Comanches.

As a precaution, he stopped Casey from building a fire.

"Not tonight," he said shortly, and Casey looked at him questioningly.

He nodded toward the sky. "Comanche moon. Full moon's their favorite time for raiding."

Casey's eyes went wide open. "Do you think...?"

"I doubt they would get this far south, but no sense sending an invitation," he said shortly.

"We had a Comanche renegade in the jail once," Casey said. "Pa wouldn't let me anyplace near him though I usually fed the prisoners. Except for that one, I only saw peaceful Indians. Comanches never came as far as Two Springs."

"You were lucky."

"Have you ever fought Indians?"

"A few times," Sean allowed, though his mouth firmed as it always did when he didn't want to talk. But Casey was too fascinated to stop.

"When?"

"During the war. I was transporting some Union rifles we'd captured through Texas."

"Was your sister with you?"

"Yes."

"I think I'd like her."

That comment made him look at her. "I think you would too, wildcat," he answered, and Casey was pleased. It was the first time he had called her that for a long time, and it was said with something like...affection? But she wished he would smile.

"I wish I had a brother," she said wistfully. "Or a sister. There was always just Pa and me."

There was such a lonely note in her voice that Sean hurt for her. Her changeable eyes held a haunting sadness, which she had not allowed him to see earlier. She had been cocky, and belligerent and stubborn and determined, but never before had she allowed him a glimpse into what must have been a near-loveless childhood.

He wanted desperately to hold her, just as he had days earlier when she had laughed so joyously. But this time he wanted to take the pain away from her life when earlier he had wanted the laughter to last. It was two sides of the same coin—to take away pain and give joy. But it was a forbidden coin, at least for now. His hand dug into the dirt where he was sitting to keep from reaching out to her, from touching her. Instead, with effort, he forced a light note into his voice. "I think Ryan often wished she didn't have one. I interfered terribly."

"Why?"

"Because we didn't agree on what was best for her."

"But she would know best, wouldn't she," Casey said simply. "It's her life."

Damn, but she was direct. And right. At least in Ryan's case, but he had a sneaking suspicion she wasn't talking about Ryan.

"She did, but I wouldn't accept it...not for a while."

"Why do men always think they know what's better for everyone?"

The question was posed innocently enough but he knew "everyone" meant "her" and "men" meant him. And he also knew she was referring to the fact that he had repeatedly made it very clear to her that he did not want her around when they finally met up with Wilson. Sean found he didn't have an answer, not one she would accept.

So he merely shrugged and chewed on some jerky, wondering how they had traveled so quickly from subject to subject, from mood to mood. He never really knew what to expect next from her. It was part of her fascination...her directness, her curiosity, her intuitiveness.

They sat together for a while, each knowing that sleep wouldn't come easily. They both remembered last night all too well, though they tried to keep such knowledge to themselves.

Sean was anguished at how much he wanted Casey back in his arms. Last night meant nothing he argued to himself. They had been coerced by circumstances into a kind of intimacy and he had taken advantage of it. Trying to force himself to stop thinking of Casey's softness, he wondered where Ty was. And if the gunfighter was all right. He wondered even more why he cared. It was crazy, but then this whole thing was crazy. Perhaps there was something to that Chinese saying that if you saved a man's life, you were then responsible for it. Heaven forbid if he were now responsible for Donaldson. He shuddered at the thought, but it also brought a smile to his face.

It was the first human response Casey had seen all day, and she tipped her head in question. "You're smiling?" she observed, making it a question in that strange sort of probing way she had.

The hat was gone, and the face, which he was finding increasingly engaging despite a smudge on her nose, was hopeful.

Sean let his smile widen. He had been surly and hostile, and except for the brief exchange earlier, Casey had been uncommonly quiet. He knew his attitude had probably puzzled and hurt her, and he felt a stab of guilt. It wasn't her fault he was feeling these flashes of desire.

"I was wondering about Donaldson," he explained.

"Where do you think he went?"

"South, probably, to start a false trail, throw off any bounty hunters." It was what Sean would have done and as much as he hated to admit it, he and Donaldson had certain things in common. He hoped not too many. "Caldwell most certainly would have posted a price on his head."

"You think there's anything that will connect you to him?"

"I think that's what Donaldson's doing right now, making sure they don't."

Casey laughed grimly. "A gunfighter with honor?" She had been taught to hate the breed.

Sean shrugged. "I'm just guessing."

"Tell me about him. Why does he wear those uniform pants?"

"To rile everyone, I suppose. He hates Southerners."

"He was in the army? He seems too young."

"The Union army. One hell of a fighter, according to my brother-in-law. They were in a Confederate prison together in Texas and tried to escape. They were well to being free when they came across a small wagon train of some ex-Rebs being attacked by Comanches. Ben went to help and Ty followed him. They saved the settlers but were recaptured. Ben was injured pretty badly. He claims Ty saved his life."

"But why did Donaldson follow him?"

"Damned if I know. Loyalty to Ben, maybe. I never could figure him out. Never much wanted to. There's something lacking in him."

Casey knew there was something else. Something he wasn't telling.

"Tell me about your brother-in-law. How did you happen to be in different armies?"

"It wasn't all that rare, wildcat," he said, noticing her slight smile at his use of the endearment. "We were roommates at West Point. There were a lot of us who fought friends, directly and indirectly. I think that was the most tragic part of the war."

"*You* were at West Point?" There was disbelief in her voice. She had met West Point officers in the past two years, and most of them had an arrogance completely lacking in Mallory. Perhaps it was just that she had resented their attitudes toward postwar Texas. Even her father, who had been quietly pro-Union, had resented their high-handed interference.

"'Fraid so," Sean said, reading her facial expression. He too had had run-ins with the governing troops.

"You said you were a rancher," she said, almost accusingly.

"I am now. I ran cattle for two years after the war. I had just put together enough money to buy land down near San Antonio, next to Ben's ranch, when Wilson raided his place. He intended to kill us all, including my sister and her children." The wry humor was now gone from his face, and Casey thought his grim look made Donaldson's feral expression seem almost benevolent.

"They…they're all right?"

"She and Ben and the children are. A good friend of mine was killed. Along with others. Wilson got away, but he vowed to return. And he will. Ryan's not safe while he's alive. None of them are."

Casey wanted to ask more, but she didn't dare push her luck. His whole body was taut, and his voice had hardened to a rasp full of dangerous promise. His eyes burned with vengeance and rage.

By common silent consent, they said no more. Casey lay on one blanket and pillowed her head on another, staring up at the silver moon and the millions of twinkling stars, which had never looked quite so bright. She thought about all he had said, and all he had not. He had never mentioned love. Had he ever been in love, been married, had children? The thought was so painful she was afraid to ask.

It was obvious he was a man who cared deeply about people, about family, and friends. Even, apparently, the enigmatic Donaldson.

But would he ever care about her? Her hands twisted

together. She had never known a heart could hurt so much from just wanting. She suddenly wished she could reach up and pluck a star from the jeweled sky above her head. But they were as unreachable as the man who lay just a few feet away.

Ty knew he was being followed. Although he had not seen anyone, he had a prickling feeling in the back of his neck. It was a sixth sense he had developed, and it had never failed him. A man in his profession didn't often live long without instincts. He continued to ride toward the Territory of New Mexico with an ease that belied the tension boiling inside of him.

He took some dried jerky from his saddlebags and slid from his horse, casually relaxing against the bay as if he hadn't a care in the world. Anyone watching him would see a man taking a few moments' rest from the saddle. His hard amethyst eyes missed little as they casually scanned the windswept plains. There was an occasional canyon, a rare broken piece of land, but mostly it was flat. It looked empty and then Ty caught a flash of light off in the distance. A piece of glass could mean Indians signaling one another. Or it could be a spyglass...which would mean a bounty hunter. Either way, it was trouble. Indians more than the other. He could easily handle one, even two, bounty hunters, but wasn't so sure about a group of Kiowas or Comanches on the rampage.

Ty slowly chewed the last of the jerky, took a swig of water from his canteen and lazily remounted. He urged his horse into a slow canter as he considered the possibilities. He didn't want those following him to realize that he was aware of their presence. Not yet, anyway. Not until he knew exactly who was tailing him.

If it was a bounty hunter, then he had made a mistake someplace, perhaps in trusting Sam. But he doubted that.

If Sam had wanted money, he would have remained an outlaw. And Sam would know that if he betrayed him, he would never have a moment's peace if Ty wasn't killed. No, it wouldn't be Sam.

Then who? One of the ranches where he had stopped? And if so, was he alone or were there more? Most bounty hunters, he knew, worked alone. They wouldn't even trust one another.

He suddenly thought of Mallory. At least his name wasn't mentioned on the posters, so apparently he hadn't been connected with the escape. Ty wondered if he had rid himself of the hellion yet. If not, Sean was as big a fool as he had been in Fort Worth when he had slipped him that pistol, and then waited out back with the horses.

That girl was a strange creature. She had surprised him with her shooting. She was appealing in a waiflike way with those large green eyes and turned-up nose. Dressed properly, she might even be pretty. And yet she was very, very confident with a gun, and he hadn't forgotten, or forgiven, that kick to his manhood. He knew she would be nothing but trouble. Women always were. And one who could shoot, doubly so. Besides, his taste ran to a different type. Bosomy and soft. Loose women who gave of their favors wholeheartedly, and didn't try to interfere with his life, or reform him. In the last two years, he had made up for the time spent in prison. Women were attracted to his dark dangerous good looks and the aura of death that surrounded him, and he had always been a considerate lover. That unexpected aspect of his nature had always surprised and delighted his bed partners and there were more than a few women who waited eagerly for his return.

The prickling sensation in the back of his neck increased and banished such fleeting thoughts, although his attention had never really been diverted from the danger that followed him. One thing about the flat plains: he couldn't be ambushed. Nor, he thought, could he be overtaken. Not on his stallion. He was convinced now his pursuers were not Indians. Indians wouldn't follow him this long for just one man and one horse.

He didn't think his tracker was aware he had been spotted. Whoever he was, the man probably planned to ambush him when he settled down for the night. Ty eased back in his saddle, his body once more relaxing as if he hadn't a care in the world. But a dark smile twisted his lips as he pondered exactly who was going to surprise who.

Ty searched for what he needed until late into the night. Finally, he found it: a small clump of brush next to an almost dry creek bed. It wasn't much, but it would provide some cover.

He leisurely made a fire, unpacked his gear and hobbled his horse, feeding him some oats. He cooked some beans and a small piece of bacon he had purchased from Sam, hoping the smell would reach out to whoever was tailing him. A man who thinks he's being tailed doesn't stop to cook, nor does he light a fire. He then rolled his gear into a blanket, shaping it carefully and placing it near a small bush, which cast a dark shadow over the "body." He slid down the creek bank where he could see into his camp although a bush disguised his own dirt-covered face. Rifle in hand, he waited.

The night passed slowly. Clouds flitted across the moon like lace, casting odd-shaped shadows on the ground. The night was completely still. Ty was afraid to move, lest he give himself away. His legs locked with cramps and sand filtered into his mouth and nose, but still he didn't move so much as a finger.

He judged it was near dawn before he heard the rustle of prairie grass, the cautious, furtive movements of an intruder. There was enough moonlight so he could see the man's legs approach his "sleeping self." And then he heard the gunshot. There was a second, then a third, and he heard another movement. The man's back was to him now, and Ty cocked his rifle. In the still night it sounded nearly as loud as the pistol shots.

"Put it down," he ordered, but the man paid no heed as he whirled, his pistol seeking a target. Ty shot, and the man whirled around again, this time not of his own accord. In a flash Ty was up, his rifle inches from the man who now lay writhing on the ground.

Ty kicked the stranger's pistol out of range and inspected his captive. The man was holding his shoulder where blood had already covered the plaid shirt. He was heavily bearded and had a livid scar that ran from cheek to forehead. Ty had never seen him before.

"Who are you?" Ty's voice was cold, his eyes merciless.

The man simply glared back at him.

Ty dug the barrel of his rifle into the man's wounded shoulder, and the stranger screamed.

"Who are you?" Ty said again, his rifle obviously ready to poke again.

"Tatum, damn you. My name's Tatum."

"Bounty hunter?"

The man's lips stubbornly closed again until he saw the rifle move. "Yes, goddammit, yes."

"How did you find me?"

Tatum moaned. "I'm bleeding to death, damn it."

"You want sympathy...after what you did to my blanket? I could catch my death of a cold that way." The tone was conversational but the menace in the words was unmistakable. "I asked how you found me. Don't make me ask you again."

"You left too good a trail heading south. I heard you wuz smart. Smart man on the run wouldn't do that." His

words died off into a moan, but they became audible again
when he saw the rifle come back down toward his wound.
"I followed that damn stream until I found the tracks coming out."

"Anyone else with you?"

"Why should I share the reward?" Tatum said. "It was
just a guess on my part."

"One you'll be damned sorry for." Ty cocked the rifle
again, and Tatum cringed, trying to back into the under-
brush.

Ty Donaldson fought with himself. He had never killed
a wounded, defenseless man. But this one not only had seen
him since he cut his hair and started his mustache, he also
had a damned good idea of the direction he was taking.

The bounty hunter, after all, had intended to shoot him
in the back while he was sleeping. But despite the coldness
that had frozen his heart, he couldn't quite take this last
step into hell. Something inside him just wouldn't let him
do it.

He searched the wounded man, keeping one hand on the
hammer of the rifle, coming up with a second gun and a
knife. He kicked them both out of the man's reach, then
lowered the rifle slightly.

"Give me one reason I shouldn't finish you off right
now," he asked coldly.

Tatum stared at him. He had known he was a dead man
since the second the bullet struck him. He had only hoped
it would be quick. Disbelief covered his face as he struggled for an answer. There really wasn't one, and he wasn't
going to beg. "I would have killed you," he said simply.

It was those words, more than any excuse or plea, that
decided Ty. He admired courage.

"If I ever see you again," he grated slowly, "I'll kill
you."

He packed Tatum's guns and knife in his own saddlebags

and saddled his horse. He didn't need to watch the man. Blood was still seeping from his right shoulder and Tatum had no weapons. But he could almost feel the bounty hunter's hot gaze through his shirt.

Ty mounted. "Where's your horse?"

Mystified at what was happening, the man was suddenly docile. "Quarter of a mile out. Staked."

"He'll be a mile now."

"My shoulder…?"

"I'm giving you a hell of a better chance than you were going to give me." Ty paused. "Tatum. I'll remember that name. And you, by God, remember my promise. If I ever find you tailing me again, I'll make you very, very sorry that you left this place alive."

Tatum shuddered at the tone. He had been told this was a kid, though a dangerous one. Kid, hell. Donaldson sounded as old as death. He watched Donaldson ride away and, despite the agony in his shoulder, counted himself lucky.

Chapter Ten

Casey thought—no, knew—she would never walk normally again. Her backside was painfully sore and she felt as bowlegged as an aged cowboy.

She had thought her father obsessed with the law and with the bitter memory of his wife, but after riding nearly two weeks with Sean Mallory she was beginning to think she had never known the meaning of the word.

The man never stopped. He was as one-minded as a thirsty mule heading for the only water hole in a hundred miles. They rode from sunrise to moonset and past, farther if the moon was bright enough. They had left Texas and were already well into the Territory of New Mexico.

There were two redeeming aspects of their journey. One was merely being with Sean Mallory, watching the muscles tighten under his shirt, admiring his easy tireless grace on a horse, secretly treasuring the wild idea of touching the golden hairs on his arms laid bare by rolled-up sleeves. Her hands often clutched the reins to keep her from leaning across the distance between them and doing just that. For the moment, it had to be enough to be his companion, to relish the magic of his presence despite the pain of deprivation.

The other distraction was the land that surrounded them. Casey hadn't traveled much since being brought to Texas when she was only a child. She had been to Fort Worth once, but that was as far as she'd gotten. Now she watched avidly as the terrain changed from flat plains to slightly rolling hills and broken canyons. She was full of questions that occasionally brought a reluctant smile to Sean Mallory's grim countenance. Her eager eyes drank in every rock, every break in the land, and her passion for wanting to know everything gave her new energy. She had vowed not to bother Sean with conversation he seemed to want to avoid, but she couldn't seem to keep it all to herself. She was particularly interested in the numerous ranchers who were so obviously of Spanish background.

"I had a drover once who came from here," Sean said. "He joined up with me last year with some cattle of his own. Said his family went back to the Spanish followers of Francisco Coronado who explored the area three hundred years ago. The land was just here for the taking, and he and his ancestors stayed, even through the Pueblo Indian Revolt back in 1680. There's a lot of them around here. They didn't leave like those in Texas did during the Texas War for Independence."

To Casey's delight, once he started talking he continued. With that wonderful slow smile he halted their journey at a strange-looking mountain, which rose starkly from the bright golden land.

The mountain was called Tucumcari, he explained. Squinting, Sean looked up, the dark bronze of his face glowing in the sun. One hand raked his gold-tinged hair in what was now a familiar gesture of impatience and Casey watched with fascination. As hard as she tried, she couldn't take her eyes from him.

But he seemed unaware of the flush of her cheeks, the

blood racing through her veins. Perhaps he just attributed it to the sun. She prayed so.

He gave her a disarming grin, and she spied mischief in his eyes. "Before the army gained control here," Sean said, "the Comanches used this as a lookout point. Tucumcari means "lookout" in Comanche. But there's a much more intriguing story."

His smile widened at Casey's immediate and intense interest and he continued.

"There's an Indian legend about an Apache warrior named Tocom, and Kari, the daughter of an Apache chief. When Tocom lost his life in a battle for Kari's hand, she first stabbed the victor, then herself. As both lay dying, the father also killed himself with a dagger, his last words echoing in the wind, 'Tocom-Kari.'"

Casey's eyes clouded at the sadness of the story.

Sean berated himself for relating the legend. He leaned over and touched her chin with his finger. "It's just a story, wildcat," he comforted. "There are hundreds of them just like it, all over the Southwest. I don't think any of them are true."

Then he made the mistake of looking into her eyes. God, they were like emeralds with facets that changed every fraction of a second. There were many emotions in them, but he could read none of them; they passed too quickly.

A glowing warmth seeped into him and ran quickly through his body. He jerked his hand away, as if it had been burned. She's not much more than a child, he reminded himself, an enchanting child who was much too vulnerable now that she was completely alone. He could not take advantage of that. He would not.

Sean forced himself to look away, his smile fading. "I want to get another ten miles today," he said harshly.

"We've dawdled long enough." He pushed his stallion to a fast trot, leaving a confused Casey to follow behind.

When they finally stopped for the night, Sean remained curt and unfriendly. But his eyes seldom left her, and he couldn't help but notice how tired she seemed, and how dirty they both were. There had been precious little water along the way, and what there was had been mostly from mud holes, which served the animals well enough but offered little in terms of washing. His own face, he knew, was bristly with several days' beard, and he touched it with distaste.

"There's a spring not far from here," he said, his face averted. "And a lake. We'll reach them tomorrow, and perhaps stay a day and rest."

He missed the sudden delight in her face. A lake! Casey had never seen much more than a river and that was usually dried up. It would be nice to stop for a while, she thought wistfully. It would be even nicer to take a bath and rest her sore self in cool water. In a lake. She wondered what it looked like, how big it was.

He made the fire, and she prepared some beans. They had found a water hole earlier, and she made some coffee, although the water was only several shades darker at end of the cooking than it had been at the beginning. The coffee tasted like mud, too, she thought. She sipped it sparingly.

The air was hot, infernally so, and her clothes clung to her like skin to a snake. The evening was not cooling off at all, although there were several thick clouds to the far east. The sky was a blood-red, like some hovering harbinger of evil. Casey shivered, wanting to move closer to Sean but afraid of the rejection she might find.

The horses were skittish, too. Sean had hobbled them, but they were snorting as though something was scaring them.

Sean comforted them with a few words, then took down

his guitar. He had not played it since they'd left the Kelloggs' although Casey had longed for him to do so. She knew it was to soothe the horses, not for her, but she didn't care. She could pretend it was otherwise.

He sang soft cowboy songs meant to comfort cattle on long drives. They were lonely songs for the most part, Casey thought as she guardedly darted looks at him. They had let the fire die and the only light came from a quarter moon and some faraway stars. The clouds stayed lazily to the east, and seemed not to move at all in the still night.

She was glad it was so dark, that he couldn't see the expression she knew must be on her face. He seemed lost in the music, his voice strong and compelling. Yet there was a wistfulness in it that reached out to Casey. She wondered at this man who was obviously so strong, so confident, yet whose music was filled with such emotion. Instead of weakening, it served to strengthen her image of him. He was a mystery in so many ways, a man who risked his freedom and life for another he didn't even like, who was now devoting weeks, perhaps months, to hunt someone who was a danger to those he loved.

Casey thought of Ty Donaldson. Both men, Donaldson and Mallory, had an aura of danger around them, a deep vein of wildness. Yet Sean's was tightly controlled while Donaldson's was unbridled. Perhaps that was what separated them.

A flash of heat lightning pierced the sky and illuminated the earth. The horses whinnied, moving restlessly. Another burst crossed the heavens and split into brilliant shards between the clouds, speeding in several directions. It was terrifyingly beautiful, and Casey found herself moving closer to Sean who had stilled his fingers to watch.

"God's fireworks," Casey said with awe, her face lit by yet another brilliant display. Her face was beautiful in the dramatic silvered light, and Sean couldn't stop himself from putting an arm around her.

He felt her tense, then relax against his body, and he thought how fine she felt there. The flashes in the sky were echoed by the throbbing of intense heat that raced through his body. His arm drew her closer, and his mouth touched the top of her head, caressing a wayward curl, when the sky crackled again with electricity, the heat hurling bolts from cloud to cloud like an angry ancient god, lighting the entire sky with fire.

Casey trembled in his arms, feeling the urgent pressure that hovered in the air, the sense of expectancy that seemed as alive as the lightning that snaked the sky and illuminated the earth. She turned her head upward, and her eyes met his. Both sets blazed with recognized desire and need.

He lowered his lips and touched hers, gently at first as he felt the tremor of her mouth. Her own lips responded, tentatively and then more confidently, and finally greedily. The kiss deepened, the hunger between them growing like a prairie fire and fueled by the excitement of the flashing sky around them.

Sean had never known such need. Her hesitancy told him only too clearly of her inexperience and it filled him with a deep tenderness.

He could taste an untapped passion that was responding to him readily. He tried to tell himself it was the strange explosive quality of the night that seemed to wrap itself around them and make them feel they were there alone in a world sizzling with a raw elemental power. He tried to stifle the groan that started in his chest and reverberated in the still electric air. No longer did she seem a child. Her mouth searched hungrily for his, and she stretched against him with instinctive yearning. His entire body was taut, his nerves sparking like the untamed sky above him. He needed her, God, how he needed her.

His tongue touched her lips, then slowly eased its way inside her mouth. It met with a puzzled response at first, then a cautious participation, and finally, an eagerness that matched his own.

Sean had never felt this explosive combination of protectiveness and lust. His hands wandered up and down her, and he felt Casey tremble with each intimate stroke, felt her hands touch his hair with a bewitching shyness before they moved on, the shyness and hesitancy disappearing. She was reaching for him, seeking to draw him closer.

Sean forced himself to slow his movements. He didn't quite understand the overwhelming magnetism between the two of them. He had always been attracted to more sophisticated women. But Casey, with her deadly combination of shyness and deepening fervor, inflamed him as never before as waves of insatiable need crowded out all his honorable intentions.

Casey's hands seemed guided by Satan himself as she found and caressed each sensitive part of him. He tried to still the throbbing need that made his loins a torture chamber, and another groan escaped his lips. As he almost ripped himself away from Casey, another light arched the sky, illuminating her face, revealing eyes full of wonderment. She reached up and touched his face with infinite gentleness, and he felt himself falling again into some bottomless pit.

"I didn't believe it," she whispered.

The whispered words jerked him like a puppet on a string from the long drop he was experiencing.

Her tone was wistful.

"Didn't believe what, little wildcat?" he finally found the strength to ask.

"That anything could be like this, could make me feel so...so wonderful and hurtful at the same time."

Sean couldn't stop himself from touching her face. It was so soft to his hand, and warm. Ever so warm.

He wanted her. He wanted her as he had never wanted another woman. And he didn't understand it. Or his need for her touch, which was so open and honest.

Casey thought she would die of wanting. How could any one live through the craving that racked her body with such tantalizing promise? There was a great fierce longing inside that quaked and trembled with urgency.

She lifted her lips once more to Sean's, wanting to feel the possessiveness that had claimed her mouth with such hungry sweetness. And this time her tongue explored as his had seconds earlier. She felt his body tighten in response and rejoiced in her power, knowing all the while it was as perilous for her as for him.

Her hand went to his neck and her fingers played a song of their own, caressing and stroking, even as she wondered at her boldness. Their mouths were still melded together and his kiss became deeper as they stretched out on the ground, trembling together in throes of need.

And for Casey, love. For she knew she loved Sean Mallory with all her heart and soul, and nothing was more vital at this moment than making him hers. Her soul craved his touch, her body his joining. Her body arched, seeking more knowledge of the hardness that strained toward her through their clothes.

Her hands continued their torment at the back of his neck, drawing a long painful groan from deep within him.

"Casey," Sean was barely able to rasp. "You don't know what you're doing."

But Casey did. Instinctively she did. She felt the shudders of his body, and she understood he wanted her as much as she wanted him. She could sense his efforts to restrain himself, but she wasn't going to let him. He was being honorable, and she didn't want honor. She wanted him.

Sean surrendered with an anguished sigh. He could no longer resist the clamoring, pulsating fires she had ignited within him, not when her eyes, her soft smile, her tempting, devilish hands all pleaded with him to continue. She had, somehow, discarded her own shirt and pants and his hands moved toward the buttons of his trousers.

He had no doubt she was a virgin. Their first kiss had told him that very clearly. He moved over her slowly, his body barely touching hers. His hand rose to her mouth, caressing it with tenderness and then it moved down between her legs and grazed the most intimate part of her with the same gentle touch. Casey felt her whole being quiver with a thousand knifepoints of exquisite agony. Her hips reached for him, but still he teased, bringing her like a fuse on a powder keg to the point of explosion.

And then he eased into her warmth, slowly, gently, reining his own needs to allow her to get used to the sensation of his hard, throbbing heat. He kept expecting fear or rejection but her every move was a plea for him to take her fully. He reached her womanly barrier and hesitated but her arms went around him, and her lips met his, and her body lifted, telling him she was ready.

He heard her small surprised cry but her hands and mouth told him to continue, and he explored deeper, feeling the passion in her grow with each succeeding plunge as she eagerly caught the rhythm of his movements. They increased the tempo, coming together in a splendor that was unlike anything he had ever felt. They were perfectly in tune, their bodies driven by instinct and desire. One explosion erupted into another, each with its own intensity and glory, coloring the skies of their own private universe.

Casey didn't know there could be such ecstasy, that every part of her body could be so swept with tides of sensation. She reveled in the strong strength of his body in hers, in the pulsating heat that filled her core and reached to her soul. She kept thinking that nothing could outdo the most recent spate of exploding sensations but then there was a final thrust and a flash of blinding light that sent her soaring higher still.

His manhood still embedded deep within her, Sean leaned over and kissed her upturned nose, swollen lips and finally, her eyes crystal bright with pleasure. Casey closed her eyes in deep contentment and lazily opened them again, watching him.

"Can we do it again?" she asked with a beguiling innocence that made havoc of the last vestiges of discipline he had left.

"You're a greedy little wildcat, aren't you?" he replied, and she could feel the laughter rumbling in the bare chest that touched her own skin with a heat that threatened to incinerate both of them.

Despite the smile that still tugged at his mouth, he could feel his manhood stiffening once more inside her. God, what was the magic that made him feel he could do anything? He looked at her face, now just barely visible in the moonlight, and he wondered briefly where the lightning had gone.

He knew she must be sore, but Casey's face was flushed with passion and her hands were already teasing him again, playing with his ear, stroking his neck. He didn't even wonder how she knew such things. She had apparently submerged a fiery passion, and now she was obviously prepared to extend her new knowledge to its limits.

She would do well as a master torturer, he thought to himself as he started to move inside her once again. He began slowly at first, as if with a waltz, then he increased the tempo, his movements growing stronger and faster until nothing mattered but the wild untamed music they were making with their bodies....

Casey was so bedazzled she couldn't think. Her world was all lightning and thunder. Things—sensations—were happening inside her that didn't have names or descriptions. How could one ever describe the cascade of feelings that whirled you to the heaven's height? Or plummeted you in wide spiraling circles? In the back of her mind the thought of hell penetrated. That's what happened, her father had told her, when you succumbed to sin. But if this was hell, she would stay forever. Her body strained to take even more of Sean Mallory, to match him movement for movement, to join him in a frantic, intimate dance.

Suddenly, Casey didn't think she could stand it. Her body arched in response to a mighty thrust, and it seemed the world exploded as her body trembled under the onslaught of ecstasy, of emotions and feelings greater than one could possibly bear. Ripples of pleasure flooded every part of her body, and she shivered with the wild, sweet violence of the climax.

Sean lay shuddering on top of her. He could feel her trembling and knew she, too, was experiencing those last tormenting quivers of exquisite delight. He slowly rolled over, keeping her melded to him. He had never felt like this before, never so wanted to prolong lovemaking, never been so reluctant to let go. He wanted to hold her tightly, to caress her, to keep her next to him. Damn, what in the hell was happening to him? She snuggled up to him, and his arms tightened around her. She felt so good, so right. Whatever else she was, she was no child. One of his hands moved upward and ruffled her curly hair. He felt its silky softness and his lips kissed the top of her head. Even now, even after days of riding, it smelled sweet to him.

Casey felt the gentleness of his touch and sensed something deeper, and her heart sang in a way she once thought impossible. She wanted to stay where she was, snuggled in his arms. She wanted to jump up and run around like a clown for the pure joy of it.

She wanted to lie here forever.

She wanted to dance and sing.

She wanted to take his hand and run like children until they wore themselves out.

She wanted him to love her.

Her finger traced a trail on his back, and his body reacted as it had before with shudders. She wondered at this peculiar power. Did it mean he loved her? Or did it happen with every woman? The thought hurt her incredibly and she suddenly had to know.

"Do you...feel this way...every time?" she questioned in an embarrassed whisper.

Sean drew back from her, an indefinable smile on his face. "No, wildcat. Not hardly ever."

He saw the disappointment on her face when he said the word "hardly," and he wondered whether it was for herself or whether she was jealous of his previous encounters.

"I can honestly say, Casey," he said with the corners of his mouth turned up in a teasing grin, "that never, never has it been like this before. You are...unique."

Casey wasn't quite sure what he meant by that, or that it was necessarily a compliment, but she liked the twinkle in his eye and the smile on his lips.

She wanted him to say more. Like explaining "hardly ever." With the turmoil still rumbling around inside her, she was consumed with the need to know. Would it be like this every time she lay with him? Would it be like this with others?

With painful shyness but iron-willed determination, she continued her questioning. "How do you feel then, when...when you...?" She searched for exactly the right words but they escaped her. "How do you feel most of the time?"

Sean watched with fascination. He wanted to laugh but she was so damned serious, and at this moment he didn't want to hurt her feelings for anything in the world.

"It's special, wildcat," he tried to explain, "when you really like someone, when you both give pleasure. You have so much passion, so much love, that you give everything that's in you. Few people do that."

Casey heard only the first words. "When you really like someone." She felt she had been handed a miracle. He liked her! He really liked her. A huge lump formed in her throat and she thought she would choke on it.

Her hand found his and clasped it tightly, afraid to let him know how much she cared about him but compelled to hold on to him in some way. She felt the gentle warmth of his hand and his other arm went around her in reassurance. Even, Casey thought, possessively. She felt dizzy with joy and fear. It would be terrible to feel these things and then have them taken away. She wanted with all her heart to tell him she loved him, but he had said nothing and she dared not, afraid she would shatter these glorious moments. She would just have to make their time together so wonderful that he would never want to leave her.

Her free hand played with the hairs on his chest. They were curly and a little coarse, and so tempting. She started licking them.

"Casey!" The sound was almost a moan, like a man in pain, and she looked up at him, surprised.

He wanted to smile at her bewildered expression. But, the devil take it, she must be damned sore and he sure as hell was exhausted.

"I think that's enough for a first lesson," he said dryly. First lesson, indeed. She was fast becoming the teacher. And what now? It was a question he didn't want to answer. He had never intended this, and now he wondered how he could keep away from her.

But Casey wasn't through. *First lesson.* Perhaps he had been disappointed after all. She had more questions, and she clung to them like a cactus needle to a backside. She stumbled over her question, but was encouraged by the warmth of his arm. "Have you bedded...many times?" she pressed.

He pulled away slightly and looked directly into her eyes. They were misty from the lovemaking, and once more he thought how enchantingly lovely she could be. She was so entirely unaware of it.

"A few," he answered, not entirely honestly.

"Was I...?" She couldn't say the word, "disappointing," but it hung in the air between them.

Sean studied the earnest face with all its fear and expectancy, and he felt his heart contract. She could be so hurt so easily, so damned easily.

"Ah, Casey. Wildcat." How little like a wildcat she was now. He wanted to tell her she was wonderful, glorious, and that he had never felt so alive. But he couldn't. Not now. Not until he made some decisions. And he couldn't do that until after Wilson was dead. His slight smile turned to a frown. He usually knew exactly what he was doing, but now his thoughts and feelings were reeling in massive confusion.

In the moonlight, he could see Casey's smile falter, but the very tentative sweetness of it twisted his heart. His hand touched her face and traced a pattern on it. "I don't know what to do with you, Casey," he said almost to pattern on it. "I don't know what to do with you, Casey," he said almost to himself, unaware of the blow he was dealing her.

She had wanted words of reassurance, of love, of shared joy. But now he sounded as if he didn't want her anymore. Raw agony made a tight ball in her stomach and she wrenched away from him. She was on her feet, running, tears streaming down her face, unaware that she was completely naked. She needed to outrun the hurt.

Casey heard him behind her, and she speeded her steps, but she was no match for Sean and she found herself caught in his arms and pressed against his chest, hot tears soaking the golden hairs she had fondled so hopefully.

He held her tight, not quite understanding all the pain but realizing he was the cause of it.

"Hush, love," he whispered and clasped her even tighter.

But Casey heard none of it. She remembered only those last, almost desperately spoken words and felt only betrayal and a yawning emptiness inside.

Still her body clung to his in need, wanting desperately to believe he cared.

He picked her up, and carried her back to camp. Laying her down he drew a blanket around her despite the heat. He didn't think he could stand the sight of her naked loveliness. And he had done enough harm to her tonight.

He cuddled her in the blanket, and she was too exhausted to protest. She lay there, her mind spinning between agony and hope. How could he be so gentle and not love her?

Her eyes finally closed, teardrops still hesitating on the long lashes. *Please, God, make him love me,* she prayed silently.

Sean's rest did not come so easily. Could he possibly be in love with Casey? She certainly stirred something inside that made him want to protect her and…and what? She was so damnably young, but he had never experienced such joy in lovemaking. And it had been lovemaking in every sense….

Love. He thought it had passed him by. Perhaps it would have been better if it had. Better for her. Better for her to explore more of the world, to discover what she really wanted.

What happened tonight must not happen again. He felt a deep ache at the thought. God, he needed time to think.

But it was impossible to think with Casey in his arms, her soft, lovely body enfolded so artlessly against his. There would be time tomorrow…in the stark light of day…to sort things out.

If there *was* a way to sort them out.

But tonight, he would give her his comfort, if not his heart. For he didn't honestly know if he could give the latter. Too many years of death had taken something from him, and he wouldn't saddle Casey with half a person. He certainly could do nothing, or say anything, until his business with Wilson was settled. He cared too much for her.

He lay awake for hours, even after she turned and her back rested against his chest as his right arm pillowed her head. After all these years of being alone, could he possibly have fallen in love? It was just the night and that strange bewitching lightning, he told himself again. Just the magic of the night.

Chapter Eleven

Covered only by a blanket, Casey woke to the golden haze of dawn with bittersweet feelings.

She had wakened several times during the night, feeling Sean next to her, treasuring the closeness while filled with fear that morning might bring indifference or, even worse, regret. She reached out for him now, but he was gone and the dawn lost its glow. She stretched, feeling an unusual soreness. Last night had been a miracle. All those sensations and feelings. If only he loved her, her world would be perfect.

She was seized by the need to be dressed when he returned. She must not let him know how deeply affected she was, how much she loved him, how hurt she was by the implied rejection of his desertion. She was suddenly terrified he might now abandon her. She must seem strong and as indifferent to last night as he apparently was.

They were together for one purpose. To get Bob Wilson. She must not let him believe there was any other reason. And yet, in the past days, her obsession with Wilson had been absorbed into a greater obsession. Not only was she no longer concerned with vengeance, she was filled with fear of finding the outlaw. For when he was found, it would end Sean's commitment to her. Or, even worse, could mean Sean's death.

"I'm sorry, Pa," she murmured. She saw her father's tortured face again, and the blood, and she hurt inside. She owed him vengeance, but how could one hate and love at the same time? Sometime in the past few days, the hate had seeped away.

Casey slowly pulled on her clothes, her nose wrinkling at the smell. They would be at the lake tonight and she could wash them. And herself.

She heard a shot, just one, and jerked out of her reverie. Her gun belt was near the saddle and she sprinted over to it, quickly buckling it over her hips and drawing the Colt. Sean's horse was gone, and hers was still unsaddled. She hesitated a moment, not sure whether she should follow on foot. She had seen Sean vault on his horse without saddle or stirrups many times, but she had secretly tried it and had only landed in the dirt.

And then she saw him riding toward her, a rabbit in one hand, the reins in the other. His eyes touched her with a kind of softness before masking over, and she felt herself trembling. She turned abruptly, not wanting him to see what was on her face. She knew she had lost her ability to hide her feelings, and she was terrified it reflected only too well the consuming need she felt for him.

But even as she turned, her eyes locked on him for a small bit of a second.

Why did he have to be so damned attractive?

Why did his hair have to shine like burnished gold in the sun?

And why did she feel rooted in the earth like a turnip?

Angrily, she finished her turn as he dismounted, her back stiff.

"I thought a fire might be ready," he said, and Casey

wondered if she heard a note of hesitation in the usual confident voice. It couldn't be. Not Sean.

Casey's chin lifted. He apparently was going to ignore last night. Well, she could do that, too."

"I didn't think we had any need for it," she said with an edge in her voice. "I thought you wanted to leave early."

Sean eyed her speculatively. He didn't know what he expected this morning, but it wasn't this tight control. Tears, perhaps? Declarations of love? He was shocked to find himself oddly disappointed. Had it meant so little to her? But her face no longer carried the flush of love, and her eyes were that secretive moss color.

"I thought you might be...a little tender, this morning," he said hesitantly, and this time she did blush, rose flooding her lightly tanned cheeks. She ducked her head in a gesture that Sean found completely unnerving. He wanted to take her, and hold her, but he was afraid where it might lead. He had decided this morning that what happened last night could not happen again...at least until he made some sense out of this mess.

It would be best, he knew, to find someplace to leave her, to give her time to understand her own feelings. It was, after all, very soon after her father's death, and he had apparently been the only family.

He was suddenly hungry to know more about her. Maybe then he could make a decision. He had been a fool to think it was only the lightning that had spurred his passion. As she stood defiantly in front of him in her shapeless dirty clothes, he still desired her more than he ever had another woman. It was the memories of last night, he told himself. But it did no good. He looked at her, and he wanted her.

"The fire," he prompted, his voice gruff.

Casey saw the muscle in his jaw flex and heard what she

thought was annoyance in his voice. She bit her lip, wishing she did not want to please him so much.

She started to nod, then something rebelled inside her. She was damned if she would be treated like a servant this morning…after last night. She wanted him to hold her, to touch her, and the only cussed thing he did was order her to make a fire.

"Make it yourself," she exploded, hurt and anger churning her insides, trying to displace her desperate need for reassurance. She turned away from him, wanting to hide the mist of tears in her eyes, the trembling lips that refused to say what she wanted them to say.

"Casey…"

She bit her lip at his tone. Pity, that was all it was…pity and displeasure that she was making more of last night than it had been.

"I'm going on," she announced. "You can do what you want."

"Casey, damn it…"

She ignored him and saddled her horse, wishing that her hands didn't shake so. She could hear nothing behind her, and she wondered whether he had moved. When she was through, she locked her face into a tight, expressionless mask and wiped away the hovering tears with a seemingly careless swipe of her arm.

When she turned back, he had not moved. The muscles in his jaw were working and the blazes of amber light in his eyes seemed to consume her.

Summoning every ounce of discipline and pride she had, she returned his look steadily. "You don't have to worry about last night." Her voice was low but clear. "I know it didn't mean anything."

Sean felt as if someone had taken a whip to his soul. There was an agonizing pain evident in her words, and the proud way she said them.

He moved over toward her, touching her chin with his fingers, lifting her head until she met his steady gaze. "It did mean something, Casey. I wonder if you will ever know how much it meant." How could he tell her that she had made him new again, young again, had filled him with hope again? That she made him smile and laugh in ways he had not in so very long? That she had taken away the smell of death and brought him the heady aroma of life? That the passionate sweet fulfillment of last night surpassed any sensation, any feeling he had ever had?

How could he when Wilson remained out there? Waiting.

He would never know a moment's peace until Wilson was dead. He could not live his life waiting for a mad dog to strike not only himself but those he loved. And that would include Casey if he did what he wanted so badly to do at the moment...to take her in his arms and ask her to share his life. The thought, which had come so quickly to his mind, shocked him with its intensity.

But he could not speak of it, not now. Not until he finished his business. In the meantime, he had to keep her safe, safe and out of trouble, and he didn't know how to do that. Damn, he didn't know.

Unless he hurt her. Unless he told her he wanted no part of her. His hand traced her cheek, the fingers full of tension, of want, as he warred with himself. And he knew he couldn't do it. Not yet. Not today. Not after looking into those wide green eyes full of hope, not after last night.

"All right. Let's get started," he said abruptly, jerking his fingers from the softness of her skin.

Casey nodded, wondering whether she had imagined that softness in his face, the gentleness of his fingers. There was none of that in him now, only a glower where the slight puzzled smile had been. But some of the hurting pain inside her was gone.

"The rabbit?" she said hesitantly. Her stomach was growling and she was already regretting her rebellion but she couldn't back down now. She knew he favored riding early in the day before it became so blasted hot.

He gave her a small rueful grin as he squinted against the bright morning sun, a flash of understanding crossing his face. They should both be starving after last night. "Since you objected so strenuously to starting the fire, you can clean the rabbit," he said as the smile stretched into a grin.

Casey's eyes narrowed. Damn but she had stepped neatly into that prairie dog hole. But she *was* hungry. Extraordinarily hungry, in fact. And if today were like every other day, they wouldn't stop for more than water and jerky until this evening. "All right," she surrendered and took the rabbit he was holding while Sean, whistling a tune, went in search of enough yucca brush to start a fire.

While Casey fried the rabbit, the silence between them lengthened. It wasn't until it was nearly done that Sean spoke, asking the questions that he had wanted to ask all morning.

"You have no family left at all?" he asked. "No one back East?"

Casey shook her head. He *did* want to get rid of her.

"Your mother?"

Sean wished he hadn't asked when he saw the misery flood her eyes. He hesitated before asking more, but he had to know. She *must* have relatives someplace. "Is she dead?" he asked gently.

The misery in her face deepened, and Sean wanted to kick himself.

"She left us," Casey said finally, her eyes looking at the ground. "I heard she died a few years back." She looked at him before continuing on. "I didn't care," she said bitterly, but the tone in her voice said she did. Painfully so.

Sean felt a new surge of tenderness. He remembered the barkeep at the saloon in Two Springs. "Damn shame the way Ray raised her..."

Embittered, the man apparently taught her to shun all things womanly because of the betrayal in his own past. He had raised her like a son, and now she was caught between the two worlds. It was so damned unfair to her.

"Is your name really Casey?"

She looked at him suspiciously. No one knew her real name except, she thought, her father. And he was dead. There was no need for anyone else to discover it. But there was something in his face, as if he really wanted to know and wouldn't laugh if she told him. Contrarily she wanted to tell him, felt compelled to. Her name was a woman's name.

Casey mumbled.

Sean looked at her quizzically.

"Cassandra," she mumbled again, this time just a tone louder. She waited for him to laugh.

But he didn't. The corners of his mouth turned up but it was not with the derision she'd half expected. There was a small bit of surprise at the unusual name, but then she saw him say it to himself and he appeared to like it.

"My mother was an actress," she said defensively.

"It's a beautiful name," Sean said.

"Well, I don't like it," she announced belligerently. Years of resentment and pain were in the statement.

But it was as if he had not heard. "Cassandra," he said, "was the daughter of an ancient king. She could predict terrible disasters, but no one would listen."

Casey seized on the explanation. "I knew I didn't like it," she said. "Who wants to know when something terrible is going to happen...?"

Sean gave her that easy smile that made her stomach turn

over. "I still think Cassandra is a lovely name," he said. "And her talent was a gift. A special gift from the gods."

For the first time in her life, Casey thought it was a pretty name, too. The way he said it, anyway. But then she wasn't Cassandra and never would be. She was just plain Casey.

"My name is Casey," she insisted, but she wasn't sure whether she was pleased when he merely nodded.

"How long did you live in Two Springs?" he questioned while she regarded him carefully. He knew she was worried about his questions; her eyes showed it. Damn, but she was like a little sphinx with her words. Yet she had milked *him* for any amount of information.

"About ten years," she admitted slowly. "There was another Texas town before that..."

"What about school?"

Casey's face grew red with embarrassment. He knew things like what "Cassandra" meant, and had gone to West Point. Her education was poor at best. "Pa taught me some," she mumbled slowly. "There wasn't a school for a long time and then I was too old. But the schoolteacher taught me at night. Pa didn't think it was needed, but I wanted to learn. Pa thought I needed to know how to take care of myself, and that was enough. He said too much learning gave people fancy ideas."

Like her mother, Sean thought to himself. He had been intrigued with Casey's curiosity and intelligence in the past weeks, and he wished right now that her father was alive so he could knock sense into the man. What he had done to Casey was near criminal. Take care of herself? She was, in so many ways, totally unprepared to take care of herself. She was too unaware of her own femininity and the effect it could have over men, and yet her skills would scare off almost any decent suitor. Her father had made sure she wouldn't really fit in anywhere.

Except perhaps with him. The idea wouldn't leave Sean.

He was bewildered by the depth of his feeling for her. She aroused many things in him: passion, amusement, tenderness, protectiveness and a curious yearning someplace deep inside himself. He wanted to reach out to her, but then he was discovering he always wanted to touch her. He wanted to soothe away that frown, to finger those curly ringlets that she tried futilely to subdue, to feel the velvet softness of her skin. He wanted most of all, at the moment, to see a smile on her face now crinkled with worry and shame.

He thought briefly about turning back, and taking Casey back to San Antonio, back to Ryan and Ben and people he knew would accept her, and adore her. A place where he could take his time, and court her as a woman should be courted and where she could learn her own mind.

But he had come too far now to turn back.

Damn Wilson.

If he took Casey home, she would also be in danger, and they would all have to live with Wilson's threat, turning their ranches into armed camps. And Sean wasn't willing to do that. He wanted to end it, once and for all.

And until it *was* ended, it would be unfair to Casey to promise her anything. He had no intentions of dying, but it was always a possibility. And despite last night's mistake, he thought it important to give her time to discover what she really wanted. There was a woman's passion in that boyish-clothed body, but Sean also knew he was the first man to awaken it. He had been unconscionable in taking advantage of it.

Despite her apparent attempts to appear indifferent this morning, he could not miss the naked longing in her eyes, and he wondered whether it was because she had never known much love or affection. Damn. Ty Donaldson was more her age, though the very thought of the two of them together sent flashes of jealousy through him. He recalled the sparks between the two and wondered for the first time whether they had been entirely hostile.

Sean stared quietly into the fire, deep in thought. Relieved to be free of his probing eyes Casey stabbed a piece of the rabbit with her knife and took a bite. Her tongue burned, and she almost dropped it from her mouth before realizing how...how ill-mannered it would look. She held it there, her tongue and the top of her mouth on fire as her eyes grew wide with the effort. Why was she always so clumsy with him? She felt like a child when she wanted to appear so much a woman.

Sean took a piece of rabbit with his fingers and realized immediately the cause of Casey's pained expression. He wanted to smile, as he often did with her, but he was afraid he would hurt her feelings. A new surge of tenderness enveloped him, and he wished it away. If he didn't do something about these damned feelings, his obsession with her could kill them both. He almost wished Ty Donaldson back. At least Donaldson would be some kind of buffer.

"Do you think you can ride?" Sean asked gruffly, reaching for another piece of meat.

Casey knew exactly what he meant, but she wasn't going to admit it to him.

"Of course," she said loftily, ignoring a little warning voice inside. She was glad his face was averted because she knew she must be blushing again. Just as Amy Caruthers, the mayor's daughter, always did. She had always thought it was part of flirting, but now she knew it for the natural reaction it was. Tarnation.

The rabbit disappeared between the two of them, and Sean rose, moving restlessly. He wanted to get going, to ride away another kind of hunger.

Casey dumped the fat out of the pan and scrubbed it as clean as possible with the gritty sand where they were camping. She would wash it tonight in the lake Sean told her about. Water. Water to wash. Clean water to drink. Her eyes cleared and sparkled with anticipation. She would wash...everything...and perhaps...just perhaps...Sean would hold her again. Hold her, and kiss her, and do all the other things that made her feel so wonderful.

Sean was there to help her mount. And she blushed furiously again. She had usually just gone ahead and mounted herself, not waiting for his help. But she *was* sore. And she really didn't know whether she could mount the horse herself or not.

His right hand felt warm on her elbow and his left steady as he offered it for her foot and confidently hoisted her on the horse. He seemed so secure in himself, so immune from any need for another person. Damn him. And damn herself for wanting him so very much.

It didn't take Casey long to realize what Sean had implied earlier. She thought she was being torn apart, and every movement of her horse made it worse. Sean had stopped several times and asked whether she wished to rest, but she shook her head. She didn't want to dismount because she knew she would never get back on. Mile faded into mile, and she made it by sheer determination.

And then it was there...like a mirage, or a mirror reflecting the sky. A huge piece of water surrounded by small bushes, a few piñon trees and some stunted cedars. It seemed miraculous. There were buffalo chips wherever she looked and, it seemed, hundreds of animal tracks. A trace of silver hurried over the water from the retreating sun, and the sky was a calm velvety blue.

Casey forgot her shyness. She kicked her horse abreast with Sean's. "Where does it come from?"

"Some kind of natural spring," he replied. "Before the army arrived, this was hunting grounds for both the Comanche and Apache. There are buffalo and antelope and God knows what else.''

Sean swung down from his horse and helped Casey down. She felt impossibly light in his arms. His hands moved over the curve of her hips and once more he felt the now familiar surge of blood. ''I'll see if I can't find something larger than a rabbit this time,'' he said, quickly mounting again. ''We'll stay here a day and rest.''

''An antelope,'' Casey said, her skin still burning from his touch. ''I think I could eat a whole one.''

Sean crooked his mouth in a forced smile. He would take his time. The longer he stayed, the shorter the temptation.

Casey built a fire of buffalo chips and the sharp thorny branches of the brush close to the water. More than one pricked her skin and she had little trails of blood on her hands and arms.

She sat on the edge of the water, watching the sunset paint muted layers of colors across a sky so different from the angry heavens of last night. The water looked incredibly inviting and Casey decided to take a bath. Her whole body was caked in dust and sweat, and her hair gritty and dirty.

The silence was almost complete; there was only a ripple of water where a fish surfaced to grab an insect for dinner, the slight rustle of the sparse bushes and the crackle of her fire. A bath would take only a few moments, she told herself. She would be clean and dry before Sean returned. She took her clean clothes from the saddlebags and placed them near the edge of the water. She then slipped from the ones she was wearing and leaned down to wash them with a small cake of soap she had brought with her. When she'd finished, she spread them over a bush to dry, and descended into the water, wondering at the coolness of it.

She carefully took a few steps. She didn't know how to swim. There had been no need for it at Two Springs. Indeed there had not even been water deep enough to swim. But she had feared little in her life, and water certainly held no terror. She was, instead, fascinated with the clean, cool feeling. She had never been in anything but river water, and river water was usually muddy, not this crystal-clear perfection in which she could see her own toes. Entranced, she took another step, wondering how deep she could see. But this time her foot didn't hit the bottom, and she fell forward, her hands and arms grasping for something solid. Her head went under and she panicked. She remembered the time several weeks earlier when she thought she was drowning in mud. Her mouth opened instinctively and she gulped a mouthful of water.

An all-consuming fear seemed to weigh her down. Her hands flailed and finally her face came to the surface, and she spat out water before her head went under again. Her feet frantically sought a hold but the struggling merely carried her down again. This time she closed her mouth and battled with herself to keep calm. As she once more surfaced, she screamed.

Empty-handed, Sean had decided to return to camp. His mind, he knew, had not been on his task and the one time he had seen a quick movement, he had been too slow to take aim. He was disgusted with himself and completely baffled by the feelings that seemed to paralyze him. He was physically exhausted, having had little or no sleep last night, and he knew he could not continue this way. He had to do something with Casey Saunders.

He was close enough to camp to see the flames from the fire when he heard the scream and spurred his horse into a gallop. When he reached the edge of the lake, he could see naught but a hand and he bolted from the horse and dived in.

Terror quickened his strokes, and he reached the place

where he had seen the hand. But she was gone. He dived underwater, grateful for its clarity. He saw her then, and his hands went around her while he kicked toward the surface. She was quiet and still in his arms, and he knew she was unconscious. Or dead.

She couldn't be. He wouldn't let her. He swam to the edge and hoisted her on the bank before scrambling up after her. Her eyes were closed and water seeped from her mouth.

Sean turned Casey over and pushed rhythmically on her ribs, watching the water come from her mouth. "Fight, Casey," he whispered to her. "Fight."

And then she was sputtering and coughing, and he was holding her tight in his arms, whispering nonsensical things to her and feeling the pain of her labored breathing. She expelled one long flow of water, then another. When she finally looked at him, her eyes were clouded with the agony of the last few minutes, and he wanted to hold her forever.

She shuddered against him, cherishing the strength that was so evident through his wet clothes. "I thought I was going to die," she finally said in a barely audible voice.

Sean held her closer. "Not possible, little wildcat. I won't allow it."

"And God wouldn't dare disagree," she chided, snuggling up even closer. She felt so safe with him.

"No," he agreed simply, and he felt her shiver, even in the heat of the summer night. "But," he added slowly, "I think I'm going to have to teach you to swim. This is the second time you've almost drowned."

Casey was suddenly indignant. "It was that gunfighter the other time," she said. "He nearly drowned me, not the water."

"Nonetheless," Sean insisted with amusement in his voice, "tomorrow we start swimming lessons and in the meantime we had better get you dressed."

Casey remembered she was completely naked, and stiffened in his arms. It had been different last night. But no one had ever seen her naked before that, and her strict upbringing surfaced, sending shivers of embarrassment up her spine. She tried to cover herself while her green eyes pleaded with Sean.

But his smile reassured her, and so did the warmth in his eyes. He stood, bringing her to her feet, holding her so she wouldn't fall. One arm was around her shoulders, one hand firmly grasping both of hers.

She had never realized how strong a man's hand could be.

How strong and yet how gentle at the same time.

She knew her legs were growing weak again but it was not the near-drowning that was causing it this time. Then Sean lifted her in his arms and carried her to where her clothes lay. She felt like a babe as he dressed her, disregarding her attempts to do it herself. He picked her up again and carried her to the fire. How good it felt to be nestled to his chest, to feel his hard strength. How strange to feel the cold breath of death one moment and so vibrantly alive minutes later.

Sean carefully sat her down, and tended the fire. He found the frying pan and cooked some beans and bacon, insisting that Casey remain still. He knew from experience she would soon be feeling nauseous and weak.

The moon was riding high in the cloudless sky, and the stars hung like jewels on a crown. Casey had always loved the evening sky but never was she so affected by it as now. She had nearly died twice this summer, and God had spared her each time. God and Sean Mallory. Suddenly she felt something rush up in her throat and she choked, retching miserably.

Sean was next to her in a flash, holding her as her body

shook. When she was through, her body trembling with the violence, Casey looked at him miserably.

He saw her apprehensive expression, and his hold tightened. "I know exactly how it feels, Casey. I almost drowned once."

She straightened and looked at him. His eyes were cloudy now, mysterious in the way they sometimes were....

"When?"

"At West Point. I was taunted into a race across a river in October. The water was freezing, and I cramped halfway across. Ben Morgan saved my life but not before I swallowed half the river."

"Tell me more about Ben," she said, snuggling up against him. "If he saved your life, I would like him."

"I think you would, wildcat, and he would like you."

"You live nearby to him?"

"On the next ranch."

"I think that would be wonderful," Casey said wistfully. "I always wanted a brother or a sister...someone who would be a friend."

"Don't you have any friends?"

"No...not like you and Ben," she replied quite simply. "I know people, but that's not the same thing, is it?"

"No." Sean ached for her. And he ached for himself, for the years that he himself had avoided friendship.

"Friendship isn't always easy, Casey," he said. "It can hurt, too."

Casey studied Sean's face and saw, for the first time, the lines of pain in it. He had always seemed so easy, so quick to smile that she had missed them before. But they were there, carved in the handsome face.

"Because you were on different sides in the war?" she asked.

"Partly that, and partly other things. Mostly a lack of

trust. Remember that, Casey. No relationship is worth anything without trust.''

''But you're friends now.''

''Yes,'' he said slowly, but Casey heard the slight hesitation in his voice.

''Something's gone forever, isn't it?'' she observed instinctively.

Sean's lips creased into a slow half-reluctant smile. Good God, she was bright. ''Perhaps,'' he allowed. ''I don't know.''

Casey, wrapped in a cocoon of his caring, looked straight up into his eyes. ''I'll always trust you,'' she said simply.

Sean's breath caught painfully in his chest. He was being given a gift of great value, and he didn't feel worthy of it, not after last night. He looked at her face, so lovely and so serious, and the pain in his chest deepened.

Whatever else he did, he would protect her. And that included keeping his feelings to himself.

''Friends?'' he said, his loins in agony at her nearness.

''Friends,'' she agreed, her heart cracking.

Chapter Twelve

Friends! Casey snorted with disgust. Hellfire!

At least it was better than nothing, she consoled herself as she desperately tried to follow Sean's instructions in the skill of swimming.

In the bright light of morning, she weighed the bond they had made last night and found it wanting. Friends. The word seemed to preclude anything else. The way he put it, anyway. For after the words were said, Sean had carefully risen, prepared the meal and slept on the other side of the dying fire. After a breakfast of biscuits, he'd insisted on teaching her to swim. With her clothes on.

Casey had never thought herself particularly slow. She had learned to use a gun quickly and accurately and to gauge where a blow would do particular damage. But with Sean standing beside her, watching intently, she was all arms and legs and none of them seemed to to go together.

Once when she went teetering into the deep water again, he caught her, but he quickly placed her back where she could feel the bottom, hands jerking at the contact, almost as if the touch of her burned him.

He was a patient teacher, and despite her clumsiness she soon began to move in the water, although not very gracefully. Within several hours she felt like a prune but she could paddle a fair distance.

Finally satisfied, Sean gave her a grin and they both returned to the bank. His eyes crinkled against the brightness of the day, Sean rolled over lazily and stretched out in the sun to let the hot rays dry his clothes. Casey dropped down beside him, tired from using new muscles and frustrated by her odd ineptness. The sun felt wonderful, its warmth flooding her like a caressing hand, soothing and relaxing.

Casey looked over to Sean and saw his eyes were closed. There was golden stubble on his cheek and his hair seemed more bronze than usual.

His wet trousers clung to his legs, outlining their sinewy strength, molding to his hard, lean hips. He was not wearing a shirt and his upper body was knotted with muscle. It was smooth, except for a ragged scar on his left chest. It must be a war wound, Casey surmised. She wanted to touch it, but that wouldn't do. She couldn't stop wondering how he came by it.

Look away, Casey. She tried. But nothing could lure her eyes away for long; they always kept wandering back. Her insides tingled and burned.

Casey forced herself to rise. He had said they would stay here today and rest. She would make herself useful and forget about Sean Mallory. Perhaps she would find some game. Some of the soreness of the day before was gone, soothed by the water. She eyed the lake. So deadly. So lifegiving. Like the sun. Like this whole country.

She looked down at Sean again. She hadn't seen him quite this relaxed before. He even looked boyish with the lock of hair on his forehead and long golden-brown lashes covering his usually wary eyes.

Casey quickly saddled her horse, checking the rifle and pistol. Both were loaded. But she always checked any-way…just as Pa had told her. She walked the horse slowly at first then kicked him into a gallop when she got beyond hearing range.

The sun was high when she finally spotted an antelope. It was headed toward the water, not yet catching the scent of man. She eyed it hungrily. They would be here long enough to smoke a large portion of it. Quietly, Casey removed the rifle from its sling on the saddle and aimed carefully. The animal lifted its head, sensing danger, its body ready to bolt when Casey shot. Its legs lifted in a beginning movement, then folded, and the animal fell.

Casey felt the familiar regret. She had never liked killing, but it had been a part of her life since she was eight and her pa first took her out hunting. She knew it was part of the life cycle. Still, it would never be easy for her. She approached the animal slowly, then dismounted. Its eyes were already clouding over, and she knew it was dead.

Casey deftly cut two large pieces of the haunch and struggled to tie them to her horse, which was sidestepping and nervous from the smell of blood. When she had packed as much as she thought she could carry, she mounted herself, regretfully leaving the remains to the predators. Despite her distaste for the job, she felt a surge of pride in what she'd accomplished. Sean would be pleased. Pleased and proud. She was sure of it.

Sean woke to heat. And emptiness. Casey was gone and the sun was already leaning toward the west. He had been so damned tired. He had had little or no sleep in the past two nights. God help him.

He checked the horses and decided she had gone looking for game. They were both sick of beans and rabbit. As long as he knew she wasn't near the water, he could relax. A little.

Sean thought briefly about going after her but quickly discarded the idea. They had been told there was little danger of Indians in this area. The army at Fort Bascomb had insured that, and Casey, he suspected, would not appreciate being checked up on. He went back to the water, thinking again how inviting it looked after all the days on the trail. He stripped off his pants and dived in, swimming with long confident strokes.

He had always enjoyed swimming, even after he'd come close to drowning at West Point. The water cleared his head but there was still one great unsolvable problem. What to do with Casey. He rolled over on his back, floating and drifting as he thought about Casey, and the vivid green eyes, and the slender lovely body and...

The five men approached Blue Hole cautiously. Deserters from Fort Bascomb, they wanted to put as many miles between them and their pursuers as possible. But their horses needed rest and water for the long dry ride south to Mexico.

Kenno, a half-Mexican tracker, held up a hand, stopping their pace. He spied a horse up ahead and knew someone was already there. And that meant food, supplies and, if they were very lucky, money.

The five left their horses and, rifles in hand, crouched down and made their way to the bushes. There were two sets of clothes sitting in the sun, but only one man in the water. Jake, who had assumed temporary leadership, gestured to two of his men to move back and keep watch. He and the other two would wait until the swimmer started to leave the water.

The deserters lay flat on the sunbaked ground, the heat sending rivulets of sweat pouring down their backs. The man in the water seemed tireless, and Jake grew impatient. They didn't have all day.

The man finally made for the bank and was stepping out when Jake rose, his pistol pointed at the swimmer's middle.

"Be very careful how you step," Jake said, registering that the man's hand automatically went to his side, where a gun belt would usually be. This was no tenderfoot even though he had been caught like one.

Sean stood there, naked and defenseless, rage smoldering in his brown eyes. "What do you want?"

"What do we want?" mocked Jake. "Everything Where's your partner?"

Sean's insides turned sick with fear. Casey. Where in hell was she? And would she have more goddamned sense than he'd had?

He had been daydreaming, trying to get her out of his system, and he had been careless. Ever since he had met her, he had lost that edge, that sense of impending danger that he had honed so well during the war.

"He left, pulled out," Sean said shortly.

"Without his clothes?" Jake said. "That don't seem too likely."

Sean ignored his comments and leaned down, picking up his pants.

"I didn't say you could do that, friend. Particularly when you don't answer my questions."

In answer, Sean hurled the pants at Jake and dived for the legs of the second man, spilling him to the ground and rolling him over on top of him for protection. At the same time a sound started deep in his throat and split the air with a strength that carried for miles in the quiet land.

One of the deserters who had heard the sound before shuddered at the memory. It was the Rebel war cry, and he had heard it at Shiloh just before his position was taken.

Ty Donaldson had finally picked up Sean's trail. He had known the general direction, and each day he had traveled deep into the night to make up for the lost time.

There were few ranchers in the dry desolate country and

he avoided them all. He lived on jerky and what water he could find, driven by a need he didn't really understand.

He was at least a hundred miles from his encounter with Tatum and felt that he had lost any pursuit. After his final look at Tatum's white pained face, he doubted the hunter would come after him, or help anyone who did. He would know what to expect this time.

Ty's mustache had thickened, and neatly trimmed black whiskers hid his strong, hard chin. He looked years older, but he would never be anything less than striking. His features were too angular, his eyes too unusual, his deadly aura too evident.

But he felt safe enough now from any comparison with the unflattering description on the poster. For a time.

When he grew close to where he figured Sean should be, he discarded his natural reticence and started asking questions. He met with resistance. This was country where many had fled to avoid recognition. They didn't like questions. So Ty tried another tactic. He described Sean's horse, claiming it had been stolen and that he was tracking the thief down.

If there was one thing ranchers didn't like, it was a horse thief. Even a friendly one. One remembered a man and boy stopping for water but it was hard for him to believe the two had stolen a horse.

Ty cursed to himself. So Mallory hadn't rid himself of the little hellion. What a fool.

The rancher suggested Ty try Blue Hole, a lake some miles away. It was possible the two had gone there. It was one of the few places in the area that would provide both water and game. He offered to go along, but with a rare smile Ty declined. It sort of amused him hanging the label of horse thief on the ever so honorable Mallory. After filling his canteen, he'd nodded to the rancher and left.

He didn't know how many miles he had traveled, but

the sun was about halfway down the western horizon when he heard the yell. It was a yell he remembered well. It had continued to echo in his dreams at night, dreams of death and smoke and blood. God, he had hated that sound.

He knew instantly it meant trouble. Mallory had gotten himself, and possibly the girl, into some sort of mess. But what? He had heard that Wilson had last been sighted far northwest of here. He spurred his horse toward the sound, his left hand on the reins, and right hand resting on his hip, just a fraction of an inch from the Colt he wore.

The sound also reached Casey, and though she had never heard the Rebel cry before she knew its source. And knew Sean was warning her. Almost without thought, she cut the meat from her saddle; she didn't want either the weight or the distraction of the jouncing burden.

She was no more than a mile from the lake, but a mesa blocked her view. She knew there were no hiding places near the water, only sparse yucca bushes, cedars and piñon trees and they gave precious little cover.

Casey saw another rider, coming fast from a parallel direction, and drew her rifle, aiming it carefully with the stock balanced on her arm. As the rider approached, she couldn't mistake the lean intensity of Ty Donaldson, and she was jolted by the sudden relief she felt. She lowered the rifle barrel as Ty pulled his horse to a halt next to hers.

"What the hell is going on?"

Casey couldn't believe how glad she was to see him. There was an assurance about him that she needed right now. "I don't know. We were at the lake…Sean was sleeping, and I decided to see if I couldn't find some game." Her head nodded toward the meat on the ground.

"How long were you gone?"

Casey shrugged. "Several hours…I had to butcher the antelope."

Donaldson looked disgusted, but didn't waste any words on his obvious thought. She had been stupid to leave on her own.

"How close can we get without being seen?" he questioned instead, his amethyst eyes glittering in the sun.

"Not very close."

"Damn."

"I'll go on in...distract them," Casey offered, ready to try anything to help Sean.

By the look on his face, Donaldson didn't like it. But he couldn't offer any alternatives. They didn't know who was there, or how many there were. And Mallory could easily be killed in the crossfire if they both rode in shooting.

The gunfighter finally nodded. "All right." He eyed Casey's slight form speculatively. She sure as hell didn't look dangerous, but he knew from painful personal experience that she had her methods. And he couldn't fault her courage.

Casey unbuckled her gun belt and tucked the gun into her trousers, pulling her shirt out over it, before handing the belt to Donaldson.

"One thing about those goddamn clothes," Ty said, "they would hide a cannon. I'll give you about ten minutes." He didn't leave room for argument.

Casey didn't waste time. There was no telling what was happening. She subdued her natural hostility at being told what to do by the likes of Donaldson. She needed him. Sean might need him.

She inclined her head once in reluctant agreement and pulled her hat down over her forehead. She kicked the sides of her horse, knowing she'd be expected to rush in after that shout.

Casey withdrew her rifle from its sling and she leaned down close to the horse's neck. In the event that someone shot first and asked questions later, she would present as little a target as possible. The water came into view surprisingly fast, and then she saw them...three men around a fallen figure. As she approached, she saw two guns take quick aim at her, and one train on Sean.

Her eyes darted quickly around, seeing another two men on the perimeter. So there were five. Not bad odds for the three of them.

She brought her horse to a stop, her own rifle aimed at the one who seemed the leader.

"Hey, it ain't nothing but a kid," one of the men said.

Casey's eyes quickly noted the army clothing before her eyes went to Sean. He was stark naked, his hands tied behind him, and his forehead covered with blood. He was struggling to sit up, and his eyes glared at her. Some part of her brain comprehended readily enough that he was furious she had ignored his warning.

The leader of the bunch eyed the rifle carefully. "That rifle's grown up enough," he said. "Put it down, kid, or your friend here dies."

Sean's face signaled her to ignore the warning, but Casey hesitated.

"And if I do...?" she asked.

"We'll leave you both alive."

Casey nodded toward Sean. "Like him...?"

The leader grinned. "It's better than being dead."

"Don't do it, Casey." Sean had barely rasped the words out when a foot caught him in the chest, and he rolled to the ground, an involuntary moan escaping his lips.

Through the corner of her left eye, Casey saw the other two men approach. The five of them were now relatively close together.

"Do you swear?" she asked in the huskiest voice she could manage. "Do you swear you'll let us go?" How many minutes had it been?

The man nodded solemnly. "No reason to kill you…not if you give me that rifle."

"No, Casey," Sean said. "Run for it." There was something frantic in his tone.

She looked over at him. "I won't leave you," she said, reluctantly handing over her rifle. She turned to Sean, her mouth slightly twisted. "Just like your other friend wouldn't. He kept turning up like a rotten apple." Casey saw Sean straighten and knew he had understood.

She slowly dismounted.

"Get undressed, kid," the leader said as he looked at the smallest man among them. "Clothes just might fit you. Gotta get rid of these army duds."

When Casey hesitated, one of the men grabbed her shirt. All the guns were lowered now. None of them felt any danger from a bound prisoner and a kid.

"Hey, this ain't no boy," the man said as his jerk on Casey's shirt outlined her breasts.

All five sets of eyes turned greedily to Casey, and Sean struggled to his knees behind them. Casey saw his movement and also saw an outline against the sky grow larger.

She pushed her hat off, and the chestnut hair curled around her face, demanding attention. She didn't have to fake the fear she knew was on her face, and it seemed to excite the men even more. One hand reached for her shirt, tearing a button from it, while she tried to turn so they wouldn't see the pistol.

"I'm first," Jake said roughly. "I get her first."

"The hell you do," another man said. "We'll toss for her."

All their attention was on their prize and who was going to enjoy her first. Their arguing covered the sound of the approaching hoofbeats.

When the figure on horseback was almost there, Casey lurched from the grasp of one of the men. She stumbled to the ground, pulling the gun from her trousers as Sean butted one of the men, who tumbled into the man beside him. A third fell to one of Casey's bullets. Then Donaldson was there, and another man was twisting on the ground while the fifth was seeking some way to escape.

Donaldson went after him, while Casey held her gun on the two men Sean had downed. One of the others was still, and the other was holding his arm. Casey saw the gunfighter leap from his horse and wrestle the last man to the ground. In minutes, he was leading a bleeding figure back at gunpoint.

Casey's eyes darted over to Sean. He had struggled to his feet and was standing with his hands tied behind his back, dried blood streaking his face. Casey's finger itched on the trigger as she saw the deep cut on his forehead and the purple bruise on his chest. His mouth was twisted in a wry smile that was half self-mockery, half appreciation at the efficient way the deserters had been handled.

As Donaldson approached, Casey could see the gunfighter's mouth twitch with amusement as he eyed Sean. "Now that's what I call an intriguing sight," he drawled. "Good thing I happened along. I would have hated to miss it."

Sean's amber eyes ignited with fire. In the past hour, he had felt true humiliation for the first time in his life, but he was damned if he was going to let Donaldson compound it. He saw Casey's worried eyes surveying the wound on his head, and he felt a fool for being taken so easily.

"Cut me loose, damn it."

"I sorta like you this way," the gunfighter mocked. "Didn't think you could get caught so easily…"

"Donaldson…" There was a very implicit threat in Sean's tone.

Casey glanced from one man to the other. The gunslinger had a smirk on his face while Sean's was livid with anger.

"It seems," Donaldson said, a leer in his voice, "that the little hellion thinks so too."

"Damn you, Donaldson."

Sean's arms flexed in an effort to break his bonds loose. It was obvious to Casey that if he did, his target would be Donaldson, not the deserters who were looking at their captors with furtive but intense interest.

Despite her brief gratitude for Donaldson's help, she felt her own indignation rise. In addition to his snide observations, he was acting as if he'd done it all when, in truth, she and Sean, bound as he was, had done their part.

Ty still had his gun trained on the man he'd captured, and Casey tucked her own gun back into her trousers, forcing Ty to switch his attention to the other three deserters. Casey found a knife in her saddlebag and, averting her eyes, quickly cut Sean loose. The grin on Donaldson's face widened, and Casey had a sudden urge to hit him where she had before.

Casting a murderous look at Donaldson and exercising what, to Casey, was supreme restraint, Sean walked over to his clothes and dressed quickly, buckling on his gun belt. Without a word, he checked the still man and pronounced him dead. Then to Casey's chagrin and Ty's disgust, he started to doctor the wounded man.

Embarrassed by her own behavior, Casey swung into action. "You keep them covered," she told Ty, "and I'll tie them up."

He started to protest taking orders from the girl, but immediately realized he could better keep them under control with the gun.

Casey found a rope on one of their saddles and told the deserter closest to her to move several feet away from the others. Then she told him to lie on his stomach and put his hands behind him. The man hesitated.

"Do it!" Donaldson's voice was like a whip, and the man hesitated no longer.

Casey quickly and efficiently tied the man's hands then his feet, finally linking them together so his ankles almost met his wrists. In minutes all three were completely hog tied.

Donaldson looked on in reluctant appreciation at her method and competence while something started nagging at the back of his mind. Sam Jones' words came back to him with the force of a sledgehammer blow. The Fort Worth sheriff had been "tied like a hog headed for dinner." It couldn't be…not the little hellion. *His ankles chained to his hands.* Not a sheriff's daughter. Not a girl, for God's sake. She couldn't have.

Just then Casey looked up with no little satisfaction at her job, and she saw Donaldson's narrowed eyes.

She looked puzzled, trying to understand the strange look on his face. "The sheriff," he said softly. "The sheriff in Fort Worth. You were the one."

Casey looked over at Sean digging a bullet out of the wounded man. She doubted he had heard Donaldson's comment over the sound of the man's agonizing yells.

She shook her head, but the look on her face confirmed Ty's suspicion. "I'll be damned," he whistled.

"Probably," Casey said with a slight sniff. "Long time ago."

"Why…?"

Casey looked back at Sean and shook her hand again.

"Later," Ty said with a grimace. Even worse than being beholden to Mallory was being beholden to a sheriff's daughter. A sheriff's daughter who had practically unmanned him.

When Sean was finished, he looked up.

"Damn fool waste of time," Donaldson said of Sean's

efforts. "What in the hell you going to do with them now, anyway."

"Give them back to the army. Fort Bascomb's not far...I wouldn't be surprised to see a patrol here soon."

"Why not just leave them here. That's obviously what they were going to do to you...if not something worse."

"Because I'm not like them," Sean said simply. "I won't leave a man to die."

The antagonism between the two was like a live thing. Donaldson was the first one to lower his eyes. "Do what you want." He shrugged. "It's your time." He knew that in those few seconds Sean had taken command again, and he wondered exactly how. He felt the old resentment rising. "Ben always said you were real good... How come they got you?"

Sean looked over at Casey who was trying to look elsewhere. She felt partly at blame for leaving him asleep.

"I went for a swim," he said simply, unwilling to make excuses for a damn fool mistake. He turned to Ty and his hard amber eyes met the gunfighter's cold ones.

"You're off the hook now," he added curtly. "We're even. You can leave any time."

Ty felt strangely desolated. He had, in his mind, become committed to the task. "You need me," he challenged. "You and this half-sized idiot who doesn't know any better than to wander off by herself."

It was hard to dispute the fact that Donaldson had probably saved both their lives but Sean couldn't dismiss the notion that he would be nothing but trouble. The young gunfighter didn't even try to hide his continued hostility, both toward him and Casey. On the other hand, another presence might help avoid what Sean wanted—no, needed—to avoid: being alone with Casey.

And they worked well together despite their differences. Casey had done fine, better than he had anticipated, but there had been no way she could have handled the five by herself, even after Sean had tumbled two of them. He still didn't understand why Donaldson persisted when he obviously could leave now, the debt paid.

It briefly crossed his mind that Donaldson was lonely. But he immediately dismissed it. Donaldson had chosen his profession. It was one that was inherently lonely, and only a man who sought isolation would choose it.

And Casey? He smiled as he remembered her words as she dismounted, then the blush, which was growing increasingly familiar. There was no question that his preoccupation with Casey had completely destroyed his usual caution. To be totally honest, he would be better off alone.

But he couldn't get rid of her now, not here. And he had a suspicious feeling that Ty wouldn't be that easy to discard, either.

"I suppose it wouldn't do any good to tell you I don't want you with me."

"None at all," Donaldson said easily.

Casey looked disgruntled. Donaldson had been a small bit helpful, but now they didn't need him anymore, and she sure didn't want him around all the time, especially now that he suspected about Fort Worth. She started to protest, and Sean's face settled into implacable lines.

"I need Donaldson until the army comes by and picks these damned scavengers up," he said. "We will talk about it again after that." And he turned and walked away, leaving the two of them glaring at each other.

Chapter Thirteen

Sean stared forbiddingly at his four captives as a ready target for his disquiet. He had tied up the wounded man, feeling that the injury was not severe enough to totally incapacitate him. The others were still hog-tied; they could move only slightly, and then uncomfortably. He was tired of hearing their curses and complaints. Sean's sympathy had extended only as far as patching up the one man; after his treatment at their hands and the intended rape of Casey, their comfort was the least of his concerns.

He considered a few curse words himself as he looked out over the plain. After he and Donaldson had buried the fifth deserter in a shallow grave, Casey had gone to look for the meat she had dropped when she'd heard his yell, and Donaldson, to their surprise, had announced he'd go with her.

Sean had watched them ride away together. They were both full of youth and high spirits after the victory, and he felt so damned old. And lonely. Casey belonged with someone Donaldson's age, someone unfettered by years of killing. But not Donaldson. Not a gunfighter with his own bitter burden. The very thought of the two of them twisted his insides.

His head ached and his wrists still smarted from the rope burns. His pride burned even worse whenever he thought of Ty's mocking eyes as he'd stood there naked and bound. It never would have happened if he hadn't been daydreaming about Casey.

Involuntarily, he relived the feel of her hands as she had washed and bandaged the gash on his head just minutes earlier. They had been efficient and cool, yet they'd seared his skin as they hesitated a moment longer than necessary.

This time his curse was violently loud and his prisoners flinched. They knew he was the one keeping them alive. The younger man would have killed them. Or left them here, bound like this, which would have amounted to the same thing. Jake recognized the breed. It had been their bad luck to encounter a gunfighter. And the girl? She had fought as well as any of them. Damn their luck.

Jake's one hope now was to divide and conquer. He had not missed the rancor amongst the three, the way the young gunfighter baited the other two. Nor the way the girl and this one had looked at each other.

"Trust them off together, do you?" he asked.

Sean whirled toward him. "Shut up."

"Don't think I would," Jake said, unperturbed. He knew men like this one. Wouldn't hit a tied man, he thought with some contempt. "Young filly and young stallion like that," he added with a smirk.

In less than the time it took for his next breath, he wished like hell he hadn't said the words. A dirty bandanna was stuck in his mouth and tied there, and his tall captor stood above him, tense with the need to do something more. Jake choked on his gag and, after looking into the hardest eyes he had ever seen, was grateful that the punishment seemed to stop there. The man's face, at the moment, made the gunfighter look almost benevolent. Jake lowered his eyes and gave all his attention to the problem of trying to breathe.

Sean struggled to keep his hands from the man as he remembered the deserter's intentions for Casey. He slowly forced himself to relax and went back to where he had been sitting.

But as his eyes again swept the rolling plain, his fists balled in longing as the ache within him grew. Where in the hell were Casey and Ty…?

God, he had been lonely. The knowledge spread over him like a storm wind, powerful and unexpected.

He'd not realized, until he met Casey, exactly how lonely he'd been.

It was as if his life had been snatched away from him, had disappeared somewhere years ago.

He had lost everything when he'd resigned his commission in the U.S. army in 1861. And it was not as if he hadn't known it would happen. He had made the decision consciously, objectively, knowing that he was tearing his soul in two, knowing that nothing would ever be the same again.

He loved the United States. He loved Texas, and when it came down to a choice, he had chosen Texas. But not without pain. And when the war was over—when the four desolate killing years had ended—he didn't have enough money left for a hotel room. He could never go back to the army; Reb officers who had attended West Point were specifically barred forever from the service. And he didn't know much else. At thirty-five he had nothing, but then he wasn't much different from thousands of other Southerners, and he hadn't wasted time on self-pity.

Instead, he and Jim Carne and others in his old troop had gone to West Texas where cattle, abandoned by Mexican ranchers, roamed wild and were free for the taking. They'd spent two long hot months building a herd. Months of eighteen-hour days and crushing heat, of injuries and backbreaking labor. The cattle didn't move in herds, and each tiny group had to be found and somehow brought into the larger group. The longhorns' reputation for ferocity had not been understated. Every moment of those two months and the subsequent drive to Iowa had been dangerous.

But they had made it, and their thousand head were among the first to reach Iowa after the war, bringing an unheard-of price of thirty-five dollars a head.

Sean had lost eight men along the way to Indians, rustlers and accidents. Increasing Indian problems and quarantines in Kansas and Missouri convinced him to try another route for the next drive, and another year was spent gathering cattle and following the Loving-Goodnight Trail through the New Mexico Territory. When he'd sold the herd to government contractors in Santa Fe, he'd divided the not unsizable profits and headed with Carne to San Antonio, bought some land from his brother-in-law and started his own ranch.

Yet the work had not brought him the satisfaction he'd expected. He now suspected it was because there was no one with whom he wished to share his life. For six years he had been the next thing to a monk while an emptiness kept growing inside him, a space that cried out to be filled. But he hadn't known how. He tried to fill it with Ryan's children—her stepson, adopted daughter and the twins—but the hole had only grown greater.

He had not been unhappy to leave the ranch, hoping to wipe away the ache that never quite went away. His obsession with Wilson had become his driving force, his reason for being, because there seemed to be little else. He had not let himself think beyond Wilson.

Until now. Until Casey had wriggled her way into his heart.

* * *

Casey and Ty found the meat the same time as the buzzards. Ty fired, scattering them just as they were descending, and Casey quickly dismounted and eyed the large chunks gratefully. It had not been much more than an hour since she'd dropped them...though it was difficult to realize how much had happened in so short a time.

Ty had dismounted, too, and was reaching for the meat when Casey shot him a murderous look. It was her kill, and she was going to bring it in.

"I'll do it myself," she told him angrily. She had not wanted him along but hadn't known how to stop him.

"Like you took care of the sheriff in Fort Worth?" the gunfighter said quietly.

Casey looked up at him cautiously, expecting to see derision and mockery in his face, but it was curiously missing. Instead, there was real puzzlement.

"Why did you do it?" Donaldson persisted.

"Certainly not because of you." Casey's voice was defiant, trying to cover up her fear that he would tell Sean...and Sean would think he couldn't trust her. But she realized from the gunfighter's eyes that it would do no good to deny it. He had read the answer to his question in her face.

"Why?" Donaldson repeated.

"Because I didn't want Sean hurt. He said he would help me find Pa's killer." Casey's voice was defensive. "I waited behind and saw the sheriff return just after the two of you rode out."

A grin spread out over Ty's face. "How did you ever chain him up?"

"How did you know?" Casey was accusing now. Damn him. He would tell Sean everything. And just when she was earning Sean's trust.

"One of the men hired to distribute posters on me told a friend."

"You have a friend?" The question was disbelieving.

"An acquaintance, then." A trace of the mockery was back but it was turned mostly at himself, and Casey reluctantly felt some of her dislike receding.

"I do have acquaintances," he added, a glimmer in his usually blank eyes. "But you still haven't answered my question. How did you take the sheriff?"

"I snuck in while he was unlocking that door in his office and hit him on the head with my pistol. The rest was easy. I used to help my father with prisoners."

Casey had not taken her eyes from Donaldson, and she was startled when his lips started to twitch. Then a chuckle escaped from his usually thinned mouth, and his cold eyes warmed and even seemed to dance a little. Casey looked at him with amazement and a little resentment. She didn't think it was funny. But he *did* look different when he laughed. Less like the cold-blooded killer she knew him to be.

His chuckle disappeared into one of the few smiles she had ever seen on him, and Casey wondered at how it softened his hard features. Damn it, she didn't want to like him.

"So I wasn't your only victim…before this afternoon. Do you always go around wreaking havoc on men?"

Casey's newfound vulnerability as a woman smarted under the question. Did Sean regard her the same way? Was that why he had been so distant yesterday? Was that why he just wanted to be friends? Her face clouded.

Surprisingly, his voice gentled. She never would have expected it. "Mallory doesn't know? About Fort Worth?"

She shook her head, unable to answer. She was completely bewildered by him now.

"Why? You probably helped save his hide as well as mine."

She hesitated.

"Hellion," he said, "you might as well tell me, or I'll not keep your secret." The softness was gone and now he was like a small boy poking at a frog with a stick.

Casey remembered why she disliked him so. "Because I promised him I would leave town and he wouldn't trust me if he found out I hadn't. Why does it make any difference to you, anyway? It's nothing to you. Why don't you just leave? Neither of us wants you."

"Ah, but you both need me."

"The hell we do," Casey retorted angrily.

"A fine pickle barrel you were in. You and the almighty Mallory." His eyes gleamed with rascality. "Fine sight he was. If nothing else, you two need a chaperon." He noted the flush on her face. "Or maybe it's too late?"

Casey started to use her knee, but Donaldson saw it coming and he twisted away. Intent on avoiding that particular weapon, he didn't see the balled fist that plunged into his stomach. Or tried to.

Ty grunted, and Casey groaned. His damn stomach was as hard as a rock. Her hand felt broken.

When Ty straightened up, his eyes flashed fire for several seconds before he started chuckling again as he saw her left hand clutching her right.

"Truce," he said with the same rare smile she had seen seconds earlier. "Or neither of us will survive."

Casey looked at him suspiciously. He was as changeable and unpredictable as a summer storm. "Are you going to tell Sean anything?"

"No." His smile was unexpectedly sweet and powerful. "Like you said, it has nothing to do with me. At the moment." The threat filled the air, and ruined the previous effect of the smile.

But she had little choice. "Truce, then," Casey conceded reluctantly, wishing he had made the offer before she'd tried to punch him. Lord, but her hand hurt.

Donaldson saw her glance down at the hand. "I'll put the meat on your saddle," he offered and without waiting for her consent did just that.

But he didn't offer her any help in mounting, not that she would have accepted any from him. When she looked over at him, Casey wondered whether she had imagined his smile. All she saw now were the same harsh, bitter lines she had seen before.

They rode back in silence.

Sean wondered if the deserter's words had the desired effect as he watched Casey and Donaldson ride in, and a feeling—something like jealousy—started gnawing at him. There seemed to be something different about them, not quite the high level of hostility that was there before, and he didn't miss Donaldson's conspiratorial look, nor Casey's resentful one as she returned it.

He was surprised at how much he wanted to hit Donaldson, almost as much as he had wanted to pummel the deserter minutes before. He thought he had disciplined the raw violence in his nature. Apparently not. It took all the control he had to keep his voice level as Casey proudly presented him with the meat.

There was so much pride in her face that his eyes softened. Her hat was gone and she was flushed, her green eyes sparkling with accomplishment. Her chestnut hair, clean and soft from the morning's swim, swirled around her face in little curls. He longed to touch her cheek, glowing in the sun, but he saw Donaldson's bemused stare and stepped back.

"I'll get a fire started," he said abruptly. "You watch them," he told Donaldson, seeing the irritation on the gunfighter's face at being ordered around. "Unless you want to leave?" he offered again.

Ty merely shook his head, and took the rifle Sean had

been holding, settling his body lazily on the ground as he curiously eyed the man with the gag. He looked over at Sean.

"He has a big mouth," Sean said simply.

Donaldson, seeing the sudden tenseness in the other man's body, merely nodded.

Sean built the fire, then cut a strong branch from one of the stunted cedars and made a spit, driving the pointed end through the meat. It wasn't long before the delicious aroma of cooking meat made them all a little giddy with anticipation. It was nearly dusk, and neither Sean nor Casey had eaten since breakfast; Ty had had only jerky during the day.

The three ate with more compatibility than they had had before. When they were finished, Ty leaned back, his hand just inches from the rifle he had brought over. The arrogant half smile was on his lips as he looked from Sean to Casey and back again. There was, unquestionably, something between the two. Their eyes lingered on each other a little too long despite their attempts to do otherwise. The little hellion and the honorable Reb captain. For some reason he didn't understand, it lessened his resentment against Sean and made the Reb seem more vulnerable.

Sometime during the afternoon, Ty realized his attitude toward Casey had changed, too, though he had fought it. He didn't want to like anyone. It scared him. That had been one of the reasons he had left Ben Morgan's ranch nearly two years earlier. But now he felt a curious tug of protectiveness toward the little hellion. Though given what he had seen of her, she was probably the last person who needed protection.

He was not physically attracted to her, though she showed signs of prettiness under the man's clothes and ugly hat. But he liked her spirit and determination, and God knew she was handy to have around. When he wasn't one of her targets. Strangely enough he had enjoyed their verbal exchanges. She seemed to touch something inside of him that had been black for a long time.

Ty did not understand why he was insisting that he continue on with Mallory. Mallory had been right when he'd said the debt was paid. It was, and he could leave anytime with his self-respect intact. He couldn't even honestly say he was staying because of Ben Morgan. It was something else. Perhaps the fact that for the first time in his life someone had done something for him without asking anything in return. He had been stunned when Mallory had helped him escape despite the danger to himself, even more stunned when the man had wanted nothing in return. It went against everything he had come to believe. And it made him insecure, opening himself up to hurt when he thought he had shut himself off from such emotions.

He stood abruptly, knowing his eyes were naked and hating himself for it. He strode back to watch the prisoners while Casey cut some pieces of meat she intended to feed them. If it were up to him, he would let them starve. He had seen Casey's torn shirt before she changed to another one, and knew what had been intended. But he had merely arched a cynical brow when Casey announced she would feed the renegades, though he was pleased that Sean insisted they not be untied.

He watched as she put pieces of meat in their mouths amid their pleas to be untied. When she came to the gagged man, she looked for instructions from Sean; she didn't know what had prompted the gag, and Sean wouldn't tell her.

Almost fiercely, Sean went over and took the gag off. Even in the twilight Ty could see how hard his eyes became as he glared at the deserter, and he felt a shiver up his spine. He would not like to be Mallory's enemy. He feared few men, but he knew now that he should fear Mallory. The man's easy manner belied what Ty sensed was a carefully controlled but explosive violence underneath. His reluctant respect for Mallory increased.

Casey had just finished when they heard hoofbeats. All three of their guns were out instantly until they saw a small column of soldiers approach.

Sean and Casey holstered their pistols, but Ty merely dropped his arm, his hand still on the trigger. He had planned to be gone, temporarily, anyway, when the army arrived. He didn't know how far the wanted posters had traveled or whether, indeed, the army would be interested in him.

An officer rode up to them. He was a lieutenant, young and officious. But cautious. His eyes swept around the camp, resting on the tied prisoners before moving to Mallory.

"I'm Lieutenant Mayburn," he said. "What happened here?"

"These...men attacked us," Sean replied simply. "We defended ourselves."

"There were five," the lieutenant stated. "Deserters."

"One's dead," Sean explained. "We buried him over there."

Mayburn looked at the three with fresh respect. Without her hat, Casey was obviously female. Two men taking five army veterans?

"We'll take them off your hands," he said. "With our thanks, Mr....?"

"Mallory," Sean said. Before the officer could ask any other questions, he continued. "This is Casey Saunders...she's the daughter of a lawman in Texas. And Donald Payton," he stated, quickly devising a new identity for Ty.

The officer nodded politely at Donaldson, but his eyes stayed on Casey. He had never seen a woman outfitted like a man before, particularly an attractive one. "Ma'am," he said politely with a gleam in his eyes.

Casey had never quite heard that note of respect before, and she liked it. "Would you and your men like something to eat?" she said, avoiding the savage looks from both of her companions. Neither wanted the army around for long, not with Ty's presence.

"We'd be delighted, ma'am," the lieutenant said, dismounting. He went over to the prisoners, checked their bonds and grinned. "The colonel sure will be glad to see them." He quickly gave orders to his men to untie the four and put them in the irons they had brought.

He turned to Mallory. "May I ask what you're doing out here, Mr. Mallory?"

"Tracking the Wilson gang."

"From where?"

Sean glanced at Donaldson. "San Antonio," he said shortly. "They raided my ranch."

"Haven't seen a gunfighter, have you? Name's Donaldson?"

Casey instantly regretted her offer of dinner. She carefully kept her eyes away from Donaldson.

"Nope," Sean said easily. "But then my cousin and I...and Miss Saunders...have been traveling rather fast. Why?"

"Man's wanted in Texas. We've been asked to look out for him."

Sean shrugged. "What's he look like?"

"Telegraph says he's thin, dark haired. Dangerous."

"We'll keep our eyes open, Lieutenant."

Mayburn looked at Mallory curiously. "You've been in the army?" The man had the bearing of an officer.

Sean grinned. "Confederate army." He looked over at Ty. "Me and my cousin both." His eyes twinkled at Ty's mottled outrage but the lieutenant's eyes had moved to Casey.

"Well...it's over now."

"Good of you to see it that way," Sean replied. "Not everyone does." Again his devilish eyes went to Ty, but the lieutenant's attention was still on Casey. "And you, ma'am? What are you doing out here?"

"The Wilson bunch killed my father," Casey said. "I aim to see them repaid in kind."

"Wilson," the lieutenant mused. "I heard he raided a small town outside Santa Fe. We've been asked to look out for him, too. Just not enough troops to go around, 'specially when we get scum like this. Seems we spend half our time chasing deserters." He nodded his head at the prisoners. "It's hell when we have to depend on ex-Rebs to catch them for us."

"My pleasure, Lieutenant," Sean said, but then his relaxed voice tightened. "How long ago was Wilson near Santa Fe?"

"Two days. We received word by telegraph."

Sean released a slow breath. So they were behind Wilson and not too far. His hunch had been right.

"Did it say where he might be heading?"

"Going north...but he could double around."

Sean shook his head. "I doubt it...not now. Was there a posse after him?"

"Everyone was too damned scared. Wasn't any law in the town they struck, and the sheriff in Santa Fe thought he ought to stay and protect the town."

Sean nodded. It was as good an excuse as any. Sheriffs all over Texas had used the same reasoning. No one, it seemed, wanted to go against Wilson.

The lieutenant drew out the visit as long as he could. Casey Saunders, for all her strange clothes, was one of the few single white women he'd seen in a long time. And the longer he looked at her, the prettier she was. She had a slow shy smile that was unexpectedly attractive. He disregarded the frowns of both the ex-Rebs, believing them merely protective. He didn't blame them.

The meat was nearly gone, and Casey yawned. The lieutenant debated briefly with himself. He needed to get back, and the moon was bright enough to travel. But Lord he would like to stay and get to know the girl better. Finally discipline won, and he ordered his prisoners mounted.

Sean, Casey and Ty watched them leave before Ty turned to Sean bitterly. "I'd rather hang than be called a Reb."

"Then why didn't you speak up?" Sean replied. "I wouldn't have disagreed." He turned and walked away, leaving Donaldson fuming helplessly.

Casey shivered at how close Ty had come to being discovered. She would not be that flippant again. If he had been discovered...

She added some wood to the fire. The water would attract any number of night creatures, and the fire would keep them away. Surprisingly Donaldson came over to help. She could feel his anger at Sean's taunting, and she looked at him questioningly, suddenly afraid he might reveal her Fort Worth adventure to Sean.

Donaldson looked back and saw Sean watching them. He gave Casey a slow, lazy wink and saw her smile gratefully in return. She could be damned pretty when she smiled, and it wouldn't hurt to give Mallory something to worry about. He wondered only briefly why he took so much pleasure in baiting both of them.

Unaware that Sean had watched the exchange, Casey went to her bedroll. Tired and depressed, she wanted Sean to hold her, to go to sleep in his arms, but knew it was impossible with Donaldson along. She took her own bedroll and lay down on it. Between swimming lessons, the hunt, the deserters, her fencing with Donaldson, and the soldiers, she was both physically and emotionally exhausted.

She lay still, but she could not sleep. Before long, she heard the soft sounds of a guitar and knew that Sean was sharing the same restless feelings. She finally rose and went over to where he sat around the dying fire, fingering soft melodies. He looked up, and his eyes were all pain, and Casey wanted to go to him.

But then he set the guitar aside and gave her a crooked grin. "Thank you," he said, "for what you did today." For a moment she thought he might continue, and she wanted him to. How much she wanted him to.

But he merely straightened up and laid out his bedroll. "Good night, Casey," he said.

Casey had no choice but to return to her own bedroll. Donaldson was no place around, neither was his rifle, and Casey wondered briefly where he might be. She was surprised to realize she even cared.

Chapter Fourteen

They were all like porcupines backing into one another the next morning. No one knew where the next quill would land.

The momentary peace they had shared at dinner was gone, and Casey, Sean and Ty were all driven by their own particular demons when the dawn came.

Sean was silent and unsmiling, having spent a sleepless night thinking about the deserter's words. "A young filly and young stallion like that..." It didn't help to realize that this new unexpected jealousy was exactly what the man had intended. He was the first to rise, and he kicked Ty awake, and none too gently. "If you plan to go along, you can damn well do your share."

Casey was the next to receive his bad humor, and her contentious nature responded in kind. She loved him, but by God, no one was going to treat her like a disobedient servant. She had planned to make biscuits—she still had some flour—but his hard glittering eyes and frigid voice hurt her, especially after the sweetness of last night, and she struck back in defensive anger.

When he told her to get breakfast, she snapped at him. "No."

"Then by hell we won't have any. I'm leaving. You can stay or come along. I'm not waiting."

Both Casey and Donaldson looked at him strangely, but he was too angry to care. He had not asked either of them to come; they had forced themselves on him.

He didn't wait to see whether they were behind him. He saddled his horse and started off, his usually reasoned thoughts in turmoil. Damn, he didn't know what was wrong with him, but he was frothing inside and he knew himself well enough to know it was leading up to an explosion.

He had always had a wicked temper, though he had learned to control it. But right now, all he wanted to do was strike out blindly.

And he didn't know exactly why. Or did he? Sean couldn't rid himself of the image of Casey and Ty Donaldson together, of Donaldson's conspiratorial wink at Casey, nor Casey's shy acknowledging smile.

During the long night, the exchange had magnified in importance. He had risen several times to feed the fire, and the last time he had remained there, staring into the flames. Donaldson, Goddammit it. Donaldson was no good for her. Not a young killer who couldn't expect a very long life, and what there was would be hell for someone like Casey. Someone raised to respect the law. The more he thought of it, the angrier he became. Donaldson was just using her, and Casey was susceptible, especially after he had so stupidly introduced her to womanhood. He didn't blame Casey. Donaldson was handsome in a dark, dangerous way, and the bitter half smile would attract someone with a soft heart. The gunfighter could be immensely charming when he tried, and Sean had seen him try several times in the past day.

But he had thought Casey had more sense than to fall for Donaldson, had even let himself believe Casey might care for him.

By the time dawn came, his pain was deep and his temper barely held in check....

He nudged his horse into a faster pace. When they reached Santa Fe, he would make arrangements for Casey to stay. If he had to hire someone to keep her prisoner. And then he could go after Wilson and be done with it...be done with it all. God, he hurt.

Sean heard two other horses behind him, and at the corner of his vision saw Donaldson approach on his right side and Casey on his left and draw up abreast. Without acknowledging their presence, he kept his eyes straight ahead and increased the pace of his trot. By God, he would wear them all out.

Casey covertly studied Sean. She did not understand him at all. He had been as taut as a bowstring this morning and the glowering visage seemed completely out of place. And now he was not even acknowledging her presence. So much for being friends. Or anything else.

The sun rose higher in the sky, and her stomach rumbled. She would have given anything to take back her retort this morning. Every time she looked at Sean's hard face, she wished she could.

She watched his lean body move gracefully with the horse, and she yearned to touch him, to make him smile, to wipe away the closed expression on his face.

Trying desperately to understand the cause of this aloof and angry Sean, she wondered briefly whether it had been the way he had been caught unawares yesterday. But she quickly dismissed that thought. Sean never took himself that seriously, and he had been at ease last night...before the soldiers came. Perhaps it had something to do with that...with memories...with regrets that he was no longer in the army. Perhaps it had nothing to do with her.

She slowed her horse as Sean did, casting another secretive look at her companion, but he had dropped back, leaving her abreast with Donaldson, and her glance found the gunfighter.

He was riding easily, a half smile on his lips as he returned her look, laughter in his eyes. There was something of a little-boy tease in him, and it was hard not to smile back, even when she felt as she did about hired guns in general and Donaldson in particular.

She had been afraid last night, when the soldiers left, that he would reveal her Fort Worth escapade to Sean. Donaldson had been angry, she knew that. She had felt him simmering when Sean called him "cousin" and said he had been in the Reb army. It had been like waving a red flag in front of a bull, regardless of Sean's reasons, and Sean had known it. He could have said something else, and with less relish.

Cascy wondered if the two men would ever drop their hostility. They rubbed each other like burrs tormenting a horse. She understood it. Ty often rubbed her the same way, though he seemed holding to their truce at the moment. She didn't, however, think it would last. She had been comforted by his wink last night. At least he wouldn't say anything until it suited his purposes. Whatever they were!

Donaldson was enjoying himself tremendously. He didn't know why he delighted in discomfiting Mallory, but he did. Especially after Mallory's own little slices the night before. He had purposely winked at Casey, knowing Sean was watching.

He continued to be intrigued by the magnetism between the hellion and Mallory. It was there for anyone with half of one eye to see, and yet the two appeared to go out of their way to ignore it. A little grin, with none of the usual maliciousness, played around his mouth.

He had no interest in the girl, not in that way. She was

too independent for his taste, too volatile. It amazed him that Mallory, of all people, was obviously thunderstruck by the girl, and that she was so taken with a man who embodied all the qualities Ty disparaged: honor and honesty and compassion, even for his enemies. Personally, Ty respected plain old-fashioned greed. You could depend on that.

Ty saw Casey look back, saw the naked longing in her eyes as they found the Reb. Sean had stopped and was stretching in his saddle, his shirt clinging to his body with sweat. He had taken off his hat, and was pushing back his bronze hair with his hand.

Ah, greed, Ty thought. Casey was, indeed, greedy, but the Texan was too honorable.

He might have to do something about that. He started laughing. Ty Donaldson. Matchmaker. He told himself it would be amusing—making Mallory jealous, sparking Casey whose temper was already trigger quick. It would be a cold-blooded experiment, something to occupy him while they sought Wilson. It never occurred to him that it could mean anything more, that someone else was beginning to matter to him. It was too crazy a thought.

His campaign started when they stopped that night. They were all too exhausted to think about hunting, and even Sean, who seemed tireless, dismounted wearily. He had given up trying to help Casey down; she usually slipped down faster than he.

But today she was slowed by weariness and depression. And when Ty offered her a hand, she took it and clung to it as her legs seemed to tremble like dandelion stems blowing in the wind. She quickly snatched her hand away, however, when she saw the glittering light in his violet eyes and thought it derision.

And then she turned and saw Sean watching them, his

face bleak, and her spirits further plummeted. Damn the gunfighter.

Dinner was bare, nothing but what little remained of the meat and some hardtack. Only Donaldson said much, and he was unusually loquacious, seemingly unmindful of the hostile stares of the other two.

"Now New Orleans," he said, "that was one beautiful city...even during the war. Took some leave there in '62, even met General Butler. Ladies weren't too cordial though." He knew it was a subject that still infuriated any Southerner. Butler had given orders that any woman insulting an Union soldier could be considered a prostitute.

But Sean had tired of Donaldson's baiting and merely shrugged. "They probably didn't care for children parading in uniform."

"I was old enough to kill my share of Rebs."

"And you think that's something to be proud of?" Sean's voice was nearly a snarl. "Killing?"

"That's what you're intent on now, Mallory," Ty replied. "You're no better than I am."

Sean's voice, when it came, was tired. "You're probably right." Sean's eyes went to Casey. Her eyelashes were drooping with weariness, and he felt a stab of tenderness so deep it cut through his anger. Tenderness and guilt. She didn't belong out here with him, with Donaldson. She belonged in a nice safe house with a yard full of flowers, and a nice safe husband who would love her and give her children. His hand started to reach out to her, but he quickly withdrew it before she noticed. He had no right.

Donaldson merely shook his head, then shrugged. "I'm going to get some sleep." In minutes the other two joined him.

They reached the Pecos River and followed it north to Santa Fe. Sean never slackened the pace. He wanted to wear Casey out so she would agree to staying in Santa Fe; he wanted to wear Donaldson out so he would stop his irritating attempts to court Casey.

It was three bone-weary travelers who reached Santa Fe, a bright city sitting on a mesa. The city was the oldest continuous seat of government in the United States, Sean told Casey when her eager eyes and questions were so impossibly appealing that he couldn't maintain his self-imposed detachment.

Sean led them up to a hotel where he'd stayed after his second trail drive. Casey lagged behind, fascinated with the sights—a long adobe building with massive walls, a plaza, a stone cathedral. She had never seen its like, never even imagined it.

She dismounted reluctantly, despite tired bones. She wanted to see everything. With a sidelong glance she noticed that the gunfighter stayed firm in his saddle, his hands resting on the saddle horn.

Sean, noticing he was alone on the sun-sheltered porch of the hotel, turned around, his eyebrows raised in question.

Donaldson, for once, seemed awkward. "I think I'll stay outside town," he said. "I'll wait for you there."

Sean's eyes burned into him. It wasn't the law, he was sure of that. He doubted the boy's own brother, if he'd had one, would recognize him now with the mustache and short, neat beard. Ty's cold eyes met his and moved away in an unusually evasive manner. If nothing else, the gunfighter was usually rudely direct.

He suddenly understood. Donaldson had once mentioned that his money had been confiscated in Fort Worth. He had taken the few coins in the sheriff's desk, but his stake had not been there. Donaldson was empty-handed and too damned proud to say anything.

Sean's hand tightened around the guitar he had just untied from his saddle. The last thing he wanted was Donaldson alone and getting into trouble again, and yet he knew an offer of charity would not sit well with him. As Ty started to turn his horse, Sean stopped him with his voice. "I want you with me," he said simply, his own pride stinging at the statement.

Donaldson's lips turned up in a quirky smile. "Now that's a rare admission," he said. He held up the palms of his hands. "But I'm temporarily out of funds." Sean's admission made his own a little easier.

"I'll loan you a stake," Sean said, adding somewhat quickly as Ty's lips tightened, "To be paid back with interest."

Ty's tense body slowly relaxed. He nodded and dismounted, his walk an arrogant saunter as he followed Sean into the lobby. Casey, who had pushed her hat down over her eyes and pulled on a shapeless jacket, once more looked like a boy and walked with somewhat the same swagger as Ty.

Sean eyed both of them with bemusement before ordering three rooms.

"Two," Ty disagreed, and Sean saw the gunfighter eye Casey. Anger rushed back into him.

"Three," he said again.

The clerk looked at the three of them speculatively. Usually cowboys bunched up together to save money, and these three certainly didn't appear more than the usual hands. "Two's all I got, and you're damned lucky to get those. Cattle drive just arrived from Texas."

Ty grinned, reading Sean's anger. But staying with Casey was the last thing in his mind. Getting Sean into her bed was the first. It had become a challenge after the past three days of mutual antagonism. He shrugged, his devilish grin growing wider. "We can bunk together," he told Sean. "You did want to keep an eye on me," he added wickedly.

"You won't find empty rooms anyplace in town," the clerk added, reading indecision in the face of the man who appeared to be the leader of the three.

Sean shrugged. He should have damned well let Donaldson camp outside town.

The rooms were next to each other, for which Sean was grateful. He could keep a protective eye on Casey. It was late afternoon, and all of them were dirty, hot and tired. Sean ordered water for each of the two rooms, watching as Ty washed, then sat on the one large bed, stretching his wiry frame and looking at the bed with appreciation.

Sean tossed him a small leather purse he took from his belt. "Take what you need," he said. Sean had a bank draft with him, and he planned to stop at the Santa Fe bank this afternoon for more money. Since the two trail drives, money was no longer a problem.

Ty caught the leather pouch and weighed it with his hand. "Such trust," he said with the half smile that never failed to irritate Sean.

"Whatever else you are, Donaldson, I don't think you're a thief."

Donaldson eyed Sean. "And what else am I?"

"Don't ask."

"You don't give an inch, do you, Mallory?"

"Not with you," Sean retorted, tired of the conversation. He looked at the dirty water with disgust. "I'm going to get a bath and shave and see the sheriff...see if I can find out anything about Wilson...and you."

"I think I'll just stay here and get some sleep. You push a damned hard trail." Ty took a few coins from the pouch and tossed it back. "Ten dollars," he said. "Plus interest."

Sean nodded and put the pouch in his pocket without checking it. He had expected Donaldson to take more, but then the man kept surprising him. "Just stay away from Casey," he warned.

"Why?" Ty questioned. "You got intentions of your own?"

Sean's lips firmed into a hard line. "Just stay away from her." He went out of the door, slamming it behind him and leaving Donaldson with a smile on his lips.

Sean hesitated at Casey's room, but he heard no movement inside and decided she must be sleeping. He should be back fairly soon.

He found a bathhouse and a barber, and had to wait on both. The town was brimming over with cowboys dusty from the trail, all apparently intent on cleaning up before spending their money in the saloons and other pursuits. Feeling better, he finally found the sheriff.

The news on Wilson was consistent with the army lieutenant's report. Sean asked to look through the posters, and he found Ty's near the top. He left, his spirits even further buoyed. There was no way in hell anyone could identify Ty from that poster. It was dusk when he returned to his room. Finding it empty he knocked on Casey's door and received no answer. Cursing softly, he turned swiftly and left the hotel. He started checking the saloons.

Ty woke a hour after Sean left. It was really too hot to sleep in midday. He started pacing restlessly, then heard movement next door.

He left his room and knocked at Casey's. It opened immediately, and he sensed an impatience similar to his own.

"Sean?" she asked.

"Doing his duty as usual," Ty said, but the sneer in his voice was not quite as bitter as before, and Casey's sharp senses caught the difference. There was a strange bright light in Donaldson's eyes. "I understand you play poker," he said.

"A little," she answered modestly.

"Let's find a game." His look was challenging.

Casey felt a light-headedness. She would love to show the gunfighter a thing or two. She nodded.

She went back in her room where she combed her hair back and hid it with the hat, buckled on her gun belt, then put on the shapeless jacket while Donaldson shook his head with despair. He wondered briefly how she would look in a dress. Something else he would have to arrange.

But he said nothing as they walked down the street. They went in two saloons and Ty silently watched the poker games in each for several minutes before leaving. Casey's opinion of him went up, at least where poker was concerned. Both games had been crooked, but only noticeable to a very knowledgeable eye.

The third place was noisy and crowded with cowboys. Ty found a table where two cowboys were leaving and he and Casey took the seats.

Casey watched as Ty put five dollars on the table, and she decided to use ten from her poker winnings from Fort Worth. Her eyes never left the gunfighter as he dealt. Competently, she thought sourly. Ty won the first hand, a glitter of triumph in his eye. A cowboy won the second, and Ty the third. His stake had grown to twelve dollars, while Casey's was down to six. She knew the three cowboys at the table completely dismissed "the kid" as a loser.

Ty's winning streak continued, his coins totaling twenty dollars when Casey decided to strike. She had bumbled through her first hands, and now with a guileless grin on her face she outbluffed the table and won one of the biggest pots of the game on a pair. Since everyone folded she didn't have to show her hand. The others put it down to fool's luck, except Ty whose eyes narrowed.

Casey could feel the atmosphere changing, tensing as the betting became heavier. She knew she might be able to get by with one more bluff and that was all. Already, Ty was watching her out of the corner of his eye, his mouth quirking with appreciation. Gradually, one by one, the cowboys left, replaced by new ones. Casey didn't try to hide her talent anymore...it was her against Donaldson. Both their winnings had increased and the contest between them was nearly equal.

The air between them was electrifying. They were both fighting for every hand; it had become a personal duel of skill. Casey had forsaken her guileless look and her face was as blank and professional as Ty's, much to his wry chagrin. Casey could tell it hurt his pride that a woman was his equal in poker.

They had drawn a crowd now, this odd couple. The boy and the man who carried himself like a gunslinger. But Casey, while noticing the growing crowd, kept her eyes on Ty's face, looking for a flicker of telltale reaction. The pot had grown as each continued to raise the other. Casey had three kings but there was a gleam in Ty's eyes that worried her. Then she made the mistake of looking up and seeing Sean standing there, his eyes full of amber sparks as they moved from her to Ty and back. She felt the familiar twist as she searched the lean, handsome face, now clean shaven, and the bronze hair shimmering in the gaslight.

"Your bet." Ty's voice was amused as he turned around and saw Sean. Casey's competent poker had demanded all his attention, but now her concentration was broken, and he saw her first uncertainty. He kept raising, and Casey, wanting to escape Sean's riveting look, folded. Ty took the pot and rose lazily, moving over to the bar and ordering a drink. Casey also sidled up to the bar and ordered a beer, feeling very uneasy about the tension that radiated from Sean. She tried to lose herself in the beer, listening half-heartedly to the rising tone of arguments around her.

Someone had brought up the subject of war, and the room visibly divided between the Texas drovers and the local ranchers and cowhands who supported the Union. Casey would never know who started it, but a fist drove into a stomach and all of a sudden the room erupted into violence.

Sean grabbed Casey and pushed her to the side of a piano, before a hand swung him around and he was amid the melee. Casey watched, crouched in a corner, knowing that this was not a time to get involved. Already shirts were torn, and she would probably be quickly identified as a woman, and Sean would be forced to defend her against Lord knew how many. She stayed obediently in the corner, against all her natural instincts.

She could see Sean and Ty pop up from time to time, but they were on opposite sides of the room. Bodies went down, and stayed down, or escaped out the swinging doors, and the crush became less. Finally there were only a few last warriors, and among them were both Sean and Ty. She held her breath as the two of them met in the middle of the room.

With no little satisfaction, Sean pulled back an already battered fist and punched Ty in the face, trying to avoid a blow to his midsection. All his budding jealousy and frustration in the past few days were in his second blow, and Ty went down, falling backward over a body. But he was up in a flash, his own hands pummeling into Sean with no little frustration of his own. Blow met with blow, as Casey shivered at the raw violence between the two.

Finally Ty fell and didn't get up, and Sean dropped to his knees. The bartender rose from where he had hidden during the fight and took a look around the saloon. Glasses, chairs and tables were all broken. Men were trying to rise. One was carrying a friend out.

All Casey could think about was the sheriff. She was surprised he hadn't arrived yet, but she was sure it wouldn't take long. And Ty couldn't get caught. She made her way across the wrecked room to where Ty and Sean were trying to rise, panting heavily. There was one fairly whole man up and making for the door. Casey stopped him. "I'll give you five dollars if you help us out the back way and over to the hotel."

"Reb or Yank?" he said.

Casey grinned. "A little of both."

"I'll take the Reb," he said.

"Good," Casey said, pointing to Sean. "He's the heaviest."

The cowboy's mouth twitched. It had been a damn good fight. "Okay," he said, taking Sean, while Casey struggled to get Ty on his feet. They went out the door at the back just as Casey heard shouting in the front. She and the cowboy hurried their two charges out as fast as possible. The hotel clerk stared at them darkly as they stumbled up the stairs but he was used to such scenes. Casey found a key in Ty's pocket and unlocked the door, helping the gunfighter stumble to the bed and fall next to Sean, whom the cowboy had already dumped there.

Casey gave the cowboy five dollars and the man quickly disappeared as she surveyed her two riding companions. Both of them had black eyes, oddly enough Sean the left, and Ty the right. Ty had blood running down his chin where his lip was split and one cheek was bruised. She suspected the rest of him was, too. Neither of them would be able to ride the next day.

The gash on Sean's forehead had opened, and blood was congealing around it. His lips were swollen and his hand bleeding. She undid his shirt, and his ribs were purple and bruised.

Sean flinched under her touch, groaning a little as he tried to sit up. He felt his sore face, first his lips, then the area around them. He looked over at Ty who was barely conscious.

"How is he?"

"That's an odd question after you two just tried to kill each other."

Sean's lips managed a smile. "I just want to know whether he's worse off."

"About the same, I'd say," Casey replied, her green eyes sparkling with mischief.

"Damn," Sean replied painfully with the lazy, slow smile that she had missed so much.

Casey laughed, pushing her hat back and letting it fall to the floor. "Men," she said, forgetting how much she had wanted to join the foray. She went to get some water and a bottle of alcohol.

It took Casey hours to clean the wounds and bandage the worst ones. Although both men complained over her "fussing," they were, for a brief time, fairly subdued. They had silently weighed each other's injuries and decided it had been a draw. Somewhere during the fight, they had expended their hostility. At least for the present. They were even a little bit sheepish.

It was midnight or later when Casey finished, and she was able to go to her own room. She slept in the clothes she had worn all day in case her patients might need her during the night.

She was so very tired that she had only a minute to recall Sean's crooked smile as she had left. She went to sleep with a special smile of her own curving her lips.

They had planned to leave the next morning, but everything was delayed. Both men slowly went separate ways after a breakfast in the small hotel dining room, leaving Casey to her own devices.

Ty didn't say where he was going. He just disappeared with the same jaunty independence he always had and a curious gleam in his eye.

Sean went to the saloon to offer to pay part of the damages, much to Ty's silent but obviously sardonic reproach. Every muscle in his body hurt, and when he had dressed this morning his body had been covered with ugly purple-and-black blotches. He doubted whether it would be possible for him to ride…either him or Donaldson. For Donaldson had also received the same punishment. Sean wondered what in the hell had possessed him the night before. But he remembered the satisfaction of hitting Donaldson, especially this morning when Donaldson grinned at him, his black eye mirroring Sean's own.

After settling a fair sum with the saloon owner who was stunned that one of the participants had bothered to return and pay for damages, he halfheartedly looked for a place for Casey to stay. The few respectable boardinghouses were filled, and he knew, in his heart, that Casey wouldn't have stayed in any event. Despite his mental threat to keep her here, even tied down, he couldn't put her at someone else's mercy. She would have to go with them…for a while… until the danger grew too great.

He smiled. She had been uncommonly gentle last night, her hands and eyes lingering on him with something more than the efficient concern she had offered Donaldson. Every touch had seared him, making him throb with exquisite pain…and not from the new wounds.

Ty Donaldson had his own errands to run. He had paid Sean back this morning and still had sixty dollars. His shirt was torn and dirty, and he decided it was time for a new one; he headed for the nearest general store. The establishment was full, but he commanded almost instant attention when he entered. It was full of women, and women had always gravitated toward Ty like bees to clover, and his battered face apparently made little difference.

Conversation came to a complete stop as he studied the limited selection of shirts and finally chose a blue one. The poster on him had said black. And then a dress in a corner caught his eye…a green one with puffed sleeves and a ribbon at the neck.

His eyes went around the store and finally rested on a young lady who looked about Casey's size. "Do you have that dress in the young lady's size?"

The storekeeper, a white-haired man of indeterminate age, looked at him with something like shock before finding his voice. "Her size?" Whatever else Ty disguised, he couldn't quite rid himself of the palpable danger that was so much a part of him, and the idea of this kind of man buying such a modest and respectable dress was incomprehensible.

Ty looked around the room and smiled with devastating impact at one young customer. "It's for my sister," he said softly. And then his voice strengthened. "My sister." Damn, but he liked the sound of that. A sister. It sounded almost real. The old need for belonging attacked him in waves. It had been a long time since he let that need surface, but it had been there…eating away at him. Last night, when Casey nursed him she had eased one pain and intensified another hidden one….

The storekeeper did have the dress in Casey's size, and he kept any amusement to himself. The girl Ty had eyed so speculatively approached, half boldly, half tentatively. "Are you and your sister staying in town?"

"I'm afraid not, darlin'," he replied, partly regretting that it was true. She was a pretty girl, dark haired, and slender like Casey.

She blushed at his answer, amazed at her own boldness, and her friends behind her giggled.

Ty grinned. "You make me wish I weren't going," he said. He was surprised at his own teasing; he didn't usually bother with that.

She blushed again and turned away, fumbling at some

dress goods while the storekeeper wrapped his package, her eyes making little darting movements toward him.

Ordinarily Ty would have accepted the challenge but he told himself he was too sore. He hated to think it might be his conscience; it was just that he didn't have time today for innocents. He took his package and left, wondering what in the hell was happening to him.

As he walked down the street, he considered the new problem. How was he going to get Casey to wear the dress?

It was easier than he thought. He reached the hotel at the same time she did and accompanied her to the room. When they arrived, he entered without invitation, much to her indignant look. He unwrapped his package and enjoyed the shock on her face as he held it out.

"What is *that*?" she asked as if he had presented a snake.

"A dress," he said easily. "For you."

"But I don't want a dress."

"That's beside the point," Ty said with his aggravatingly snide look. "I was struck with the strange desire to see you in one."

"Struck senseless," she retorted.

"Perhaps," he said. "I had the same thought but still... And don't worry about the money...it's what I won off you after you stopped paying attention." Laughter danced in his eyes.

"I won't wear it."

"You will unless you want Mallory to know all about Fort Worth."

"You wouldn't."

"Wouldn't I?" There was so much implication in his words that Casey shuddered. She remembered Sean's look last night. Damn Donaldson.

"That's all I have to do?" she asked skeptically.

"On my honor," he replied.

"You don't have any."

He laughed. "You're right, hellion. But you don't have any choice."

"How long do I have to wear it?"

"Just today."

"I wish I'd left you on the barroom floor last night."

He ignored the comment. "Deal?"

Casey nodded resentfully, and he left the room, hearing the door slam behind him.

Casey viewed the dress with apprehension. It had been years since she'd worn a dress. It was pretty, though. Something in her longed to try it, but something else was afraid to. How could she be something she was not?

She felt her hair. It was dusty and matted. There was water in the porcelain bowl and pitcher, and she washed her hair as best she could, brushing it until it dried and swirled around her face. Then she tried the dress.

It was a simple cotton, but the emerald-green pattern and ribbon at the collar emphasized the bright greenness of her eyes. It fit perfectly, wrapping seductively around her slender curves. It felt strange, having skirts impede her movement, but there was something that made her feel... different. She tried to see herself, but there was only a half mirror, and she instantly felt she was betraying herself by even wanting to know. She was, after all, doing it under duress. What was happening to her?

She didn't know how long she sat there before there was a soft knock on her door. And a voice. Sean's voice.

Casey wanted to die. She wanted to disappear through the window. He would think she was trying to be something she could never be. A lady.

The knock grew more insistent and she forced herself over to the door. She opened it slightly and met his puzzled eyes as he looked at her face. She saw them soften, then grow puzzled again as they wandered downward, and the door opened all the way.

Casey stood there, her hands nervously locked behind her, her head defiantly high but her eyes reflecting her uncertainty.

Sean had known she was pretty, even beautiful at times when she wasn't hidden by all those shapeless clothes. But now she was truly lovely. Her eyes were full of wistful magic, her rich red-brown hair glowing in the stream of sunlight from the window. The dress flowed easily over her perfect body. His hand reached up and touched her cheek. "You're beautiful."

Casey felt as though her heart had just burst into a Sunday morning hymn at the Two Springs Baptist Church, and she searched his face for confirmation. It was there, in the heated blaze of his eyes and the tender smile on his lips.

He touched her shoulder. "The dress?"

"The gunfighter." After all that had transpired between them, she still didn't feel comfortable with calling their fellow traveler Ty. It would mean she approved of him. And she didn't. Not even now.

Sean recalled how Donaldson had suggested he go after Casey, to see whether she was all right. What in the hell was he up to now? Donaldson never did anything without a reason. But now he didn't care, he didn't care about anything but Casey. For five days he had been curbing the terrible urgency within him, the need to touch her and laugh with her, and make love to her. It had been Donaldson's presence that had held him back, that and the fear he was being unfair to her, and the suspicion that she might now prefer the younger Donaldson. The days had been among the most miserable he had ever spent. But her love had shone in her eyes last night, and now they were misty with the same longing. He leaned over Casey until his lips met hers, and he felt their eager response. His kiss deepened and his hands played with the soft curls of hair before they went around her compulsively, roughly, possessively, joyfully. And then they turned tender as if he were holding a gem of infinite value.

He wondered at the great surge of feeling that rocked him to the core, the happiness bubbling and spreading throughout him. And peace. An uncommon peace, full of wild jolting emotions, yet peace nonetheless...a sense of coming home, of being where he belonged at last.

His lips caressed her eyes, then the soft satin of her cheeks, before once more finding her mouth. They met with a soft wanting harmony, which almost immediately exploded into a hungry, exhilarating need. Somehow they moved toward the bed. He wondered briefly if Donaldson was waiting for them downstairs, and then he smiled to himself. He suspected he wasn't.

Chapter Fifteen

Casey woke up in Sean's arms, feeling a happiness and satisfaction she had never known before. Even last night did not have this perfection, for last night had been fire and storm, and this morning a rainbow of incredibly lovely feelings.

She didn't want to move, didn't want to break the hold of his arms around her, of his body, which fit hers so perfectly.

He had been so extraordinarily tender, tender and rough, gentle and demanding. She had leaped from one star to another under his touch until she thought she could bear no more, and then they were swallowed in an enormous sunburst of sensation.

She felt his hand now, moving languidly over her hip, and her own hand caught it and brought it to her mouth. She nibbled on him happily as she felt his mouth on her hair.

"You're beautiful," he whispered.

She turned to look at him. She knew she was no such thing, even though he had made her feel that way last night.

"No," she denied seriously.

An anguish struck Sean. Casey's only sense of worth lay

in activities that were inherently destructive. She had no idea how pretty she was, how entrancing that mixture of shyness and passion, how much character and strength were in her face. She should have been told long ago that she had the rare kind of beauty that lasted, not the china-doll perfection, which faded so quickly.

"Oh, Casey...you are so wrong."

"You don't have to say that," she said, burrowing herself in his arms. "I know I'm not. It doesn't matter."

But Sean could tell it did, and his pain intensified. If he could give her nothing else at the moment, he wanted to make her believe in her own beauty and worth. Even if it meant he would lose her.

He turned her toward him and wouldn't let her duck her face, which she tended to do on the rare occasions she was uncertain. "Have I ever lied to you? To anyone you know of?"

"Yes."

He stared at her, his eyebrows furrowing.

"When you lied about Donaldson's name to the lieutenant."

"Would you rather I'd told the truth?"

"That's not the point," she said logically. "You lied."

"Damn it," he said in frustration. "Well, I'm not lying about this."

"I know you don't think it's lying. It's a...a kindness." If nothing else, Casey had always been brutally frank about herself.

"A *kindness*?" he exploded. He let go of her and sat up abruptly, looking at her in complete puzzlement. Then he stood and picked Casey up, carrying her over to a mirror.

"Look," he demanded.

His anger was such that Casey looked. And she wondered if it was truly her in the mirror. Her hair swirled about her face in mischievous little curls and her eyes were a deep dark green from last night's passion. Her face glowed with a special brightness, and Casey was startled. She did look…well, better than usual.

Sean saw the little shy smile make its way to her eyes.

"You make me feel pretty," she confessed. "It's you, not me."

Sean shook his head at her obstinacy. "The first thing you have to learn is never to doubt a compliment."

"But I know…"

"Casey, you are an attractive young woman, and you've driven me to hell and back in the past week. I've been crazy with jealousy…"

Casey felt a thrill run through her. Sean? Sean jealous?

"Why?" The word finally managed to emerge.

"Donaldson, damn it."

"The gunfighter?" The amazement in her voice was so genuine that he started chuckling.

"I think some women would think him handsome."

"A gunfighter?" she said again, stupefied at the very idea. She had been so lost in her yearning for Sean she hadn't given Donaldson much thought, except to dislike him and the fact he kept Sean from her.

And then she thought of last night, and how Donaldson had bought the dress. She had bitterly resented him then, hated him for forcing her to wear it. Now she wondered why he had done it.

It was as if Sean read her thoughts. "He's a strange man," he said softly.

Casey still hated to think anything nice about Ty, even after what they'd been through together. He'd obviously had some nefarious purpose. But she didn't want to talk about Donaldson. She had something else in mind. Her tongue darted out and licked his chest.

But Sean, though aching for her once more, had regained some sanity. He had lain awake much of the night, worrying about her. He knew that his plans for Wilson could well result in his death. But he saw no alternative. And he couldn't leave her with child.

His head leaned down and he kissed her lightly, then set her back on her feet. "We should leave," he said, but his hand lingered on her arm, reluctant to let it go. He wanted her so damned much.

He spun away and hastily pulled on his clothes. Without another look at her, he turned the doorknob. "I'll see if Donaldson's awake. We'll leave in an hour."

He didn't see Casey look back in the mirror, didn't see the glow fade in her face. She looked at the dress on the floor and suddenly hated it. Slowly she dressed in her own shapeless clothes. She started to push the damned dress under the bed, then reconsidered and, instead, stuffed it in her saddlebag. It had worked magic once. Maybe it would do so again.

Sean didn't stop to knock at the door of his own room. He merely used his key and when he opened it there was a gun aiming right at him.

"You should know better than that, Mallory," Ty said in the old mocking manner. He was half dressed, his tight trousers buttoned, but the belt not yet buckled. He was shirtless. "I thought you would be a little longer."

"What game are you playing, Donaldson?"

"Game? Me?"

"The dress. Asking me to check on Casey."

"I got tired of seeing you two lusting after each other," Ty replied. "It was ruining your concentration." The half smile disappeared. "Why in the hell don't you take her home…revenge isn't worth her life."

It was a different Donaldson standing there, Sean knew. The mockery, the arrogance was gone, and Sean saw something like real concern in the gunfighter's eyes. Once more, a twinge of jealousy stirred in him.

"If it was just revenge," Sean said quietly, "I would agree."

"Then what?"

"Wilson vowed to kill my whole family...anyone and everyone I love. She would be in just as much danger if I took her home today. He's already struck at us twice. At least this way I might be able to protect her."

"But he's going north..."

"He goes north frequently...apparently has a hideout up there...he heads back when he thinks it's safe again."

Ty was silent. Thinking. He didn't know when it had happened, or why, but now he cared. It was damned unsettling.

"And the little hellion?"

Sean smiled at the word. "I wouldn't trust her to stay here. And she's promised to do as I say."

Ty looked at Sean dubiously. Did he know about Fort Worth? Ty knew he should probably tell him, but he had promised the girl and he kept his promises slightly better than Casey. He grinned, and the old mockery was back, as if he was ashamed of the momentary lapse. "What are we waiting for?"

They were closing the gap between themselves and Wilson. They followed the Rio Grande up to Taos where Sean discovered the outlaw gang had stayed several days, selling cattle they'd rustled, drinking and whoring. Taos was the perfect spot for it; it had long been the gathering place of mountain men, prospectors, Indians and outlaws. It was an open town, free and easy, with little law.

As in Santa Fe, Casey was awed by the streets of golden adobe buildings, the plaza where an American flag, nailed to the pole by Kit Carson during the war, still flew. Every-

thing, in fact, fascinated Casey—the violet-purple mountains to the north and east, the steep canyons etched by the
Rio Grande, the golden beauty of the region. Never had she
seen mountains, and their rugged beauty entranced her.

But Sean left little time for appreciation. Since Santa Fe,
it seemed to Casey he was pursued more than ever by demons. He stopped only when he thought the horses needed
it. She had stopped protesting when he helped her down,
partly because she wanted his touch, partly because she
loved the possessive look in his eyes as he did so.

They usually slept side by side, but in the week since
Santa Fe, Sean did little but wrap his arms around her. They
were both too exhausted to want much more. For the moment, it was enough to see his eyes light when they turned
on her.

Ty came and went, sometimes bringing game, sometimes
information. Casey found herself watching for the rangy
form on the big bay. He could still infuriate her as no one
else had ever been able to…with his knowing half smile
and caustic comments, but then she would see a sudden
confusion in his hard amethyst eyes and wonder if she was
beginning to trust him. A little. But then he would make
another nasty observation about her appearance or abilities,
and she would remember he was still a hired gun, a man
without compassion or honor.

After leaving Taos, Sean had new confidence, as if he
knew exactly where he was going.

"Fortitude," he had replied when she asked.

"Fortitude?"

"It's a mining camp in the south Colorado mountains."
He had heard in Taos that Wilson was heading to Fortitude,
and it made sense. "Fortitude was solidly Southern during
the war," he explained. "Everyone with Northern sympathies either left voluntarily or involuntarily…there were
even a few lynchings. Wilson likes to think he's a wronged

Southern patriot and I expect he uses that, although now I hear he has both Yankee and Southern renegades with him.''

Casey asked the question that was beginning to haunt her day and night. "What are you going to do when you find him? How can the three of us do anything?''

He looked at her sharply. "The two of us...Donaldson and I. Remember your promise.''

It took all her will to reply mildly, but she had to know. "The two of you, then?''

"I have an idea or two.''

She didn't say anything but her face begged him to continue.

"I think Wilson's base is up there, and he raids into Texas whenever he needs money...or he starts itching about me again. He couldn't do it unless he has the protection of the town. I just have to convince them that Wilson will turn on them before long. There's a great deal of money there, and Wilson's a very greedy man. I don't think he will ignore it for long.''

Casey looked dubious. "But if he feels safe there, why would he risk...?''

"Because someone's going to tempt him into it.''

"Someone?''

"Donaldson," Sean said with some satisfaction.

"But he's a Yankee...you said...''

"He's also a wanted man...I took a poster from Santa Fe. I think Wilson will welcome him fast enough. Donaldson's Satan himself according to the poster, and that's exactly the kind of man Wilson wants.''

"But isn't it dangerous?''

Sean's glance was gently inquisitive. "I thought you didn't care? He's just a gunfighter.''

"Well," Casey stated defensively, not quite able to express her contradictory feelings about Donaldson, "he's kind of *our* gunfighter now."

Sean laughed, his eyes warming at the reluctant admission. He still, at times, had lingering doubts about Donaldson...and a troubling, nagging sense of rivalry where Casey was concerned, but he had tried to cast them aside. The bickering between Ty and Casey was like that between competing siblings; there had been times he and Ryan had engaged in similar matches. That neither Ty nor Casey recognized the bond growing between them was not strange. Neither of them had ever had much of a family, and he had sensed the stark loneliness in both. They didn't know that teasing was often part of affection.

Astride his bay, Ty looked down at the isolated ranch in the valley below. He had seen two in the last four days and he wondered at the determined hardy people who risked Indian attack, outlaw bands and loneliness for a piece of land.

He had separated from Mallory and Casey, according to plan, and ridden ahead, cautiously talking to the few ranchers or riders he had seen. Except for several reticent Ute Indians, most were more than willing to talk. Loneliness was a given in these mountains, and a new face was cause for rejoicing.

Ty knew he was right behind Wilson's gang, probably no more than a day, according to the tracks. He thought about trying to catch up with them now, join the gang immediately, but discarded the idea. The first problem was survival. On the trail, he could easily be shot on sight, no questions asked. In Fortitude, he planned to cultivate the gang until he was asked to join.

So he had circled around and rode what he believed was a parallel trail. He glanced down again at the ranch. It looked tranquil and welcoming in the twilight. There were horses in a nearby corral, looking like toys in the distance. He watched as two figures, one small and slim, one larger with a bad limp, took several of the horses inside a barn. He thought about going down, but the terrain was rough and broken, and it was getting dark. His bay was tired and Ty didn't want to risk his stumbling. He would stay up here tonight and go down in the morning for water.

He unsaddled and hobbled his horse. He poured water from one of his canteens into his hat for the animal, then nibbled at jerky and hardtack. He was too tired to try to hunt, and it was warm for a fire. Instead, he sat, his back against a tree, and considered the last few days.

Sean Mallory had consistently surprised him. When they had first met two years earlier, Ty had considered Mallory just another defeated foe, and had payed little attention to Morgan's respect for the man. He had always thought that Mallory was soft.

And he had thought him a fool when he'd helped him escape, then said he was going after Wilson. Alone. Only a fool would do that, a fool who wanted to die.

But after listening to Sean's plan, he had slowly, reluctantly comprehended the devious brilliance behind it, and decided that Sean was not a fool. Nor was he in any way soft. He had not missed the reckless gleam in the man's eyes as he unfolded every detail. Sean's music and peculiar sense of honor had misled him into underestimating the Reb's unique talents. He had been startled to learn that Sean apparently shared his affinity for danger.

And Casey. She was also a surprise. She was so damned competent at everything except being a woman. But apparently she was learning fast. And it was strange how well the Reb and she fitted. He never would have expected it. Yet they seemed right together in a way that made him ache with loneliness. He had not missed the way they touched at every opportunity, and he wondered if he would ever feel that way.

He doubted it. He had closed his heart a long time ago, and it was too late to change. And his profession precluded attachments. He was honest enough to know that his future was not promising. He was fast with a gun, but there were others faster. There was always someone faster. And now he was even more a target with the bounty on his head. An ambush, a shot in the back, a posse. All were possibilities. No, probabilities.

It didn't matter, anyway. No woman, no decent woman, would have anything to do with him. He had placed himself outside such things, and for the first time he had doubts regarding the path he had chosen. But what the hell, it was done.

Tired of the self-searching, Ty stretched out on a blanket and went to sleep.

Something woke him at dawn. Catlike, he sprang to his feet, every sense instantly alert. Perhaps it was the quiet that woke him. It was perfectly still, too still. He didn't hear the usual morning sounds.

He crawled to the edge of the steep hill and looked down at the ranch below. There were five men approaching the house where a curl of smoke rose, blending into the soft hues of morning. Every sense he had told him there was something menacing about the men, something deadly.

They had to be some of Wilson's men hunting for fresh horses. Ty cursed as he watched two of the men make for the corral and the rest approach the front door.

It was none of his affair. If he attempted to interfere now, he could ruin Sean's whole scheme. But then he saw the door start to open and close, saw the men push it open. There was a shot, followed by an agonized scream. He quickly removed the hobbles and saddled his horse, cursing every second it took. He vaulted into the saddle and urged the bay down the incline, his Winchester in his hand. Somewhere back in his mind the thought occurred to him that a month ago he wouldn't have bothered.

Whatever was happening inside the cabin was occupying the three men. The fourth man was in the barn, and a fifth standing watch at the corral.

The outlaw at the corral stood easily, his gun holstered, apparently expecting no trouble. He drew his pistol when he saw Ty but it was too late. Ty's gun was level and a bullet caught the outlaw's chest and slammed him against a wooden pole of the corral. At the sound of the gunshot, the second man rushed from the barn, his gun drawn, but the sun caught his eyes as he came from the dark and he was momentarily blinded. Again Ty's rifle found its target and ripped into the outlaw's neck, killing him instantly.

The noise of a scuffle came from inside the cabin, and another scream, then two men poured out, one holding up his trousers with one hand and carrying a pistol with another, the other carrying a shotgun aimed directly at Ty.

Ty kicked his feet clear of the stirrups and fell as the gun roared. He heard his horse scream and he rolled over several times before stopping and grabbing for his pistol. He had dropped his rifle in the wild scramble. The two men in the door had been joined by a third, and all three were shooting at him as he darted under a fence rail and behind a water trough. He aimed at one of the men, gratified as his target went down against another of the outlaws, deflecting his shot. Ty aimed again and the fourth man went down. Before he had time to get off another bullet, the fifth man dropped.

Ty rose cautiously, looking around him. There was blood everywhere. He checked the two men at the barn. One was dead and the other soon would be. His gun still leveled, he carefully made his way to the ranch house. All three men were dead. He looked into the open door, wondering where the last shot had come from, and then he saw her.

A woman stood just inside, swaying slightly as if she were about to fall. She clutched a shotgun tightly as if her fingers were glued to it. She was wearing only a torn shift now spattered with blood, and her face was as white as the garment had probably once been. Her dark brown hair hung around her face and her hazel eyes were glassy. Ty moved to catch her as she fell.

He cradled her in his arms, then looked around for a place to put her. There was a man on the floor, blood on the upper part of his body, and Ty knew it was the figure he had seen last night with the woman he was now holding. Father? Husband?

There were curtains to the left and right off the main room. He went to the right and pushed through the flowered material to reveal space that held little but a bed, table and a mirror, but the bright curtains and quilt gave it a warm and comfortable feeling.

Ty set her down gently, feeling curiously protective. He stood and watched for a second, then went to check on the man in the other room. He was still breathing. Damn. The girl, the man, his horse, all of them needed attention, but the man needed it more at the moment. He tore the man's shirt open and studied the wound...not that he knew much about them. But he did know what was fatal and what was not, and this rancher was damned lucky. The bullet had gone through his side, just to the left of his heart. He must have been knocked unconscious when he fell because Ty didn't think the wound itself was that severe. He found a towel and pressed it tightly to the man's chest, soaking up some of the blood. Then he went back to the girl. Her eyes were still shut and he walked over to the table where a pitcher and water bowl sat. The girl had apparently been disturbed washing because there was water in the bowl while the rest of the house was neat and clean. He took a towel from a hook, wet it and went over to her, gently cleaning her face, waiting for her to regain consciousness. He didn't want her to be alone when she did.

Her eyes finally fluttered open, so full of raw pain that he wished they would close again. "My brother?"

Ty felt a sense of relief flood him at the identification. So he wasn't a husband. "He's injured," Ty said, instantly sorry he did not know any other words of comfort. He felt awkward and uncertain. "Did they...? Did they hurt you...?"

A grimace of a smile appeared on her face. "If you hadn't come along when you did..." She tried to struggle up. "Where...? Why...?"

"I was just riding by," he said, "and heard your scream."

"They're dead? All of them?"

He nodded. The man at the corral should be dead by now. He had felt no obligation to help him.

The young woman shivered although the morning was already stifling hot. "Did I kill that...?" She couldn't quite say "man."

"Yes." Once more, Ty knew he should give some words of reassurance, but looking down at her he felt like a stammering child. She was not beautiful, but her features were soft and pleasant, and her hair was like mountain mahogany, rich and dark with red fire.

"Kurt?" she said, trying to rise.

"Your brother?"

She nodded. "Is he badly hurt?"

"He'll live."

A tear started down her cheek. "It happened so quickly," she whispered. "Thank you. Thank you for coming. They would have killed both of us."

Or worse, Ty thought, something inside him constricting.

"I killed a man. I never..." Now there was more than one tear.

Ty felt completely helpless as tears slid down her face but he was astounded at her reasoning. She wasn't crying because of what happened to her, but because she had killed one of those animals. He wanted to tell her the man had deserved to die, but he sensed that was not what she wanted to hear at the moment.

"You didn't have any choice," he said softly, instead. "You saved my life."

Her eyes, a mixture of light green and warm gray, begged for assurance, and he smiled, a gentle smile that was new to his face.

She struggled to rise again. "I have to see Kurt. I have to help him." But then she noticed her near-nakedness, and she blushed furiously, trying to cover herself. She once more recalled everything in a vivid flash, and her lips trembled. "I... They..."

"I know." His voice was soft and soothing, and more than anything else the girl wanted his presence nearby. He was her security in a sea of fear and shame and violence.

"I'll help your brother onto a bed," Ty said. "And then I have to see about my horse. Will you be all right?"

She wouldn't. She would never be all right again. She had been pawed and touched and nearly raped. She had felt the hot noxious breath of a man who had forced her to the floor and had been ready to enter her. She had seen her brother shot. She had killed a man. But she looked up at the strong, kind stranger who had appeared from nowhere to protect them, and couldn't tell him that. She nodded.

Ty's bay had been hit, but not badly. He wouldn't, however, be able to carry any weight for several days, and they all needed to get the hell out of here.

Ty half carried, half pulled the brother into the other

room and up onto a bed before hurrying out to the corral.
He briefly checked the outlaw with the chest wound who
had joined the others in death. Ty knew he was damned
lucky they'd all died. There was no one left to identify him,
and he wondered briefly what he would have done if his
aim, and the girl's, had not been quite so accurate. He
would have had to kill them. Or abandon Sean's plan. He
was glad he hadn't been forced to make the choice, particularly in front of the girl.

He led his horse to the barn, reassuringly rubbing the
animal's muzzle. He found some salve and spread it over
the several wounds inflicted by the shotgun blast. A shotgun was a particularly nasty weapon, and he was lucky that
one of the outlaws had left his inside when the ruckus
started. Ty smiled. His mistake.

He had to get rid of the bodies. If they had, as he suspected, been sent by Wilson to obtain fresh horses, they
would be missed. He had to make Wilson think the ranch
had been abandoned and the five men had just decided not
to return empty-handed, or that they had stolen the horses
for themselves.

His eyes traveled over the stable area and found a shovel.
He cleared the corral, placing the horses in the barn, and
started digging a wide, deep trench deep enough for five
bodies.

By the time he was through burying the men, sweat
caked his shirt, and dirt clung to his boots and trousers. He
let the horses back out and shot his gun several times so
that they trampled and packed the new grave, leaving little
evidence of the recent violence.

The girl had dressed in a light gray dress that matched
the gray in her eyes, and her hair had been tamed into a
knot at the back of her neck. Her hands moved efficiently

over her groaning brother, and only her still, too-white face gave any indication of the ordeal she had suffered.

Ty lounged against the wall of the brother's bedroom, feeling dirty and hot and clumsy. He had no idea of how to talk to the girl. When she turned to him, her eyes were calm but questioning, her lips firm, the trembling gone. They tried a small smile, but didn't quite succeed.

"Kurt and I can never thank you enough, Mr....?"

Ty tensed. He hadn't thought about that. That they would want to know his name. One fist balled behind him. He didn't want to see the warmth disappear from her eyes. "Jim," he said finally. "Jim Tyson."

The man on the bed struggled to sit up, and he offered his hand. "Mr. Tyson. As my sister said, we can never repay you. My sister...she told me what almost happened..."

Ty felt more awkward then ever. He wasn't much better than the men buried out there, and he knew it better than anyone. Not knowing what else to do, he walked over and took the hand, finding it unexpectedly firm.

"Can you ride?" he asked abruptly.

The man looked at him questioningly.

"I think they're part of a larger bunch. When those five don't return, you might have more visitors." Ty looked at the girl who just stood there, waiting.

The man straightened upright, wincing as he did so. Ty saw that he had a bandage over the wound, and he moved stiffly. "I'm Kurt Monroe. This is my sister, Jennie."

Ty nodded. The name suited her. Soft but strong. "We need to leave as soon as possible," he pressed. "Do you have someplace to go?"

"There's a ranch about fifty miles to the east. They're friends of ours."

Fifty miles. It would take at least two days with a string of horses, a woman and a wounded man. That would put him far behind Sean's schedule, but he had no choice. He couldn't leave them now. Sean would just have to wait.

"Let's get moving."

Kurt Monroe stared at him. "You're going with us?"

"I don't think you can manage on your own," Ty replied.

There was puzzlement in the man's eyes. "I don't understand why you're doing all this." The young man completely baffled him. He wore his gun strapped down like a gunfighter and he had the same deadly menace as the earlier invaders. But for some reason he appeared to be taking their part.

Ty heard the wariness in the man's voice, and he understood. Monroe was no fool, even if he had brought his sister unprotected to the middle of nowhere.

"You need me," he said simply and stalked out of the room, confused by his own actions.

He had been with that damned Mallory too long, for God's sake. He was even beginning to act like him. Ty scuffed the dirt in front of the house in disgust before heading to the corral to ready the horses for travel.

Chapter Sixteen

Sean pulled up his horse and looked at the small town of Fortitude. Worry was gnawing away at him.

He had not seen Ty Donaldson in three days although they had planned to meet once more before entering Fortitude to work out the final details of his plan.

Where in blazes was he?

Despite his reputation, Donaldson had been consistently reliable in the past weeks, and Sean had acquired a healthy respect for him. As much as he had hated to admit it, he was glad to have the gunfighter with him. Ty had grasped the plan immediately; it had been odd, in fact, how well their minds had worked together. It had been a little disconcerting.

It seemed unlikely Donaldson would disappear willingly, especially knowing their plan depended upon him. Sean had thought to remain out of sight until Ty had firmly established himself in Fortitude, but now he needed to get down there and see if there was any word of the young gunfighter. And if, indeed, he had been right in thinking Fortitude had been Wilson's destination.

And what to do about Casey?

As if she'd heard his thinking, she moved her horse up beside his own. "You're worried," she observed.

He had given up hiding anything from her. "Donaldson should have showed up before now."

"Do you think he lit out?" There was disappointment in her voice although she had never really expected much from him.

"That's the hell of it. I don't think he did. He must be in some kind of trouble, and I don't know where to start looking."

Casey's gaze met his. "You can't go down there... Wilson knows you."

"He probably already knows I'm on his trail. I've been asking a lot of questions."

"What about me? He wouldn't know about me."

"He's probably been told there's a boy with me," Sean said. "And he saw you in Two Springs. You told me that."

Casey lowered her eyes to the saddlebags as an idea entered her head. She would have to present it carefully. Very carefully.

"He saw a deputy," she said slowly. "And it happened so quickly, I don't think he ever suspected I was a woman."

Sean comprehended quickly but his eyes were already clouding with denial.

"You know I can take care of myself." Casey used her trump card. "And you know I can find out things no one else can."

Sean's eyes narrowed, but he didn't say no.

Sensing her advantage, Casey rushed on. "I can say I'm looking for an uncle, that my pa had died." She had another idea, but didn't think Sean was ready to hear it.

Sean relaxed slightly. It was an interesting proposal. A mining town like Fortitude was always hungry for women and miners were generally respectful of women. Casey had none of a loose woman's mannerisms, and Sean did not doubt that she could protect herself if someone got out of line.

But he knew he would never forgive himself if anything happened to her. The sooner this whole affair was over, the sooner he and Casey could go home.

He saw her hands tighten on the saddle horn as she waited for his answer, and he knew how important it was to her. She wanted to help, needed to help, and if he left her here, she would find some way to get involved...some way in which he wouldn't have control or knowledge.

Sean nodded slowly.

Ty knew they could go no farther. Kurt Monroe was almost falling from his saddle and pain etched across his face.

They had gone perhaps twenty miles, Ty leading a string of twelve horses, and Jennie Monroe and her brother following behind. Ty had chosen a rocky route where hopefully they would lose any trackers. Jennie had understood and had gathered the droppings deposited by the string of horses and dispersed them among the rocks.

Ty was struck by the girl's composure. He had never met anyone like her. Once her shock wore off, she quickly understood their need to leave and had followed his every suggestion—cleaning the porch, covering the red stains in the living room, and packing what she and her brother would need—without questions or tears, her eyes conveying her total trust and lack of suspicion.

Her brother did what was asked of him although his face clearly showed his doubt. Kurt Monroe knew their benefactor was right, that someone quite possibly would retrace the steps of their attackers, but there was something about Jim Tyson that bothered him. His sister had told him what had happened, how the stranger had come out of nowhere and killed four men. He was grateful, even as he wondered what kind of man killed so efficiently and, apparently, without the slightest regret. And why was the stranger going out of his way to see them to safety? It didn't make sense, and Kurt didn't like things that didn't make sense. But for the moment, he tossed aside his fears. The man had saved his sister.

When they stopped, Ty helped Kurt Monroe from the saddle, afraid that he might otherwise fall and further injure his shoulder. Then he helped Jennie, his eyes catching hers as she slid easily into his arms. For a moment, he held her there. She felt so soft and her hair smelled like flowers. Damn. What was he doing? He abruptly let go, turning around and seeing the watchful gaze of her brother.

"I'll see to the horses," Ty said shortly.

When Monroe tried to help, the rancher swayed and almost fell, and Ty told him he was more trouble helping than not. With a brief grimace Monroe agreed and went back to where his sister was unpacking supplies. Ty unsaddled the three horses they had been riding and grouped them with the others on a makeshift picket line. When he returned, Jennie Monroe had spread out the food she had brought from the ranch—fresh bread, cheese and beef.

When Ty was finished, Kurt Monroe was waiting for him. Despite the exhaustion and pain he was feeling, the rancher started asking the questions that had been plaguing him during the past hours. He didn't like the way his sister and Tyson looked at each other, not without knowing more about the mysterious man.

"You from around these parts, Tyson?" he queried, trying to sound indifferent.

"No," Ty replied, not offering any additional information.

"Cowhand?" Tyson looked like anything but a cowhand.

"No," Ty said again.

Monroe's hand dug into the dirt in frustration. He tried to relax. The man had, after all, saved his life, his sister's life…and his string of Thoroughbreds. But the hard purple-blue eyes sent ripples of apprehension through him.

He tried again. "Need a job? When this is over with, we'll be needing a hand."

"No."

Jennie was irritated with her brother. He had always been very protective of her, but she was twenty now, fully grown, and could look after herself. And he had no right to question a man to whom they owed so much. Her eyes pleaded with him. She didn't know what it was about the stranger, but she was drawn to him in some inexplicable way. And his reticence only increased her fascination.

He was remarkably striking looking with his glittering bright eyes and dark hair, mustache and short-trimmed beard. She had never liked facial hair before but on him it was very attractive. She had secretly watched him during the day, noting the lean grace of his body and the way his hand frequently went to his gun as if to assure himself it was still there.

He had been so gentle in the ranch house just after the shooting. And then he had turned all business as he'd disposed of the bodies and the evidence of the violence. The efficient hardness made those earlier moments so much more vivid in her mind.

She changed the subject. "Do you really think some… more of those outlaws will go to the ranch?"

"It's likely," he said tersely, and Jennie ached to have more words come from his mouth.

"Do you think they will follow us?"

"Not if it's too much trouble."

"You seem to know a lot about them," Kurt broke in, a question in his voice.

"Some."

Kurt's apprehension was growing by the moment. "How?"

"I listen," Ty said with his lips twisting with humor.

Jennie wanted to laugh. It wasn't often someone so completely thwarted her brother.

Ty decided he had had enough questions. He started his own attack.

"What were you doing out there with no help? Don't you know how damned dangerous it is for a woman?"

Kurt flushed. "I had some...they left a few days ago for the mine in Fortitude."

"And you were going to stay there...alone?"

"I was going to Denver, see if I couldn't find more hands."

"How long have you been ranching here?"

Monroe wondered how the conversation had turned so abruptly from their benefactor to himself. "Seven years," he slowly replied. "Our father started the ranch...he died three years ago."

Ty's eyes swept him coldly. They held all the intimidation he had honed to an art, and Jennie was fascinated. She had never met anyone so cool and assured...and deadly. She felt jolts of lightning spark through her and wondered what it would feel like to run her fingers through that thick dark hair. The notion startled her; she knew she ought to fear the quiet menace that surrounded him.

But she also knew, from the moment he had taken her in his arms in the ranch house, that he was the one she had been waiting for, the reason she had turned down so many others although she had never known exactly why. He was not what she had envisioned. She had always thought the man she would choose would be gentle, educated, caring, but except for those few minutes this morning there was nothing gentle about this hard-eyed stranger whose mouth and words mocked, and who obviously knew more about guns than poetry.

She wanted to know more about him, but she knew questions were not the way. The last few moments had proven that.

"That's a beautiful horse," she remarked, looking at the bay, which was grazing with the other horses.

The stranger's mouth relaxed into the first real smile she had seen. "The bay?"

"Does he have a name?"

"I call him Trouble because he was so damned hard to break." Ty flushed as the curse word left his mouth. "Beg pardon," he mumbled.

Jennie wanted to smile at his expression. But she was pleased that he worried about her reaction. She sensed he rarely cared what anyone thought.

"I live on a ranch, Mr. Tyson," she said gently. "I've heard the word before. I've even been known to say it myself."

Kurt looked at her incredulously. She had never said it and had often winced when he and his hands had. He studied her face. It had a softer look than he had ever seen before, and her eyes were dreamy. He glanced at the man who called himself Jim Tyson. He was staring at Jennie as if he had never seen a woman before.

Kurt yawned, and both his sister and Tyson looked at him, startled as if they had been wakened from a dream. "I'm going to get some sleep," he said. "Jennie?"

She nodded, wanting suddenly to close her eyes and think about Jim Tyson and remember the way he had held her this morning.

Monroe rose and turned to Tyson. "I'm sorry we're so much trouble to you. We'll be at Dave Michael's place tomorrow, and you can be on your way." He reached out his hand. "Thank you again."

Both Jennie and Ty knew he was making it clear that tomorrow they would go their separate ways.

Jennie knew that wouldn't be the end of it.

Ty was afraid it would be...and even more it wouldn't.

When Ty woke at dawn, he saw Jennie Monroe sitting on a rock overlooking a meandering stream. He sat up and looked around. Her brother was still sleeping, his blanket askew as if he'd spent a restless night.

Ty rose and went over to her, knowing somehow that she knew he was there.

"It's beautiful, isn't it?" she whispered, looking toward the sun peeking over a mountain, spreading soft pinks and golds across the rich green carpets of grass that surrounded them.

Ty had never thought about it before, had never paid much attention to sunsets or sunrises. It was either dark or light, and light was preferable because you could see danger coming. But now he looked down at Jennie where a beam of light caught the red in her hair, and saw the beauty.

They were silent, Ty at a loss for words, not knowing how to make gentle conversation.

"Where are you going?" she asked softly.

Ty, his mind on her, answered without thinking. "Fortitude...I'm already late." The words escaped him because he had been worrying much of the night about Sean and Casey. They would think he had deserted them and for some reason the idea pained him.

"Late?" she asked.

He was instantly sorry he had spoken. He would leave them at their friend's ranch and never see her again. It was better that way. He nodded curtly. "An appointment."

"Will you be back this way?" She held her breath as she waited for an answer.

Ty looked down at her face, into the warm hazel eyes

that held such hope. It was a serene face, an accepting face, and he wanted to touch it as he had never wanted anything before.

Speechless, he shook his head.

"We would like an opportunity to thank you better," she said, a little breathlessly.

"Are you going back to the ranch?"

"It's all we have," she said simply.

"It's dangerous. It will always be dangerous, especially until you get some hands."

"You won't consider...?"

"I'm not a cowhand, miss." The tone was abrupt.

"What are you, Mr. Tyson?"

He stared at her a long time before he spoke. "Not much of anything. Not much of anything at all." And he realized for the first time how true the words were. A man without friends, a man who killed for a living. He was less than nothing.

Filled with an emptiness he had never quite recognized before, he turned to leave, but she caught his hand. "You *are* very much, very much, indeed, Mr. Tyson," she said quietly. "You saved my brother and me. You didn't have to do that. You didn't have to help us now." She felt her hand burning from touching him, and she reluctantly released him. "You're a good man, Mr. Tyson," she added as her face softened into something beautiful.

Ty felt his chest contract, and a lump lodged securely in his throat. He had been called many things in his life, but never that, and never in such a gentle way.

"You don't know anything about me," he finally managed in a choked voice.

"I know all I have to."

Ty ached with all his being to touch her, to believe her. But he knew the moment she discovered who he was, she would recoil in horror. The knowledge made his voice rougher than he intended. "You know nothing," he said, strolling away with angry, jerky movements. He finally turned, his hopeless yearning barely under control. "Wake your brother," he rasped. "We leave shortly."

Casey slowly pulled on the dress, which she had packed in her saddlebag. Sean had been quiet, too quiet, and she knew he disliked what she was going to do. She also knew he was worried about Ty.

Casey didn't know why. Although she was disappointed in the gunfighter, she wasn't really surprised. Men like that had few loyalties. He had simply been amusing himself during the past weeks, and now he had tired of it. It was that simple.

Sean had turned away while she changed clothes. She wished he hadn't. He had come to mean so much to her, had, in fact, become her life. She didn't think she could live if anything happened to him. Her fingers suddenly trembled as they sought to bring together the buttons and holes on the front of her dress. Finally she completed them and stared at Sean's stiff back. How straight it was, how straight and strong and proud. She walked over to him, and put a tentative hand on his arm. He spun around, his face for once uncertain and hesitant. Her breath caught in her throat.

"I don't like you going down there alone," he said, his fists knotting.

"It's the only way," she said simply. "Unless you want to go back."

He groaned. God, he wanted that. But it was no use. This was something that had to be settled.

"I'll be all right," she said. "Don't forget I was a deputy for my father. I've handled drunks and outlaws and deserters." The last was said with a grin.

"I know," Sean said. "But I'll miss you."

Casey stretched up on her toes and kissed him. "And I'll miss you."

All of a sudden, she was in his arms, being clutched fiercely to him. "I love you, Casey Saunders," he said, before his lips pressed tightly, demandingly, on hers.

Casey's heart swelled to bursting. It was the first time he had mentioned love. She wanted to tell him she loved him, too, but her mouth was blocked by his and instead she told him with a wickedly mischievous tongue and the desperately tight hold of her arms.

She was the first to pull away this time. If she didn't go now, she was afraid she would never go. And he wouldn't be truly hers until they were through here.

He gently touched the short curly hair. They had devised a story about that, how she and her gambler father had come down with the fever. He had died, and she had lost much of her hair. Now she visited the mining camps in search of an uncle, her only living relative. Mining towns, such as Fortitude, usually had so few women Sean knew she would be accepted immediately and probably treated like a queen. Still, he didn't like it.

"I'll try to ride up here day after tomorrow," she said, knowing his part was the hardest. Waiting.

He nodded, his hand touching her cheek one last time. She looked so damned pretty in the dress, her hair framing the vibrantly alive face. He helped her into the saddle, and she blessed the wide skirt, which, even astride, fell to past her knees where her boots came.

Casey rode away without looking back.

It was easy.

Casey rode into town, seemingly impervious to the stares that followed her. She studied the ramshackle collection of rough-board buildings and tents. Two proclaimed themselves saloons.

Casey had not told Sean her real plans...working as a dealer in a saloon. She suspected he would not approve although that was by far the best place to pick up information. Swallowing her guilt at the deception, she pulled up to the larger of the two establishments and dismounted, noting with some amusement the crowd of men gathering around the building. Without paying them any mind, she entered the saloon. Aware of all the heads turning her way, she went up to the bar.

A barkeep, obviously befuddled at her entrance, hemmed and hawed for a moment. The woman looked like a lady, but ladies didn't enter saloons.

"I'm sorry, ma'am," he said awkwardly. "Women aren't allowed in here."

Casey flashed him a blinding smile, and the barkeep thought his legs would buckle under him as it traveled up to the vivid emerald eyes. "I'm looking for the proprietor," she said.

A man rose from a table nearby and came over to her, his hat in his hands. He made a small bow, his cautious face full of curiosity.

"Ma'am," he said. "I'm Michael Kelly, owner of this poor establishment. How can I help you?" His eyes were running over her appreciatively, noting the slender yet shapely build and the striking face. He had never seen a woman's hair that short, but it seemed to fit her, the way it swirled around in tousled curls.

She hesitated, letting her eyes mist a little with sadness. "I...I'm looking for a job...as a dealer."

Kelly's eyes went wide open.

"I'm very good at it," she hurried on. "My father was a gambler...he taught me."

"Where is he now?"

"He...he died. A fever." Her hand went self-consciously to her hair. "I had it, too, that's why..."

Michael Kelly thought he had seen and experienced everything. Now he wondered. This girl looked like anything but a gambler or a saloon girl.

It was as if she read his mind. "That's all I do," she said. "Nothing else. I just deal cards." There was such an edge of steel in her voice he believed her.

"Why Fortitude?" Kelly asked, studying her intensely.

"I've been looking for my uncle...I heard he's in one of the mining camps...I've been going from one to another, but I don't have much money." She stopped, her wide green eyes pleading with him, and he felt his reservations fade away with their impact. Lord, she would draw customers in here. He would put the other saloon out of business.

He grinned. "Let's see how good you are." He took her arm and led her to a table where he had been playing with two other men. Both jumped up, taking their hats off, and standing awkwardly.

"Sit down, gentlemen," Kelly said. "Miss...?"

"Brannigan," Casey said without blinking an eye, deciding instantly that Brannigan would appeal to a man named Kelly. "Kathleen Brannigan."

Michael Kelly smiled, and Casey thought him attractive for the first time. He was a large man, but she doubted whether there was any fat on him. He was just large boned. His dark, almost black eyes were flat until he smiled, and that changed his hard-lined face. "Ah, Irish," he said appreciatively and introduced the two men at the table as "Curly" and "Bob." He handed her a deck of cards and watched her movements with narrowed eyes.

Casey shuffled them with quick professional skill as the other men in the saloon crowded around the table. "Five-card stud," she announced and dealt the hand.

Thirty minutes later she had the job. Kelly took her into his small office. Offering her one of the two chairs, he took the other. "I'll stake you," he said, "and take half your winnings."

Casey arched an eyebrow. "Half?"

He grinned, and she decided she liked him.

"Forty percent, then."

Casey nodded.

"How long will you stay?"

"Until I can find out if my uncle's anyplace around."

"That won't be so easy. There're claims all over and some miners are damned secretive."

"I guess they're afraid of claim jumpers or outlaws," she probed. "I heard there's a bunch heading this way."

"Oh, that's the Wilson gang. They don't bother us here. In fact, they're sort of a blessing. They keep others away."

"Oh," she said in a small voice. "Outlaws...here?"

"Like I said," Kelly reassured her. "They don't bother us. We don't bother them. They're some of our best customers."

Casey let just a bit of fear show. Too much wouldn't do, not after riding boldly into town alone and seeking a job as a dealer in a saloon.

Kelly understood. Or thought he did. The girl was obviously making the best of a poor situation, and he respected her gumption. And the Wilson bunch did have a fearful reputation. He had often wondered himself whether the town was wise in ignoring its presence. But he was willing to take their money as long as they behaved themselves.

"Do you have anyplace to stay?" he asked now.

Once more, Casey let uncertainty cloud her face as she shook her head.

"I have a couple of rooms upstairs," he said. "You can have one."

She met his eyes. "I meant it when I said dealing is all I do."

He nodded, although there was a trace of disappointment in his face. "There's a lock on the door," he replied, all the time wondering how long it would take to seduce her. But now he kept his eyes blank, his mouth only slightly appreciative.

She smiled, and he was struck once more with its radiance. She was pretty enough, but when she smiled, something truly splendid happened. It affected his barkeeper, too, and the other men in the saloon.

"I'll show you the room," he said, thinking he needed to get back to work. The Glory Hole would be brimming over with customers tonight, he thought to himself with no little satisfaction.

Chapter Seventeen

Ty was hurting

Jennie Monroe had ridden beside him much of the morning, and he was dreading the moment he would leave. It had amazed him at first how much he enjoyed her easy company, and he couldn't seem to stop looking her way. She was so damned pretty and she made him feel... well...worth something.

He wanted to touch her. Her skin looked so soft and warm, her eyes so bright, her mouth so tender. And he was the recipient of it all.

He really hadn't understood those electric charges he'd felt passing between Casey and Mallory until now. He wouldn't have believed it possible that he himself would be struck by such damn fool nonsense. He was acting like a schoolboy.

They stopped frequently along the trail. He told the Monroes it was because Kurt needed rest, but it was really just an excuse to help Jennie down, to touch her and feel her momentary reliance on him.

"Mr. Tyson?" The sound of her voice interrupted his thoughts, and he turned toward her, something in him trembling as he did so.

"Is there anyplace you call home?"

Home. It was an alien word to him. Home and family and love and everything that went along with it. His hand clenched the reins. He had never thought he wanted such things. He had thought being alone and self-sufficient and independent was enough. He had gotten used to the idea that was all he would ever have. He had believed Sean weak because he let a woman into his life, and he had watched the whole process with amusement. But the amusement was now gone, and he felt a terrible hunger and thirst he had never known. The fact that it was new did not reduce its intensity.

His mouth was dry when he finally answered, his eyes avoiding hers. "No," he replied with his usual brevity.

"You must have been born someplace," Jennie said with total frustration. "Or did you just spring from the sky to smite the wicked?"

At that, Ty spun around to face her and saw her puckish curiosity. He had to smile at her question.

Jennie thought how much it changed his face, softened it into approachable lines, and his eyes showed something of a puzzlement she sensed was rare.

"Not exactly," he said, his mouth still twitching slightly as he thought how beautiful her eyes were. How soft and inviting her lips. Damn.

"Then where?" she persisted, encouraged by the smile, which still hovered on his lips.

"Missouri," he said finally.

"Do you always go around rescuing people?"

His lips trembled again with his effort to keep them from smiling. "You're my first," he admitted.

"You do it very well."

Ty didn't know what to say. Jennie Monroe confused him, intrigued him, delighted him, frightened him.

Frustrated him. He liked her more every moment, and

she was stirring up feelings better left undisturbed. But he felt an exhilarating lunacy that made him throw caution to the wind. For the first time in his life, he felt alive, really alive.

It seemed now that his past had been nothing but darkness. There had been a brief opening of light with Ben Morgan but he had fled from that as he had fled from everything that threatened his bleak perception of the world.

Mallory and Casey had chipped into that wall. Sometime in the weeks they had traveled together, Ty had felt a new sense of belonging, despite the bickering. He had never cared enough before to argue or fight or banter with anyone, and he had never felt accepted for what he was. Mallory and Casey may not have liked him, or approved of him, but they had accepted him.

Desolation struck him as he wondered what they were thinking now, as he realized they must assume he had abandoned them...just as Casey had always suspected he would. For some reason, despite Sean's early hostility, Ty knew that the Reb trusted him in an odd sort of way.

They were waiting for him, Mallory and Casey, and he had let them down. He had to get back, and quickly. But when he did, he would lose forever the brief magic of Jennie Monroe.

Ty ignored her last comment. "How far are we from your friend's ranch?" It was a terse question and all hint of a smile was gone from his face.

Jim Tyson's expression was so dark and glowering after his brief smile. Jennie felt as if he had slammed a door in her face.

"A few hours," she guessed.

"I'll see if your brother thinks you can make it the rest of the way alone."

Jennie's smile faltered. She didn't want him to go.

"Please..." she said softly. "I didn't mean to pry."

He didn't say anything, but neither did he spur his horse back to where Kurt trailed the horses. Instead he regarded her with a steady gaze. There was an invitation in her eyes, not the kind that he had seen in saloon girls, but a deadlier one. One to enter her life. Her wide eyes pleaded with him not to go, and her lips trembled as she waited his answer. He wanted to stay, God how he wanted to stay.

But he had to go. Now...before he risked any more of himself, before she found out who and what he was. He knew her brother already suspected. There were some things you couldn't hide, and the aura of death and violence around him was one of them.

"I'm already late," he said. "You should be safe from here on...they would never have followed this far."

There was something implacable about his voice, and Jennie knew he wouldn't change his mind. "Will I... we...see you again?"

Not if you're lucky. Ty kept the bitter thought to himself, but his reply was no more comforting. "No."

"But..." There was a world of longing, of bewilderment in that one word. Jennie had found the man she wanted, and she wouldn't let him go easily.

Ty's voice softened. His hand reached out. "You're special, Jennie Monroe. You deserve something special. I hope you get it."

Throwing all caution to the wind, Jennie, for the first time in her life, was bold. "I don't want you to go, to disappear..."

Ty knew he should tell her who and what he was, but he couldn't do it. He couldn't bear to see the distaste cloud her face.

"I'm a loner," he said instead. "My home is the next town, and it will never be any different."

"I don't care," she said stubbornly, even as she amazed herself by saying such things to a near stranger. But he wasn't a stranger. He was already a part of her, would always be a part of her.

"But I do," he was telling her now. "I travel alone. There's no room for anyone else."

Neither of them wondered how the conversation had got so serious. They had known each other less than two days, but each had already captured the other's thoughts. At least some of them.

Ty's eyes, trained for so many years to hide the loneliness and quiet desperation, remained curiously blank, hiding the raw biting need to take her in his arms and hold her there. Only his hands, unusually rough on his horse's reins, showed his anguish as he untied the rope of the string of horses from his saddle horn and attached it to hers. He rode to the back of the string where his horse was tethered. He dismounted quickly, checking to make sure the animal was fit to ride. In several quick movements, he changed the saddle from the Monroe horse to his own, and mounted.

He looked at Jennie, drinking in the sight, locking it inside of him to recall during the lonely nights ahead. He nodded briefly and turned back to Kurt.

Unable to go after him with the string of horses tied to her saddle horn, Jennie could merely watch as the two men exchanged some words, and Jim Tyson tightened his knees against his horse and galloped out of view, taking her heart with him.

Sean Mallory paced beneath the trees with profound impatience and frustration.

He hated waiting more than anything else, always had. He was impatient by nature, used to action and activity, and now he could do nothing but sit and wait...and worry.

Worry about Casey. Worry about Donaldson.

It was not in him to be a bystander and he was being

forced to do so now. While Casey could be in danger. And where in the hell was Donaldson?

He had fought himself bitterly on the matter of Casey, and what she wanted to do. He had always been driven to protect those important to him, sometimes too much. He had to restrain himself from doing the same with Casey.

He knew he would never be able to entirely protect her. The things he loved most about her—her independence, her stubbornness, even her impulsiveness—would always send her catapulting into adventure. Thank God she was so damned competent.

When he had finally accepted the idea that he loved her, he had also accepted who and what she was, and that he couldn't change her, even if he wanted to. He smiled now at the memory of her stubborn insistence that she would do her share of the hunting, at the way she'd deliberately exposed herself to the deserters. She would always insist on sharing both work and danger, and while he knew it would probably mean many uncomfortable hours for him, he was inwardly challenged and pleased at the prospect.

Life would never be dull with Casey.

But God, he would be glad when this was over.

And Donaldson. Damn the man. He didn't know when or how it happened, but Donaldson had become important to him. It had hurt his pride to admit it, but Ben had been right and he had been wrong. There was more to Donaldson than appeared on the surface.

In the past few weeks, Sean had uncovered a few chinks in Ty's armor and knew, despite Casey's reservations, that Donaldson would never have willingly disappeared at this point. Something had happened, and while Casey was in Fortitude Sean couldn't go in search of him. She might need him.

It was nearing evening when Ty approached the town. When he left the Monroes that morning, he had ridden hard but he was at least two days behind Casey and Sean, and he had no idea how to find them. He had circled the small mining town but found no sight of them. There were any number of places to hide in the surrounding mountains and forest.

Tense and wary, he cursed himself for letting them down. Yet he had had little choice. He could only hope that Sean and Casey had waited before attempting anything on their own. But why would they? There was no reason for them to trust him. None at all.

His sense of worth, never very strong, plummeted at the notion. He excelled at one thing and one thing only, and he knew how fleeting and empty that was.

He stopped at the first saloon, knowing it was the place to collect any information. He tied his horse to the rail and walked in, his eyes immediately assessing the place and going instantly to a young woman dealing cards. His tight lips relaxed into the usual half smile. Goddamn. The hellion. In *his* dress. The smile spread into a grin as he swaggered over to the table.

All the places were taken so he stood in back of the crowd watching the players as he assessed Casey Saunders. He had not seen her in the dress, and he congratulated himself for choosing well. She looked almost beautiful, especially without the god-awful hat. Her eyes frequently swept the onlookers and Ty knew they had found him, and he silently applauded the fact that she showed no recognition. There were others waiting for a place at the table; in fact, most of those in the heavily populated room were either watching Casey or waiting for the privilege of playing with her. And apparently losing their money. The pile in front of Casey was substantial. No one, however, seemed to mind.

He backed away and went to the bar, taking a place next

to a tall man dressed in black who was watching the game with no little satisfaction. Ty assumed immediately he was the owner.

He ordered a whiskey and leaned against the bar. "How long she been here?" he finally asked the black-clad man.

"Since yesterday," the man answered. She's already increased my business fifty percent. Word gets around fast."

"Any chance I can get in that game?"

Michael Kelly eyed the newcomer. He didn't look like a miner, not the way his holster was strapped to his thigh. He had seen gunmen before and recognized the breed. "You with Wilson?" he asked cautiously.

Ty was surprised at the openness of the question. So Sean was right. Fortitude did tolerate the outlaw gang's presence. He wondered if it was through fear or greed. "Not yet," he replied.

"You looking to join up?"

Ty shrugged, leaving the answer up to interpretation.

Kelly appreciated caution. "Perhaps if I have a name, I can pass it on."

Ty eyed him speculatively, as if he were weighing whether he could trust the saloon keeper. "Donaldson," he said finally. "Ty Donaldson."

Kelly stared. He knew the name. There had even been a dime novel based on one of the gunman's more famous duels. "Any way to prove that?" he said. Kelly was a brave man...you had to be out here...but he instantly regretted the words when he saw the strange amethyst eyes turn to violet ice. He didn't doubt the man's identity another moment.

"Calling me a liar?" Ty asked.

Kelly had always known when to retreat. "No," he said. "I'll pass the word along. Come with me."

He took Ty over to Casey's table. "Anyone want to give their seat to Ty Donaldson?"

Two chairs were instantly vacated. With a slight mocking smile, Ty took one, nodding his head once in recognition of the favor. The second man remained standing. He didn't want to play in a game with the notorious gunslinger, not even for the girl's company. Mike Kelly slid into the seat instead, with a smile of his own. This should prove to be damned interesting.

Casey paid little attention to either, dealing the cards smoothly as if there had been no change. Only an eyebrow lifted toward Ty when he opened.

The game went on for another hour, the stakes climbing steadily until only Casey, Ty and Michael Kelly remained in the game, and the entire room was gathered around.

"Mr. Donaldson?" Casey asked politely, as she raised once more. There was more than five hundred dollars in the middle of the table. Ty nodded and raised again, Kelly folded, and Casey called.

Casey had three queens, and Ty three jacks. She grinned as she raked in the money.

Ty gave her a wry smile. "That about finishes me, Miss…"

"Brannigan," she said smoothly. "I'm going to take a break," she announced to a disappointed table.

"Can I buy you a drink?" Ty made the offer softly.

"I don't drink with customers," Casey replied huffily.

"Not even for consolation?"

"No. If you'll excuse me…?" Without another look, Casey swept away from the table and up the stairs to her room. In its privacy, she quickly penned a note, which she tucked in her sleeve, then sat down for a moment.

Donaldson had surprised her. She had really thought him long gone. And she was amazed at how pleased she had been to see him. Because they needed him, she told herself.

It was definitely not because she had felt a tiny bit of loss when he'd disappeared. She pinched her cheeks and bit her lips to put color in them, and returned back downstairs.

He was standing at the bar, surveying the room carefully. She went over to him. "Are you playing again, Mr. Donaldson?"

"I'm afraid you took everything I had," he said. "I underestimated you."

"People frequently do," she replied, her lips twitching. "You must have something else...like a horse. I'll loan you a stake against it."

Kelly, who was standing next to Ty, started to protest. It was against the policy of the house. But then he looked at Donaldson's hard face, and Casey's attractive one. He didn't want to infuriate the first or lose the second. He nodded.

Casey took a piece of folded paper from her sleeve, writing the terms and giving it to him. After glancing at it, he signed it and handed it back to her.

Ty's luck changed. He won the first hand, then the second, and finally recouped most of his loss in a third hand. He rose lazily. "I'll take that paper back," he said, and Casey gave it to him with a small smile.

"It's been a pleasure," he said. And left.

Casey rose very early the next morning. She hated to put on the dress for riding, but she had no choice. It was all she had other than her man's clothes, and she didn't dare use those. Not anywhere near town.

She suspected she was early enough to avoid any questions or persistent gallants. Every time she stepped outside the saloon, there were numbers of men asking to escort her, telling her how dangerous it was. She slipped down the stairs, outside the unlocked door and over to the stable. It was, as usual, empty. She had found that the owner, like most businesses in Fortitude, could not find help because of the more lucrative mining. Horse stealing was not a problem in Fortitude, however, and the stable was often left untended.

Casey saddled her horse, mounted awkwardly because of the dress and rode out of town at a trot, grateful that all the shutters were still closed, and only a couple of drunken miners lay sprawled against the saloon.

The sun was just peering over the horizon when she reached Sean's camp. Tucked away in a thicket of trees, it was well away from any trails. She didn't see him at first, and was struck by a stab of fear. Then something moved, and she saw him emerge from behind a tree, his hand holstering his Colt.

He strode quickly toward her horse. The now empty hands reached for her, then lowered her gently before his lips met hers. Sweetly. Hungrily. All his fear and worry transferred into need, and his arms held her to him like a vise.

"Ah, love." The cool, amused masculine voice jerked them apart.

Sean spun around. "Donaldson!"

"I take it I haven't been overly missed." It was a statement not a question.

"Where in the hell have you been?" Sean questioned, his frustration making the question harsher than he'd intended.

Ty dismounted and sauntered over. "There was something I had to do," he said simply.

Sean studied him. There was something different about Donaldson, something perhaps not quite so hard. But it was obvious he wasn't going to say what. He smiled slowly. "I didn't think I would ever say this, but I'm glad to see you."

Casey, who had resented Ty's appearance at the particular moment he chose, saw something strange dart across the gunfighter's face. Something new and appealing. She took Sean's hand and nodded.

Ty stood absolutely still. He hadn't thought Sean would ever admit it, much less Casey. He swallowed, and apologized for the first time in his life. "I'm sorry I'm late."

"It's not important," Sean said.

Ty glanced over at Casey, her hand tight in Sean's. "You look kind of pretty in the dress," he said awkwardly.

Casey's eyes softened. "Thank you...for that and the dress."

"My pleasure," he said as he had the night before. And meant it.

The three of them went over the plan. Over and over again. Sean wanted nothing left to chance. It had changed, because of necessity. From what both Casey and Ty had learned, the two doubted whether Wilson could be provoked into attacking the town. He was too entrenched there, felt too safe.

"Then we'll have to make sure the town thinks he's turned on them," Sean said as Ty looked at him with something akin to admiration.

"There's a mine payroll a week from today," Casey said. She had been gathering bits and pieces of information. "And the gold is brought in every Saturday from the Lucky Lady Mine by wagon."

Sean, Ty and Casey talked another hour before Ty rose to leave. He had the definite impression that Sean and Casey would like to be alone.

Sean walked with him over to the horse. "It all depends on you," he told Donaldson. "Whether you can get in with Wilson and come and go freely."

"I'll manage," Ty said.

Sean hesitated, then offered his hand.

Ty didn't smile as he took it, but he felt its strength and

confidence and friendship, and his own hand tightened its grip.

Neither man had to say anything else. Ty mounted silently and rode away.

Sean watched him disappear before taking Casey's hand and leading her over to a tree. He guided her down and they both sat, Casey leaning against Sean's chest, feeling his arms go around her possessively. It was enough at the moment to rest her head against his heart and hear it beat, to feel the whisper of his breath against her hair. A fear grew inside her so painful she wondered how she could bear it.

She had seen the look in Sean's eyes as he'd talked to Donaldson. There was a brightness there, echoed by one in Donaldson's, and she knew it was because of the prospect of danger. She could feel the simmering violence in him, something she had sensed in him earlier but not quite to the extent she did today. Now he was like a caldron, ready to boil over, and it scared her.

She had never felt that excitement at danger, though she recognized it. It had been a part of her father, part of the reason he had stayed in a job that paid little. Casey had only felt fear, pure unadulterated fear, unblessed by any stimulation she knew others felt. It scared her now, this anticipation in Sean for a confrontation that could mean his death.

She took Sean's hand, studying it, caressing it. It was bronze from the sun and callused from work. Her lips touched each of his fingertips, as her fingers made patterns on the back of his hand. It was so strong, strong and capable and oddly gentle as he returned the featherlike touches. The tenderness was so at odds with those other feelings she knew were brewing in him.

Casey twisted around and met Sean's eyes. "You're looking forward to this, aren't you?"

Sean took a moment to answer. "I'm looking forward to it being over," he said slowly.

"No," Casey contradicted as she searched his eyes. "You like the danger...as Ty does."

His hold tightened around her. "Perhaps," he admitted, surprised at her insight. "It's been my life for so damned long. I don't know anything else...and it's also this waiting. I've always hated it, particularly when you're in town, and I'm sitting here...."

"When it's over...what...?" Casey was afraid to finish the question. He had never said anything about the future.

Sean's arms tightened about her once more, but he said nothing. He loved Casey and wanted her as his wife. But it would be so unfair to say anything now. If anything happened to him, it would make things much worse for her. As painful as it was, he had also resolved not to make love to her again. He could not leave her pregnant. But God, his body ached for her.

He kept his voice even as he returned her steady gaze. "I'm going to give you a letter. If anything happens to me, I want you to take it to my sister and her husband."

Casey started to protest, but he put a finger against her lips. "I want you to promise me you'll do that. Or else I won't let you have any part of this."

"Nothing will happen to you...."

She said it with such confidence he smiled. "No," he agreed. "Still, I want your promise."

Casey didn't want to consider the possibility of anything happening to him, but she saw from his expression how important it was to him. She nodded. "I love you," she whispered, knowing she had to say it now. She had to let him know. She couldn't hold back any longer. No matter how hard she tried.

Sean didn't answer. There was only a flicker of pain in his face before his lips drew toward her and touched her cheek and then her lips. At her fervent, almost desperate response, he surrendered to his own needs and the kiss deepened, spurring to painful awareness the hurting ache that had gripped him for the last several weeks. All his resolve melted in an overwhelming urgency to bring her as close as possible to him, to share feelings he had never shared with anyone before.

His hand reached for her hair, feeling its silkiness in his fingers before it moved down and his arm went tightly around her neck and shoulders, clasping her to him as if he would never let her go.

He felt her hand going inside his shirt, and he trembled at her touch. He knew he couldn't stand much more, not without succumbing to something more. Reluctantly he pulled his lips from hers and took a long deep breath. She was looking at him with a lazy catlike glow.

"Casey," he whispered with a slight sigh. "You would tempt an angel and God knows I'm not that."

"Good," she said with satisfaction, and he had to laugh at the smug look on her face.

"Not good," he replied. "Not now."

"Why?"

It was said with such complete candor that he smiled again. "Because," he said, giving her the only explanation he thought she might accept, "you distract me, and that's not wise at the moment."

"Hmm. Do I really distract you?" Her hand started playing with his ear, and Sean felt the impact of little needles jabbing his senses.

Perhaps she deserved some of her own medicine. His tongue went to her ears and he licked them, feeling her stiffen in his arms. Her hand found its way down his back, tracing patterns among his muscles and nerves. He felt her hand lowering...lowering...

* * *

Sean watched Casey dress slowly. Good Lord, but she was beautiful and grew more so every day. Her face was flushed a rose color and her lips were full and red from his kisses. A contented smile curved them in a very bewitching way as she completed her last buttons.

His own smile, he knew, must be rueful. He hadn't meant this to happen, but at least he'd had enough small willpower to keep from spreading his seed in her. He pulled on his own clothes, remembering the feel of her, the way the fires had kindled quickly into an inferno of senses. He didn't think he would ever get enough of her. Never. If he had the chance...

Chapter Eighteen

During the next six days Casey rode out of town every morning at dawn under the guise of visiting the various claims and searching for news of her uncle. Most of town was asleep at that hour, and she didn't have any trouble with unwanted protectors.

And Michael Kelly had been helpful. When she rode back the first morning, he had been pacing the floor of his saloon and was horrified to learn she had been riding alone. It took her an hour to convince him that she could take care of herself and that she enjoyed riding and would continue to do so. Given no choice, he reluctantly quieted, but he made it known that if anything happened to Kathleen Brannigan the offender would answer to him. And Michael Kelly had no small reputation of his own.

Casey knew she would have little trouble from the miners and cowhands that frequented the town. She wasn't fool enough, however, not to worry about Wilson's men.

Michael didn't have to point them out. They wore their guns slung low and were quarrelsome and trigger-happy, and they had more money than most. But none ever stayed overnight, and Kelly kept a tight rein on them. No one seemed to want to tangle with the saloon owner.

There was no law. No formal law, at least. Casey had discovered that the first day. Instead, there was a committee of townspeople, led by Kelly, and a miner's committee, which took care of their own disputes. She supposed that Kelly's position was what kept Wilson's men reasonably well behaved. They didn't want to lose their sanctuary.

The town itself was composed of tents and hastily constructed buildings: two saloons, two general stores, a blacksmith, an assay office, which doubled as a bank; a boardinghouse, which housed several ladies of dubious virtue; an eating place run by a rough-voiced widow, and a shack where a Chinese man did laundry. The latter three establishments, Casey suspected, made more than most of the miners. There were always long lines in front of all three.

She had purchased a new dress at the general store. There hadn't been many to choose from, and they had all been obviously selected with the boardinghouse ladies in mind. She knew a little about sewing, and managed to cut the excess material from the large garment and fill in the low-cut bosom. Despite Michael Kelly's protection, there was no sense further tempting the hungry male appetites.

The skirt was narrow, so she wore the new dress at night and the dress Ty had given her when she went riding.

For five days, Casey did as she told Michael Kelly and visited the mining sites, inquiring about her nonexistent uncle. She was always met with goggling eyes but respect, and was usually asked to share some food. She had a way of putting the miners at ease and she had to admit she enjoyed the admiration shown in their eyes—not for her skill with a gun but for her appearance. She knew it had something to do with Sean. She desperately needed to feel desirable.

On the sixth day, she cautiously went to Sean's camp. The waiting period was worse for him than for either herself or Ty. At least they were doing something.

Although it had only been a few days, it seemed like weeks, and she missed him with all her being. She knew his helplessness must be tearing at him but she had news for him, and she hoped it would soothe that restlessness that rubbed him raw.

She heard him first. The wildly pulsating notes of the flamenco music she remembered so well echoed through the trees. She knew his patience was nearing an end to take the chance that someone might hear. She halted her horse and listened, fascinated as before with the passion behind the music, with the beauty of the haunting melody, which emerged from the strings, so rapidly at first, then slowly, lingeringly. It never ceased to amaze her...this hard man who coaxed such magic from a piece of wood. Warmth curled inside her, and she had to bite her lip to keep from riding pell-mell into camp and throwing herself into his arms. Instead she urged her horse into a slow walk, and straightened her face into some semblance of dignity as she approached.

The music stopped and she knew he heard her approach as she also knew his gun would be ready. She whistled the signal they had settled on earlier.

He was standing, his hand still on the guitar, his eyes dark and hooded. Gently laying the guitar down, he strode over and caught her as she slid down, holding her tightly for a moment before letting her go and spinning away. He took two long steps and stood, his back as tense and taut as a bowstring.

"I've got news," she said.

Sean turned, and Casey could see his tightly pressed lips, the muscle straining against the drawn skin of his cheek.

"Ty's ready," she said quietly, and Sean noted absently that it was no longer "Donaldson" or "the gunfighter." He arched an eyebrow in question.

"He was in the saloon last night. He apparently has been totally accepted."

"No problem with his Union background?"

"Like you said, Wilson's mainly interested in his reputation. Ty told him that he was caught robbing a store and was forced into uniform. You were right. It was something Wilson understood."

"Anything else?"

"I only had a few minutes to talk to him. He said he's been trying to goad Wilson into taking the mine payroll, but Wilson won't do anything in Fortitude. He feels safe here."

Sean's eyes narrowed. "Then we just have to change his mind. Does Ty have any problem getting away?"

"They all sort of come and go," she said. "There's no reason to keep him there."

"And Wilson? Does he ever come in?"

Casey eyes turned glittering green. "No. Apparently he isn't interested in the ordinary vices, only in what he can take in violence, and he steers clear of that here. Ty says he has some grand illusion about becoming a cattle baron. He already acts like the king of the valley." Casey's voice was bitter. She hadn't known what she would do if she saw the outlaw in person, whether then she could control the hatred that still simmered inside her. It had ceased to be the important thing in her life, but it was still there, hovering like some kind of bird of prey.

"When is the next mine payroll?"

"In three days. They'll bring in a load of silver and return with a payroll."

"How many guards?"

"Three and a driver. One goes ahead, one stays with the wagon and one rides drag. I watched them last time. They don't expect any trouble."

"Saturday, then," he said. "You can let Ty know?"

"He'll be back. He knew that would probably be the target."

"How is he?"

Casey looked directly at him. "Different somehow. Still cocky and arrogant but there's something changed about him."

"I'd like to know what in the hell happened those days he disappeared," Sean wondered aloud.

"Maybe we're just imagining it."

"No," Sean said abruptly. All three of them had softened. And it worried him more than he wanted to admit. He knew the problem between himself and Casey. He could only surmise about Ty Donaldson. They all needed their wits about them. "Maybe we should call this whole thing off?" Sean continued, voicing his inner doubts.

"No," Casey said. "We've come too far."

Sean studied her determined face, and he knew she was right. They had been committed far too long to turn back now. They—he and Casey—could never begin until the other thing ended.

He nodded. "We'll meet here Saturday morning."

She held out her hand, and he took it, holding on to it tightly before drawing her into his arms. After a long moment, he pulled himself away. Neither needed any more distractions. Not now. And in five days it would all be over, and they could begin again.

Casey winced at his withdrawal. In five days it would be over between them.

Jennie listened to her brother in dazed delight.

"I don't think we should go back until we get some hands," he said.

Jennie knew he hated to make the admission. Kurt was independent, so independent he had decided he didn't need any help when the hands had left for the mines. But now one arm was useless, and he knew he couldn't adequately protect his sister. And they couldn't stay with friends forever.

"Fortitude is the closest town," he said. "I'll ride in tomorrow and see if we can't find some disenchanted miners or cowhands."

Jennie had a feeling that Fortitude would be the last place Kurt would go if he knew that was Tyson's destination. Though grateful to Tyson for his assistance, he had made no secret of his disapproval of Jennie's obvious interest in the drifter.

After watching her mope for several days, he had confronted her. "He's a gunslinger, Jennie. Anyone can see that."

Her chin had jutted out in unfamiliar defiance. "I don't," she said. "Gunslingers don't stop and help people as he did."

"How do you think he was able to kill four men? Four, Jennie. And without a qualm."

"Would you rather they'd killed you and raped me? And don't forget I killed one. Does that make me a gunslinger?" There had been acid in her voice, and he'd looked at her with surprise. Jennie was usually sweet tempered, and defiant only when something or somebody she loved was endangered. Jennie's heart had always been much too soft, he thought now. Yet she was strong in other ways. It took a strong woman to live out here, to bear the loneliness. He saw the steel in her hazel eyes and wondered just how strong she was.

He had changed the subject, and days had gone by without mentioning Jim Tyson's name. Kurt Monroe believed that they would never see him again. Despite his gratitude, he was secretly pleased the man had disappeared.

When she asked to go with him to Fortitude, he readily agreed, glad to see a smile back on her face. She had had few enough diversions and perhaps she could find some material for a new dress. She deserved some pleasure.

They left early the next morning. Jennie borrowed a side-saddle so they could ride instead of taking a buckboard.

As she mounted, she thought of the sleepless nights she had spent since the attack on their ranch. Jim Tyson's curious little half smile never left her, not even at night, nor did that haunting loneliness she had glimpsed in his usually frozen eyes. Dear God, she prayed. Let Jim Tyson still be there. Please.

Ty took the proffered drink from Bob Wilson.

The outlaw leader had poured it with his left hand. His right hand was no more than a claw in a black leather glove.

There was something inherently evil about the man's face, Ty noted and was instantly surprised at his observation. He had never really thought much about good or evil before. If he had he would have classified himself as the latter. His perspective, he noted wryly, had changed in the past few days.

"I understand you're anxious for some excitement," the outlaw said in a gravelly voice.

Wilson was bulky but there was still a quickness about him. His eyes were pale blue and empty, but Ty didn't underestimate him. He had run free for three years, three years of robbing and killing, and Ty knew the outlaw's freedom wasn't all luck. There was an animal cunning emanating from him. Cunning and hatred.

Ty shrugged. "I heard you kept your men busy and rich."

"They needed some rest," Wilson said. He eyed his newest recruit speculatively. He had heard of Ty Donaldson's reputation for years and what attracted him, even more than the rumored speed of his draw, was his reported intelligence and ruthlessness. If he was going to get Ben

Morgan and Sean Mallory, he needed someone like him. It galled him that he had failed twice. It wouldn't happen on the third attempt.

"I'll make it worth your while," he told Donaldson. "I have a job for you here, and then one in Texas."

"How much worth my while?" Ty asked.

"There's a ranch I want near here. I want you to help me get it. When that's done, I plan to return to Texas." His mouth tightened. "There are two men there I want dead. I'll pay you a thousand dollars a month now, and a bonus of five thousand when the two men are dead."

"What two men?"

Wilson stared at him. "It's none of your concern. I'll tell you when the time comes."

Ty stood, waiting for him to continue. "In the meantime...?"

"There's a ranch south of here. Owned by a man named Monroe. I want it. The last men I sent there didn't come back. Do what you have to, but make damned sure I'm not connected to it."

Ty's stomach turned over. So that was the reason for the raid on the Monroe ranch. It hadn't been the horses, after all. He nodded. "I'll ride up there Sunday."

"Why not now?"

"I lost some money last night. I aim to get it back."

Wilson grunted. "Not from that damn skirt I heard about, I hope. Half my men have lost money to her. She seems to bewitch them. I thought you had more sense."

"I don't think it's witchcraft," Ty said. "She's just a good poker player, and it helps that she's pretty enough to distract them."

"And you? Does she distract you?"

"Nothing distracts me where money and a job's concerned," Ty replied coldly.

Wilson was the first to drop his eyes. He believed Ty Donaldson.

"Take as many men you need Sunday," he said. "And don't disappear like the others. They probably stole Monroe's Thoroughbreds." Wilson's eyes grew uglier. "Don't let something like that happen to you, Donaldson. I'll find the others and cut their damn hearts out. I'd do the same to you. No one betrays me. Remember that."

Ty's lips curled in an icy smile. "I will. You can depend on it." With an insolent tip of his hat, he left.

Casey had started planting the seed her first day in town with Michael Kelly. Now it was time to reap the harvest.

When she returned from meeting Sean, she changed her clothes and went down to the almost empty saloon for something to eat. Kelly was there, standing against the rail, his dark eyes fathomless. He asked to join her for the noon meal and as soon as they sat, Casey started her attack. "They scare me…the men who ride with Wilson. I've heard some of the things they've done."

"Been accused of," Kelly corrected soothingly. "They've never so much as fired a gun here."

"But maybe they're just waiting for their chance…when no one expects it."

"Don't you worry your head about it," Kelly said, though there was a small frown on his face. He had worried about the same thing himself.

"But…"

"I've made it real plain no one's to touch you," he said, his smile gentling. He liked Kathleen, liked her more every day. She was a challenge. So far, she had sidestepped every advance he had made, although she did it with charming shyness. He was beginning to wonder whether she was a virgin. She certainly acted like it, and paid little attention to any man...except perhaps that gunfighter who had come to town a few days after she did.

Michael Kelly was an excellent judge of human nature. It was a necessary talent for a saloon owner, who made his living off the vices and weaknesses of others. There was little he missed, including the fact that of all the men seeking Kathleen's attention, only Ty Donaldson had captured it...even if only for a few moments. There was something guarded about Kathleen Brannigan's eyes when Donaldson sat at her table, something that was not there with other customers. It made him wonder.

He did a little probing of his own. "Donaldson's joined Wilson, you know."

Her green eyes betrayed nothing. She only nodded. "I'm not surprised. He's a gunfighter, after all."

"I thought you might like him?"

"A gunfighter? Never."

There was conviction in her voice, and Michael Kelly relaxed. "Will you have dinner with me tonight?"

Casey started to refuse, then changed her mind. She hadn't missed his pointed question, and she wondered when she had made a mistake. Perhaps she could further plant her seed of distrust.

"I would like that," she said. Finishing the stew she was eating, she excused herself. She still had the better part of an afternoon before she would start dealing tonight. Her winnings had grown. Perhaps she would go over to the general store and buy a ribbon for her hair. Strange how she had started to think about her appearance.

Guided by impulse she found herself at one of the general stores. There were a couple of miners there, and a young couple she had never seen before. The man was medium height and stocky with rust-colored hair. His arm was in a sling. The woman was very pretty and Casey felt envy strike her viciously. As Casey went up to the counter.

the woman turned, and Casey noted the sweet features, the striking hazel eyes, the easy smile.

"Hello," she said to Casey and turned to the man. "Kurt, why don't you go to the saloon and see if you can find some hands. I'd like to look at material."

Casey noted the man gave her an affectionate smile, not the burning kind Sean sometimes gave her.

"All right," he said to his companion. "Stay here until I come for you, and we'll eat together."

The girl nodded, and Casey thought she saw relief skitter across her face. When the man had disappeared, the girl leaned over the counter to the storekeeper.

"Have you heard of a man named Jim Tyson?"

The storekeeper shook his head. "Can't say I have."

Casey watched as the young woman's face fell.

"But you must," the woman persisted. "He said he had an appointment here."

Casey watched the woman's hands join and clutch into a desperate ball. "Jim Tyson," she asked, interrupting the two.

The woman turned, her eyes wide with hope. "Have you met him?"

"Tall?" Casey asked. "Slender with black hair and a beard?"

The woman's mouth spread into a wide smile, her eyes lighting, as she nodded.

"Donaldson. Ty Donaldson." The storekeeper's fist came down with a bang. "You're talking about that gunslinger. Why didn't you say so? He's gone off and joined the Wilson bunch."

There was a blankness in the girl's face, then shock, and finally realization as the light slowly faded from her face. "Wilson?" she said, her voice faltering. She had heard of the outlaw bunch, of the killings. Her brother thought Wilson might be the one responsible for the raid on their ranch.

Casey watched the changes in the girl's face. This girl was obviously part of the days Ty had kept so quiet about.

Now she was grasping the edge of the counter. "I don't...believe it," she repeated, but her eyes said she did.

"Come with me," Casey said.

"But I...I'm to wait for my brother."

Brother, was it?

"We'll go sit outside...you can get some air. I'm... Kathleen Brannigan," Casey said, almost revealing her name.

The girl looked at her blankly, then caught herself. "Jennie. I'm Jennie Monroe."

There was a bench on the porch outside and Casey led Jennie to it. "Why don't you just sit for a moment."

A tear started down Jennie Monroe's face. "I don't believe it...I don't believe he's an outlaw. Not after what he did for us."

"What did he do for you?" Casey asked softly.

"A few weeks ago, a band of outlaws attacked our ranch. They shot my brother...they were going to..." She stopped, unable to say more to a stranger.

"And..." Casey prompted.

"This man...Jim Tyson...came from nowhere. He killed four of them.... I...I killed one. Then he helped us reach a neighbor." Her face clouded with confusion. "I can't believe...he's one of them. He was so kind."

Well, well, well, Casey thought. So that was where Donaldson had disappeared. No wonder he didn't say anything. It would shoot his hard image to hell in a basket. Donaldson. A knight in shining armor. Damnation!

As she was pondering this new aspect of Ty's nature, she was startled by a new outburst from her companion. "I don't believe it. It must be two different men."

Casey couldn't mistake the longing in the other woman's voice, not when she felt the same thing for Sean. "I think you might be right," she soothed, her mind running up and down one dead-end trail after another. She hadn't been wrong in sensing a new melancholy in Ty. So he had been smitten, too! Damn, he had tried to help her with Sean. She could do no less for him. But how, without giving the whole scheme away?

"Will you trust me?" she asked suddenly.

Jennie Monroe turned, her hazel eyes misted. The face before her was so earnest, so caring, so determined, she managed a weak smile and nodded.

"Are you leaving today?"

"I think so."

"Going back to your ranch?"

"If my brother can find some hands."

"Tell me exactly where it is."

Jennie, her face thoroughly confused but somehow filled with hope, gave her explicit directions. "Do you know Jim Tyson?"

I wonder if anyone does, Casey thought to herself but she merely nodded. "Yes," she said out loud.

"He isn't a..."

"Would it matter if he were?" Casey asked abruptly. She had to know before she went any further.

Jennie remembered Jim Tyson's gentleness after the attack, then the bitterness in his voice the next morning when they had watched the sunrise together. "You're a good man," she had said then. And she'd meant it.

She knew she was right. Regardless of what anyone said, regardless of what Jim Tyson had been, there was something in him that was good and right. "No," she returned with complete certainty. "It wouldn't matter."

Casey smiled, and Jennie felt its intense warmth.

"Look for him...Monday," Casey said.

Jennie searched her face. She wanted to ask more, but for some reason she trusted the woman. She also sensed she wouldn't be told anything else. "He's not...you're not...?"

"No," Casey said. "He's just a good friend." It shocked her to know she meant it.

Jennie started to ask something else, but she saw her brother coming across the dirt street with some men. She seized Casey's hand. "Thank you," she whispered. "I'll be waiting."

Casey nodded and turned away. She didn't want to answer any questions from Mr. Monroe.

Despite her preliminary reservations, Casey enjoyed dinner with Michael Kelly. He was openly admiring, something Casey was not quite used to but immediately decided she liked. Sean had told her she was pretty at the hotel in Santa Fe but she still needed reinforcement. And Michael, which he insisted she call him, was very interesting company.

He had been a riverboat gambler until the war made that means of travel hazardous. Feeling no commitment to either side, he had come west, using his winnings to start the saloon. Like any river gambler, he was a dangerous man, well prepared to defend what was his, and tolerant of the behavior of those who didn't interfere with him.

"But there's so much gold in this town...don't you think they'll turn on you?"

"Wilson's bunch?" He shrugged. "They haven't yet. If they do they'll get more than they bargained for. There isn't a man here, or a miner in the valley, who isn't a member of one of the protection committees. Enough of that. I want to know about you."

Casey blushed and Kelly once more wondered whether it was an act or real. It was difficult to imagine a woman working in a saloon who still blushed, but there was something about this woman that kept the miners respectful, an innocence that survived the dark, smoke-filled, often vulgar environment of the saloon.

"I've told you everything," she said slowly.

"Very little. Very, very little. Like how long you plan to stay?"

"Until I know my uncle's not anywhere around here."

Kelly leaned back in his chair. "Would you consider staying longer...if I gave you a piece of the saloon?"

Casey stared at him. "Why would you do that?"

"You've doubled my business." His hand inched over to hers, hovering above it, his eyes asking permission. "And I don't want you to go." His voice was soft.

Casey's eyes fell. She did not like lying. Particularly to someone who had been kind to her, someone she was beginning to like. Her hand withdrew perceptibly, and Kelly understood. "That wouldn't be part of the bargain," he said, a little stiffly.

She looked directly into his eyes. "I can't," she said. If only he knew what trouble she was bringing him, him and the whole town.

"Do you know where you're going next?"

She shook her head numbly. It was a question that haunted her hourly. Where would she go? She couldn't stay here. It wouldn't take long for the townspeople to figure out what had happened. And she would likely be tarred and feathered if she was within grabbing range.

She had known Sean was right. The people of Fortitude had made a pact with the devil and would eventually pay for it. When the town was of no more use to Wilson, he would raid it as ruthlessly as he had Two Springs. And then the miners and townsmen would be unprepared. At least Sean was giving them a chance. Still, her conscience nagged at her.

"Kathleen...?"

She jerked her head up, knowing she had been day-dreaming. She looked at the gambler questioningly.

"Anytime you want to come back...the offer's open."

"I won't," she said softly, "but thank you. You've been very kind."

"Not nearly as kind as I would like to be."

Casey smiled and the all too rare flash of light seemed to blind him. Kelly wondered exactly when he had been so affected by a woman before. Years, he knew. Too many.

"Thank you for a wonderful dinner," Casey said. "But I think we should get back."

The disappointment in Kelly's handsome face was obvious, but he merely nodded and rose, pulling out her chair for her. "As you wish," he said. "But remember...if you ever need anything..."

"Thank you," Casey said simply.

Ty was in the saloon and Casey saw his eyes narrow as she and Kelly entered, his hand at her elbow. The gun-slinger stood and ambled over lazily. "Are you ready to play, ma'am? I have some money to win back."

"Or more to lose," she answered tartly, resenting the knowing look in his eye.

"Maybe," he acknowledged with the familiar curl of his lips.

Casey found her regular table and sat while Kelly went to his office for some fresh cards. For a moment she and Ty were alone. "Saturday," she said.

He nodded. Then grinned. "Have a nice dinner?"

"It's none of your business," she snapped. "I didn't ask you about those days you disappeared."

The smile faded from his face, and Casey noted the shadow that fell over it. She was *right*. He did care.

But she had no more time to puzzle it out. The other chairs at the table were being taken and Kelly was approaching with the deck of cards.

Two more days.

Chapter Nineteen

Saturday dawned bright and clear. Casey stopped her horse on the way to Sean's camp and looked down on the town. It looked so peaceful in the quiet pastels of morning. She shivered, thinking once more of Two Springs and the violence of Wilson's raid. It seemed almost as though gun smoke drifted over Fortitude already.

It would have come sooner or later, she told herself.

She felt fear nibbling at her. Fear for Sean, for Ty, for herself. Fear of what she was bringing to the town. Fear of what would happen after. Fear of being alone again. Fear of losing Sean.

To take her mind off the next twenty-four hours she started thinking of ways to get Ty and Jennie Monroe together. She thought about Kelly's offer, but after today it would be impossible. They would all be lucky to escape Fortitude with skins intact.

Sean. She wished she could displace the constant presence he was in her heart and thoughts. She loved him so much.

Her shoulders straightened. Her nightmare would end soon. Her nightmare and her dreams. She would help destroy the man who had killed her father, and Sean would free his family. Then they would go their separate ways. With pride. She would make sure of that. She would not make it difficult. But Casey knew it would be the hardest thing she had ever done.

An hour later she rode into Sean's camp and noted with dismay that Ty was already there, and Sean was drawing something in the dirt with his knife.

Sean looked up, a tight distracted expression on his face. "Casey," he acknowledged, his voice cool.

Ty looked up and grinned. "You're late," he observed, and Casey started to bristle.

"You're early," she retorted.

"I left Wilson's camp yesterday to go look over a ranch for him. Figured it would be better if I left yesterday. Less chance for anyone to connect me with you two. Damned if I want all of Colorado on my tail, too."

Casey slid down from her horse, and her dress caught in the stirrup. "Dratted women's clothes," she muttered as she turned to unhitch it, missing the sudden warmth in Sean's eyes as they crinkled in amusement.

Sean moved quickly to her, his hands efficiently freeing her as he smelled the fresh sweet scent of her hair. He cursed himself. He was trying so damned hard not to let anything show, not to grab her and feel her lips, not to tie her to a tree and leave her there. He could do none of them. He couldn't leave her bound because he might not come back. And if he didn't she would follow them. He should never have let her come this far. He would never forgive himself if anything happened to her.

Casey read his thoughts. "I won't stay behind," she said. "You know you need me for the playacting."

Sean's hands lingered on her. She looked beautiful as her hair caught flashes of the sun and her eyes matched the rich green of the grass in the valley. Her chin tilted in the defiant way he had come to love. Despite all his resolve, his lips touched hers tenderly before he wrenched them away.

"You let Ty and me take care of the guards," he warned. "I don't want you to appear until that's done. Agreed?"

Casey looked at him stubbornly. "I'm as good..."

"I know," Sean said wearily. "You're as good as either of us, but I can't help looking out for you and I might well make a mistake. Please, Casey."

She finally nodded. Pulling a small tin from her saddlebags she held it out to Ty. "For your horse."

Ty reached up and took it. "What is it?"

"Boot polish. That blaze on your horse is easy to identify. Neither Sean's horse nor mine is any different from most of those in town."

Ty looked astonished, then embarrassed. It was something he should have thought of. "Thanks," he grumbled as he took the tin and strode to his horse, studying the white blaze before methodically applying the red-brown paste and watching it disappear.

Sean's arm went around her. "I think that's a first," he whispered.

At her quizzical look, he continued, "The thanks."

"Why don't you try it?" she said impudently as she reached back into her saddlebags and brought out three black silk masks.

Sean took one and studied it. The silk cloth had been doubled to hide their features. Holes had been made for the eyes, and the masks had ties to keep them in place. Casey had not wanted them to go blind at an awkward time.

Sean rubbed the soft material with his fingertips, and looked at Casey. "What in the devil was this?"

"Don't ask," she replied with a devilish grin. "I don't think anyone will ever connect it with you."

Her eyes were sparkling with mischief, her face flushed from his approval. Lord above, but he loved her. He hated himself for putting her in danger, but he saw no way out. Not now.

Casey and Sean stood there for several seconds, his hand resting on her shoulder, their eyes devouring each other. Ty had finished and turned to look. He groaned and the noise startled both Sean and Casey from their reverie.

"I don't like interfering," he commented wryly, "but I think Casey had better change clothes."

Casey turned, resting her eyes on Ty. "Someone was in town looking for you."

Ty raised an eyebrow. "Bounty hunter?"

"Not unless they come in a dress and with long dark curly hair."

Ty had been at ease but he was suddenly as taut as a stretched spring. He reached out and grabbed Casey's wrist, and she flinched at the pain. Seeing her discomfort, he immediately let it go but his eyes were cold and merciless.

"Who?"

"She said her name was Jennie. Jennie Monroe."

Ty whirled around, away from a stunned Casey and a mystified Sean. Casey had not expected this kind of reaction or she wouldn't have said anything. Not now. She watched the muscles in his back bunch and saw his fists tighten into white balls.

She took a step forward. "Ty..." Her voice was softer than it ever had been with him.

"What did she want?"

"She said she was trying to find you...she said you saved her life."

"Does she know who I am?"

The words grated out painfully, and Casey suddenly ached for him. "Yes."

Ty swung back around, facing her. "Did you tell her?"

"No. She described you to the storekeeper. I was in the

store at the time." She thought it wise at the moment not to include her own conversation with Jennie Monroe.

"What...what did she say...when she heard who I was?"

"I don't think it mattered that much."

"Of course it mattered," Ty rasped. "Why would a decent girl have anything to do with dirt like me?" There was so much pain and fury in the words that Casey flinched. She hadn't really considered what his reaction would be. She had naively thought he would be pleased.

She tried again. Awkwardly. "Why don't we go back by the ranch? You can talk to her."

Ty's eyes were full of pain. "You know why Wilson wanted me? To kill her brother and take his land. Men like Wilson think I'm one of them. And I am, damn it. I'm not good enough for someone like her. I'm not good enough to wipe her feet."

"But you are!"

Casey's defense went unheard. Ty had turned around and stalked away.

There were tears in her eyes when she turned around and faced Sean. "I didn't mean to..."

"I know," he said softly. "Give him some time...he needs to get used to the idea that he's not entirely the devil incarnate." His mouth turned up in a wry smile. "I thought you didn't like him."

"He sort of grows on you."

"Like poison ivy."

"Something like that," she admitted.

Sean's voice lowered. "He was right. You need to change clothes...if you're going."

Casey wiped away a tear. "Damn him," she said.

Sean leaned down and kissed away a second tear. "I love you, Casey," he said.

Her eyes flew wide open. "You...what?"

His hand traced the curves in her cheek and then cupped her chin in his hand. "I love you," he said again.

Then why didn't he kiss her? She reached up on her toes so he would. But he merely held her chin up and his intense eyes said little she understood. "After..." he started, and stopped almost immediately.

"After...?" she queried, her heart nearly stilled.

He forced his voice back to normal. "We'll talk when this is all over."

"But..." She couldn't leave it there.

"We're going to miss the payroll wagon," he said. "You change. I'll talk to Ty."

She nodded slowly.

Sean followed the direction Ty had taken and found him leaning against a tree, staring bleakly off into the woods. His eyes changed into the old icy blankness when he sensed Sean's presence.

Ty's voice was mocking when he spoke. "Is the hellion ready?"

Sean grinned. Ty's nickname for Casey suited her. "In a few moments."

There was a strained silence. "I'm glad you're with us," Sean said finally.

Ty merely shrugged.

"Any plans after tomorrow?"

"We might not be alive tomorrow."

"Let's assume we are," Sean replied dryly.

"I think I'll head north. I've had my fill of Texas."

"You're welcome to come with us."

Ty arched an eyebrow. "I don't think so."

Sean knew it was none of his business, but Casey's comments had intrigued him, almost as much as Ty's violent reaction. "That girl Casey mentioned...why don't you stop by there?"

"And do what?" Ty said. "Ask her to hitch herself to a hired gun, to someone who doesn't know anything but that?" His voice was empty, devoid of bitterness. There was only acceptance of what he was. "There's a price on my head. I'll never be free of bounty hunters."

"Ben can help with that. There were enough witnesses to prove you were framed."

There was another silence as if Ty was trying to believe. Then he shook his head. "I chose to be what I am. And when I did I knew it meant being alone. There's no going back."

"It doesn't have to be that way," Sean said softly.

Ty spun on him, his amethyst eyes bright and glittering. "You should have been a damned preacher," he spit out. "Don't interfere with my life. Not now, not ever."

Sean nodded and turned around. He took a few steps. Not hearing any following ones, he turned back to Donaldson, who was still leaning against the tree. "Coming?"

Ty's eyes darkened as he straightened up and ambled lazily toward Sean, the old half smile back in place. It was as if the scene had never happened. "Why not?" he said.

The three of them rested their horses on a hill above the dusty dirt trail leading to the Lucky Lady Mine, the largest mine in the area. From their vantage point they could see two points of the trail, two winding miles apart.

The wagon, filled with supplies and the payroll, appeared at one point, and Sean noted with satisfaction that the established pattern was holding true. There was one man in the lead, far enough ahead to be out of sight of the wagon on parts of the turning, twisting road. Another was behind, again frequently out of sight. An armed guard rode beside the wagon, and the driver had a shotgun lying next to him on the seat.

Sean bent his head toward Ty. "You take the back rider.

I'll take the front. Casey will come with me and tie up the first guard. We won't have quite as much time as you. He pointed at a spot in the road. "Meet me there and we'll take the last guard and the wagon."

Ty nodded, and the three of them pulled on the masks, tying them firmly. The horses separated, Ty heading left and Sean and Casey right.

The back guard, Rich Goodman, let the wagon disappear. Damn but he was thirsty. He stopped his horse in the middle of the trail and dug in his saddlebag for the flask. Nothing ever happened on these trips except his rump getting sore. It wouldn't hurt to take a swallow.

Ty watched the guard for several minutes, wondering why he was lagging so far behind. Then the man stopped and raised the flask...with his gun hand. This was going to be easier than he'd thought. He eased his horse onto the trail.

As Goodman started to lower the flask, he saw a masked man holding a gun on him and his stomach turned over. The flask tumbled from his hand.

"Throw your guns down," a muffled voice ordered, and Goodman, noticing the steadiness of the gun hand, obeyed quickly.

"Now put your hands up and slide down from the horse."

Cursing under his breath, Goodman complied again. No job was worth his life and there was something about the robber that scared the bloody bejesus out of him.

The gun now waved him over behind some rocks and the guard started to tremble. His fear caused him to stumble.

"Do exactly as you're told, and you'll live through this," the man on horseback said. The mask gave him an almost unearthly menace. Goodman fought to keep from being sick and stumbled on.

"Stop there. Sit down and take off your boots." Ty was amused at the readiness of the man to do so although his hands shook. Ty dismounted lazily, his slim build disguised by two added shirts for bulk. "Put your hands on your head and stand up."

Again Goodman complied, though he was mumbling a prayer. He watched with terrified eyes as the masked man transferred his gun to his left hand and took a knife from his belt. The man tried to hide his fear but was afraid he wasn't succeeding. He didn't even think he cared. He just wanted to survive.

"Lower your hands, carefully, and take off your belt," the robber said. "And listen hard. I shoot as well with my left hand as my right."

Goodman nodded, hope battling with fear. The robber wouldn't be asking this if he was going to be killed. Unless the man liked to torture his victims. His hands trembled as he tried to unbuckle the belt and pull it through the loops. When he finally succeeded he let it slide through his fingers to the ground. The knife flashed, and his heart stopped. But instead of going to his throat or heart, the knife went toward his stomach and he almost fainted until he saw it neatly slice the buttons of his trousers. He knew a painful kind of humiliation as his pants fell to his ankles and he stood there shaking in his long underwear.

Despite himself, Ty felt a small twinge of remorse although his cynicism told him the man deserved it for his carelessness. He tucked the knife back in his belt and, still holding the gun steady, went to the saddle and took a rope from it. "Hands behind you," he said curtly, and the guard obeyed with alacrity.

Ty quickly tied the man's hands behind him, then his

feet, hooking them together as Casey had the deserters in New Mexico. It was, he had to admit, effective.

He took the man's bandanna off and gagged him. "Don't worry," he said. "I expect someone will be along before long." Those were his only words of comfort as he strode away and disappeared, leaving Goodman struggling on the ground.

Sean and Casey weren't so lucky. Their guard took his duties seriously and he rode with his right hand resting on the gun in its unstrapped holster.

Sean wanted no noise to alert the wagon, and he didn't see a way to ambush the man without the possibility of a shot. He finally settled on an outcropping of rocks over a turn, which would put the wagon out of sight of the guard for several minutes. He dismounted and told Casey to stay with the horses. Then he climbed to the top of the rocks, ready to leap onto the guard.

When the guard was directly underneath him, Sean leaped, one hand aiming for the man's right arm. The guard was alert for those around him, but not above, and he fell from the horse with an oath, struggling against the arm that pinned his gun hand to his side. He tried to kick, but the fall had partially stunned him, and the black-masked man had the advantage. He tried to fight, but then there was a blinding pain and everything went black.

Sean didn't waste time regretting the blow. He put his gun back in its holster and dragged the man from the road, noting with approval that Casey had darted onto the trail and was leading the guard's horse out of sight. They had just reached the safety of the rocks when they heard the wagon clattering by.

"Tie him up like I told you," Sean said quickly, then swung up on his horse. "Ty and I will be at the next pass."

Casey nodded. They had gone over the plan any number

of times. She checked the guard's wound. It would be painful but not fatal.

With a rope she tied the guard's hands behind him, took away his belt and slicked the buttons off his pants. She got down to the man's feet and started pulling off the boots, a harder task than she had imagined. It took several minutes and she cursed each one of them. She finally succeeded and tucked them in her saddlebags. She then tied the man's feet, hitching them to the rope on his hands. Casey decided it was unnecessary to gag him. He would be unconscious for several more minutes, much too long to warn the wagon.

She regarded her handiwork with wry pride and mounted quickly, spurring her horse into a gallop.

She was late. The wagon had been stopped, apparently without a shot, and Sean and Ty had ordered the mounted guard to the ground. The driver was still on the wagon seat but his shotgun was on the ground, and his hands were up. Both guard and driver looked furious.

"The miners won't stand for this," the driver said.

Sean shrugged and turned to Casey. "Take him over to the rocks and tie him up," he said, pointing to the guard standing in the road. He turned to Ty. "You go along."

With the two of them, it only took seconds, and the guard was hog-tied out of hearing of the wagon.

When they returned, Casey went to the wagon where Sean was still holding a gun.

"Get the strongbox," he told her, and Casey climbed on the wagon, passing the box to Sean.

"That's all, Reeve," she said in a voice an octave lower than usual.

"Goddammit...now you've done it," Sean exploded. "We have to kill him now."

"But, Reeve..."

"You know Wilson's orders. No one was to know who

done it. Damn. He's nervous enough already about Sunday and the bank.''

The driver stiffened visibly at the words. The fact the gunman had mentioned a bank meant he was a dead man. His hands pulled tighter on the reins.

"But I ain't never killed anyone before," Casey whined from behind the driver.

"Time you start, if you're going to stay with us. I'll go finish off the driver. You take care of this one."

Sean disappeared, and Ty was a distance away. Casey leaned over the man. "I don't want to kill you, mister. You promise not to say anything, and I'll just pretend. When you get to town, you say I missed you and you don't know who it was that robbed this payroll."

The man would have agreed to selling his soul at the moment.

"You do say something, and I will kill you," she continued. "Understand." The man nodded again.

Casey leaned down. "You jest keep those reins in your hand and when I shoot you slump over. The horses should start running and when you're out of sight, you can take control again."

"Thanks…I won't forget this," the shaky voice barely managed, and Casey felt a stab of guilt.

"You jest stay grateful." She hopped down and, pointing the gun at him, shot just past him. The driver slumped and the horses jerked into a gallop. The wagon went flying down the trail, and Casey prayed he could get control back.

Ty brought her horse over. "Not bad," he drawled.

Through the mask, her voice was worried. "I just hope he doesn't keep his word."

"He won't," Ty assured her. "You won't be able to shut him up when he gets to Fortitude. Not with that gold shipment in the bank."

"Are you heading to town now?" Casey asked Ty as

Sean approached. He stopped next to her, his arm going around her as if it belonged there.

"I don't think any of Wilson's men will be welcome in town after this," Ty said. "I'll meet with Sean this evening before I head back to Wilson's camp with the bad news." He chuckled. "I've got to give it to you, Mallory. It worked like a charm. Wilson will be livid with rage."

Casey wanted to say something but didn't know exactly what. She might not see Ty again. "Ty...?"

"Yes?"

"Be careful."

The mask covered the small twisted smile she knew was probably there.

"I'm always careful."

"I know," she said softly. She wanted to say something else, but there was something about the tilt of his head that warned her against it.

"I'll see you tomorrow."

Ty hesitated and then said cautiously, "I want to talk to Sean a moment."

Casey eyed him suspiciously.

"We might not be able to meet later. They might close the town. It's a message for Ben Morgan, nothing to concern you."

Still wary, Casey moved away while Sean went to Ty's side.

"What are you going to do with her tomorrow?" Ty asked abruptly, removing the mask.

"She's promised to stay out of it."

"You're a fool, Mallory. She promised you in Fort Worth, too, didn't she?"

Sean nodded, his eyes now searching.

"Well, she didn't keep it. She stayed, and she saw the sheriff go back to his office after we left. She hit him over the head and hog-tied him."

There was silence.

"She probably saved both our lives," Ty said, feeling like all kinds of a traitor for having betrayed Casey. But he didn't want her hurt. "If you want her out of it, you're going to have to knock her out or lock her up. Otherwise she will be right in the middle of things."

Sean's mouth had turned grim. He nodded. "Thanks. I'll see you later. If I can't leave town tonight, we'll meet tomorrow after everything's over."

"I may not be there."

"You will," Sean said. "I've found it's not so easy to get rid of you."

A slight smile tugged at Ty's lips. He inclined his head in farewell and turned his horse around, urging it into a fast trot. He didn't look back.

Sean helped Casey mount and they rode to a gnarled tree and dismounted again, Sean lifting the strongbox from the saddle. They had gone through the plan over and over again, and neither needed words. Time was limited. Sean started digging with his knife as Casey changed clothes. She put the dress back on and bundled her man's clothes into her saddlebags, then went over to watch Sean.

His sleeves were rolled up and his shirt was pasted to his upper torso with sweat. She leaned against a tree, content to watch the strong, even strokes of the knife. His eyes glinted when he glanced up at her with the smile that had been missing for so long. There was something rakish about him this afternoon, and it made her heart spin with longing.

He was finally satisfied with the depth of his hole and he lifted the small strongbox inside, covering it up and spreading the spare dirt around. When he finished he grinned, and Casey knew it was because the waiting was finally over. She went to him. His shirt was open to the waist and she thought she could hear the pounding of his heart. His eyes shot amber sparks and his hands reached for her, then retreated.

He shook his head. "I'm filthy," and he was. Wet dirt clung to his shirt and hands, yet Casey felt such an elemental pull to him that she could scarcely bear it.

"It doesn't matter," she said and loved the crook of his mouth as it turned even farther upward.

"Ah, but it does. You don't want anyone to think you fell from your horse...or held up a pay wagon." But he brushed a hand against his denim trousers, and cupped her chin.

"You were wonderful."

Casey felt a moment's elation before tumbling back to earth. So she was. Wonderful at holding up wagons. Wonderful at tying up people. Wonderful at scaring drivers half to death. Not so wonderful at being a woman. Her green eyes clouded.

The devilment fled Sean's eyes. "I don't want you going back to Fortitude. Why don't you go to my camp and wait for us there?"

"No," she said simply.

Sean knew he couldn't change her mind, especially after what Ty had told him. Nor did he want to betray Ty's confidence. The only way to keep her out of tomorrow's action would be to tie her up. In the morning he would have to find a way.

"You're a very special lady," he said softly.

Casey's heart stretched and reached for him, her eyes telling him how very special he was to her.

But a cloud fell over his eyes and Casey was left with an indefinable chill.

She looked so pretty, Sean thought. Her hair, now freed from the scarf, was as soft as angels' wings as it curled around her face. God, he loved her. He would never forgive himself if anything happened to her.

He tried again. The worry made his voice harsher than he intended. "You'll stay out of the street. Behind cover."

"What about you?" she said defiantly.

"I'll face Wilson." The hard lines were back in his face, his mouth grim and unyielding.

"Then I will, too."

He faced her and his eyes were like agates, stony and emotionless.

Casey shivered at the change in him. He was suddenly so cold and distant. She reacted the only way she knew... with anger. Hellfire, he wasn't the only one with reason to kill Wilson.

"I'll do what I want," she said, disappointment and pain swamping her. He only wanted to control her. There were no soft words, no promises of tomorrow. She spun around and rushed blindly for her horse. As she stumbled, his strong arms caught her.

"Casey, please."

If she hadn't felt so discarded, she would have heard the pain in his voice. But she jerked away and mounted swiftly. "It's my battle as well as yours, Sean Mallory," she said bitterly. "And neither you nor anyone else can keep me from fighting it." She dug her heels into her horse and sped away.

Chapter Twenty

Casey rode fast, wanting the wind to dry the tears that flowed down her face.

She didn't understand all the emotions that were tumbling out of her. She had always kept them firmly to herself, as her father had taught her, and now they were flying free like the wind.

Anger. Love. Uncertainty. Hope. Hopelessness. Fear.

Fear was the greatest. Fear of losing Sean. Fear of never seeing him again after tomorrow. She didn't know if she could bear that....

But in the last several days, he had been so distant. She couldn't help but feel she might have disappointed him in some way. And why not? She had no experience. She didn't know the soft words and the ways to pleasure a man.

But he said he loved you.

Like a sister. Didn't he say she reminded him of his sister?

She knew he would take her with him. He was too honorable to do anything else and he felt responsible for her. But she couldn't stand that. Not now. Not ever. Not the way her body ached whenever he neared.

She wished she could be something different. She wished

she had agreed when he had asked her to go to his camp, to wait there. But she could no more do that than she could stop loving him. She had tried to change, but she couldn't.

She was Casey Saunders. Ray Saunders' brat. More boy than girl. That's what they had all said. And they had been right.

She dug her heels, urging her horse into an even faster speed, bending low as her tears dried in the hot wind.

Sean watched her race away, thinking what a superb horsewoman she was. Lord, but she was like quicksilver. She had so many different moods, and he loved them all. Mischievous child, efficient gunman, passionate woman. He grinned at the last. She was magnificent. After this was over, he would let her know how much.

But first, he had to keep her alive. She would be furious tomorrow, for he had no intentions of letting her become embroiled in a bloody shoot-out. He knew how competent she was but tomorrow was different. There would be bullets everywhere and he didn't intend for her to be in their way.

He also knew Casey might never forgive him, might turn to someone else. She had traveled weeks for her chance at Wilson.

But he couldn't forget their first meeting…in Two Springs. The bartender had told him how Casey had rushed to her dying father's side, taking Wilson's bullet in her leg. She would do it again, no matter what she promised. It had only strengthened his resolve when Ty had told him about Fort Worth. Casey didn't know what restraint meant.

Tomorrow. Tomorrow it would all be over. Months of searching for Wilson. Weeks of being with Casey, of feeling her rob one part of his heart after another.

By sundown tomorrow, either he or Wilson would be dead. Casey would be furious. But alive. That was the important thing. And if she would listen, he would ask her to

marry him, to go back with him to the ranch in Texas. Even
with the uncertainty hanging over him, he could feel the
unaccustomed joy rising in him. She was everything he had
ever hoped for, ever wanted. A partner in the fullest sense,
a friend as well as lover, a source of laughter and delight.

He swallowed. *Think about what's ahead. It's no time to
make mistakes now.* But he couldn't put Casey from his
mind.

And Donaldson. He wished he could do something to
help Ty. It was startling to discover how much he had
started to care about the gunfighter he had once despised.
Sean's lips twitched. Preacher, Donaldson had called him.
No one had ever called him that before. The twitch became
a smile and a chuckle started deep in his throat.

A mile outside of Fortitude, Casey slowed her horse. It
would not do to ride helter-skelter into town. She looked
at the lather on the horse with self-disgust. She turned the
horse off the trail and dismounted out of sight. She wished
she had something to rub him down with, but Sean had
taken the clothes she had used in the robbery. He would
take them back to his camp where he would change his
own clothes before coming into town. They wanted nothing
to link them with the payroll robbery.

She walked her horse until the lather dried, and mounted
again, once more cursing the clumsy skirt. She rode slowly,
in the most ladylike manner, into a town boiling over with
anger.

Casey heard the first account at the stable. By the time
she'd reached the saloon, the number of bandits had increased to ten, all of them huge and fearful.

Michael Kelly was huddled in one corner with a group
of men. Five of Wilson's men were tied together in another
corner guarded by two glowering miners.

Casey could barely withhold a smile. Sean had been right

in judging the indignation of Fortitude. Nothing was quite as galling to men as to know they had been wrong in trusting someone.

She was ignored so she made her way to her room upstairs. The green dress was stained with horse sweat and dirt and she quickly changed into her other dress and went back downstairs.

The group around Kelly had grown. She inched herself up to it and listened.

"We should have known better, trusting a bunch of coyotes like that," the stable owner was saying.

"We all enjoyed their commerce," Kelly said reasonably but there was a new hard edge to his voice. "The question now is what do we do about it?"

"Joe said they planned to rob the bank tomorrow. Everything I have is in there."

"He was damned lucky to get away, damned lucky he could tell us who done it."

"Said he ducked just as the robber shot at him and got the horses running. Didn't think he had it in him."

"We all owe him something…if that robber hadn't identified Reeve Taylor we would all be sitting ducks tomorrow."

"Those men we sent out to search for the guards should be back soon. Maybe they can tell us more."

"If they're alive."

"No reason to kill them if they were masked. The only reason they tried to kill Joe was 'cause he heard the name."

"Don't make no sense. None at all…why…after the past two years…?"

Kelly shrugged. "Maybe they intended to leave…not come back. Now is a good time, what with the payroll and the gold in the bank. I suppose it was bound to happen.

You can't trade with the devil. We should have known that.''

Casey silently blessed him.

"What now...should we get a posse?"

Kelly hesitated. "They don't know that we know what happened," he said slowly. "If we keep his men here and take any more who come in, we can keep them from knowing. Then when Wilson's bunch rides in tomorrow, we can ambush them. It would be hell of a lot safer than trying to take him in his valley."

There was a chorus of consent.

"I'll go get the miners," one bearded man said.

Kelly nodded. "Be careful who you tell. We don't want word getting back."

"Don't worry. Wilson won't have a friend left after today."

Kelly nodded. He told two men to round up the others and station sentries on both sides of town. If any of Wilson's men entered town they would be taken captive in one of the two saloons. No one would be allowed to leave.

As the men dispersed to their assigned duties, Kelly noticed Casey.

"What happened?" Casey asked innocently.

"You were right," the saloon owner said ruefully. "Wilson's bunch held up the pay wagon...seems they plan to attack the town tomorrow." His black eyes observed her carefully. "You didn't see anything when you were riding this morning."

Casey's heart stopped beating. "No."

"Thank God you didn't run into them...they apparently don't care about the rules anymore."

Casey's heart started again. He had just been worried about her safety.

"Maybe you'd better leave town," he said slowly.

"Looks like it might be more dangerous out there than here," she replied. "Besides, I can shoot."

Kelly grinned. She had shown him the gun tucked in her boot when he had questioned her about how safe she was working in a mining town. He also knew about the rifle she carried when she went riding. B'God, she was a woman and a half. He wished once more that he could break the reserve around her.

"You're probably right," he said. "But I want you to stay in your room tomorrow."

Casey's indignation rose. Why was it that every man thought she was incapable of defending herself? She would show them. All of them.

But she kept her thoughts to herself and merely nodded as Kelly rushed off to help the others. If he only knew that just hours ago she had held up the pay wagon. The thought coaxed a small smile from her.

Casey felt his presence before she saw him. Perhaps it was the sudden tenseness in the crowded saloon where men had been gathering all day. The stores had all been closed, and the miners were slowly drifting into town. The sole topic of conversation was the robbery. She could feel the tension...and the excitement that reverberated in the room. She had seen it before: the titillation of danger, the rush of blood. She wondered if she were changing...becoming more like the men in the room. She didn't want to be like that. She didn't want to anticipate the shedding of blood. Casey shivered as she turned from her game.

Two miners had Sean by the arms and were pushing him toward Kelly. When they reached them, Sean shrugged the arms aside and stood alone. Good Lord, he was handsome, Casey thought as he stood proud and strong, the familiar lock falling over his forehead.

Kelly looked at the newcomer slowly. "Who are you?" he asked without preliminaries.

Sean leaned arrogantly against the bar. "Do you treat all strangers this way?"

One of the miners grabbed his arm again, but let go when Sean's hard agate stare fastened on him. "Answer him," the miner said.

"Why?"

"So you won't hang," Kelly said lazily.

Sean seemed to weigh the answer, then drawled slowly. "My name is Mallory. I'm from San Antonio."

Kelly studied the worn leather holster. It was empty, the gun already confiscated by the miners. "And what do you do in San Antonio?"

"I'm a rancher," Sean replied with obvious reluctance.

"And what is a rancher doing in Fortitude?"

"That's my business." Sean's jaw clenched.

"Now it's ours, mister. And we're in no mood to argue." A gun was poked into Sean's ribs.

"I'm looking for a man named Wilson."

If the atmosphere had been tense before, it was deadly now.

Kelly's voice was deceptively soft. "And why would that be?"

"It's none of your damned business."

Kelly nodded to the miners. "Lock him up with the others." Wilson's men who had been unfortunate enough to be in town had been tied up and locked in the back room of the stable.

When the miners grabbed him Sean struggled just enough to be convincing. "You're in league with him, damn you."

Kelly held up his hand, stopping the miners. "What do you mean?"

"I heard this town was protecting him...I just didn't believe it...."

Everything was still in the bar now. Casey's hands had stopped playing with the cards.

"Just what is your business with Wilson?" Kelly's voice was still soft but there was a hint of uncertainty to it now.

"He raided my ranch, killed my friend, tried to kill my sister. I've been hunting him for months."

"Any way you can prove that, friend?"

"My pocket," Sean said, wary of making any moves.

Kelly reached inside the indicated pocket and pulled out a paper, looking it over carefully. "A bank draft from a San Antonio bank. In the name of Sean Mallory. It seems," he said slowly, "you might just be in the right place at the right time." His dark eyes raked Mallory. "You were going after him alone?"

"I was hoping to hook up with some law."

Kelly laughed. "There's no law up here...'cepting miner's law."

"Then alone," Sean said.

There was a dangerous gleam in the stranger's eyes that Kelly recognized. This man was no mere rancher.

"The war?"

Sean nodded.

"Which side?"

"Does it matter?"

"No. You just don't look like a rancher."

"I've been fighting a hell of a lot longer than ranching."

Kelly accepted the explanation though he was not yet prepared to totally accept the stranger. Not yet.

"Tie him up."

Sean started to protest.

"No one's going out of this town tonight," Kelly said tightly. "Wilson's planning to raid the town tomorrow and we'll have a little surprise waiting for him. If you are who you say you are, you shouldn't object too strenuously. You can join us tomorrow."

Sean didn't resist as his wrists were tied in front of him. "Should we put him with the others?"

"No," Kelly said. "Leave him here. If he's telling the truth, they would kill him." He turned back to Sean. "Sit over there." He nodded to a table in the corner. "Try anything and you're dead."

Sean allowed a grim smile and went over to the corner, folding his long body into one of the chairs, watching carefully as two of the miners took chairs opposite him.

He and Ty had considered this possibility, and in a way he was gratified. The leader apparently was very careful and had everything under control. Casey had said he would be, but still an angry town was difficult to handle.

Sean knew Ty would wait until sundown. If Sean hadn't appeared, the gunfighter would assume the town was doing exactly as planned and return to Wilson's camp to complete his role.

Sean's eyes swept the saloon, resting on Casey, who had returned to her table. Damn it. Neither Ty nor Casey had told him she was working in the saloon. Would she ever stop doing such damned rash things? It was still another reason to keep her out of tomorrow's gunfight. But his expression revealed nothing as he turned to one of the guards. "A woman dealer?"

One nodded while the other glared distrustfully.

"She looks about as busy as I am," Sean said wryly as Casey looked anywhere but in his direction. "Do you think I might play?"

One guard looked at the other. "Ask Kelly," he finally shrugged.

"Kelly..."

The gambler appeared at the table.

"He wants to know if he can play with the lady?"

Kelly grinned. He felt reasonably certain the stranger was not one of Wilson's bunch. There was a certain feeling of integrity about him, and Kelly prided himself as a judge of character.

"Why not? He has the money." The bank draft was for unlimited funds.

Sean raised his bound wrists. "Can you untie me?"

"Nope," Kelly said, cordially enough. He walked to Casey's table and leaned over her. Sean felt a twist of jealousy. The saloon owner was a good-looking man, and he bent over Casey with a familiarity that wrenched Sean's gut. Especially as Casey looked up at him and gave him that blinding smile that he had not seen for days. Then she stood and walked with Kelly over to his table.

"This is Kathleen Brannigan," Kelly said and Sean stood, lowered his eyes and waited as Casey sat down.

"Sit down, Mr...."

"Mallory," he said, wondering how she was so composed. Nothing showed on her face except a cautious interest. No wonder she was so damned good at cards.

During the next hour, he found out how good.

Ty paced the ground Sean had designated. The sun was almost at the horizon, and the sky was a vivid scarlet. Sean obviously wasn't going to make it.

Ty mounted his horse. He would have to ride hard to reach Wilson's camp before nightfall. At this point, he could only assume that all had gone according to plan. It was up to him now to convince Wilson to raid the town tomorrow. The name "Mallory" was to be his trump card.

Wilson had chosen well. The valley he used had one easily guarded entrance. Ty called out the password as he passed beneath rocks where Wilson posted his sentries.

A curl of smoke was rising from the ramshackle cabin Wilson used. The outlaw leader came out as he heard a warning shout from his sentries. He watched as Ty Donaldson galloped to where he was standing.

"Trouble," Donaldson said.

"What kind of trouble?" Bob Wilson asked, still unconcerned. He had been careful not to rile the miners, not yet, anyway.

"A payroll wagon's been robbed. They're blaming you."

Puzzlement crossed the outlaw's face. "Get down and come inside."

There were two other men in the cabin. The three had obviously been sharing a bottle. One was Reeve Taylor.

"What in the hell are you talking about?" Wilson said, glaring at his newest recruit.

"Some men robbed the mine payroll. One of the guards heard Reeve's name."

Reeve spun out of the chair. "I haven't been out of here all day."

Wilson's eyes narrowed and he looked at Donaldson suspiciously. "What are you up to, Donaldson?"

"Damn it, I'm trying to warn you. They've already locked up all your men in town. The miners are forming a posse, plan to strike in the morning."

"And why weren't you locked up?"

"I was just leaving, taking the backdoor to see a woman at the boardinghouse. I got a whiff of what was happening and got the hell out. It was too late for Lewis and the others. I don't think anyone realized I was there, much less heard anything."

"A posse, you said?"

"They're sending after every miner in the area."

"Goddammit," Wilson swore.

"Could it be any of your men...on their own?" Ty posed the question carefully.

"They wouldn't dare," Wilson growled. "Someone else

did it. When I find out who, I'll make them wish they had never been born.''

''There might be a way you can benefit,'' Ty said slowly. Carefully.

Wilson glared at him.

Undaunted Ty plunged on. ''They plan to attack in the morning...the town will be empty. And there's a gold shipment due to go out Monday.''

''No,'' Wilson said. ''We'll wait here. Ain't nobody can get to us in this valley.''

Ty shrugged and turned to go, then stepped back. ''Another thing...strange. They said the guards weren't hurt. But the robbers took their belts and boots and cut their trouser buttons. They'll never be able to hold their heads up again...'' Ty reached the door.

''Donaldson.'' The word was as cold as the roar of a blizzard.

He turned around.

''Have there been any strangers in town?''

Ty paused, as if to search his memory. ''No...yes...there was someone. Tall, rangy, light brown hair. Keeps to himself.''

''His name...?''

Ty shook his head. ''I never heard it.''

There was a long string of curses. ''Mallory. It had to be Mallory.''

Ty's eyes were questioning.

''The captain of my troop during the war. The bastard. He used to treat our prisoners like that. Should have just killed them, but he was too damned soft.'' The voice was a whisper now. ''Mallory, by God.''

Ty was silent, as he raised an eyebrow in question.

''Will he be coming with the posse?'' Wilson asked.

Ty shrugged. ''They were rounding up all your men and

anyone they didn't know.... Probably locked him up with the rest.''

Wilson's eyes glinted and Ty couldn't miss the cold satisfaction in them. "They think he's one of us?''

"They aren't taking any chances.''

Wilson chuckled. It was a cold, hollow sound. "Mallory. Sitting there jest waiting for me. Like a rat in a trap.'' He looked at his ruined hand and remembered the day it had happened...and the pain. Mallory had shot him to protect his Yankee prisoner...a goddamned Yank. Hate welled and spurted like a fountain, contorting his face, twisting his lips.

"Maybe we'll take the town, after all,'' the outlaw leader said. "Call the men together.''

Chapter Twenty-One

Casey stood at the window of her room, looking over the mountain peaks. They seemed so peaceful, so tranquil this bright sunny Sunday morning.

She wore only a shift, one she had bought several days ago to wear under the dress. She had also bought a corset, but had promptly discarded it. Casey did not understand how women could wear such an imprisoning garment. She thought about such things because it took her mind from more important matters...and from the fear. Fear for Sean. Fear for Ty. Fear for the aftermath of this day.

Was it only two months ago that she'd first met Sean? Since she'd basked in his warm, lazy smile and joined in his fierce sense of purpose...since she started to realize what being a woman was all about, how her body could come alive with a look, a touch?

How strange that the three of them had melded together so well when there had been so much antagonism in the beginning. She would miss Donaldson terribly...he had, in some mysterious way, become the brother she had always wanted. And Sean. She was so confused about him, afraid that he would feel tied to her out of responsibility, or guilt. He was a respected rancher, a former army officer, and she would be an embarrassment to him. She knew nothing about being a wife, or choosing nice dresses, or riding side-saddle, or any of the other things that made a lady. She leaned her head against the wall, and blinked back the tears. She wondered how she could survive without him. She would lose her heart if she lost him, yet...

Casey wondered how he was faring this morning. Somewhat ruefully, he had lost four hundred dollars to her last night during their poker game, forty percent of which went to Kelly. That fact had mellowed his host's feelings toward him. Although Kelly had left Sean's hands tied, the saloon owner had lodged his prisoner in a bedroom above the saloon, locking the door and setting a guard at the windows outside. Kelly didn't figure a guard was needed outside Sean's room because it led only to the saloon, where dozens of trigger-happy miners continued to gather. Kelly was inclined to believe Sean but was not yet willing to take a chance with the lives of those entrusting themselves to his leadership.

More than anything, Casey wanted to steal over to the room, but she didn't dare run the risk of ruining everything now. The plan was going too smoothly.

She knew Sean had commanded guerrillas during the war, and now she understood why. He was a brilliant planner. He had even anticipated the possibility of being linked to Wilson, but the pure charisma of his personality had noticeably disarmed Kelly, and Casey suspected he would be free before long, certainly in plenty of time to participate in his long-waited confrontation.

Casey went over to the bed and took her pistol from under the pillows, checking it, as she always did, to make sure it was loaded. She could not join the men in the street. Again, it might spur suspicion, and the three of them—Sean, Ty and herself—were, after all, guilty of robbery. She doubted their reasons would mitigate the offense if discovered. But at least she could shoot from the window.

She trembled as fear once more flooded her. Sean would take chances. He wanted Wilson badly enough to risk everything. Her hands clenched, wanting the minutes to speed up, wanting them to slow down. She could see figures darting in the street, the shadows of men perched among the roofs and behind curtains. It reminded her of a day two months ago—an age ago—when her town in Texas waited for the Wilson gang, the day her father had died. Oh God, she prayed, don't let anything happen to Sean.

Sean paced impatiently across the room he had been given. His hands were still bound, though he knew he could probably free them if he really tried. But he wanted no suspicions now. Kelly had indicated he would release him once the opportunity to warn Wilson had passed, and he believed the gambler. There had been an instant recognition between the two of them, one of those rare moments of understanding and respect between two men who sensed a certain integrity in each other. In a strange way, it pleased Sean that the man was cautious. Casey had told him how respectfully Kelly had treated her, and how well he maintained order in his establishment despite his rowdy customers. Sean had tried to understand how Kelly allowed the town to tolerate Wilson until he remembered how he, himself, had done so for more than a year during the war. Even when he knew how dangerous Wilson was, Sean had thought he could keep him under control. He imagined that Kelly accepted the outlaw on somewhat similar terms.

He heard the rasp of a key in the lock, and the door opened. Kelly looked as impeccable as he had last night though Sean knew he had probably not been to bed. He had heard loud voices arguing throughout the sleepless night.

The gambler stood to one side, and a bearded miner entered behind him, a smile stretching across his face.

"Captain Mallory. Good glory, am I glad to see you."

Sean stared at him for a moment trying to place the face.

"Rufus Denning," the miner said. "I was there when you were wounded near Richmond." He turned to Kelly. "Weren't no better officer than Captain Mallory... wounded real bad when he tried to save our lieutenant. Glad to see you made it, sir."

"Denning? Corporal, wasn't it?" Sean remembered now and was rewarded by a wide smile and a nod.

Kelly took a knife from his belt and cut the ropes around Sean's wrists. "Guess you're who you say you are. We would appreciate any help you can give us."

Sean rubbed his wrists, grateful for the freedom. His thoughts turned immediately to Casey. "Miss Brannigan?"

"In her room. I asked her to stay there." The question didn't surprise Kelly. Mallory had played with the girl long into the night, and everyone seemed to have a tendency to become protective of her, including himself.

Might as well ask a squirrel not to chatter, Sean thought wryly. "I'll be down in a minute," he said to Kelly, then turned to Denning, stretching out his hand. "Good to see you again, Rufus."

"You, too, sir. Especially now. Bad business. All of this. Heard Wilson killed a friend of yours."

"Sergeant Carne," Sean said abruptly. Jimmy Carne had been with him at Richmond.

"I'm sorry, Captain. He was a good man, a good sergeant."

Sean merely nodded. There was nothing else to say.

When the two men were gone, Sean kneaded his wrists a couple seconds, then quickly slipped from his room and knocked softly at the door he had seen Casey enter the night before.

When she opened it, he strode inside and closed it again, locking it behind him. She was dressed in the green dress. Her chestnut hair glowed with red and gold from recent brushing, and her eyes seemed to embrace him with a special tenderness. She was so alive, so vibrant. He hadn't meant to, but he couldn't stop his lips from reaching for hers, as his arms wrapped around her with a need he couldn't tame. He had seen her yesterday, and yet it seemed forever.

Feeling her in his arms, Sean knew what he had to do. All night, he had thought of Two Springs, of her running in the street, of bullets catching her. He remembered the way she had galloped into the nest of deserters at the Blue Hole, and how she had stayed behind in Fort Worth, attacking the sheriff on her own. He could risk losing her love, but not her life. Not this time. Still he hesitated, wanting to treasure the sight and smell and feel of her.

Their kiss deepened. In passion, in urgency, in desperate yearning. A violent shudder shook his body and a groan escaped his throat.

Minutes. They had only minutes before someone would be looking for him. God knew how long before Wilson would be coming, if, indeed, he did.

Sean tore his mouth away from hers and stood, memorizing the flushed features, the shining eyes, the trembling mouth.

Almost before Casey realized what was happening he had whipped off his bandanna and his hand grabbed her wrists, tying them quickly together, while his mouth stilled any protests. His mouth still melded to hers, he picked her up and strode over to the bed, gently lowering her. One hand covered her protests, as the other tore cloth from the bedclothes, and a gag replaced his hand as she fought him. In several more economic moves, her hands were tied to one of the bedposts and her feet to the end of the bed.

Her eyes accused him, screamed at him, begged him.

A muscle flexed in his cheek. "I'm sorry, Casey. I won't see you hurt."

A small desperate sound came from inside the gag, and Sean wondered if she would ever forgive him. A tear started down her cheek and he didn't know if it came from rage or humiliation or grief. His heart stopped beating as he looked at her, possibly for the last time.

He wanted to say something but couldn't. Given Casey's temperament, she would probably despise him for this. He wanted to say he loved her, but he couldn't. Not with the possibility that he would die in a few hours. Better that she hated him.

She should be safe here. Certainly safer than anyplace else. Given the element of surprise and the current manpower in town, Wilson's bunch didn't stand a chance of getting up here. Without looking back at the squirming, struggling figure, he went to the door, opened it and closed it firmly behind him.

Ty was waiting for his horse to falter. When it finally happened, he wasn't surprised. He had, before daybreak, placed a stone under the shoe and knew it was time, past time, that it would have started eating into the tender part of Trouble's hoof.

He was riding at the front of approximately sixty men, on the left side of Wilson. Reeve Taylor was on the right. The sound of so many hooves was like thunder in the quiet Sunday morning, threatening and menacing.

He had been surprised at Wilson's lack of suspicion, particularly for a new member of his bunch. But then he had his own reputation to thank for that. A reputation as a cold-blooded killer for hire. A reputation he deserved. A reputation that would repel Jennie Monroe. Desolation and loneliness cloaked him as completely as a shroud when he thought of her reaction when she learned he was a fraud and a liar.

Trouble's faltering gait turned into a decided limp, and Ty leaned over to Wilson. "Must have picked up a stone. I'll get it out and catch up."

Wilson nodded, his thoughts focused on Sean Mallory and the pleasure he intended to take in slowly killing his former officer. The trail was full of loose stones, and Wilson knew Donaldson was as anxious as any of them for action. He should be back before they reached Fortitude.

Ty let the outlaws pass before dismounting. With his knife, he quickly dislodged the stone. Trouble's hoof would be sore, but he could travel. Ty waited until the last of the dust settled along the trail, then mounted and turned in another direction. His face was known in Fortitude. If he entered town, he would surely be shot or captured, no questions asked. He would wait for Casey and Sean at the camp. He would then lose himself in the northwest. He thought about leaving now, but he would never cease wondering if Casey and Sean had succeeded. He told himself it was just curiosity, nothing at all to do with emotional feelings, for he had schooled himself not to have any. He wanted to see whether Sean was really as good as everyone said he was. Just that. Nothing more.

Sean and Kelly had established a network of signals with the lookouts. They saw the flashing now, and Kelly, in his black suit, walked down the town's one street, his hand motioning to the miners and townsmen hidden on roofs and in windows. Hidden behind the buildings at both ends of the street were men with wagons, ready to block both exits from town.

Wilson stopped within sight of Fortitude. Donaldson had told him the posse was gathering at 10:00 a.m., and it was now 11:00 a.m. by his watch. The town should be empty. Wilson and his men had circled around to avoid the posse. They would hit the town with speed, taking the assay/bank office first, then robbing each of the stores. Wilson himself planned to take the shack where Donaldson said Mallory was detained along with his own men.

He had sent several scouts ahead and they reported back, saying the posse must have left. Things were abnormally quiet, even for a Sunday morning. Wilson signaled his men to proceed at a gallop. He wanted to take the town by surprise. He looked around for Donaldson, wondering what had delayed him, but his blood lust made the question inconsequential. He dug his spurs into his horse.

Wilson was at the edge of town when a sudden blind instinct made him swerve from the road. His men, caught up with the excitement of the charge and prospect of looting, didn't stop but swarmed past him into town.

Wilson was about to follow when he heard the gunfire. There was far too much for his men alone. He remembered the town in Texas several months earlier when so many of his men had been killed. It was another trap. Rage filled him as he watched a wagon pull across the street and heard the gunfire and screams. This time, none of them would get away. And he had almost been among them.

Mallory. Jesus Christ, he should have known. A sickness slowly enveloped him. Mallory. And Donaldson. Donaldson had led them into it, like lambs to slaughter. And he had fallen for it. Donaldson would pay. Just as Mallory would pay. No one betrayed Bob Wilson. No one.

His hate and revenge increased with the echo of every gunshot, with every scream. It echoed in his head like thunder, pounded at his senses. Donaldson. The gunfighter had dropped off about a mile away. Wilson swung his horse around. He would find the trail and follow it. He would find Donaldson, and tether him like the Judas goat he was, and then wait for Mallory. And then he would take great, prolonged pleasure in killing them both.

Sean dropped his pistol and walked to one of the dying men in the street, stooping down beside him.

"Wilson?" he said curtly.

The man merely groaned, barely stopping a scream as hot flame licked his insides.

"Wilson...where is he?"

"Doctor..."

"When you tell me where Wilson is...."

"He was...with...us...I...please...a doctor..."

Sean's jaw locked. He had planned everything so carefully...and Wilson had somehow escaped. He had checked every dead, wounded or captured man.

The man on the ground groaned once more, then sighed, his mouth releasing a long, painful breath. And died.

Kelly came toward him. "Did he say anything? All the men we captured say they don't know anything about the robbery. Or where Wilson went."

Sean shoved his conscience in a dark hole. "This one...said the money was buried out near where the robbery took place. Under a gnarled tree."

The saloon owner whistled. "I was beginning to wonder...must have been just a few of them. Did he say anything about Wilson?"

"Just that he had been with them."

Kelly looked at Mallory's drawn face. "I'm sorry, Mallory. We'll got a posse together...maybe he went back to the valley."

Sean laughed bitterly. "Not a chance. He's probably miles from here. He's real good at that, lighting out and leaving everyone else to pay." He felt dead inside. More searching. More wasted months, perhaps years.

"Maybe we can pick up his trail," Kelly said. "I'll send a couple of men to search for the payroll."

Sean nodded. It would be strange if he didn't go with them now. "I'll be with you shortly." He went into the saloon and up the steps to Casey's room. She was lying quietly, although the messed condition of her bed and the red welts on her wrists said she had struggled mightily. He untied her quickly, his amber eyes meeting her angry ones.

"Damn you," she spit out.

"At least you could say you're glad I'm alive," Sean said mildly, avoiding the task of telling her they had failed.

"I would," Casey said, "if I were." Sparks flew from her eyes.

She had died a thousand times during the last hour...during all the firing and yelling, and, most of all, during the quiet that abruptly ensued. And then he was here, acting as if nothing had happened. She hated him. She loved him. She despised him. They had been partners, and he had betrayed her. The words couldn't get past the lump in her throat, but her eyes told him how she felt. It was the final proof that he had never actually accepted her as she was.

Sean had to look away. There was hurt and betrayal in her face. He wondered if she would forgive him. Especially now that Wilson had escaped. He remembered the first time he'd met her. She had wanted the outlaw as badly as he. He had had no right to take the opportunity away from her. But he would do it again.

"We got most of them," he said finally.

"Wilson?"

Sean shook his head slowly. "He got away. I don't know how. We're going after him."

"I'm going, too," she finally managed.

"You can't, Casey," he said softly. "Not unless you want to give everything away."

"I don't care," she said stubbornly.

"Think about Ty, then," he said softly. "If not about yourself or me. You and I could go to prison. Ty would be sent back to Texas and hung."

Casey's defiant face collapsed as she realized he was right. "Do you always get your way?" she asked desperately.

Sean's face creased with pain. "No," he said softly. "I have to go, or Kelly will wonder," he added. "Stay here until I get back."

Frustration filled her face but she didn't protest further, and Sean took her silence for consent. His hand cupped her chin. "I won't be long." He stroked her cheek as he bent down and kissed her lightly. "Wait for me," he said.

Casey waited until the sound of the last hoofbeats disappeared in the mountain breezes. She slowly went to the window and looked out. Several bodies were still lying on the ground, others were being carried into the saloon. For medical attention, she supposed, though there was no doctor in town, only an old veterinarian. She slipped from the room and hurried to the stable. Only a few horses remained; the rest, she supposed, had been taken by the posse. She quickly saddled her horse and mounted.

She wouldn't stay here any longer. She would go up to Sean's camp where Ty was waiting. Perhaps he would have an idea about Wilson. Perhaps the two of them could go after the outlaw together. It would be a freezing day in hell before she would wait meekly for Sean Mallory. Never again. And never again would she trust him. He had proven himself to be just like other men. She had thought she had his respect and trust if nothing else. Her anger and disappointment grew as she rode hard out of town.

Wilson was a superb tracker. As boys in Tennessee, he and his younger brother learned to fish and hunt when they were very young. It was the only way they'd managed to survive. Their father was a circuit preacher whose gospel was fire and brimstone. When he did occasionally show up he seldom brought food, only his fists, which he used against his wife and children. Wilson had eventually killed his father, and he and his kid brother had turned to hunting men as well as animals. They had been arrested during the first year of the war and given the choice of prison or enlistment in the Confederate army.

The two brothers had found a new purpose in war. Their skill in tracking and killing earned them respect for the first time in their lives. Their audacity was legendary. But they had no lofty motives; they just enjoyed the killing. When his brother was killed at Manassas, Bobby Wilson's internal rage accelerated, encompassing all Yankees and everyone in authority. When Captain Mallory handpicked members for a special guerrilla force, Wilson applied, believing it would mean less authority and more action. He hadn't counted on Mallory being such a noble bastard. Wilson had delighted in finding ways to thwart him until, at last, he tried to kill their Yankee prisoner, and Mallory had shot him, ruining his hand. He looked at it now, twisted and scarred, and cold fury choked him. He had tried for years to pay Mallory back, and every time he had failed. Now his plans to take over this valley were in ruin, his entire band gone. All because of Mallory...

He found Donaldson's trail and followed it cautiously although he doubted whether there was another trap. No doubt Donaldson thought the plan had worked.

Wilson traced the gunslinger's trail up a winding path, then decided to continue on foot. Tying his horse deep in the woods, he made his way soundlessly through the trees, gun in hand. He saw an opening up ahead and got down on his hands and knees and crawled toward it.

* * *

Waiting was always the hardest part of any job, Ty told himself. But it had never been this bad. The sun was high in the sky now, casting streaks of silver through the trees. Sean and Casey should be here any time. He had unsaddled his horse and rubbed him down, more for something to do than any need. Now he decided to resaddle Trouble, so he would be ready to leave as soon as Casey and Sean appeared. He had already buried whatever they didn't need and covered signs of their presence. If everything went as expected, no one would be looking for them, or for any sign of strangers.

His hand clenched tightly at his side as he pondered his next moves. Texas was out. Colorado was also dangerous now. When they didn't find him with Wilson, there would probably be another wanted poster. His options were becoming more and more limited. He thought of Jennie. It was such a soft name. Soft and fresh like a warm spring breeze. He let himself wonder briefly how it would feel to touch her, to make love to her, to come home to her.

Damn you for a dreaming fool, he told himself as he swung the saddle from the ground to the horse's back. His thoughts dominated by a pretty girl with dark hair and gentle hazel eyes, he never heard the soft footsteps behind him, and he sank unconscious to the ground as a gun crashed down on the back of his head.

Chapter Twenty-Two

Sean stayed with the posse for half a day. Wilson's valley was deserted except for the few men he had left to guard it, and they quickly surrendered when faced with a posse or more than a hundred men.

When he returned to town, he learned the payroll had been unearthed and that Casey was gone. There was a letter in her room to Kelly in which she thanked him for his kindness but had determined her uncle was not here, and she had left to look further. Sean couldn't miss the disappointment on Michael Kelly's face.

Sean was momentarily nonplussed by her absence, but then thought it just as well. He knew she had been angry, and she must have gone ahead to join Ty. He didn't think Ty would let her get in trouble, and it was far better that they leave town separately. He made his own farewell to Kelly, ignoring the questions in the saloon keeper's eyes, and said he planned to continue to hunt Wilson.

Deep inside, he wondered. It would take Wilson time to rebuild, and now the outlaw would be wanted badly in two states. Sean wondered if it was worth it, to continue after Wilson, particularly now when he wanted nothing more than to marry Casey and keep her safe. He was tired of the hunt, of bloodshed, of violence. Even that brief surge of stimulation, the sense of danger that had once made him feel so alive, had an ugly, bitter taste. He wanted peace. And love. And a family. He wanted Casey. More than anything in his life, he wanted Casey, and the brightness and love she had brought into what had become an empty life.

But did Casey want him? Would she be content to be a rancher's wife? He had seen how very angry she had been this morning when he had tied her up, as well as how competently she had handled the men in the saloon last night. And, he thought with renewed jealousy, how fascinated Kelly had been by her. She was just discovering her own attractiveness as a woman, and she might well want to go her own way. Especially after he had tied her this morning. He knew she considered it a betrayal. But he had had no choice.

The thought knotted his insides and he felt unbearably anxious. What if she were gone? What if she had been angrier than he thought? What if she had gone on after Wilson alone? Casey. Be there. Wait for me. Be my wife. To hell with Wilson. Let someone else take him. With anxiety tearing at him, Sean rode like the furies toward his camp. She *had* to be there.

Ty felt as if someone had taken a hammer to his head. It wouldn't stop pounding and every time he moved it only made it worse. He tried to move his hand, but it was locked behind him with the other one. He stilled, keeping his eyes closed, preventing a moan from escaping his lips.

How could he have been so careless?

He listened for sounds, for some clue. Was it a posse? A bounty hunter?

He felt a boot kick his stomach, heard the gravelly sound of Wilson's voice. "I saw you move, Donaldson."

Ty opened his eyes and stared up at the voice. Wilson stood there, his lips twisted into a sneer.

"Or is it Donaldson?" Wilson asked. "Was that also a lie?"

Ty struggled to sit. His hands were tied tightly behind him and attached to another rope looped around a tree. Wilson kicked him again, and this time a soft moan escaped his lips.

"I asked whether Donaldson is really your name."

"Yes," Ty whispered through clenched teeth.

"And what is a gunfighter doing with Mallory?"

Ty's lips pressed together as another wave of pain assaulted him. He didn't know which hurt the most now, his head or his ribs.

He knew seconds later when Wilson's boot once more hit the damaged midsection.

"Answer me, damn it."

"Go to hell."

"Oh, I'm going to enjoy killing you, Donaldson," Wilson said with relish. "But I'm going to wait until your friend gets here. And then I can play with both of you."

"No one's coming," Ty said. "Why don't you just kill me and get out of here before the posse shows up?"

"Ah, such concern for my well-being. No, I just think I'll wait awhile." He took out a knife and ran its sharp edge across Ty's neck, drawing a thin line of blood. "Tell me, gunfighter, how does a man like Mallory exact such loyalty from someone like you?"

Ty was silent. He damned well didn't know. What he did know was he had to warn Sean and Casey. If only he could get Wilson angry enough to shoot. Perhaps the noise would alert Sean. Otherwise they would all die.

The knife pierced deeper at his neck and Ty could feel the warm blood flow down his front. "You were eager enough to talk at my camp," Wilson said.

"You're dirt, Wilson."

"And you're better than me?" The point was now a raw, fiery pain at his throat.

"At least I know what I am," Ty whispered. In one desperate effort, his knees came up and drove at Wilson's middle, and the outlaw fell over, dropping the knife. Ty struggled to reach it, but the rope binding him to the tree was too short.

Wilson rose, cursing. He drew his hand back and hit Ty's mouth, splitting his lip.

It took all of Ty's effort but he managed to sit once more and whisper through his broken mouth. "Brave, aren't you, Wilson. To hit a bound man."

Wilson glared at him. He was tempted to kill Donaldson. More than that, he ached to kill him. But now was not the time. He took off his bandanna and gagged him. "I need you alive a little while longer," he said. "You're my sacrificial lamb." And then he kicked him again before disappearing behind some trees.

Casey approached Sean's campsite with little caution. Anger was still boiling inside her. She rode into the clearing, her eyes going instantly to the bloody body on the ground. She slid down from the horse, running to him. Too late, she saw him shaking his head, saw the warning in his eyes. She whirled around.

"Another one." Wilson stepped out from the trees, the gun in his hand. "You alone, missy?"

Casey stared at him, remembering the broken hand from Two Springs. The outlaw's eyes were flat and unmoving, like a snake's. The man's gloved hand reached out and shoved her away from Ty. "What did you do to him?" she demanded.

He looked at her curiously. "And who might you be, missy? What's your part in all this?"

Casey looked desperately at Ty. She started toward him again.

This time Wilson backhanded her, and she went down. She could hear Ty growl from behind the gag and saw him try to struggle to his knees.

Wilson looked back at him. "Don't like that, huh?" His attention went back to Casey. "Do you belong to him? Or to Mallory?"

Through a blackening eye, Casey saw Ty nod at her. "I was running away with him," she said, nodding her head toward the gunslinger. "Mallory doesn't know nothing about this place. He blackmailed both him and me into helping him. Wasn't nothing against you."

Despite his suspicion, Wilson was interested. "What did he have on you?"

"Ty's got a five thousand dollar bounty on his head from Texas. And me?" She shrugged. "He caught me cheating at cards."

"You're the new woman been dealing at the Glory Hole?"

Casey nodded.

"Maybe you're telling the truth, maybe not. We'll wait and see. If Mallory doesn't get here by nightfall, perhaps I'll believe you. It doesn't make any difference for Donaldson. He's dead either way. No one betrays me...I don't care why. Lie down on the ground, missy."

Casey's eyes were suddenly frantic.

"Oh, I'll take my enjoyment all right," Wilson said, "but first things first. Sean Mallory heads the list. If you're lying, and he does come in here I'll take great pleasure in taking you in front of him. In front of both of them." His voice was like a whip. "On the ground, I said."

Wilson was so intent on Casey that he didn't see Ty stretch out as far as the rope would allow him, or see the leg swing up at his crotch, but he did see Casey's eyes flicker, and he turned, his gun swinging toward Ty. As Ty's boot hit him, the gun exploded, and Ty crumpled over.

Sean heard the gunshot and spurred his horse into a gallop, drawing his gun from the holster. He didn't stop to think. Casey. Casey must be in danger. Nothing on earth or in heaven could have stopped him. He saw the clearing and two figures struggling as the burly one tried to dislodge the slender one from his back. Casey had her arms around his man's neck and was holding on for all she was worth.

She saw Sean riding straight at them and suddenly let go, knowing it would send Wilson off balance. And then Sean was on top of the outlaw and they were rolling on the ground, over and over. Fists pummeled one another. Casey couldn't tell who was winning. She knew both men were wild with fury and they kicked and gouged until she didn't know how either could survive. Blood was spurting from both men and yet the fight went on. Seconds seemed like minutes and minutes like hours. Both Sean and Wilson had dropped their guns on the ground. Casey had been able to reach one but the two fighting men were between her and the other one. Both combatants tried to reach it, each jerking the other's hand away before they could get a firm grasp.

Casey leveled the gun she had seized, trying to get a shot, but the two men were moving too fast, and she was afraid she might hit Sean. She saw Wilson grasp a rock and swing it, Sean ducking just in time for it to glance off the side of his head. Stunned for a second, he faltered. Wilson lifted the rock again, and Casey took aim. But before she could fire, a shot rang out and she saw Wilson fall on Sean.

There was a moment's silence. Everything seemed absolutely still. Sean. Ty. Wilson. Even the birds had stopped their flitting from tree to tree.

"Casey." Sean's voice was more a pant than a word. "Are you all right?" His breath came in small gasps, and Casey knew he was near exhaustion.

"Sean, oh yes." Filled with bubbling gratitude to God, Casey took one of Wilson's hands and rolled him over, seeing the large bloody hole in his chest, the still-hot gun in Sean's fingers. Wilson's gun. Somehow, Sean had been able to grab it.

Sean just lay there for a moment, unable to move.

There were cuts all over him. His cheeks were purpling, his nose tilted to one side, one of his eyes was blacker than the one in Santa Fe. And his hand had gone to his ribs, feeling them tenderly. As painful as all his hurts must be, Casey saw no major injuries, and her hand touched his face lightly in grateful relief. And then she ran over to Ty, who was motionless on the ground. She cradled his head, not caring if the blood from his wounds soaked her dress.

Donaldson moved, moaning lightly.

Too exhausted to move, Sean watched with aching, hurting jealousy. So that was the way of it. He had lost her. Perhaps he had never even had her. Slowly, he finally rose and painfully walked over to Donaldson, kneeling to investigate the gunshot. He pulled Donaldson's shirt down, and wiped away blood with his bandanna, studying the bullet hole in the gunfighter's right shoulder. It would be a while before he could use his gun arm again. The bullet had torn through muscles and tendons and apparently was still lodged inside. Ty's mouth was bleeding as were several deep cuts on his neck.

"I've got to take the bullet out," he said curtly to Casey. "Start a fire."

Ty's eyes were open and staring at him. "You?"

"Unless you want to go back to town and take a chance of hanging." Sean's lips were grim.

Ty closed his eyes for a moment, fighting the waves of

pain. "You any good at it?" he said when he opened them again.

"Not much."

A small rueful chuckle started in Ty's throat at Sean's laconic answer. It ended in a bloody cough. "You always were honest, Mallory. Painfully so."

Sean stared down at him. Donaldson's face was pale and strained, his jaw locked against pain. "I'm sorry, Donaldson. I never should have involved you."

"You forget, Reb. I involved myself. And this is my own damn fault. Like you in New Mexico. Taken so easily...it's what happens when you're thinking of a woman..." His voice trailed off as the pain in his shoulder struck with renewed vengeance. He grasped Sean's outstretched hand until Sean thought it would break.

Casey, Sean thought, momentarily glad of the distraction of pain. Forgetting about Jennie Monroe, Sean immediately assumed Ty was referring to Casey. How could he have been so blind? He felt the pressure on his hand increase again, and he tightened his own grip even as he felt the old loneliness flood him.

A fire was going now. Sean could feel its heat behind him. With his free hand he took the knife from his belt and handed it to Casey who was leaning down over them. "Put it in the fire," he ordered shortly.

"Ty," he asked softly. "Do you have any whiskey in your saddlebags?"

Ty nodded.

Casey needed no more instructions. She quickly went to where Ty's saddlebags lay...near the fallen saddle. Her hands searched through the belongings until they found a small flask. She handed it to Sean, who checked the contents, satisfying himself there was enough for his needs. He handed it to Ty. "Take a few swallows. Not much. I'll need most of it for the wound."

Casey leaned down and helped raise Ty's head enough to drink. He winced at every movement.

Sean noted how gentle Casey's hands were, how her face suffered at every change in Ty's face, and he suffered his own agonies. He wished he could hate Donaldson, but he couldn't. Not after all they had been through together.

"Get the knife," he told Casey abruptly.

Sean took it from her, and poured some of the whiskey on it, hearing the hiss as the liquid cooled and purified the knife. When he could touch it, he turned to Ty. "It's going to hurt like hell, but that bullet has to come out."

Ty nodded, one fist digging into the ground.

Sean looked up at Casey. "Get him a piece of wood to bite on, then see if you can't find something to use for bandages. I don't want you watching."

Casey looked from one man to the other. Sean's face was as strained as Ty's. A muscle jerked in his cheek. She knew from the stiff way he was sitting that his ribs must be agonizing. Any rebellion at his curt order faded with concern. "All right," she said obediently, and Ty and Sean looked at her in startled surprise.

She found a branch thick enough that Ty wouldn't bite through it, gave it to him and turned away. Even if Sean hadn't ordered her away, she couldn't have watched. Instead, she quickly changed to her man's clothes, and started ripping the green dress into bandages, tensing with her own private agony every time she heard a moan from the direction of the trees. Her hands tightened against the cloth as the moan turned into a muffled scream.

She heard Sean's low curse, and finally a grunt of victory. "Got it."

Casey forced herself up, taking the makeshift bandages with her. Ty was unconscious, and she was glad. Blood was everywhere, on the ground, on Ty, on Sean. She watched as Sean poured alcohol on Ty's wound, then took her bandages and bound it tightly, finally lashing Ty's arm close to his chest to immobilize it. He stood stiffly and swayed slightly, and Casey quickly grabbed one of his arms, pulled it around her neck and walked him over to a tree, helping him down.

"Now," she said severely, "it's your turn. Take off your shirt."

He was too tired to object. And he hurt too damned much. With Casey's help, he painfully took his shirt off and she looked at his bruised ribs with concern. Taking a wide strip of cloth she bound his chest tightly, then swabbed at his various cuts. It was the second time she had performed such intimate functions for him, and her hand lingered just a trace longer than necessary on some of the bruises, ignoring his protestations that Ty needed her more. She wished she could take some of his hurts on herself, make that stern mouth smile, ease the lines around his eyes.

But his eyes were unfathomable and hooded, their amber sparks stilled. She wanted to kiss him, to soothe his sore, hurt body with her hands, but his expression was forbidding. And his words, when they came, were curt.

"We can't stay here long. They're combing the hills and we can't be found together."

Casey looked at his bound ribs, then Ty, and shook her head. "Neither of you can travel far." Then she remembered Jennie Monroe. Their ranch wasn't far away, according to the girl's directions. It would be just the place to deposit Ty, she thought with a mischievous glitter in her eye. And he would be too weak to protest.

"I know a place," she said, and Sean regarded her doubtfully.

"We can't go back to Fortitude..."

"I know. Remember those three days Ty was missing?" Sean nodded.

"Well I found out what happened. Some of Wilson's

men raided a ranch south of here. Ty rescued the ranchers and killed four of the outlaws.'' There was a note of pride in her voice.

"Did Ty tell you that?" Sean said sourly. He liked neither the pride nor the fact that she knew about it when he didn't.

"No," she said, wondering at his peculiar attitude. She had thought he would be pleased. "I met someone in town who told me." She didn't see any reason to tell him it was the same girl whose name had wrought such a strong reaction from Ty a few days before.

"Do you think we can trust them?"

She nodded.

"All right, we'll try it. There's a full moon tonight, and we can travel late. In the meantime I'll get some rest. Wake me when you think Ty can move." He longed to reach out and gather her to him despite the pain. He needed her softness to chase away the despair.

But she was angry with him, perhaps angry enough to turn to Ty.

"Sean..."

His eyes regarded her warily.

"I was so glad to see you...so grateful you weren't killed."

There was something tremulous in her voice, and his grim mouth softened. "You almost had him yourself, little wildcat. Go see to Donaldson." He turned around so she wouldn't see the pain in his eyes.

They left at dusk. Sean had to help Ty into the saddle, and he tied him there. He didn't want him to fall, not with the shoulder as it was, and Ty was weak from loss of blood. That he protested little and didn't even ask their destination told both Casey and Sean exactly how weak.

Sean was still drained, physically and emotionally. It was

over at last, his long search for Wilson ended. The man would no longer be a danger to him and those he loved. But there was no sense of victory, only a deep, dark emptiness. He had had only a few hours of restless sleep in the last couple of days, and the fight with Wilson had completely enervated him. Perhaps it would dull the pain of losing Casey, of knowing they would soon be going separate ways. She had become a part of him. He didn't know how he could bear the loss.

Even now, she was unnaturally quiet, her attention riveted on Ty, and he felt the gulf between them.

He tried to think of other things...of San Antonio, his ranch, his nephews and nieces. But the thoughts only pierced him with new regret.

Sean was leading Ty's horse, and he stopped to check on the injured man. Even in the moonlight, Ty's face was unnaturally pale and his lips compressed in a straight, tight line. He tried to smile when he saw Sean's eyes on him. "I'll make it, preacher," he mocked painfully.

"Want to rest?"

"I'd never get back on," Ty replied through clenched teeth. "How much longer?" He had been drifting in and out of consciousness, barely aware of his direction.

"Casey says not far."

"Ah, Casey," Ty said. "Hell of a woman."

Sean felt the knife dig deeper. "She is that," he answered hollowly, then started the journey again.

It was dawn when they came to the Monroe ranch. Ty was unconscious, slumped over the saddle. They were nearly to the house when challenged by two men who seemed to appear from nowhere, their rifles aimed directly at the three newcomers.

Casey leaned down and spoke to one of them, but Sean couldn't hear her words. The man turned to his companion, said a few words, then hurried to the house, leaving the other with his rifle trained on Sean.

The door of the house opened slightly and Casey caught a glimpse of Jennie Monroe. Casey couldn't hear the conversation, but she saw the door bang against the outer wall as Jennie tore down the steps and ran across the yard to where the three of them waited. She went directly to Ty, her own face turning almost white as she curtly ordered the two ranch hands to untie him and take him inside.

A man followed her out of the house. His face full of questions, he approached Sean.

Sean leaned down. "My name's Sean Mallory. I understand you know Ty, that we might be able to rest here."

Kurt Monroe offered his hand. "I'm Monroe," he said. "Jim Tyson's welcome here…and any friends of his." He looked curiously at Casey, and back at Sean. "What happened?"

"The Wilson gang."

Monroe's face tightened. "Are they behind you?"

"Wilson's dead. The rest are either dead or captured."

"Thank God for that. Come in. You both look tired and hungry."

Sean's smile was only a shadow. "I would…we would…like to see how…Jim is."

"I think my sister's probably taking very good care of him. We owe him a lot."

"I'd like to hear about it," Sean said slowly.

"And I would like to hear about Wilson," Monroe replied grimly.

When they reached the inside of the house, Sean and Casey could hear Jennie Monroe moving around in another room. Casey looked at Monroe. "Maybe I can help," and again Sean felt a sting of jealousy as she left the room.

When Monroe lifted an eyebrow in question, Sean said

simply, "Casey Saunders. Wilson killed her father. We and…Jim…had been tracking Wilson for months."

"What happened?"

"The good people of Fortitude," Sean said wryly, "decided they would no longer tolerate Wilson and his bunch…thanks in part to Jim's efforts. Wilson got away and ambushed Jim and Casey."

"Who killed him?"

"I did," Sean said flatly. "But not before he shot Jim. I appreciate you taking him in."

"You and the girl look half-dead yourselves."

"I need some sleep, then I'll be on my way."

"You're welcome to stay."

"My business is finished," Sean said bleakly. He stared at Monroe for a moment. "Tell me about Jim Tyson. What happened here?"

Monroe briefly related the events, leaving out the fact that his sister had been pining away ever since Tyson had left. He had mixed feelings about their benefactor. Gratitude, certainly, but also a certain fear.

"Who is Jim Tyson?" he asked suddenly.

Sean pondered the question carefully, not knowing exactly why it was asked. The answer, when it came, was as much for himself as for Monroe. "A man," he said quietly. "A strong man. A loyal friend. There's no one I would rather have by my side."

Sean was so damned tired he didn't notice Monroe's sigh of relief at his answer. He absently ate the breakfast that was put in front of him and accepted Monroe's offer of a bed in the bunkhouse.

Casey watched Jennie's gentle hands take the bandage from Ty's shoulder. Despite her care, the pain of taking the sticking cloth from skin jarred Ty back into consciousness.

He started to curse, and then his eyes found hers and opened wide in disbelief.

"What...? How?"

"Be still," Jennie said. "I'll try not to hurt you."

Even his pain seemed to seep away with the miraculous sight of her. How he had dreamed of this, of those hazel eyes looking at him in that tender way, yet he didn't want her to see him like this. So weak. So helpless.

His gaze moved and found Casey at the end of the bed, a familiar gleam in her green eyes, like the times he had played poker with her. Damn her interfering, anyway.

And then he felt Jennie's hands on him again, soothing hands that were feather light against the hurts and bruises of his skin. He saw something in her eyes and his breath caught in his throat and lodged there until he thought he would burst. "Jennie," he said achingly, hope and fear battling within him. She didn't know who he was, not really.

It was as if Jennie Monroe recognized the dread in his eyes and understood it. "Casey told me everything, Ty Donaldson. I think you're the bravest, most wonderful man I've ever met."

Utter confusion spread over Ty's face as he slowly comprehended the words. A smile started on his lips and spread to his eyes, softening the hard face.

Casey felt a tear as she saw the untapped love in him springing forth. She left the room, knowing that neither Jennie Monroe nor Ty Donaldson were aware of her presence.

Sean was gone, and Kurt Monroe said he was in the bunkhouse. A wave of desolation swept over her. She had wanted to feel his arms around her so badly. After seeing Jennie and Ty together, she longed with all her heart to see the same look in Sean's face, to rekindle the fire of his touch. What had happened in the past few days?

But then he had never spoken of a future. Never indicated there would be anything beyond Wilson's destruction. She had been a fool to think otherwise. With sudden determination, she turned back to Ty's room. She would say goodbye, leave before Sean woke. Pain churning inside her she spun back into the bedroom, waiting until Ty and Jennie finally noticed her.

"I want to say goodbye," she said in a tight, strained voice. "I'm leaving."

"With Sean?" Ty's voice, usually so strong, was weak but full of concern. "He shouldn't travel yet."

"No," Casey said. "I'm going alone."

Ty looked at her determined face. Her pain was clearly visible. He tried to sit, groaning as he did so. He turned to Jennie. "Will you leave us for a moment?"

"Casey," he said as soon as Jennie had retreated behind the curtain. "What in the hell...?"

"I'm just a responsibility to him," Casey cried out desperately. "I'm not...I don't know how to be..."

Ty was stunned. After weeks of watching Casey and Mallory together he was amazed at Casey's stupidity. But then Sean had been acting strangely, too. He started to say something, but Casey interrupted. "I just...just wanted to say goodbye... I'll... Goodbye." Tears streaming from her face, she ran from the room.

"Jennie..." he shouted.

Jennie had seen Casey's tears as she ran from the house to the stable where her horse had been taken. She hurried back into the room. "What..."

"Those two fools," Ty said. "Help me up."

"You can't."

"I can," Ty said, wincing as he tried to stand.

Jennie hesitated, wishing Kurt were here, but he had

gone outside minutes ago. Seeing the determined look on Ty's face, she knew she couldn't stop him.

He leaned on her and they walked out the door as Casey and her horse disappeared from sight. Ty started a curse, then swallowed it as he looked at Jennie, struggling under his weight. He banged into the bunkhouse, searched quickly for a body and lowered himself next to the only one there. His hand jerked Sean awake.

"Casey's leaving," he said as Sean's eyes opened.

"Casey? Where? Why?"

"Because she has some damn fool notion you don't want her."

Sean's face creased in pained confusion. "But...you and Casey..." Then he saw the way Jennie and Ty were holding each other, the quick warmth that passed between them.

"Damn," Ty said with disgust. "You two deserve each other. Go after her, Mallory, or you're a bigger fool than I thought."

Sean needed no more urging.

"Kurt's horse is outside," Jennie said. "Already saddled."

Sean looked at Ty and Jennie and smiled slowly. Then he was gone.

"You have some strange friends," Jennie observed quizzically.

Ty grinned through the pain that was, once more, making itself only too well felt. "I do, don't I," he replied, and the two of them stumbled back to the ranch house.

It took Sean an hour to catch up with her. Casey had stopped and dismounted at the top of a hill overlooking the Monroe ranch. She couldn't quite let go, not yet. The future seemed impossibly bleak. She didn't know where she would go.

She did have several hundred dollars from her gambling.

Perhaps she would go to California and see the ocean. The thought left her even more depressed than before.

Casey heard hoofbeats and turned, her heart leaping like a frog as she saw Sean approaching.

She took a step backward as he bounded from the horse, disregarding his ribs, his hurts, his exhaustion. His eyes never left her face as his hand cupped her chin.

"And where do you think you're going?" he asked softly.

"California," she said defiantly.

"Such a long way?"

"I've always wanted to go to California," she said.

"Texas is better."

"Texas?" she said in a small voice.

"If you don't think being a rancher's wife would be too dull."

"A rancher's wife?" she echoed, dumbfounded.

"My wife," he said, holding his breath.

"Your wife."

His mouth lowered to hers and caressed it persuasively. "Hmm," he murmured.

She reluctantly tore herself away. "I don't know how," she said, shame in her voice.

"I didn't think there was anything you couldn't do," Sean countered with the lazy smile she loved.

Hope started to build within her but fear still remained. Her green eyes clouded with doubt and misery. How would she ever make an acceptable wife for someone like Sean?

"Will you marry me, Casey?" Sean pressed.

"You…you're just repaying a debt. You don't have to, really you don't."

"Debt, damn it. I've heard enough about debts to last me a lifetime," he growled, suddenly angry. "I hope I never hear the word again."

"But…"

"I love you, Casey...I think I have almost from the beginning. I love your shining smile, and those green eyes..."

"But..."

"I love everything about you...your independence and stubbornness, your curiosity, your warmth. But I wanted you to be sure... I saw you with Kelly...and Ty...and you're so damned attractive..."

Casey saw the uncertainty in his face. *He* was unsure about *her*. Her heart trembled with the sudden comprehension. He, who was so sure about everything, was afraid.

The hope expanded. "I love you," she said shyly. "But..."

She was stopped once more by his lips. When he finished nuzzling them satisfactorily, he drew back. "I was afraid you loved Ty."

"Ty?" she replied, amazed at the thought. Ty, who was like a brother?

There was so much astonishment in her voice that he knew, as Ty so indelicately put it, he had been a fool.

"You were so angry..."

"Not anymore."

"And you're so young..." He stood there awkwardly, wanting to make her aware of her choices while inwardly terrified he might lose her.

"You're my life," Casey said, and leaned against him, feeling his arm go around her. She felt the tenderness that made her go weak at the knees. She loved his strength, his gentleness, his easy way with people. She loved the way he smiled and crinkled his eyes, and the way his strong, lean fingers caressed a guitar.

Now, leaning against him, she drew his hand to her cheek, pressing it against her skin. She felt the fingers tracing intricate patterns, felt the love in the touch, the quiet wonder and need in their tentative query.

Casey looked out over the valley. The setting sun was

turning the sky the color of honey. A color of peace. Of richness. Like the richness she felt inside.

Casey turned to Sean. Only he could ever make her soul sing like this. She could barely stand the sweet agony of loving so much.

His lips touched hers with infinite promise. "Casey, my love," he whispered. "Cassandra. The daughter of gods…will you marry me?"

"A foreteller of the future…" she teased. "Are you quite sure you want that?" Her voice was husky with a promise of its own.

"Only if you are part of it," he said.

"Now and forever," Casey whispered and felt his arm tightening around her. They both looked out over the valley, seeing the soft hues of the sunset ignite into splendid layers of cinnabar and crimson.

Like their love, Casey thought with sudden insight. She loved Sean in so many ways. In so many wonderful, tumultuous, challenging ways. Yet there was a harmony there, too.

His soft voice was like a teasing breeze. "Then you will marry me? It's a hard life." He still was hesitant to believe she could be content with him.

"Not as hard," she retorted slyly, "as protecting you, I suspect."

"Especially against my will. Ty told me about Fort Worth. Will you ever obey?"

"No," she answered, her green eyes sparkling. "Want to take back the offer?" She saw the answer in his eyes.

"And ruin the challenge?" he asked lazily, an invitation in his eyes. "I don't think so."

Once more, his lips touched her mouth and he knew how true the words were. There was something about her that made him feel alive, that made each day a heady adventure.

Ever since he had met her, each day had been brighter, the sun more brilliant.

"You make the world glow," he said, and Casey leaned contentedly against him, telling him wordlessly, it was their love that made it so.

Epilogue

January 1868

Dear Jennie:

It's good to hear that you and Ty are safely settled in Montana.

Sean wants you to know that Ty no longer has any legal problems in Texas. Ben Morgan went to Fort Worth as soon as we returned, and discovered that Mr. Caldwell had died of a heart attack. With the old man gone, he found witnesses to testify to the fact that the younger Caldwell provoked the fight, and all charges have been dismissed.

Sean also checked with the law in Colorado. Since Ty didn't show up in town that Sunday, no one could directly connect him with Wilson's doings, and he was never charged.

As for me, I couldn't be happier. Sean's sister, Ryan, has been wonderful. I was terrified at first that she would think Sean had made a mistake. When we arrived I put on a dress and petticoats and even a corset. It was even worse than I'd imagined. We had to take a buggy over to the Morgan ranch. Sean couldn't stop grinning and I wanted to murder him. Ryan was so nicely dressed and she tried to be friendly but I didn't know how to talk to her. It was the worst hour I've ever spent in my life. I was almost crying when we left. When we got home, I took off the clothes and put on a pair of pants and headed for the stable.

As I left the house, a lone rider came into view. It was Ryan, and she, too, was wearing pants. She just stared at mine and started laughing. It seems we were both trying to impress the other, and neither Sean nor Ben chose to tell us differently. It probably would have gone on for weeks if Ryan hadn't decided I should meet her as she really was. No wonder Sean was in stitches. I could have killed him that night.

You would like Ryan. She and Ben have a houseful of children, a son of Ben's, a girl and boy they adopted, and a pair of twins who are always in trouble. But irresistible. Ben spoils them all dreadfully. I've never seen a gentler man with children...or with his wife. They're so in love, it hurts to watch them.

Ryan said the same thing about Sean and me. I never thought I could love him more than I did that day at your ranch, but it seems the love between us just keeps growing. We are working hard to fill our own house with children.

I hope this letter finds you and Ty well. Tell him I miss him. But only a little.

Please write.

Casey

April 16, 1868

Dear Casey:

It took two months for your letter to get here, and Ty and I are both grateful to you and Sean and Ben Morgan. But Ty doesn't think he will ever return to Texas. He is just too well known there.

Here, he's just Jim Tyson, rancher and sheriff.

Yes, he's been elected sheriff. Not because he's fast with a gun. He never completely recovered from that wound, but because the people here like him. In the seven months we've been here, there's scarcely a man he hasn't helped. He often curses Sean bitterly, blaming it all on him. But secretly I think he's rather pleased with himself.

We have a foreman to help with the ranch, and there's not much danger in the sheriff's job. It involves mostly settling small disputes. There isn't even a jail.

I told Ty I was writing to you and he said to ask the preacher and the hellion if they would be godparents to our first child. In about six months.

Let me know your answer.

Affectionately,

Jennie

* * * * *

Against the Wind

Chapter One

Independence, Missouri
June, 1866

The woman's eyes opened wide, suspicion clouding their soft hazel color, when she heard Seth Hampton's drawl. The hopeful, even eager look on her face froze.

With a sinking heart, Seth Hampton waited for the condemnation he sensed was coming. God knew he'd heard it all the way to Independence. General Lee had surrendered, the Confederacy had collapsed, but he wondered now whether the war would ever truly be over. He had traveled several thousand miles to escape it, but now he saw something close to hatred reflected in eyes that were much too wary, much too weary, for a young woman.

And much too familiar. They were part of what he'd hoped to escape: the years of pain and violence and grief. And the memories. And the nightmares.

Kate MacAllister. That was her name, according to the wagon master. It fitted her. No-nonsense. No frills. Although with those lovely eyes she probably could be quite pretty, her hair was drawn back and well covered by a sunbonnet that did little for the oval shape of her face. And her dress, though clean, was so faded he could barely tell what color it might once have been. But it fitted slender curves, and she moved with a grace that was appealing.

So was the inherent strength in her face. It was written all over the determined jaw and the strong, firm line of her mouth. But now, a hostile expression had spread across her face, and a sense of sad futility swept through him. Nothing had changed in the past year, nothing at all.

"Is that a Southern accent, Dr. Hampton?"

He nodded once, keeping his eyes as expressionless as he could. He needed her. She needed him. It should have been that simple, but nothing was simple these days. "Does that make a difference, Miss MacAllister?"

Her eyes grew even more frosty. "Did you fight for the Rebels?"

Seth's jaw set. "I doctored for the Confederacy."

Her chin jutted out. "Did you fire a gun?"

He had. Several times, in fact, when a wounded man on the ground was being threatened. He didn't know whether he had killed. He'd prayed to God he hadn't. Seth nodded.

"We don't need you, Doctor," she said abruptly. "We don't need a traitor." She turned her back to him and started to walk away.

Seth reached out a hand to stop her. He felt her tense as she stilled and turned back to him, and he tried to measure his words. "The war is over, Miss MacAllister. We've all suffered, but now it's over."

"Not for me," she said, in a voice that was obviously just barely under control, as her hazel eyes flashed with anger. "Nearly my whole family is dead. Two brothers dead, a third brother dying. My parents dead of broken hearts. My fiancé lies somewhere in Pennsylvania. All because you Southerners wanted to keep slaves." Her voice broke. "And you think it's over? Forgive and forget? Oh, no, Doctor. Not ever! We don't need help from the likes of you. We'll find another way to get to California.''

"There is no other way," he said quietly. "Not for you. Or me. Not this year."

"Then we'll stay here." There was the slightest sheen in her eyes, as if she were fighting back tears, and for the first time she looked vulnerable, despite her anger. Seth didn't even try to stop her when she turned again, not until she stumbled slightly, and then he took two long steps to steady her with his hand. Her head swung toward him, and he saw the tears, no longer hovering, but splashing down a face filled with despair. She made a futile effort to wipe them away with her hand, then jerked from his grasp and almost ran toward a group of covered wagons clustered in the shade of a grove of trees.

Seth felt as if a fist had plowed deep in his stomach. But the wagon master had warned him. No one wanted a Southerner on this trek west. But he'd had to try.

"I'm sorry, Doc. I really hoped it would work." The wagon master's voice was sympathetic. He had been hovering nearby, hopeful and anxious over the outcome of the meeting.

Seth turned to see Cliff Edwards. He shrugged. "Maybe I'll try it on my own."

"I wouldn't advise it," Edwards said. "There's been numerous war parties—Arapaho, Cheyenne, even Sioux out there. Indians think too many folks are coming onto their lands, and there was a massacre of Indians last year at Sand Creek. Didn't make them feel too kindly toward us. And even if there weren't Indians, you'd need some kind of guide to get you through the mountains and deserts. Why don't you just go back home?"

Home. Seth smiled crookedly. How could he tell him there was no longer a home, just a house where his brother and his brother's wife, the woman Seth had loved for years, lived?

"Guess I'll just wait around and see whether anyone else needs a hand," he said instead.

"Doc, I'd give almost anything I have to take you along with us. These folks don't know how badly we'll need a doctor before we reach California, but rules are rules. You have to have the required wagon and supplies. You being a Reb doesn't make them amenable to changing that, nor to any family taking you on."

"You don't feel that way?"

"Hell, it wasn't my war. I didn't lose anyone. But most of these people did."

"I did, too," Seth said. "A brother. Another brother fought for the North."

"Hell, maybe I should tell her that."

"I don't think it would do any good," Seth said wearily. "I've seen that look too many times."

"Her brother needs you. I wish I could make her see that."

Seth's interest was immediately piqued. "What's wrong with him?"

"Lungs, I was told. Got real sick in a prison camp. Andersonville. God-awful cough. Miss MacAllister said the army doctors claimed he wouldn't survive another winter in Illinois. But I just can't take them without another man along. He can't pull his weight. It takes a lot of strength to drive one of those wagons across this country. That's why I suggested you. God knows she's going to need you. Or someone like you."

Familiar pain coursed through Seth. He had thought he was escaping from the constant ache at the waste and destruction of war. At one time, he had even thought he might become immune to it, and he'd known many army doctors who had, who had even become callous about it. But he had realized back then that he didn't want that, for he couldn't accept the opium of indifference. He wanted to care. He wanted to keep his soul. No matter the price. And the price was high. So damnably high. The nightmares never stopped, and neither did the aching sense of loss. And now there was the rejection, even hatred, that he constantly faced.

But after the war, after his duty ended, he'd known he couldn't stay in Virginia. There were too many shadows there among the hills he had once loved, too many memories of shattered men and screaming horses. The once-joyful innocence of his life had been mutilated beyond repair.

The West. It had beckoned to him as the North Star had once beckoned slaves to freedom. An untouched land in need of doctors. A promised land without reminders of sweet, beautiful Blythe, or the time when he and his brother might have killed one another in the name of duty. A healing place.

He wished he could help Kate MacAllister. He wished he could help her brother. He wished he could heal just a few bitter wounds, both in himself and in the raw, agonizing aftermath of war. Fool's thoughts. His brother had called him a Don Quixote. Perhaps Rafe was right. Perhaps he was running from all the wrong things, rather than, as he'd thought, to the right things. But then Rafe had always said he had been running against the wind all his life.

Seth turned his attention back to the wagon master, who was looking at him oddly. Had so much time gone by while he was wool-gathering? "Do you think she might let me look at her brother?"

"I don't know," Edwards said. "You might ask her."

Seth figured he already knew the answer. He tried again on his own behalf. "You can't use a scout—?"

Edwards shook his head. "We have our two. And you

have no experience. Even if I did, some of these people would be mad as hell if I used their money to hire on a Reb. A private party, like the MacAllisters, taking you on... now that would be different.''

"You're leaving in four days?"

"Yep," Edwards said. "We're already late. Won't be any more trains this year, not unless they want to winter in the mountains. I hated delaying this long but we needed the time to get the wagons in top shape.''

Seth hesitated. The thought of the MacAllisters nagged at him. "The doctor said Miss MacAllister's brother can't stay here another winter?"

"That's what she told me."

"You can't...take her anyway? Even without me, or someone else?"

"The MacAllisters can't pay much. Few men are willing to take on that kind of responsibility and hard work without a damned good reason. Now you—you look responsible. I was willing to take a chance on you, but not some of the others she talked to. Got fifty families depending on me. A weak link can get people killed. You break your rules once, you might as well not have any at all. Sorry, Doc.''

"Which wagon is she?"

Edwards paused. "You sure you want to do that? Try again?''

Seth shrugged. "I've spent four years getting through a war. I suppose I can survive another one. In any event, maybe I can help the brother.''

Edwards searched his face. "I hope you can—if they will let you. I feel damned bad about this. They've already bought the wagon and supplies, but then Jeremy got sick real bad. I just can't risk it, Doc. I can't.''

Kate had nearly beaten the material to oblivion. She had meant only to wash it, but now, as she looked at Jeremy's shirt, she noted with dismay that she had nearly ruined it. There were new rips in the cotton cloth, which was already threadbare.

She couldn't quite make herself wish it was the Reb, rather than the shirt, that she was thrashing. She had never physically struck any living thing in her life. But she felt totally justified in striking out at this innocent piece of cotton cloth. For a moment, it represented her loathing for anything—and anyone—Southern.

She was particularly bitter at the thought of showing the Reb her disappointment moments ago, of showing even a hint of frustration. She hated the thought of tears, much less exposing them to a—a hateful Reb. She hadn't really cried since the disasters started, the disasters, one after another, that had caused her to leave the only home she'd ever known, the place where she had once felt safe, so long ago.

She'd had to be strong for her brothers, eleven-year-old Nick and nineteen-year-old Jeremy. She couldn't show any weakness, because she feared that if she did she might shatter into a million pieces, like a collapsing dam. She often felt like that these days, full of cracks and on the verge of breaking. And if she did, what would they do?

So she had armed herself with whatever weapons she could find—mostly anger against the Rebels who had caused all this. They were the target to blunt all the sorrow and grief and anguish of the past four years. Anger had helped her survive and had given her the strength to keep the farm going for Jeremy—even if it meant working twelve hours a day in the fields. And then Jeremy had come home so wounded in body and soul that even that goal was gone.

She had learned to block away other emotions, bottling them so tightly that they couldn't get out. This way nothing would weaken her purpose in saving what was left of the

MacAllisters. There was no longer any laughter, tears, or even smiles. She knew deep inside that her stoicism was not good for Nick or Jeremy, yet she didn't know how to undo it without coming apart altogether.

She nurtured harsh thoughts toward Cliff Edwards for even suggesting the Reb to her, for building hope that perhaps she had finally found a hired man he would accept. Mr. Edwards knew what had happened to her family, knew that Jeremy had almost died in a Reb prison. How dare he suggest she hire a—a traitor? Even Jeremy had agreed with her decision when she told him minutes ago, though he couldn't hide his own disappointment.

Kate needed some relief from the anger and frustration she felt. She had to get Jeremy to California. She had to. But not through the help of a man who'd helped destroy him. She took a pair of pants and started to pound on those.

Taking a Reb with them to California! She'd rather take the devil.

But, dear God in heaven, what would they do now?

If they will let you. Cliff Edwards's last words. If the MacAllisters would let him help. After meeting Miss MacAllister and watching the anger boiling in those expressive eyes of hers, he knew it was a very big *if*.

Seth returned to the rooming house where he'd left his medical bag. The room was cheaper and cleaner than those in the hotels, which had sprouted everywhere, it seemed. And the cost included meals such as he hadn't had in a very long time. Here he had found little hostility, at least once he'd said he was a doctor. The proprietress, Mrs. Rose, had had no kin in the war, and the city of Independence had leaned toward the south in its sympathies. He'd soon discovered, though, that Mrs. Rose didn't have much use for either side, after surviving both the Jayhawkers and the Bushwhackers.

Her husband had died years earlier in a mining camp where he had gone to make their fortune. He had sent her enough money to join him. The money and the news of his death had come on the same stage coach. So she had invested the money in a house in which she could establish a livelihood. Hence, she'd begun to mother her boarders, as well as her two children. One had just survived measles through the help of a doctor, and she would hear no wrong said about any of them. She had taken Seth to her quite ample bosom with the express intention of coddling him and fattening him up.

She greeted him now as he came in, her face beaming as she told him she had, just this minute, taken an apple pie from the oven. Seth, as usual, didn't have the heart to argue. Hers was one of the very few friendly faces he had seen since Kentucky, and her pies were very, very good.

He gave her his most engaging grin. "Do you suppose I can buy half that pie from you?"

"No," she said. "Absolutely not. But you can take it as a gift."

"Mrs. Rose," he said, thinking the name fitted her perfectly, with her plump cheeks and happy disposition, "that just isn't right."

She puffed herself up, obviously used to controlling her boarders. "And who are you, Doctor, to tell me what's right?"

He backed down quickly from her indignation. "Then I thank you." He rose and went to the sink, pumping some water into his hands. "I'll be back a little later."

"Is that wagon train working out?" she said. "You know, this town needs another doctor."

"I know," he said, "but..."

"I know." She sighed. "The call of the West. I know it well."

"You're wonderful, Mrs. Rose," he said.

"Aye, and you remember that, Doctor."

Seth got together his medical bag and the half pie and rode his horse back to where the wagon train was camped, hesitating only a moment before dismounting and approaching the MacAllister wagon with his peace offering. He would probably end up with more pie than he wanted, and not exactly in the the place it belonged.

A boy was whittling outside the wagon. Seth guessed he was twelve or so and, upon noticing that he had the same hazel eyes as Kate MacAllister, decided he was probably her brother. The boy's eyes opened wide as he watched Seth approach, and then his nose wiggled as he sniffed the delicious smell that came from the pie. He glanced suspiciously, however, at the doctor's bag in Seth's other hand.

Greed was obviously battling with personal loyalty. "You that Reb my sis talked to?"

"I'm afraid so. I brought a peace offering, and hoped I could take a look at your brother."

The boy gave him a dubious look, but his eyes remained on the pie. "Kate's down at the river washing clothes."

"May I see your brother, then? And you could watch the pie for me."

"I don't know if I should do that. Kate said you was a Reb. She doesn't like Rebs."

"What about you?"

"I don't like 'em, either. Killed my two brothers."

"My brother was killed, too."

"He was?" Morbid interest shone in his eyes, although his back was stiff.

"Yep. And I have another brother who fought with the Yanks. Doctored a bunch of them myself. Mr. Edwards said maybe I could look at your brother." Seth offered a brief prayer for forgiveness for his lie.

"He did?" The boy obviously had made Cliff Edwards

a hero. "I guess it would be all right, then. Jeremy's not feeling so good. He's inside."

Seth nodded and handed the boy the pie. He looked at the piece of wood the boy was working on. "That's a fine-looking dog."

"That's Blacky," the boy said. "He died." It was said in the same singularly blank voice that Seth had heard too many times before, a voice that spoke of a kind of numbness to death. He felt the same pain he'd experienced earlier. No boy should have to take the fact of death so... naturally.

"I'm sorry," Seth said, but the boy only nodded, as if it didn't matter. "And who should I tell your brother gave me permission to enter?"

"I'm Nick. For Nicholas," the boy explained solemnly.

"Well, Nick, you take care of that pie for your brother, all right?"

The boy nodded and watched as Seth moved up to the wagon flap and rapped against the wood before pulling the canvas back and entering.

It was dark inside. And hot. A man was asleep on the one visible bed. His breathing was raspy and his color, even in the filtered, dim light, pale and unhealthy. Seth drew in his breath. The man on the bed looked so young—probably not more than twenty.

He stooped down next to the poster bed that rested along one side of the wagon. He noticed two additional mattresses rolled neatly underneath the bed, along with several boxes. Every square foot of space was utilized.

With a slight sigh, he listened carefully to the young man's breathing, and he knew the other doctor had been right. The lungs were damaged, probably by pneumonia or some other lung disease.

The young man moved slightly, his foot brushing a broom, which fell, and he woke up, slowly focusing his eyes on Seth. His eyes were brown, not the hazel of his siblings'. Seth recognized the wary look in them. Eyes that had seen too much.

"Who are you?"

"A doctor."

The man coughed—it was a hacking, painful cough—and reached for a cup next to him, sipping its contents slowly. His face showed his struggle to contain the cough.

Seth leaned down and opened the bag and took out a powder. "Here, add this."

The man looked at him suspiciously. "What is it?"

"Snakeroot. It might help. If not, we can try quinine."

The man was obviously going to refuse, but then he started coughing again, this time nearly gagging. He didn't seem to notice as Seth took the cup from his hand and mixed in the powder. He held the patient's head and guided the concoction down his throat. The coughing slowed, and the man looked up at him, his forehead beaded with sweat. "You're that Reb Kate told me about?"

Seth nodded.

"I thought she told you nothing doing."

"She did, but the wagon master said you were sick, and I thought I would see if I could help. Just temporarily. Unless you have a doctor?"

The man, Jeremy MacAllister, as Seth recalled, glared at him. "You're not wanted."

Seth smiled grimly. "So I've been told."

"Then get the hell out of here."

Seth ignored the anger. God knew he'd done it before, especially when he'd had to perform amputations. "Cliff Edwards said you were at Andersonville. Pneumonia?"

MacAllister coughed again, but it did not have the force of the previous episode. "Yeah, I was in that hellhole of yours."

"Was it pneumonia?" Seth insisted.

"How in the hell do I know? No doctors...at least none worth a damn. Even if there was, there was no medicine, no shelter, no food. I just know I was damned sick the whole time." His words came in short breaths, as if each came only with difficulty, and his voice was deepened by the constant coughing.

"When did this last spell start?"

MacAllister turned away from him without answering.

"When?" Seth's voice was sharp, authoritative, and the man—more a boy, Seth thought sadly—turned back to him.

"Two weeks ago," he finally said reluctantly.

"The cough's been getting worse?"

MacAllister nodded.

Seth could almost guess what had happened. The MacAllisters had arrived three weeks ago from Illinois. The strain of the trip and then the work involved in preparing for the trek west had probably sapped what little resistance and strength Jeremy MacAllister had had.

He went back into his bag. Nearly every penny he had was invested in that bag, and in a larger one in the rooming house. He pulled out another bottle of the powder he had just given MacAllister, and a bottle of liquid. "I'll leave this with you—it's snakeroot. And this is quinine. Use the latter sparingly. And rest." He straightened up. "I'll be in town a few more days. Cliff Edwards knows where. If you need anything—"

Seth didn't wait for parting words. He didn't want to give Jeremy MacAllister time to refuse his offerings, and that was exactly what he expected. He quickly stepped out of the wagon, noting the young boy still hovering nearby. The half pie was next to him, but there was a big thumb mark where he'd apparently tasted. Seth smiled to himself. At least there was enough boy left in him to do that.

He found his mount contentedly munching grass. Sundance had seen him through the last two years of the war;

he was one of the few surviving thoroughbreds from the
Hampton farm, which had once raised some of the finest
horseflesh in Virginia. Sundance, a bay whose coat had
once fairly shimmered in the sun, was still too thin. Even
a year after the war's end, the stallion had never reclaimed
the sleek beauty that had once been his. Instead, there was
a muscular gauntness that spoke of too many lean years.

Seth took just a moment to run his hand down the animal's neck, receiving a reassuring whinny in response as
Sundance moved his head to nuzzle him for a brief moment. Seth tied down his medical bag and swung into the
saddle. "We still have a long way to go, boy," he whispered. "Just maybe we'll do it by ourselves. What do you
think of that?"

Sundance flicked his tail in seeming agreement.

Seth sighed. It was pretty damn bad when your only
friend was a horse. Well, it had been worse.

"Let's go see if there's more pie," he said, and Sundance willingly trotted down the road back to Independence. Seth just wished he really cared about that pie but
he suspected that he wouldn't be able to eat any, and if he
did it would taste like ashes.

Balancing her wash in one hand and a bucket of water
in the other, Kate MacAllister emerged from the woods
along the river to see the Reb emerge from her wagon.
Anger, hot and violent, seized her, and she started to increase her pace, disregarding the water slopping out of the
bucket. But before she reached the clearing, she suddenly
stopped as she saw him run a hand down his horse's neck.
There was something about the way he did it that made her
watch, a sort of wistful communion with the animal, which
responded in kind.

And then he swung up into the saddle, and she thought—
reluctantly—that she had seldom seen a more natural horse-

man. There was so much grace between the two, a continual flow of movement that she couldn't contain a certain admiration and even envy.

He was bareheaded, she noticed, his blond hair glinting gold in the sun. She suddenly thought of his eyes, vivid blue-green eyes that had viewed her earlier with something close to compassion.

She shook her head. She didn't want to think of him in any favorable way. He was a Reb, part of the catastrophe that had destroyed most of her family and ruined the few remnants. Jeremy, Nick and herself. So much of their beings had been stolen away by the war: Jeremy's health, her future with the man she loved, Nick's childhood. Sometimes she thought the only thing that sustained her was hatred. Yet how could it be otherwise, when her mother and father and two brothers lay buried? How else could she not succumb to loneliness and fear?

Kate moved again, noticing that Nick was no longer outside. He must have stepped into the wagon, she thought. He had been wonderful with Jeremy—patient and uncomplaining, always turning down invitations to play with boys from the other wagons to sit with Jeremy or try patiently to tempt him with food.

Dear heaven, he was only eleven, so young to have lost so many. At least she and Jeremy had had their chance to be young. *Don't cry. You can't let Jeremy see you cry.* Kate forced down the threatening tears and pasted a smile on her face.

She stepped up on the short ladder into the covered wagon, wishing with all her might that they had not bought it. They had spent so much of their small hoard of money on the wagon and supplies, and now...

Kate had consumed most of the morning going to the suppliers, hoping they would repurchase the wagon and the other goods, but none were interested. A deal was a deal.

And she knew there would be no more takers, not this year. She hated to think Jeremy and Nick would have to spend the winter in this wagon, but they could not afford to rent even the meanest of rooms now, not and have enough money left to make a new start in California, if they ever arrived. Choices. All of them equally harsh. She felt so completely helpless.

There *was* the Reb. But that was no choice at all, no matter what the wagon master thought. She couldn't stand being so close to someone who had been in any way involved with what had happened to those she loved. She couldn't put her family in the hands of someone like that. She couldn't.

He's a *doctor,* a traitorous part of her mind said.

But he said he'd fired a gun. He was as bad as any of them.

A doctor. A doctor for Jeremy.

She couldn't. She'd already discussed it with Jeremy. He'd agreed with her. His one experience with a Reb doctor had been horrible; the prison doctor had been an incompetent and a drunk, and had probably killed more Union soldiers than disease had.

Jeremy was sitting up, which was an improvement, and he and Nick were arguing about something. Kate's eyes rested on an object in Nick's lap.

"What is that?"

Jeremy gave her a sullen look. "That Reb doctor came by here. Tried to bribe Nick with that damned pie and me with some medicine. Probably just flour, or something."

But Jeremy did look a little better. Not quite as flushed as he had hours ago. Kate looked at Nick's hopeful face. Perhaps she shouldn't have been so tight with the money. It had been so long since he'd had any kind of treat. Part of her wanted to take the pie and throw it in the Reb's face another part looked at Nick's too-thin face and anxious eyes and wanted him to have everything in the world.

Her voice softened. "I think we can keep it. There's no sense wasting good food out of spite. I don't see any obligation. We've already told him no."

That was all Nick needed. He quickly found a knife and cut three pieces, offering the first to Jeremy, and the second to Kate. But Kate was afraid she might choke on it, no matter what she'd told Nick. "I'm going to save mine for tomorrow. You go ahead and eat while I hang up these clothes."

"You sure, Kate?" Nick said.

"I'm absolutely sure," she assured him as Jeremy looked at her warily. He, too, had looked a little longingly at the slice, sniffing it with more enthusiasm than she had seen him show toward food in days. She ducked out before either of her brothers could say any more and moved toward a rope stretched between two trees. She stretched upward, wishing she were a bit taller, and hung their clothes up.

She heard eager talk coming from the direction of the other wagons, and she tried to close her ears to it. She had depended so much on this trip—on the chance to take Jeremy to a warm, dry climate where he could improve. She hadn't realized how much she'd been depending on it until Cliff Edwards reluctantly refused them a place in the train. She had argued. She and Nick could manage. They had managed the farm alone these past two years. She'd done everything a man could there—plowed, harvested, even repaired fences.

But she hadn't controlled a team of four oxen, Mr. Edwards had retorted, not up mountain trails and across rivers. If only she could hire a man...

She had tried. Dear God, how she had tried. She had put up notices all over town. But they were going to California, and available single men were heading to the gold and silver finds in Colorado. No one was willing to take on the responsibility of a woman, boy and invalid for months.

No one but a Southerner, an ex-Reb, a lean man with hair of gold and a wistful smile. A dangerous smile, she was already discovering, since she couldn't seem to dismiss it from her mind. There had been something lonely about it, something that touched her in a peculiarly poignant way.

Her brothers would turn over in their graves. So would her mother and father, who, she was convinced, had died of grief as they lost one son after another. The doctor said it was her mother's fever, and her father's heart, but Kate knew the real culprit.

How could she even think of hiring him? It would be a betrayal of everything she'd loved. Her chin set. They would make do. She'd try to talk to Mr. Edwards again. Reason with him. Even beg if she had to.

But she just couldn't force herself to hire the Rebel.

Chapter Two

In the end, Kate had to swallow her pride. It did not endear Seth Hampton to her that he made it easy. She didn't want it to be easy.

She wanted it to be hard, so that she could hate him.

But after a talk with Cliff Edwards and then a conference with Jeremy and Nick, she'd known she didn't have any choice but to approach the Reb. Time had made her see reason, but it hadn't made her like it.

Another factor had prompted her surrender. Jeremy had improved the next day, after another dose of the medicine and the mixture of quinine. But she did not fool herself. If they ran out of medicine, which they would, and they stayed in the wagon during Missouri's cold winter, she could lose her brother.

Pride and dislike weren't as important as Jeremy. She'd thought of the word *hate,* but she'd eventually had to dismiss it. It had such an ugly sound, and, she'd been taught, hate was unworthy of the MacAllisters, who were—always had been—God-fearing people. Still, she couldn't help considering that particularly unwholesome emotion, and she didn't like Seth Hampton one bit for being so darn nice about her surrender.

She went to him the next afternoon. She had gotten nowhere with Cliff Edwards, not with pleas or with tears. He was even less sympathetic than before, now that he knew she had an option—an option he very much favored.

"Give the Doc a chance," he'd said. "If he doesn't work out, well, then we can leave him at one of the forts along the way."

Clenching her teeth together, she'd said she would talk to her brothers about it. Nick, strangely enough, had been in favor. Jeremy...well, Jeremy had argued and then understood the necessity behind it. It was either accept the Reb's offer or stay here, and Jeremy didn't want Kate to have to live in this wagon all winter. They didn't have time to try to find anyone else.

So Kate finally asked Cliff Edwards where Seth was staying and made the long walk into Independence. His landlady said Dr. Hampton was in the stable, and Kate, feeling dusty and sweaty and reluctant, went inside.

He was currying his horse, talking to it all the while, and she tried to listen, since he obviously didn't see her. "Miss Virginia, do you?" he was saying. "So do I, but just wait until you see California. They say it's the promised land for fine fellows like you. The richest grass you'll find anyplace. You'll get all prime and frisky again—" His words stopped, as if he had sensed something, and he turned around slowly, his eyes becoming wary when he saw her.

"Do you always talk to your horse?" She couldn't stop the question. She never heard anyone do that before. Horses were for working.

"We've come a long way together," he said noncommittally.

She hesitated. "I talked to Mr. Edwards."

He waited, he green-blue eyes steady and patient.

"I—we—don't have any choice but to hire you, if you still want to come."

"Accepted," he said. His eyes remained on her, but it was clear that he was demanding nothing more.

"We don't have much money to spare...."

"I don't need any," he told her. "I just needed a place on the train."

"No," she said abruptly. "We have to pay you."

"Food will be enough," he said, turning back to the horse.

"Mr.—Dr. Hampton?"

He turned back to face her.

"Thank you for the medicine you left. It did seem to help."

"I'm glad," he replied simply.

"But—"

"But you're still not happy that I'm going along with you?"

"No."

He sighed, and the sound was resigned, sad. "At least we have honesty between us."

"Neither is Jeremy pleased," she added, a little desperately. She was suddenly feeling addlepated in his presence, strangely susceptible to his easy charm. *Southern charm.*

"I know." Again Kate heard his resignation.

Kate wished he wasn't so reasonable, so infernally understanding. Resentment grew, but so did something else as she discovered that her gaze didn't want to leave his solemn one. She found herself studying his face and finding it difficult to dislike. His sandy eyebrows were thick, and arched in such a way that they gave him a relaxed, even lazy look. His features were regular, except for a cleft in his chin that made him look sensuous and vulnerable. He had a mouth that she suspected usually smiled easily. It had, the first time she had seen him, but now, while not grim, it had firmed into a straight line. His striking sea-colored eyes appeared depthless, as if they contained a hundred secrets.

"Why do you want to go west, Dr. Hampton?"

"Is that important?"

"Yes, to me it is. We have to trust you."

"Do you, Miss MacAllister? Trust me?"

"No," she said flatly. "I feel like I'm being blackmailed by Mr. Edwards."

"I think we both are, Miss MacAllister. We'll just have to live with it."

"You'll have to sleep outside. You understand that?"

"That's fine," he said easily. "I've been doing little else during the past few years."

It was the wrong thing to say, and he knew it almost immediately. She didn't need reminders of the side he had taken during the war.

"Miss MacAllister. Please understand one thing. I could just as well have served on the Union side. My only concern was saving lives."

"But you weren't on the Union side, were you, Doctor?"

"It didn't make any difference to me. I doctored the wounded from both sides."

"So our boys could go into your prison camps." Her words were bitter.

He shrugged. There was obviously no use arguing. "Did Edwards say when you're leaving?"

"Sunrise, day after tomorrow."

"I'll be there."

She hesitated. "There's not much room left in the wagon for your belongings."

"I don't need much. I came all the way from Virginia on horseback. Two bags, that's all. Mostly medicines."

She looked at him curiously. "All the way to California?"

He looked amused. "I don't need much, Miss Mac-Allister."

"Why are you going?" she asked again.

"There was no reason to stay in Virginia," he said. The amusement had left his eyes.

"No family?" She didn't know why she asked that. She didn't want to know. She didn't want to know anything about him. She didn't want anything to do with him but what was absolutely necessary.

"Two brothers, two sisters," he said. "Three in Virginia, one in the New Mexico Territory."

"You're lucky," she said, the bitterness creeping into her voice again as she turned around. "I'll tell Mr. Edwards he has his doctor."

"If your brother needs anything before then," Seth said, "send for me."

He received only a curt nod for his trouble.

Ten days passed on the journey, and speech between Seth and Kate and Jeremy MacAllister remained at a minimum. Only Nick seemed willing to give Seth a chance.

Each morning, Seth tied Sundance behind the wagon and drove the team and wagon over heavily rutted roads, his backside feeling every one of the ten to twelve miles they made each day. He longed, instead, for the saddle and the easy gait of Sundance.

He rode Sundance each night after the wagon train stopped for the night. Kate MacAllister had made it very clear that she wished to spend no more time with him than necessary, so he usually disappeared with one of the scouts, picking up tales about the trip west, about Indians, or about the buffalo that were being slaughtered by white hunters. It was usually very late when he returned to find a plate of food on the driver's seat of the wagon. Usually his bedroll had been placed next to the wagon and Kate had disappeared for the night.

Each family prepared its own food, although after a few days several families started to join together in the cooking duties. The MacAllister wagon, however, was usually avoided. The guides said it was because Kate was a single woman and he was a Reb. Neither were welcome additions to the train.

Jeremy continued to improve from the snakeroot and quinine. And, Seth thought, rest. At Seth's insistence, the MacAllister wagon led the train, so that the dust wouldn't irritate Jeremy's damaged lungs. It had caused some grumbling among the other families, but Cliff Edwards's orders were law.

This part of the journey was flat and dry. The only scenery was a few farms, including some that had been burned by either Confederate or Union sympathizers. The scars of war were still with them and did nothing to reduce the lingering bitterness in the MacAllister wagon.

Seth drove himself physically, never going to his bedroll until he was so exhausted he knew he could sleep. The nightmares that had haunted him since the war stayed at bay, however, and each morning he murmured his thanks for that fact.

He welcomed young Nick's company. Restless and bored with the slow pace, the boy often sat up on the seat with him, while Kate MacAllister stayed stonily inside the wagon with the older brother. There were endless questions, which Seth enjoyed. He had always liked children for their innocence and curiosity and open-mindedness. And that was particularly true now.

"What is Virginia like?"

"Green and lush, with rolling hills and wide rivers."

"Did you have slaves?"

"Nope. My family didn't believe in slavery."

"Then how come you were a Reb?"

Seth hesitated. Slavery hadn't been the issue to him. Loyalty to Virginia had. Loyalty to friends. But if he'd actually had to fight, he might well have chosen the North, as his brother had, because he, too, believed in the Union. As a doctor, though, he didn't see that sides made any difference. Just saving lives. Blue or gray. But he didn't know whether he wanted to explain that. His pride prevented him from saying anything that would even sound like an excuse.

"Doctors have no sides," he said.

"That's not what Kate believes."

"What do you think?"

"I don't know," Nick admitted. "I think I like you, even if Kate doesn't."

The honesty of childhood. Seth felt both pleasure at the boy's reluctant acceptance and a kind of aching hurt at Kate's continuing rejection. It was going to be a long, long trip. It already had been, in fact.

That night, Jeremy was well enough to help gather wood for the fire. Seth stayed at the campfire to keep an eye on him, rather than take his usual ride out. Some color was coming back into the young man's face, and his light brown eyes had life in them again.

Kate had taken off the sunbonnet she wore almost constantly, whether to keep the dust from her hair or for some other reason Seth could only guess at. He immediately thought someone should burn the damn thing, for her hair was her best feature, light brown and seemingly touched with gold. It softened her features, and she looked pretty and young, especially when she looked at Jeremy with something close to pleasure. She even spared Seth a look without the usual censure.

Scattered fires lit the dark night sky, and the haunting sound of a harmonica from one of the wagons drifted over the various campsites. Kate had made beans and biscuits, which had become their staple diet at night. Cliff Edwards said that once they left the farming country the men could start hunting and fresh meat should be available. But compared to the meals Seth had had during the war, the dinner, which tonight was hot, was a feast indeed.

Conversation remained stilted, however, as if a fence had been erected and the MacAllister side posted against a trespasser named Seth Hampton.

Yet there was a softness to the evening. A half-moon reigned overhead amid a sea of stars, and a soft breeze had brushed away the bruising heat of the day. Talk from the various wagons had stilled as the travelers listened to the sweet, sad strains of "Lorena," a song sung by both the Reb and the Yank sides during the war.

Kate sat still, her head tipped back, her eyes gazing into the distance, and Seth remembered her words that first day. A fiancé lost in the war. Jeremy, too, looked lost in time, in memories, and Seth felt an aching sadness of his own. He thought of Blythe and his brother, Rafe, and their child. But the hurt was not as strong as it once had been, the loss not quite as bitter. But the loneliness was still there. Deep and painful. He felt as if part of him were missing—the strongest, most giving part.

Kate looked up at him, and for the brief moment their eyes met, a sudden acknowledgment of loss and pain was exchanged—a second of understanding. But then, with a will Seth couldn't help but admire, Kate almost visibly pulled away, her face suddenly confused.

She almost leapt to her feet. "I'm going for a walk," she said.

"I'll go with you," Nick said eagerly.

She shook her head. "Not now. Why don't you go play with some of the other boys?"

Nick hesitated a moment, as if weighing the currents in the air, currents obvious even to him. But the boy's reluctance to join the other boys was clear. Seth realized then that he'd never seen Nick join boys his age.

"How about helping me find some wood for the fire tomorrow morning?" Seth asked. "Maybe we can find something for you to carve with."

Kate threw him an angry look, as if Seth were stealing something from her, and Seth merely shrugged, his own anger beginning to rise. Nick was still a boy, but he had been caring for his brother as if he were an adult, and no one seemed to notice. He suspected that Kate had so much on her hands herself that she had forgotten what it was to be young, to need some security and pleasure.

"He can go with me," Kate said ungraciously.

"Why don't we all go?" Nick asked.

Jeremy, who was leaning against the wagon wheel, looked interested. He had been barely civil to Seth in the beginning, but had now progressed to a wary acceptance.

"Miss Kate?" Seth inquired politely.

It was clear to him, and probably Jeremy, if not Nick, that Kate's whole reason for a walk was to avoid his presence. Yet this time he was not ready to let her off lightly.

Kate looked at her two brothers, one mildly curious and the other eager. It was Nick's face that helped her decide. He asked for so little and had gone through so much. She supposed she could tolerate the Southerner's company for a brief while. A very brief while!

She didn't understand, however, why the prospect wasn't as distasteful as it should be. She had watched him in the past ten days as he'd befriended Nick and even eased Jeremy's resentment. Both facts had stiffened her own resistance. And yet...

Seth Hampton had one of the most striking faces she'd ever seen. Though not classically handsome, as her betrothed's had been, it had a kind of integrity that she'd tried not to notice and a kindness that was difficult to ignore.

But he was still a Rebel. A traitor. One of those who had robbed her of everything, and part of her couldn't let go of that fact. She had stayed as far away from him as possible in the small area they inhabited, and she had even been a little grateful for the way he disappeared each night. She had also felt an odd disappointment. That made her even angrier. And more confused.

And tonight, when he had looked at her with pain in his eyes, with a loneliness that she instinctively knew matched her own, she was flooded with unfamiliar feelings—a rush of warmth and even empathy. Worse, she felt a flooding confusion she hadn't experienced since the war had started and so much had fallen on her shoulders. She'd been so sure she was right in disliking and resenting Southerners. In some way, it had made things easier to have an object to blame.

But Nick looked so expectant. Kate decided to tuck away her own feelings for the moment—just for the moment. "All right," she said as she put her arm around Nick's shoulder, effectively closing out Seth Hampton. If he noticed, he didn't show it. He just fell into step alongside them as the harmonica music changed from a ballad to a merry jig.

Nick, catching the mood, twisted loose of Kate's arm and darted ahead toward the stream. There were no woods here, only plains that bordered a narrow, shallow waterway still thick with mud stirred up by the many animals that drank from it.

The sky stretched to infinity, with a million stars sprinkled across its rug of blue velvet. For a moment, Kate felt a kind of peace she hadn't known in a long time, since the news arrived that her two brothers had been killed, along with her betrothed, and Jeremy, at sixteen, had run away to avenge them.

Now, however, as she looked at her brother skipping

stones, she felt a little tranquillity seep back into her soul. Jeremy was unquestionably better. They were bound for a town called Sacramento, a place of unusual beauty and opportunity, she'd been told.

Perhaps it was time to stop thinking of the past and start thinking of the future. It would be better for both Nick and Jeremy, and for her, too. She heard another splash, and looked up. Dr. Hampton had moved away from her and was stooping next to Nick, his hand returning to his side after evidently skipping a stone of his own.

A Reb skipping stones like her brothers had? But he wasn't like them. He didn't believe in the same things. The old anger refused to surface, though, and again a peculiar warmth curled unexpectedly through her. She saw the side of the Reb's face, its expression intent and serious as he searched the ground, like her eleven-year-old brother, for the perfect stone to make the perfect skip. There was something terribly endearing about the act—a wistful return to childhood that touched her in ways she didn't want to be touched.

He apparently found what he sought and picked it up, turning to her with a tentative grin. "Would you like to try?"

She surprised herself by taking it. One of her older brothers had taught her to skip a stone, but that had been a long time ago. She pulled her arm back and tossed, but the stone fell into the stream like a...like a stone. Nick tossed her a disgusted look and Kate felt a moment of chagrin before another stone was dropped into her hand and her arm was drawn back. The touch on her arm was gentle but firm, and it seemed to burn a hole in her skin.

"It's in the twist of the wrist," the Reb said solemnly, as if he were discussing a matter of the greatest importance. The gravity of his deep voice sent tremors through her. He had no right to be disarming. No right at all, she thought as she followed his instructions. She saw Nick's eyes on her, widening slightly at her apparent willingness, and she wondered whether she had been that much of an ogre these past months. She moved her wrist as instructed, and the stone still sank, just like a stone.

"You need a lot of practice, Miss Kate," Dr. Hampton said chidingly, his soft, drawling words curling around in the air like molasses dripping from a bottle. Dr. Hampton, she warned herself. Dr. Reb Hampton. She refused to think of him as Seth, even after these past ten days. She turned around and found herself inches from his face, from a sensuous mouth that was smiling slightly and eyes so bright that even in the night she felt they could light the sky by their own power. She had the worst urge to move ever so slightly so that their lips would meet....

The sound of the harmonica was still drifting through the air. Now, the notes were more plaintive, sad and filled with longing. Kate felt the sadness to the tips of her toes. She felt the whisper of Dr. Hampton's breath, warm and clean, and the tingling along her spine grew in intensity.

Dear God, was she that lonely, that foolish? She suddenly jerked away from his hand. She was as much a traitor to her family as he was to his country.

"I have to go back," she said, hating the trembling in her voice. "We'll be leaving at sunrise."

"Ah, Kate..." Nick said, his voice so normal that Kate envied him desperately.

Kate turned away from the eyes that looked into hers so steadily. She didn't want to look at Dr. Hampton. She didn't want to betray herself, and that, at the moment, was exactly what was happening.

"Come on, Nick. We have to check on Jeremy."

"No, we don't. He's doing fine."

"Nick!"

This time, her brother didn't protest, but Kate saw th

shadows return to his face, and once again she felt guilty. She transferred that guilt into her anger, which she directed toward this man who stirred feelings she didn't want. Or understand. "Leave us alone, Doctor. Stay away from me and Nick."

He stepped back, and his lips, which had been smiling, turned grim. "As you wish," he said. For a contrite moment, she watched him stride quickly along the stream, his stiff back counterpointing the usual easy grace of his walk. She felt something new throbbing inside her, not the sharp sword of loss, but rather an inexplicable poignancy. Was it for something that could never be?

She wished with all her might that they didn't need Seth Hampton. Perhaps by the time they reached Fort Walker they wouldn't. Perhaps then she could tell Cliff Edwards the arrangement just wasn't working. Hopefully, it would be too late then for Mr. Edwards to abandon them. It was a plan, at least. A plan that might help her keep her sanity.

For the briefest slice of time, Seth had felt whole. He'd felt real again, like someone who could accept pleasure. He had thought he had lost that simple feeling.

He had gone home after the war, to what had once been home. The farm that the Hamptons had built back in 1816 had been destroyed, and although his brother had asked him to join him in rebuilding it, he simply hadn't had the heart left. He had tried. Dear God, how he had tried, because it was so important to Rafe and Blythe. They'd wanted him as a partner to rebuild the family's reputation for breeding fine horses, and Seth had considered it. But he, too, had once loved Blythe, and he knew he would never really be comfortable with them. There would always be an ache in his heart if he stayed, a reminder of what he had lost. He loved his brother too much to be jealous of him, but neither would their house ever be his home.

His brother had wanted to give him money for his share of the land, but he had demurred. It would take Rafe a great deal of money to rebuild, and Seth didn't need much. When Rafe felt financially comfortable, he could then send Seth what he felt fair. Rafe had tried to change Seth's mind, but Seth had simply left one morning, leaving only a note behind. He didn't like goodbyes. There had just been too many of them in the past years.

Since then, he had molded his hopes and dreams and steered them in one direction: west. They didn't include anyone else, or even much expectation of happiness. Too much had been extracted from his soul after four years of bloody war.

And then, tonight, he had opened himself up again, only to have someone else slam closed the door of light. The shadows were back, clouding his mind with familiar images. He knew as well as he knew death always followed life that the nightmares would return tonight.

Seth would walk several miles, and then perhaps take a ride. Maybe he could wear himself out tonight, passing the dark hours awake. He didn't wish to wake up screaming, not with Kate MacAllister nearby. He had gone through that once with Blythe and had seen the pity on her face.

Seth didn't think he could stand that again. Even if Kate MacAllister had any pity left to give.

Chapter Three

The sound of moaning woke Kate. Her mind felt dense, and it took her a moment to clear it. Sleep had not come easily last night. She had found herself lying awake, listening for sounds under the wagon. She had been tense and confused, still bewildered by those womanly feelings of hours ago. Feelings she shouldn't have for an enemy.

It was growing increasingly difficult to think of him that way, and yet she must. She could never reconcile her bitterness toward the Confederacy and anyone who had been a willing part of it.

But still she'd wondered about him. He had looked so alone when she had torn herself from his grasp. She had heard him telling Nick he had family and she wondered why someone with relatives would leave them? He had spoken of his brothers with affection. But then, there was so much she didn't know, because she hadn't wanted to ask. She had told herself she knew everything she'd needed to know. He was a Southerner. But that argument wasn't working as well as it once had.

It had been very late when she finally fell asleep, and now she had to shake the heavy cobwebs from her mind to fathom the low cries she was hearing. Her first thought was Jeremy, but as she adjusted her sight in the dark wagon, she saw the he was breathing better than he had in weeks. Nick, too, was peacefully asleep.

The noise, almost a sobbing, was coming from below. Kate hurriedly pulled on a dressing gown. It was a worn, almost shapeless garment she'd had for years, but at least it covered her. She quietly moved to the opening of the wagon and lifted the flap.

The approach of dawn had lightened the sky to a dull gray, brightened only by a splash of light to the east. There was some movement near the horses and oxen, but she didn't know whether the disturbance was merely the early wakening of the beasts or the men already tending them. She jumped from the wagon and stooped to where she knew Dr. Hampton had been sleeping since they had left Independence. He had chosen a place nearby in case Jeremy needed him. As she watched him in the dim light of dawn, Kate felt an aching sense of shame. She had offered him nothing, not an extra blanket or pillow or anything to provide more comfort. He was thrashing now, and she saw the glint of something wet on his face. He was muttering— No, it was a moan. "No more," he was rasping out. "Please, God, no more."

And then: "Morphine!" It was almost a shout. "Got to have morphine!" His body shuddered, as if preparing for unbearable pain, and Kate thought her heart might break at watching such personal agony, such hopelessness. Even her own losses seemed less terrible at the sight of his racking grief. She swallowed the lump in her throat and reached out, touching his arm lightly.

He woke immediately, his eyes wide open and perceptive. He was so much quicker than she in reaching the same level of alertness minutes ago, and she realized he must have been aroused this way many times before. Necessity? Training? He looked toward her, and then his hand went to his face, and she knew he was searching for the wetness there, as if this nightmare had occurred before. She turned away, instinctively knowing he didn't want sympathy, or even acknowledgment of what had happened.

"I'm sorry," he said in the deep Southern drawl that had so infuriated her the first time she'd heard it. But now it had the slightest hesitation in it, and the unexpected vulnerability it implied was appealing. "I didn't mean to waken you."

"Of course you didn't," she said. "I was just going to start a fire."

Dressed in nightclothes? The unspoken question hovered between them.

He turned his face away from her, and she moved away to give him privacy, but not before she saw his arm go up and his sleeve brush against the dampness on his cheek.

Kate leaned against the wagon and looked up into the sky. The stars were fading now, and the moon looked nearly transparent as the first thin line of light started to spread over the horizon. She was hearing more noise now, as people were beginning to stir. Soon, one of Mr. Edwards's men would be knocking at each wagon, telling the occupants they had only a short time before departure. There would be the smell of coffee, perhaps some bacon, or even eggs that some of the women had purchased from farms along the road.

She sensed, more than saw, Dr. Hampton standing beside her. "I'll start the fire," he said, his voice firm again, with no trace of the previous hesitation. She turned. He was tall, about six inches taller than her own height, which was greater than most women's. She seldom had to look up at a man, but now she did, as she studied his lips, which twisted into a small, abashed smile, much like Nick's when he had been discovered doing something he shouldn't.

At the same time, though, Kate sensed he didn't want

any questions. His usually clear eyes were clouded and strained, and lines that shouldn't frame the eyes of one his age had etched trails in his face. His usually clean-shaven face was slightly bristled now, which, instead of making him look slovenly, had the opposite affect. She wanted to reach up and touch them, to feel those bristles across her cheek....

Good heavens above, what was happening to her? She was standing in her nightclothes before a man she detested and imagining the most absurd things.

"I'd better get dressed," she said, and turned, fleeing from him. Fleeing from herself.

Seth took up his former habit of riding Sundance at night and keeping a certain protective distance, in attitude if not always in geography, from Kate MacAllister and her family.

He had felt exposed that night when the nightmare returned. He had hoped, when he'd finally lain down in the wee hours of that morning, that he had exhausted himself enough to keep it from recurring. But, perhaps because he had allowed his emotions free rein that night, the nightmare had attacked even worse than usual.

The dream took him back to the medical tent during the last battle for Richmond. They had run out of chloroform, the most popular anesthetic, and morphine. There was only whiskey for amputations, and nothing for stomach wounds. The cries were haunting, and there was so little he could do without medicine. He could only try to save a few lives, often in such agonizing ways that he often wondered whether it was worth it. And then there were more wounded. Always more.

Seth didn't want to surrender to the nightmare, but sometimes even during a hot day he broke out into a cold sweat and memories bombarded him like the shells that had once rained on so much of Virginia.

Jeremy was growing stronger day by day, taking over some of the tasks Seth had performed. He unhitched the oxen at night, watered and fed them, and usually started the fire. Seth didn't protest. The boy—and Seth couldn't think of Jeremy in any other way—needed a certain amount of exercise or he would turn into an invalid for the rest of his life.

And this assumption of chores meant that Seth could spend more time away from the wagon. He started taking his evening meals with Cliff Edwards, listening to him talk about the trail and California.

Seth was also being called upon now for his medical skills by others in the wagon train. The first mishap occurred three weeks out of Independence, when one of the children was bitten by a water moccasin along a river. Two days later, a woman's arm was broken. And then there was a foot cut that went unreported and unattended until the foot had swelled to nearly twice its usual size.

Reluctance to call "the doc" disappeared gradually. He first charmed the children with his patience, and then the women as their children succumbed, and finally some of the men, one by one. His opinion was asked about stomach aches, gout, rashes, sunburn. But the thaw didn't quite reach Kate MacAllister's wagon, except for Nick. If anything, the atmosphere became more tense.

Seth understood what was happening. He recognized the attraction between him and Kate, no matter how hard she tried to fight it. Because she *did* fight it, he did, also. He was through with lost causes. God knew he'd had enough of them in his life. He was tired of fighting the wind— much less the tornadoes—that swirled around him with fury. He wanted peace. Dear God, how he wanted peace.

He also wished he could stop wanting Kate MacAllister.

Although she looked nothing like Blythe Somers, his first love, the two women had many similarities. Strength. Stubbornness. Total commitment to those they loved. And Kate could be damnably pretty when she took off her sunbonnet and allowed that sun-tipped hair to fall around her face, framing the hazel eyes that flashed and glowed.

Her eyes had been soft that morning after his nightmare. Even compassionate. But he didn't want her compassion. He wanted her acceptance. If she was unwilling to give him even the slightest chance to prove himself, then to hell with even trying.

Still, he wished his body didn't react as it did when she was around. It didn't do the same thing with the other marriageable young ladies on the train; in fact, more than one had signaled interest once he seemed to become socially acceptable and no longer just the "damned Reb."

But with Kate, it was always "Dr. Hampton," that stiff title combined with a deliberate coldness that conversely seared even more scars on his heart. Jeremy, on the other hand, while not burning up with gratitude, was at least following his suggestions without the glaring hostility that had accompanied their first days on the trail.

Over the next few days, the pace of the train quickened as much as possible; the wagons left before sunrise and didn't stop until sunset. Tempers grew short, but Cliff Edwards repeated the same litany over and over again. "We have to get across the mountains before the first snowfall."

They were nearly across "Bleeding Kansas," where they often passed burned-out farms and roving bands of men. Renegades, according to Mr. Edwards. The wagons were ordered to move closer together, and the dust was as thick as in a sandstorm, even at the front wagon. Earlier wagon trains had stirred and pounded the land into fine powder, and the slightest wind sent it sailing in swirling clouds that set everyone to coughing.

Jeremy's cough worsened again, and Seth fashioned him a face mask from a gunny sack and took back all his old duties, driving the oxen each morning after tying the canvas over the wagon to keep out as much of the dust as possible. The resumption of duties meant he couldn't go for his usual long rides, but those were now frowned upon by Edwards, in any event. Many of the guerrillas from both sides had taken up open banditry after the war, and the wagon master didn't want anyone wandering far from the main group.

Kate often took over the reins as Seth sat in back with Jeremy, spooning him various mixtures he hoped would help. But even the snakeroot didn't help much now. He gave him brandy to help him sleep and applied mustard-seed oil to the chest, as well as mixtures of stramonium and hickory leaves.

Kate's overt hostility softened at night as they worked together to get Jeremy to eat some broth, while Nick whittled silently in the corner, his hazel eyes shuttered, his usual questions silenced. Nick worried Seth as much as his brother.

Seth would lean back against the bags of flour and corn-meal and listen to Jeremy's breathing, trying to take the boy's mind off the effort. He discovered that Jeremy had enlisted at sixteen and that he was now only nineteen. He looked years older—except when he slept. But then, Seth knew he looked years older than his age, too. So did a lot of men now. He also knew why the boy sometimes fought sleep, because he did the same thing.

"What are you going to do in California?" Seth asked Jeremy one evening, as Kate sat in a corner mending a shirt in the light of a lantern.

"If I get there," Jeremy said.

"Oh, you'll get there," Seth said. "You're going to be my best advertisement."

Jeremy gave him a faint grin. "Not looking for any patients, huh?"

"Are you decrying my skills?" Pleased at the boy's banter, Seth gave him a devilish smile and continued, "I propose to parade you up and down the streets of Sacramento as evidence of superior ability. I wouldn't take it kindly if you interfered with that plan by not getting thoroughly well."

Jeremy's grin widened. "I'll do what I can, Doc."

Pleasure sifted through Seth at Jeremy's grin. It was the first time the boy had been more than civil to him. It also showed a new attitude, a hopeful one. "You'll have to see to that." He hesitated, then repeated his earlier question. "What do you plan to do when you get to Sacramento?"

"Become a storekeeper, if my sister has anything to do with it." Some of the light left Jeremy's eyes.

"And if she doesn't?" Seth felt Kate's eyes boring into his back. But he knew Jeremy needed his own dream to survive.

"A farm. That's all I ever wanted to do—farm," he said slowly. "But Kate thinks..." His words trailed off.

"You might be surprised how much better you'll feel, when you get out of this dust," Seth said. "I think you might be able to do a lot more than you think."

Jeremy turned away, as if unable even to think of such a miracle. And Seth leaned back against a lumpy sack of something and wished he could make the boy believe.

When Jeremy finally fell asleep, Seth nodded to Kate and stepped down out of the wagon. He needed a walk, to exercise the stiffness in his legs from sitting all day. He was surprised when he heard a voice behind him. "Dr. Hampton..."

He turned. Kate was behind him, her hair in one long braid in back. The embers from the fire on which she'd cooked a meal flared up, and he saw the anger in her eyes.

"Why are you giving him false hope?"

"It's not false hope."

"He'll never be able to plow and..."

"Miss MacAllister," Seth said patiently. "Don't ever tell him what he can't do."

"You want to kill another Yank?" she asked, her voice suddenly harsh and unforgiving. She knew she was being unreasonable, but she couldn't stop herself. He had trespassed on her life, and her brothers' lives as well. She didn't know whether her anger was directed at him or at herself for allowing him to make such an impact on them. On her.

"Don't be a fool," he said, venting the anger that he hadn't known was building up inside. "You'll kill him yourself if you coddle him. You'll drain the life from him."

"What do you know about his life, or our life?" she asked bitterly, "or what it was like before the war." They were beyond the wagons now, walking along a small bluff that overlooked the dry camp. "It's my family, not yours, damn you."

It was the first time she had ever cursed in her life, and she heard herself with horror. This was his fault.

"Is that it?" he asked softly. "Do you think I'm trying to take your family away?"

It was entirely dark now. They were beyond the campfires, and the sky was cloudy, hiding the moon and the stars and blocking out their light.

He heard a small sob. "I don't know what I think," Kate said, sounding like an abandoned child. His anger melted under the sound, replaced by tenderness.

He couldn't see her eyes. He could barely make out her features. The air was already tense, signaling a coming storm, and he felt the heated air vibrating with energy. His body was radiating the same heat, the same energy, the same tension.

"Ah, Kate," he said, his fingers reaching up and touching her chin, rubbing it ever so lightly. "You don't always *have* to know. Confusion is sometimes healthy."

"Someone *has* to...."

"Give Jeremy a chance. He's a man who's been at war. He's no longer a boy."

"But I want him to be." The cry was plaintive. "He should be. And Nick..." Her voice trailed off.

"Is much too old for his age," Seth interrupted, "but there are so many children like that now. My sister-in-law took in ten children during the war." He hesitated, knowing what she thought of Southerners. She had said it often enough. "Black and white, all of them had been abused one way or another, and by one side or another. Some renegade Southerners had killed the parents of one, Yanks had raped a runaway slave girl of thirteen. There was a boy, Jaime—he still lives with her—who reminds me of Nick. So much had happened to him, he tried to shut out the world. But he couldn't. None of us could."

"Why did you leave?"

He was silent for a long time. "Remember that nightmare I had?" he asked.

"Yes," she said.

"Virginia is beautiful. God's country. But after the war, whenever I looked at it, I saw death and destruction. It was everyone's battleground. Southern troops destroyed the homes of those loyal to the North, and Northern troops those homes that sheltered Confederates. I could never look at it and see the peace I once knew there."

There was such infinite sadness in his voice that Kate found herself hurting with him. She didn't want to. The South had brought on its own misery. But now she saw what he saw, and she found herself aching at the uselessness of it.

His fingers had moved now to trace her cheek, and again

she felt the gentleness in his touch. So sensitive, so light. Her head tipped up toward him, her eyes seeking the face she now envisioned nightly in her own dreams. She hadn't wanted to admit that, and had told herself it was an aberration. So was this. So was this need to comfort.

His lips came down and touched hers, searchingly at first. And then more firmly, as if finding what he was seeking. Kate found herself surrendering in a way she had never surrendered before, not even to the man she had planned to marry. She hadn't had this need then, nor this sudden hunger to right things that were so very wrong, not only for her, but also for him. She wanted to ease him as much as she wanted to ease herself.

All thought escaped her mind completely as she lost herself in his kiss—in the heat that enveloped them as if they had fallen into the heart of a volcano. The attraction between them exploded into flames so greedy they consumed everything in their path except their unexpectedly desperate need for one another.

Seth deepened the kiss, and what had started as a natural extension of those empathetic moments between them became something else altogether.

He felt her body respond as it unconsciously leaned against his and flamed a desire that was entirely unique in its depth and complexity. He hadn't thought he would— could—love again, not after Blythe, but what he was feeling came close to that. Very close. The physical feelings were even stronger than they had been with Blythe, perhaps because when he had kissed Blythe so many years ago she had been so young and innocent, and he had been careful not to go beyond the bounds of propriety. After that, he had loved her from a distance, because she was engaged to his brother.

But Kate MacAllister was not seventeen, and she responded in all the ways of a woman, although he knew it was not entirely willingly. He didn't want to think of that. He didn't want to think that once more he was pursuing something that was totally elusive.

He couldn't stop, however, not with her body yielding to his, just as her lips were, even though he knew that this was a mistake, that it was too soon. Her resentment and grief were still raw. But it had been so long since he had held a woman this way, so very long, and she was life and hope and pleasure. He needed all three to the core of his soul.

He knew she felt the same magic he did, the same momentary sense of something being essentially right. As his tongue nuzzled her lips, her mouth opened to his and her body melded itself into his masculine one. His arms went around her and his fingers played with her braid and then moved up to her neck, massaging with tender, sensuous strokes.

Kate had thoroughly confounded herself by opening her mouth to his, and now she found the taste and feel of his tongue dizzying. She felt her body quivering in the oddest way. She needed his steadiness and strength to keep on her feet, and she therefore, quite sensibly, leaned farther into him.

Nothing else, though, was sensible. The world was swirling with sensations she'd never known existed. She felt the strength of his arms and the movement of his muscles against her, which did things to her body that made her blood feel like liquid fire.

He took his mouth from hers long enough to whisper, "Pretty Kate," and the two words were immediately locked forever in her memory. They had been said so warmly, as if he really meant them. She had never really felt pretty before, and had never been told so. Not even by the man she was to marry.

Somewhere in the back of her mind, she tried to remember he was the enemy, that what she was doing was a betrayal of her family, but her mind, her heart and her body were not listening to each other. For this moment, nothing mattered but this wonderfully rich awareness that washed away all the worry and grief. She was so alive. So incredibly alive. His hands were so gentle, and yet each touch was deliciously painful.

His mouth settled easily on hers again, and she found her lips—her tongue—responding instinctively, seeking to explore every one of these extraordinary feelings. She craved more, and wondered at sensations that kept increasing in intensity, one feeding on another until her body trembled with expectancy, with the need to know how much more there was. Thomas Beck, her fiancé, had never aroused these kind of feelings.

The thought was invasive—and destructive. Thomas was dead, lying near her brothers, in Southern earth. Guilt, the most terrible kind of guilt, washed over her, making her feel unworthy, damned. She stiffened, and she felt the same reaction in him.

His mouth left hers. "Kate?"

Why did her name have to sound so pleasant on his lips, the quite ordinary word transformed into something lovely? That Southern drawl. Music. Deadly music.

She pulled away. "I'm sorry. I can't."

She felt his body still, as if he'd turned into a statue, and she couldn't move, either. They were locked together in a battle of wills.

"Because I'm from the South?" His voice was softly angry, and that was more intimidating than if he'd shouted.

"Because you *fought* for the South." She tried to make her voice steady. She didn't know if she succeeded, because her heart was still quaking.

All Seth's feelings of hope died. *Damn. It would never*

be over. Never. But he tried. One more time, he tried. "The war's been over for a year, Kate."

"It will never be over for Jeremy—for a lot of men."

"Let Jeremy decide that, damn it."

"My older brothers, then," she said desperately.

"And your fiancé," Seth added bitterly. "Well, lady, keep fighting your war. But don't make Jeremy and Nick fight it, too. I'll take you back."

He turned around, taking her arm with none of the tenderness of moments before, merely determination. Kate held back a moment. "Dr. Hampton—? Seth—?"

Seth stopped, hesitated.

"I'm sorry," she said. She wanted to say more. She wanted to say it wasn't the war, not now, but her own guilt, guilt at acknowledging all these forbidden feelings and the sense of betrayal they created in her. How could she care for him and still be true to the memory of her brothers, her parents, and Thomas? Perhaps that was the worst guilt of all. Thomas. She'd thought she loved him, but she'd never had these kinds of swirling, dancing, aching feelings with him. Never.

He sighed, and Kate could sense the regret in the sound. "I'm sorry, too. I should have—" Just then thunder roared across the sky, followed immediately by a streak of lightning. "I'd better get you back to the wagon," he said abruptly. "At least rain will settle the dust. It should help Jeremy." His voice sounded professional, impersonal, and Kate felt a devastating loss.

She wanted to reach out to him, and her fingers flexed with that need—but she couldn't. Especially now, when his voice was curiously cool after having been so warm only moments ago.

So she tried to make her legs move in an ordinary fashion. They objected, and she stumbled just as another roll of thunder seemed to shake the earth, and rain came, suddenly and in torrents.

Kate felt his arms steady her and then gather her up as if she weighed next to nothing. She started to object, but one look at his face now lit by a flash of lightning dissuaded her. His face was set in hard, unyielding lines, his mouth grim and his jaw rigid. He seemed not to notice the rain that plastered the thick hair around his face.

Her head was next to his heart, and she heard its steady beating, a sound that made her feel safe and warm. Even now. Even with the bitterness still alive between them. But soon that safety would be gone, and in a moment of honesty she realized how much she, and her brothers, had come to depend on him, how they all had come alive again in their own ways.

Why couldn't she accept her own feelings?

They reached the wagon and he helped her inside and then assisted her and her brothers in securely tying down the canvas to shut out the rain. He worked silently, his hands deft. As he tied the cords in one corner, Kate thought that his hands had a peculiarly masculine beauty of their own, his long, sure fingers capable of both strength and gentleness.

When he finished, he quickly examined Jeremy and told him he wouldn't need the mask tonight. Seth mixed the now-familiar snakeroot in water and handed it to the younger man. Then he gave Nick an irresistible smile that Kate wanted for herself. But when he turned back to her, it was gone. His face was grave and his eyes were hooded. "I'll be leaving."

"You can't sleep outside." She didn't want him to go. But she couldn't bear to have him stay, either.

"I don't plan to," he said simply. "I'll be bunking with Edwards, if you need anything." He paused. "I think I'll be leaving the train at Fort Kelly, in Colorado. I've been talking to young David Cochran. He's learned a lot in the past month. He'll help you out.''

"Mr. Edwards—?" Kate started to protest, but something in his face stopped the words. There was a harshness she hadn't seen there before, an unbending firmness.

"But, Seth—" This protest came from Nick, whose expression was disconsolate. Kate wondered when Dr. Hampton had become Seth to Nick.

Even Jeremy looked dismayed, and Seth almost rethought his decision. But he couldn't. He would only end up hurting them all the more.

"Fort Kelly's a few more weeks away," Seth said. "By then, we'll be out of the dust, and the weather should be dry. I'll leave enough medicine. You'll be fine."

"But you were going to Sacramento with us," Nick persisted. "You said you were."

Seth smiled ruefully, but the usual warmth didn't reach his eyes. "Things change, Nick. I thought I might try Denver. The scouts say it's a booming place that needs someone like me, and I think your brother's going to be just fine after getting to the mountains." He hesitated. "I—well, I think it's time to find my own way. Might even go goldhunting."

Kate was too shocked to say anything. When had he made this decision? Why? Because of tonight? Or because of the way she had treated him throughout this journey?

What would they do without him?

He had become a member of her family. Without any of them actually realizing it, he had carved himself an important place in their lives. A Southerner. A Rebel. And she didn't want him to go. And yet she couldn't ask him to stay. She knew what would happen if she did, and she also knew she would hate herself if she allowed it to happen. So, apparently, did he.

As he stepped out of the tent and she retied the flap, she looked back. The crowded interior of the wagon was suddenly very, very empty.

Chapter Four

As Seth made his way through the driving rain, he knew he had made the right decision in leaving. He had been thinking about it for the past few days, although he had continued to hope that things might change. There had been changes, a lessening of hostility with Jeremy, and even, at times, with Kate. But, after tonight, he knew nothing had really changed, at least not with Kate.

Part of him balked at making that decision, the decision to leave, to give up. He had never been a quitter. But, God, he was tired of fighting wars. He didn't need another in his life. And he wasn't going to torture himself again by wanting someone who loved another, or who didn't want him.

For a while, he had allowed himself to think about the valley Nick and Jeremy talked about, the Sacramento Valley, which was supposed to be so fertile and beautiful. But it had been a fool's dream.

Kate MacAllister had made it very clear that she would never accept what he was. And he couldn't change that attitude. He had tried. He had thought time might help, but it had been more than a month now, and despite the obvious attraction between them, he couldn't pierce the wall she'd constructed against him.

He didn't think he could stay in such close proximity to

her and resist doing what he had done tonight. When he was around her, his fingers ached to touch her, to make the look in those eyes soften, to bring much-needed laughter to them. And that, he'd discovered, was disastrous for both of them. He had not missed the pain in her eyes tonight. Whether it had been for him, or for the man who had been killed in the war, he didn't know. He didn't think he wanted to know. He only knew that if he stayed, the pain would probably grow deeper, and he wanted no part of making it so. It was not easy to be torn by loyalties; no one knew that better than he.

The mood in the Edwards wagon, occupied by Cliff Edwards, the man who cooked for him, and the scouts, was gloomy. The rain was hard and steady, and probably long-lasting. They would miss valuable travel time.

Seth gratefully agreed to a game of poker. The stakes were low, which was fortunate, since he couldn't concentrate.

He was down five dollars when Edwards threw in his cards. "Time to turn in," he said. "What about you, Doc?"

Seth shrugged. The last thing he wanted now was sleep. The nightmares came when his mind was in turmoil. And God knew it was roiling now, as much as the storm outside.

"How's the MacAllister boy?"

"This rain will help settle the dust. That should help."

"Hmm... I hope so," Edwards said. "He seemed so much better for a while."

"Once we leave this dust behind..."

"I'm sure glad you're around, Doc. So are the other folks, now."

Seth hesitated. "Not all of them."

"I ain't heard any grumblings lately."

"I'm thinking about leaving, taking off toward Denver."

Edwards looked at him sharply. "Not you, too. Gold-hunting don't seem your style."

Seth grinned. "It's not. But doctoring is. You have, what, a hundred people? Most of them fit. I hear the gold camps are crowded, and they don't have any doctors." It was a plain, bald-faced lie. He didn't know whether they did or not, but it seemed logical.

"What about the MacAllisters?" Edwards watched him closely, and Seth kept any emotion from his eyes.

"Once in the mountains, Jeremy should be fine. And David Cochran could help them out. I've been keeping an eye on him. He seems willing and competent."

"You made a bargain," Edwards said.

"Predicated on things working out," Seth reminded him. "They are not."

"Miss Kate, you mean?"

Seth shrugged. "Her resentment is natural enough."

"I don't think that's all of it," Edwards said shrewdly. He had seen the way his two most interesting passengers looked at one another when they thought they were unobserved. He hadn't missed the need in their eyes, a need that they seemed bound and determined not to allow each other to see. Pride was a terrible thing, he thought. So was obstinacy. They had three more months to go on this trail. At least three months, and time could do a lot for obstinacy. If he could only tempt Seth Hampton into staying. But, looking into those determined eyes, he wondered if he could.

And he sensed that now was not the time to argue. So he only nodded. "I can't hog-tie you and make you stay, but I sure would be sorry to lose you." He rose, then added, "I'm going to take one last look around camp. Check on the sentries. Make sure none of them have ducked into wagons."

Seth felt his usual restlessness. "I'll go with you."

Cliff Edwards threw him a poncho. "Damned if I want *you* to get sick."

Seth smiled wryly. "I never get sick. Four years of war, sleeping in snow sometimes, riding in icy rain. Never even a fever. Sometimes..." The smile disappeared, and Seth's face looked bleak.

Edwards winced inwardly. He liked Seth Hampton. He liked the dogged persistence with which the soft-spoken doctor convinced former enemies to trust him, to let him help them. Hampton had an unusual compassion that drew people to him, regardless of their prejudices. Edwards also liked Kate MacAllister and her dedication to what was left of her family. Both of them had gone through a crucible of fire, and both had been made strong by it. Now they needed tempering. Maybe by a third party.

He had three weeks to do it.

"Come on, Doc," he said. "Let's go."

The rain continued for three days without cessation. The road became impassable, and the heavy wagons bogged down in mud. The wagon train made a total of only eight miles in those three days. The only good news was Jeremy, who, as Seth had predicted, improved dramatically. Despite his protests, he was still ordered to stay inside the wagon. A cold would be catastrophic for him.

Seth drove the wagon the few miles before Edwards disgustedly called for an early stop. Nick rode in front with him, despite the rain. He didn't say anything—didn't even ask any of the usual questions—but silently worked at his carving, glancing over occasionally at Seth's face.

When Seth checked on Jeremy, he didn't stay long, just measured out the medicine and kept his conversation to a minimum, asking only whether the boy had passed a good night. He was always aware of Kate's presence—too aware. Tension radiated between them, as neither of them was willing to risk even the slightest overture.

The rain was lessening at the end of the third day. Tempers throughout the wagon train were short as a result of the enforced confinement in too-small wagons. There was no hot food, nothing for children to do, no way to stretch stiff limbs. Men had to go out into the pouring rain and feed and water the miserable oxen and other livestock or stand for hours at sentry duty. Cases of dysentery broke out, and Seth believed it came from a stream where some of the travelers had refilled their water kegs. Previous wagon trains—there were so many of them—had used the streams carelessly and left them polluted.

He had made sure the MacAllisters filled their kegs well upriver of the main trail, and had advised others to do the same, but apparently some had paid no attention. Cliff Edwards had ordered, henceforth, that all families were to follow Dr. Hampton's orders, or they would be asked to leave the train at the next fort or town.

In the meantime, Seth prescribed calomel for the worse cases of dysentery, and arrowroot and other indigenous astringents for the milder cases. By the fourth day, nearly everyone was well again.

The rain finally stopped, and the train moved on slowly. The road was still muddy, which made it difficult for even the oxen to pull their loads, and streams were hard to ford because of high water. They were now approaching Big Sandy Creek, and Edwards feared the heavy rains might make the usually placid creek difficult to cross.

It was. They camped overnight along the rushing waterway, hoping it would go down during the night. By evening, it had dropped a little, but was still chest high at the fording place, and the current was strong.

But Cliff Edwards felt they couldn't delay any longer. The skies were cloudy again, and there might well be more rain, pushing the water level even higher.

Loads were exchanged; the stronger teams and higher wagons took goods from other wagons. Wagon boxes were raised from the bolsters to keep provisions from getting wet. Ropes were attached to the riggings of each wagon to steady it as it crossed the creek.

Although the MacAllister wagon had been first in line, it was now moved back so that heavier wagons could go across first. One wagon overturned in the water, and everything not tied down went floating downstream. Kate, who had been watching from the bank, went back inside her wagon and tied everything down that she could. Flour, cornmeal and bacon had already been transferred to wagons with higher beds.

When she finished, she rejoined Jeremy and Nick, who sat on the bank watching as the wagons moved slowly across the river. Seth was across the river, helping with the ropes balancing the wagons. Kate could see him perfectly from where she was. He was helping pull ropes stretched taut around trees for leverage. He and several other men had taken off their shirts in the humid heat, and the sun hit the glistening beads of sweat on his chest like tiny fragments of gold. His blond hair, so like the golden corn her family had once grown, was tousled as if he'd been running his hand through the curling tendrils that fell over his forehead.

He was magnificent in his concentration, in the way his muscles moved and in the manner in which he grinned at something someone said to him. Need seethed within her, need so potent that she clenched her fist into a ball so tight she felt she might break her own fingers. No matter how hard she tried to dismiss that craving, she couldn't. She just couldn't. It was there, something so sweet and wild and impossible that she ached in every feeling part of her. How could she let it go so easily? Let *him* go?

One of the wagons started to tip, and she heard a scream and then the terrified bark of a dog as it fell from the wagon. The current caught it and started to sweep the animal toward where they were sitting. Before Kate could do anything, Nick was up and running for the edge of the stream, apparently in an attempt to grab the animal. But he fell into the water, and then he, too, was tumbling over in the heavy current.

Kate heard her own scream as she got to her feet. "He can't swim!" she screamed as she ran down to the edge. Neither could she, and though every instinct pushed her to go into the water, she knew she would only make things worse.

Then Jeremy was there, ready to go in, but Seth, on the other side, yelled at him, "Stay there, I'll get him!" With movements so fast Kate could barely follow them, Seth was in the water, his strokes strong and fast. Kate felt Jeremy's hands on her.

"He'll get Nick," he said, and there was such confidence in his face that Kate believed him. She had to. Dear God, she couldn't lose Nick, too.

Two other men were in the water now, but Seth had been the first and was the swiftest swimmer. Kate saw him grab something and shove it toward one of the other men and then swim on. In another moment, she saw two heads, a small one with brown hair and a larger one with gold. A few strokes, and Seth stood up in the water and moved rapidly toward the bank. One of the other men held the drenched dog.

When Seth reached the bank, he put the boy down. Nick was coughing up water, nearly doubled over. Seth turned him over so that the boy lay on his stomach, and he pounded on the boy's back as Kate and Jeremy reached them.

Seth, water dripping down his face and naked chest, looked up. "He'll be fine," he said, with that disarming grin of his. "I'm going to have to teach him to swim, though, particularly if he's dead-set on jumping in first and thinking later."

Nick groaned, coughed again and then tried to sit up. "The dog?"

"Probably a damn sight better than you," Seth said. "Mr. Cochran's got him." His hand moved up to the boy's shoulder and lingered there. "Promise me you won't do something like that again."

Nick looked sheepish—sheepish and pale—but still his eyes lit at Seth's offer. "You'll really teach me how to swim?"

"Promise," Seth said.

"Then you'll stay with us?"

Seth hesitated. "Let's just say I'll make sure you know how to swim."

Nick grinned, and Kate knew it would probably take him a very long time to learn how to swim.

She found herself hoping so. Really hoping so.

Seth stood, pulling Nick up as he did. "I'd better take you across myself. I don't think I want to try that again."

"On your horse?"

"On my horse, Nicholas," he confirmed. "If your sister approves." He looked over at Kate.

"His sister approves," Kate said. "Thank you." She hesitated a moment, and then added, "Seth."

Water was still running down from his hair, over his bare skin, and her gaze was drawn to where golden, curly hair made an arrow pattern down to his waist. Reluctantly her gaze moved upward again, to sea-colored eyes that were suddenly blazing with challenge.

A self-conscious tremor rumbled through her body. So did something else. Waves of desire that went way beyond gratitude. *It's just that he saved Nick,* she argued to herself, and saw him grin, as if he knew exactly what she was thinking and knew she didn't believe it for a second.

"I'll take you, too," he offered quite easily, but there was a teasing note in his drawl, the drawl that no longer offended her.

The thought was terribly tempting. Holding on to him, her arms around that hard body, those cabled muscles. But, as tempting as the image was, it was also unnerving—too unnerving.

She shook her head, unable to utter the refusal. "I'd better stay with the wagon."

Kate saw his eyes cloud, and she knew instantly that he had taken it as another rejection, when it wasn't that at all. She simply no longer trusted herself with him.

But before she could say anything he turned away, and she knew he was going to get his horse, which he had tied on a long rope to graze as they took the wagons over. She saw Nick tag along with him, and she wished with all her heart she could be as easy with him, that the tension wasn't so thick between them. But she had made it that way, and now she didn't know how to change it.

The campfires burned merrily that night. They had made it across with only a few goods lost, and no lives—thanks, they all knew, to the quick action of Seth Hampton.

The family who had lost some of its supplies had them replenished through contributions. The Cochrans, who owned the dog that had fallen from the wagon, brought the animal to see Nick.

"This is Betsy," Edie Cochran said, shyly introducing the dog to Nick. "She's going to have puppies. Would you like one of them?" The young girl looked at Nick as if he were the next thing to God.

Nick swallowed deep. "Would I!"

"You can have your pick," Edie offered graciously. Nick's eleven-year-old face went three shades of red, but his eyes glowed.

Kate wanted to cry. It had been so long since she'd seen real pleasure on her brother's face. And now twice in one day. A miracle. Seth Hampton's miracle.

One of several, she realized. Not only Nick's rescue today and the smile now, but Jeremy, who looked on contentedly and who hadn't coughed the whole day.

And herself. She hadn't realized how much she had locked her heart away, her feelings. When she had watched so many die, she'd had to, or she couldn't have gone on. But then, she realized, it had become a habit. She didn't know now when she had looked at a sunset or a sunrise and seen beauty instead of a long day of work ahead. Even this trip. Years ago, it would have started as a wonderful adventure, but when they had actually left, she had felt almost dead inside, because she was leaving everything she knew and loved behind.

And she hadn't realized how much her own attitude had

affected her brothers, how bitterness had replaced the innate sense of joy she'd once had.

But now it was coming back into her, day by day. That sweet appreciation of everyday things. There was a pleasure in living again, in hearing the sad strains of a harmonica, in watching Seth Hampton simply ride a horse, or now, particularly, in seeing a smile transform Nick's face.

She only wished Seth were here to see it. She felt a poignant sadness that he was not. But, as he had done so often recently, he had chosen to eat with Cliff Edwards and his hands. He was quite deliberately and consciously separating himself from the MacAllisters, and she was responsible.

Kate had not even thanked him properly for saving Nick or helping Jeremy. She swallowed the thick gob of remorse threatening to block her throat.

She looked at Nick, who was now absorbed with Edie Cochran. Jeremy was talking to Daniel and David Cochran. She realized how isolated they all had been. She had been so concerned with Jeremy or so wrapped up in her own mixed emotions that she had made little effort to make friends, and again it was her brothers who had suffered. Nick had taken on so much responsibility and had become so withdrawn. She had constructed a shield of grief and loss and bitterness so thick that she hadn't even noticed.

Fighting back tears, Kate slipped off and walked down the wooded bank of Big Sandy Creek. The water was still high, rushing to join some other ribbon of water. Night had fallen, and the earlier threatening clouds had dispersed, leaving the sky cleansed and clear. Stars blinked lazily, and a three-quarter moon sat benevolently overhead, its image reflected in the water, which now appeared equally benign. It was difficult to think she'd almost lost her brother to it hours ago.

If not for Seth Hampton. Seth Hampton. The name was like him. It had a warm sound to it.

"Miss MacAllister?"

Her last name sounded odd now, too formal after so many weeks. When had she started thinking of him as Seth? This afternoon? Weeks ago?

She swung around to look at him. It was almost as if her thoughts had summoned him.

His eyes were quizzical, but his lips smiled, a wonderful sensuous smile that seemed to light the world—at least her world. She shivered under its impact, warning herself.

"I...came for a walk," Kate explained sheepishly.

"Nick?" Seth inquired.

She couldn't stop a smile of her own. "He has a disciple now, a nice young lady, and the promise of a puppy. I would say he is very well—thanks to you."

He looked uncomfortable. "There were others who helped."

"But not as quickly as you."

He shrugged off her gratitude. "I'm just glad he's all right."

"I think he'll be much better now."

He raised a questioning eyebrow.

"I'm beginning to realize a few things...namely, that I haven't been fair, not to Nick or Jeremy. Or you."

His eyes, which were wary, softened. "You had reasons."

"I thought I did," she said slowly.

He moved closer to her, his hand touching her chin softly. "Don't," he said. "Don't feel guilty."

"It's just—"

"Just what?"

"I don't like myself very much at the moment."

"I do," he said simply, his hand moving to the side of her cheek before dropping and taking hers. "Go for a walk with me, Miss MacAllister."

"Kate," she told him softly, and she matched her steps to his as they walked beyond the campfire and the voices. He found a fallen log and gestured to her to sit down. She nodded, and he helped her down, then gracefully settled next to her.

Kate looked out over the creek, then at the sky overhead. "It seems so peaceful now." She chewed on her lip. "I don't think I could have survived losing someone else."

Seth pulled her against him, holding her lightly, but with a warmth that seeped through to her soul, a soul that was increasingly hungry for that kind of touch.

"Tell me about your home," he said.

Kate didn't know if she could. The silence stretched between them, but, strangely enough, it wasn't an uncomfortable silence.

He prompted her. "Is your name really Kate, or is it Kathryn?"

How had she ever thought his drawl offensive? It lingered in the air now, fine and comforting.

"Kathryn Mary," she said, "after my grandmothers."

"Kathryn Mary," he repeated. "I like that."

She shrugged. "Everyone called me Kate. My brothers started it when I was small."

"How many were there?"

"Four. The two oldest were twins. John and Jacob. They were four years older than I, and they always looked after me. Jeremy came four years after me, and then, of course, Nick. There was one other girl, born two years before me, but she died of a fever when she was only one. So John and Jacob always felt..." Her voice died away.

"Protective?"

She nodded, then added painfully, "They both died at Gettysburg."

"I'm sorry, Kate," he said.

"It nearly killed my mother, and then Jeremy ran off at sixteen to avenge them, and that *did* kill her. She lost her will to live. My father, he just didn't seem to care about the farm anymore. The twins and Jeremy had loved it and had always worked with him. When they were gone, he lost heart. Nick found him dead in the barn one morning."

Pain washed through Seth, pain for her and for young Nick. But there was more. He remembered her mentioning a fiancé. He wanted to know. He had to know.

"You said you were betrothed?"

"He died at Gettysburg, too," she said. "Practically the whole unit from our county died that day. I grew up with Thomas Beck. It was always expected that we would marry. Have children." She hesitated. "But I think a part of me always ached for something else. There seemed so much more to the world than a farm in Illinois. But everyone expected…"

She turned and looked up at him. "And then they were all gone, and no one expected anything, and all I felt was loss. I could finally see the world, but all I wanted was my family back, and everything the way it used to be."

The tears she hadn't shed before started coming, and she felt him put his arms around her, pulling her close to him, allowing her to soak his shirt with long, heaving sobs. He didn't try to stop her, or even comfort her with words, but merely let her release all the anguish inside.

She didn't know how long she cried, but she felt his lips against her hair, his hands soothing her in that sure, compassionate way of his. There were no questions, no demands. There was only a haven of acceptance. Somewhere deep inside, she realized for the first time that she had blamed herself in some way for what had happened, feeling that her dream of seeing the world had somehow caused the demise of her family.

She wondered now whether her anger against Seth was really anger against herself.

The tears were finally spent, and for the first time in a very long while she felt a wonderful relief. But she also felt exposed in a way she'd never been before.

She straightened. "I'm sorry," she said, and then gave him a weak smile. "I've said that several times now, haven't I?"

"There's nothing to feel sorry for. I suspect you've needed to do that for a very long time."

"Still—"

His hands played with a tendril of hair that had escaped from her braid. "Still nothing," he said. "You don't know how many times I've wanted to do the same thing."

"You?"

"There's a certain advantage in being a woman, you know."

No matter how hard she tried, she couldn't imagine Seth Hampton breaking down, or even showing the slightest weakness. Her face showed her doubt, and he gave her that easy smile of his, the one that always wriggled its way into places it shouldn't.

"I think I'd better get you back to the camp, or I might do something I shouldn't."

She wanted him to. How much she wanted him to, but despite these moments of tenderness, there was an uneasiness about him now, a quiet reserve that had been there since she'd broken away from him the other night.

She could still feel, however, that compelling, magnetic attraction between them. She knew he wanted to kiss her. She also knew he wasn't going to. The strength of will that was so evident within him wasn't going to allow it. With a desolation that crept through every crevice of her heart, she knew that nothing had changed, that he still planned to leave, that he had offered something before and wasn't going to risk its being refused again.

Kate also knew she couldn't offer anything herself. She wasn't sure yet whether she wouldn't run away from him again—for whatever reasons. Perhaps she was afraid of her own vulnerable emotions, or of losing him as she had lost so many others. She felt racked by so many conflicting feelings.

It was as if he read her mind. He rose with that grace that was always so sensual, pulling her up easily. She wanted him to pull her into his arms, but he didn't.

He did, however, catch her face in his hands and lean down to kiss her lightly. "Don't ever doubt yourself, Miss Kate. You're a very strong lady. And you have a lot to give. Don't run from it. Don't ever be afraid. And don't ever, ever feel guilt for something you can't help."

He walked her back to the wagons and gave her that wry smile of his, the one that always went straight to the core of her being. Then he turned, striding off again. Alone. Always alone. Just like her.

Chapter Five

Seth stayed as far away as he could for the next week and a half, mostly scouting with Dallas Terry, learning as much as he could since he'd soon be on his own.

He had to start weaning himself away from the Mac-Allisters and the growing feelings he had for all of them. It would be damned difficult to leave them, but he envisioned only pain for himself, and for Kate, if he remained with them. Her beliefs were simply too ingrained, her feelings too deep and her loyalties too strong, for her to ever to give herself freely to him. And that was the only way he would have her.

He'd known since that evening they had walked after Nick's mishap that he could probably bed her. But then she would probably hate him for a lapse she would consider traitorous, and he couldn't stand that. So he found himself wandering out more and more.

Since Jeremy had been feeling so much better and had eagerly assumed most of the duties Seth had once performed, Seth mostly limited his contact with the Mac-Allisters to teaching Nick to swim when they camped alongside a stream or river. Nick was a quick learner, despite his attempts to pretend otherwise, and Seth felt confident that he now knew enough basics to never again repeat the mishap at Big Sandy Creek.

After one such lesson, Nick, feeling extremely proud of his growing competence, begged him to stay and take supper with them. Kate, he said, had cooked a particularly tasty stew.

Seth was about to decline when he caught sight of Kate. She was stepping out of the wagon, a shapely ankle revealed as she stepped down and a pretty green dress gracefully swishing around her slender form. Her hair was tied back with a matching green ribbon, and the green in her hazel eyes warmed when she saw him. He felt his intended refusal die on his lips, to be replaced by a certain immediate arousal throughout his body.

But, although she smiled warmly, she seemed flustered, saying little as she dished out a stew that was a great deal tastier than that prepared by Cliff Edwards's cook. Jeremy, too, was quiet, although he was obviously feeling much better, his face now a healthy tanned color.

Seth tried to keep his eyes on the food, but it was more than a little difficult. Whenever he glanced up, his gaze met Kate's, and he had a damnable time moving it. Her face, like Jeremy's, was slightly tanned from the sun and now flushed from the fire. Her eyes were lovely, filled with an uncertainty and vulnerability that moved him immensely. But then, everything about her seemed to affect him in some lunatic way. He wasn't usually speechless, but there was so little to say now.

Now that he planned to leave. He knew how damned difficult it would be. To leave not only her, but also Nick, who had wormed his way into his heart, and even the reticent Jeremy, who watched him with such cautious eyes.

Seth carefully avoided conversation on Fort Walker, or the future, or his planned departure. He also avoided mentioning the recent war. And Kate's family.

But Nick chattered on about the puppy he was to have,

and even Seth was caught up in his eagerness and enthusiasm.

"Did you ever have a dog, Seth?"

Seth looked into Nick's eager eyes. "Many of them. Even had a baby fox a friend of mine rescued from a trap."

"What happened to it?"

"Well, I—we doctored it, and I kept it until it was well enough and old enough to be on its own, and then my brother took it deep into the woods and released it. It's probably a pretty old fellow now."

"Your brother?" Kate asked.

Seth looked embarrassed. "I'd gotten attached to it," he said simply and was startled—even a bit stunned—when Kate's lips broke out into the most spontaneous, open smile she had ever given him. It was so incredibly lovely, like a sunrise, full of light and quiet, glowing beauty.

"You doctored a baby fox?" Kate's question was spoken softly, almost wistfully. "And wanted to keep it?"

He winced at the sentimentality of the image. "I was a boy."

Kate smiled. "I think you would probably do the same thing today."

"At least I've progressed enough to turn it loose myself," Seth said with a chagrined smile.

"Have you?" The question came from Jeremy, and his question went far beyond the obvious. Jeremy had the smallest grin on his lips and a kind of searching look in his eyes.

Seth nodded slowly, trying to tear his eyes away from the tender look in Kate's eyes. He liked it...very much. And he wasn't sure how long it would remain there.

"And your brother?" Kate asked, interest shining in her eyes and making them lovelier then ever.

"I had four of them. Rafe and I were the closest, since we were only a year apart. The others were considerably older. I think he was destined to be a lawyer, as I was a doctor. He could argue any point of view."

"And you?"

He found himself trapped by the bright interest in her eyes. He shrugged. "Rafe always said I was single-minded, that once I decided on something, nothing would change it."

"Is that true?" Her eyes had changed. They were no longer tender but intense. And he knew she was asking another question altogether. He knew all the MacAllisters were waiting for an answer. Was he really going to leave them at Fort Walker?

"Yes," he said simply. "Rafe found that out." Seth didn't know why he added that last statement. He knew it invited another question, and perhaps it was time to answer it. Time they knew more about him. About exactly how doggedly stubborn he could be.

There was a silence, a kind of pall that fell over each one of them before Nick broke it. They all sensed there was a Pandora's box here.

"How?" Nick asked.

Seth looked directly at Kate as he answered. He wasn't going to apologize for anything, not for his role in the war, not for his loyalties, not for doing what he'd thought he had to do. "My brother joined the Union army—in the West, so he wouldn't have to fight his friends. But toward the end he was moved back into the Shenandoah Valley, where I was posted. I didn't know it, not then, nor on Christmas Eve, when I and a wounded Confederate general escaped a Union ambush and took refuge on the farm of a friend of mine."

Seth was watching Kate's eyes, saw them widen a little at his choice of words, but he didn't give her time to wonder long.

"Rafe knew the area, and he was ordered to track us down. He didn't know his quarry was me, of course, any more than I knew he was in Virginia."

Seth paused, and the three listeners seemed to move closer, their faces obviously fascinated at the drama of the story. "He found us. I would have shot him before I let him take my patient."

It was Jeremy who fastened on the words *would have* and urged him to continue. "But you didn't—?"

A muscle twitched in Seth's throat and his lips firmed in a tight, narrow line before speaking again. "That's not the point. I would have, and he knew it."

"What happened?" Nick prodded.

"Interference—from two armies. A standoff. I was able to take my patient away." He knew his voice softened as he remembered that remarkable Christmas, when two armies had confronted each other and a ragtag bunch of orphans Blythe had gathered had made both sides remember their humanity. For a few hours, anyway. And then the wedding. The wedding of Rafe and Blythe, his own love, that same day.

"And now?" Kate's soft voice interrupted the bittersweet memory.

"We're friends again. We both did what we had to do, and we knew the other had no choice."

"Would he have shot you?"

Seth shrugged. "He would have taken me prisoner."

"Why didn't you fight for the North, too?" Kate asked, and Seth grimaced as he realized again that his decision five years ago was always going to stand between them.

"It didn't seem to matter much to me what side I chose," he explained once more. "I was a doctor. There's no right or wrong about wounded. I thought the Confederacy needed me more."

He stood. "Thank you for dinner," he said abruptly, and he left before he saw the familiar condemnation in her eyes....

He left the next morning with Dallas again. Before sunrise. Before he saw her. Before a brief glimpse of hope surfaced again. Before his body started reacting in wanting ways again.

Damn. Loneliness was now a constant ache within him. Less than a week and he would be on his own again. The thought was agonizing. They rode together most of the morning, both in silence. Seth was preoccupied, and Dallas's attention was completely on the trail ahead.

Unfortunately, Dallas's concentration left Seth too much time to think. It was becoming more and more difficult to stay away from Kate MacAllister, especially after that evening when he'd tasted her tears and glimpsed her wistful vulnerability. He had realized then that he loved her, but he also knew he couldn't live with that anger against the South, and Southerners, he sensed was still simmering within her.

It was late afternoon when a squad of blue-coated soldiers approached. A lieutenant introduced himself as Roswell Campbell and reported they were on a mission to alert travelers about a band of Cheyenne that had been attacking army supply wagons and civilian wagon trains. The fort was still eighty miles away, five or six days by wagon train.

"Can you accompany us to Fort Walker?" Dallas asked. "How large is your party?"

"Fifty wagons about a hundred and fifty people."

Lieutenant Campbell shook his head. "You should be safe enough if you keep your people together. They're selecting easy pickings—a lone wagon, perhaps two or three. There's a damned lot of movement, and gold fever has made folks careless. We're urging the smaller parties to join up with outfits your size—at least to the fort. Do you think your wagon master will agree?"

"I can't speak for him," Dallas said. "Why don't you ride on back—they're only about ten miles east—and talk with Cliff Edwards? Take a bit of supper with 'em. We still have to scout out another campsite."

The lieutenant's face brightened. "It will be damned good to have something besides hardtack and beans." He started to turn his horse away, but then he glanced back. "Be careful."

Dallas nodded. "Always am."

Once the soldiers were gone, Seth turned to Dallas and asked about the Cheyenne. He soon wished he hadn't.

"There's been trouble for years," Dallas said, "and it came to a head two years ago. The Cheyenne believed too many whites were coming through their territory, and some young hotheads started raiding. Stage lines, stations, wagon trains. The Colorado militia, under the command of a man named Chivington, went after them. Instead of finding those who were guilty, he attacked a peaceful camp, slaughtering men, women and children. Even mutilatin' them. Some Cheyenne ain't forgotten that. I don't blame them none," he added. "Despite a treaty last year, some ain't ever forgiven the white man for that day. Don't suppose they ever will. So keep your eyes open, Doc."

With that, he spurred his horse ahead, and Seth followed, wondering whether there was peace any place in this country.

Kate helped prepare the meal for the soldiers who arrived just as the train stopped for the evening. She was grateful for the distraction, for a few new faces, for something to do. She'd missed Seth terribly since he'd left so abruptly last night.

Her body had felt tense all night, hungry in a way it had never been before. Her mind was muddled and bemused by the man, who was both so stubbornly gentle and so maddeningly resolute. She had so wanted to touch him last night, especially when he had talked about his brother with such sad affection.

She had wanted to comfort him as he had comforted her, to feel his arms around her as they had been the other night. But she didn't know how to tell him. He had made it clear that he didn't want to stay with them, that he preferred to strike out on his own.

She felt an emptiness that grew in intensity each day they came closer to Fort Walker.

She wished she had the right to ask him to stay. But he had made it clear that he wouldn't, and she couldn't find it in herself to beg. Not to a Southerner. She still couldn't quite get over that obstacle. No matter how much she tried, it kept returning to haunt her. It seemed such an utter betrayal to those she had loved.

Kate used some of the dried apples she'd been hoarding and made two pies, one for the soldiers and one for her family. They all needed a lift—including Seth, whom she hoped would join them again tonight.

But he didn't appear, not for supper, or even later, when an impromptu dance was held. Members of the train brought out their instruments: harmonicas, fiddles, even a flute. The soldiers were very gallant, paying attention to all the single women in the party, and particularly to Kate. She had brushed her hair and tied it back with a ribbon and put on her one good dress—the green dress that had so obviously met Seth Hampton's approval the night before. She tried to enjoy herself as she danced with the young lieutenant and then a sergeant, but she found herself looking for the gracefully tall man with the golden hair and the sea-green eyes.

Others were, too. All the young women of marriageable age, and even some who weren't, were asking where "the doc" was? For the first time in her life, she knew the terribly bitter taste of jealousy, though she realized she had no right to do so.

When a large number of the men also asked, Kate realized how many friends Seth had made on this trip, despite the hostility he'd braved during the first few days and weeks. He was no longer seen as "the Reb," but simply as "the doc."

"Miss MacAllister, will you honor me with another dance?" The lieutenant had an eager look on his face, one difficult to refuse. She nodded her head, took his proffered hand and found herself twirling around to the music.

When they slowed just a bit, the lieutenant gave her a

disarming grin. "There will be another dance at Fort Walker. There always is when a wagon train comes in. I hope you will save me several dances then."

Kate hesitated. She could not even think of Fort Walker now. They would lose Seth there. "I'm not sure, Lieutenant...." She went red as she realized she'd completely forgotten the man's name. She'd never done that before, and especially not when someone had been kind enough to ask for a dance. But all her thoughts had been of Seth, for Seth. *Where was he?*

But the lieutenant didn't seem to mind. "Campbell, Roswell Campbell. My friends call me Ross."

"Lieutenant Campbell," she acknowledged.

"Ross, please."

She smiled at his eagerness, wondering whether she could have appreciated it more weeks ago. Before Seth. Now, everyone paled beside him.

"It'll depend on my brothers, whether Jeremy's well," she said, "but thank you for asking."

"That was wonderful pie tonight."

Kate wished someone else thought so, and then she scolded herself for thinking so. Why? Why, for dear Heaven, could she not erase the Southern doctor from her mind?

She looked up at the young officer and saw admiration reflected in his eyes. He was a handsome man, handsomer than Dr. Hampton, but he didn't have the charisma that Seth Hampton had, nor the lines of character carved into a face molded by adversity.

"Thank you," she said. She thought again of Seth Hampton out riding alone, or with only one or two scouts. "Are there really hostile Indians out there?"

The laughter left his face. "I'm afraid so. But you don't have anything to worry about here, not on a train this size."

"Have—have you seen any?"

His expression sobered. "Aye," he said, with a trace of a Scottish accent. "There's been a few skirmishes. We were sent out to escort a supply train and came upon some Cheyenne attacking it. But when they saw us, they galloped off.''

''Is there danger...for the scouts?''

''I wouldn't worry if I were you, miss. I heard that Cliff Edwards hires only the best. They know what they're doing.''

But Seth Hampton wasn't the best, not as a scout. He wasn't a scout at all. He was a doctor. She swallowed hard, and tried to lose herself in the dance steps.

The soldiers were gone in the morning. Despite the revelry of last night, Cliff Edwards had everyone up before dawn. He wanted to make at least sixteen miles today, he said. Because of the roving Indian raids, he felt it more important than ever to get under the protection of Fort Walker as quickly as possible.

Everyone was now ordered to stay with their wagons, and Cliff Edwards kept the wagons as close to each other as possible. Nick sat up on the wagon seat along with Jeremy, and was told to watch for any cloud of dust, for any large group of horsemen.

Kate walked alongside the wagon for a while. She was terribly restless and apprehensive, although she didn't really understand why. She only knew she'd felt like this before—once about the time she'd learned that her brothers had been killed, another time just before her father's death.

She felt that same sick dread now, and found she couldn't sit inside the wagon. Nor could she sit patiently beside Jeremy and Nick. Particularly Nick, who had grown quiet again. He, like her, kept looking for a horseman on a bay horse.

Keep him safe, she found herself praying. Please keep him safe.

Dallas Terry slowed his horse, and Seth followed suit. After a day and night on the trail, there were almost back to the train, according to Dallas. No more than a couple of miles at the most, especially if Cliff Edwards had made the time he'd intended.

In the past thirty hours, they had traveled probably a total of forty-five, fifty miles, looking first for a good campsite for the next two nights and second for any sign of the Indians the army had told them about. So far, there had been none.

They were riding back to the wagon train from the north, making a sweeping movement. It was something with which Seth, after years in the army, was familiar.

But now it seemed that Dallas sensed something odd. He had been unusually tense during the past few minutes, almost as if he sensed danger. He was leaning over the side of the saddle, scrutinizing marks in the ground. Suddenly he dismounted and dropped to the ground, looking more closely at a scattering of tracks. "Unshod ponies," he said. "Not long passed."

"Cheyenne?"

Dallas shrugged. "I don't know. Could be Arapaho. Even Sioux, though they don't usually come this far south."

"How many?"

"'Bout ten ponies here, but that don't mean anything. Could be more around. Goddamned Chivington. Doc, you go back and warn Cliff. I'll scout on ahead, see if I can find any more tracks."

Seth hesitated, not liking the idea of Dallas going on alone. "I know how to use a rifle, if you're worried about that."

Dallas looked at him with amusement. "Doc, I didn't doubt that for a moment, or you wouldn't be with me. Cliff sizes up a man real well. I just think he should be warned. May be nothing at all. But then again..."

Still Seth hesitated, and then his attention turned to the left, to low hills dotted by grass. A flock of birds was rising, almost as one, up into the air.

"Christ," Dallas said, and swung back up on his horse

just as a group of horsemen suddenly appeared on the hill. No more words were necessary as they spurred their horses into a gallop and rode for their lives.

Seth soon realized they would not outrun their pursuers. They both had been riding most of the day, and their horses were tired. Sundance no longer had the speed and endurance he'd had before the war. He glanced around, and the riders behind were closing. His glance went to Dallas, just as his companion's horse stumbled and went down.

He whirled his own horse around and saw that Dallas had managed to jump free as the horse fell, an arrow in its side. Seth raced back and leaned down, offering a hand to Dallas, who swung up behind him. Seth made for a small hill to the right. He had his rifle out now, and as they reached the hill, both he and Dallas jumped down. Seth regretfully slapped the haunch of his horse, sending it racing away as he and Dallas fell down lengthwise on the ground.

Dallas had lost his rifle, but he had his pistol, and ammunition in his gun belt. Seth had a repeating rifle, his prize possession from the war, but the additional shells were in his saddlebags. Confederate General John Mosby himself had given him the rifle after Seth had rescued a wounded general. He hadn't used it in war, but he had hunted with it, and, like most Southerners, he was an excellent shot.

The Indians were almost on them when Seth and Dallas started firing. There were eleven of them, and Seth took aim at the leader. "I'll take the one in front," he said to Dallas. "He looks like the leader."

The scout nodded. "I'll try for him, too."

"Thought you trusted me," Seth said wryly.

Dallas grinned. "I do, but sometimes *I* miss. One of us might take him. Then you fire to the left, and I'll fire right."

Their guns exploded almost simultaneously, and the Indian fell as Seth found another target to the left and squeezed the trigger. The Indians were still coming—just a few feet away now—and both Seth and Dallas brought down the two riders directly in front of them. They hugged the side of the hill as the hoofs went around them, and then they turned, each taking aim at the back of one of the attackers.

The riders also turned, and a hail of arrows fell around them, along with a lance. Seth felt a burning sensation in his shoulder, and another in his side. He knew the gun was slipping from now-numb hands, and he felt a terrible sense of sad irony. Four years of war, and then, when he thought he was fleeing it at last....

"I'm sorry," he heard himself whisper to Dallas. I— Tell Kate..." But then waves of pain wiped away every conscious thought, and the earth went spinning around. He tried to keep his eyes open, but the sun was disappearing, and the light. And then the blackness was total, and he sank into oblivion.

Chapter Six

The sound of gunfire reached the wagon train, and Cliff immediately stopped the long line of wagons and told the men to prepare to circle the wagons.

There were too many shots, too close together, for anything but trouble. And Dallas and the doc were late. Edwards's instincts were all tingling.

He went from wagon to wagon, asking for a few volunteers and emphasizing that they were to be under his scout's command. They were not, under any circumstances, to instigate an attack unless it was necessary to save themselves or someone else.

Kate listened silently, her heart freezing with fear. She knew. She knew to the depth of her soul that something had happened to Seth Hampton. Dr. Hampton. The Rebel. She knew, and she was sick with the knowledge. She felt everything inside her clench into a hard knot.

"Sis?" Nick had moved next to her and was looking up anxiously at her. Kate couldn't answer; the words were locked in her throat.

Jeremy, who had been driving the wagon, looked toward her. "Can you handle things here? I want to go with the volunteers."

The Kate of several weeks ago would have objected. Not

Jeremy. Not Jeremy, who had struggled so desperately to get well, who had already seen too much war.

But this Kate couldn't. Let them live their own lives, Seth had said. *You have to let go.*

And she knew that she herself would volunteer if she thought she could be of any help. But she couldn't. She was a terrible rider and a worse shot, although she had tried to learn before they left Illinois. She would have to wait, and she knew it would be as hard as anything she had done in her life, as hard as the times when she had waited for others to return. She didn't know whether she could survive another loss.

So, her heart in her throat, she merely nodded at Jeremy, refraining even from saying "Be careful." He was a man who had fought a man's war.

"Do you suppose it's Seth?" Nick asked tensely.

"I don't know," she finally managed to say. For Nick. Only for Nick could she present a brave front, when inside she was trembling. "I hope not."

"But you don't even like him," Nick said, looking defiant and angry, his eyes tragically large and lost-looking.

"Yes, I do," she said, putting her hand on his shoulder. "In the beginning, perhaps I didn't. I didn't really know him then."

"I liked him even then," Nick said. "Even if he was a Rebel."

"I know," Kate said. "Sometimes you're very wise, you know?"

"I want to go with them."

"I do, too, Nick, but we would just slow them up."

"I want to do something."

"Why don't you carve him something?" she suggested. "He thinks you're very good, you know. He told me so. I think he would like to have something of yours."

If he comes back, and if he does, for when he leaves. A remembrance when he leaves. The trembling inside turned to sickness, a sickness that churned in an expanding pit of loss, of emptiness, of fear. *Oh, Seth. Stay alive. Go if you must, but please stay alive.*

Nick's face brightened slightly, and he disappeared inside the wagon to find a proper piece of wood.

As she started to guide the team of oxen into a circle, she watched as the volunteers rode off on horses provided by Cliff Edwards's remuda, the extra mounts brought along for the scouts and for hunting parties. Jeremy looked good in the saddle. Sure and strong and healthy. So different from when they had started this journey. Was it the trip? The dry weather? Or Dr. Seth Hampton, who had provided not only medicine, but hope, as well? She whispered a quiet prayer as they rode off.

Kate finished guiding the oxen into the circle, as they had already practiced doing several times. When she braked the wagon, she scrambled down from the seat and walked over to where Cliff Edwards stood, a growing group of travelers around him. Every man had a weapon at his side. So did some of the women.

Edwards was giving instructions to those who held guns. To the others, to the children and the other women, he gave alternate directions. His practical, unemotional voice was soothing.

"You, Miss MacAllister, can you take some of the children?"

Kate nodded.

"Play a game with them—keep them busy?"

Kate wondered whether he was also trying to keep her busy, to keep her from screaming, from running after Jeremy and Seth. She wondered whether her face showed all those things. But she only nodded and took six children whose parents held guns.

A story. That's what they need, she thought. She tried to remember back to her own childhood, to the cozy nights in the farmhouse when the family had gathered together, when her brothers had teased and played. As the only girl— the only sister—she had been spoiled shamefully by them, and by her mother and father, too. She had been wrapped in a cocoon of safety. When it was torn away, she had been so utterly naked and exposed.

So she had constructed a new barrier, so that the hurt wouldn't be so vulnerable to new wounds, one of resentment and anger. *Please come back, Seth. Please come back.*

A story! Think of a story. Don't think of Seth. You can't bear that now. She blinked back tears. Fairy tales. Fantasy. Happy endings. She needed all three now. She needed to believe in them. She had believed in so little for so long now.

She settled the children around her. "Once upon a time," she began, "there was a girl named Snow White...."

There was the sound of gunfire again in the distance. Kate's hand tightened around that of a small girl next to her as she continued the tale of the seven dwarfs.

She tried to keep her eyes from the plains, from the direction of the gunfire. She tried to keep them on the fidgeting children, who, despite the story, wore fear on their faces.

"And the prince leaned down and kissed Snow White, and slowly, so slowly, she opened her eyes...."

As she had. Seth had slowly brought her back to life again. Don't destroy it now, she prayed silently to God as her voice droned on with the remembered words of the fairy tale while her mind was someplace else. *Please keep him safe.*

Her head snapped up as she heard some shouts and looked out again. Horsemen were coming in, moving rapidly toward them. She tried to pick out a bay stallion, a golden head, among them, but she couldn't. And then she saw Seth's horse. It was running alongside the others, its saddle empty.

"No!" she found herself screaming, and she was up, ignoring the children for the moment as she ran toward the opening between the wagons.

And then she saw him. He was being held by Dallas

Terry in front of the scout's saddle. He was slumped over, his head bent, and she knew he was unconscious. Or dead.

The horsemen came straight to Cliff. Dallas helped lift Seth down to a group of standing men. Kate saw the broken ends of two arrows sticking from Seth's body.

Terry's jaw was tight. "Saved my life. He could have gotten away, but he came back for me when my horse went down. Damn fool."

Cliff looked over him. "He's still alive."

"Bleeding like a stuck pig, though," Dallas said.

"Indians?"

"A small band. What was left of them went skedaddling when they saw reinforcements. The doc here did pretty good with his gun."

As they were speaking, Cliff was checking the wounds. "Got to get those damned arrows out. Wish to God we had another doctor. I'll have to do it. Dallas, you heat a knife, make it two knives. We'll have to cauterize it. I can't sew like the doc here."

Kate stood frozen, looking at Seth's white face, then at the blood thickening and drying on his shirt and pants. She'd never noticed what long lashes he had, or how much he looked like a boy with his hair tousled and his eyes closed. But then, how would she have? She had banished him, over and over again. Her heart swelled with an anguish she thought she would drown in.

She knelt and took his motionless hand, the one that had such gentleness in it, and she tried to give to him some of her own strength. Live, she demanded silently. *Live!*

She sensed, rather than felt, Jeremy hovering next to her. And Nick. But then some men moved in and picked Seth up, carrying him over to the cook wagon, where a fire had already been started.

She wanted to do something. She had to do something. "Mr. Edwards, please, is there anything I can do?"

"Get his medical bag. We'll need chloroform. Thank God we have that."

Kate hurried off to do his bidding. She knew exactly where he kept it, along with the larger bag with additional medicines. She found it quickly and returned at a run.

His shirt was gone now, cut off, apparently so as not to disturb the arrow. His pants had also been lowered to show the second arrow. Blood seeped from both wounds.

She looked at Cliff. "Should I wash it?"

He nodded. "Pour whiskey around it, too. Dallas will get you some."

Someone handed her a bucket of water, someone else a cloth. Everyone was gathered around, concern written on their faces. Everyone was praying for him. She knew that as she looked from face to face. He had made himself a member of her family, but he had also apparently made himself a member of everyone's family.

Dallas, grief written all over his hard face, was also kneeling now as he handed Kate a bottle of whiskey. "Come on, Doc," Kate heard him saying. "Ain't no one died for me yet. Don't want that on my ledger, you hear me?"

But Seth didn't seem to be hearing anyone. Wake up, she wanted to scream at him. Don't do this to me. And then she realized what she had silently said. To me? Everything had been to her. Everyone had taken from him, herself most of all. No one, she thought, had reached out to him. Her hand took a cloth and gently, so very gently, cleaned the blood from around the two arrows. They were so ugly, those protruding pieces of wood that were draining the life away from Seth Hampton.

When the old blood was cleaned away, fresh blood continued to leak from the wounds. She took the bottle of whiskey and looked at Cliff Edwards. He nodded, encouraging her.

She hoped Seth would remain unconscious. She had seen alcohol poured on wounds before, knew the extreme pain involved, but she did it anyway, reluctantly. He didn't move, and she'd wished he had. He was so unfamiliarly still, all that restless energy quieted.

"Miss Kate?"

She looked up at Edwards in question. His expression was compassionate.

"You better move now."

"I want to stay."

"It won't be pleasant. I don't want a fainting woman on my hands."

"I won't faint," she said firmly, "and I've helped with calving."

"This ain't nothing like calving, Miss Kate," he warned.

"I'll stay," she insisted.

"Okay. I guess you're as much family as anyone. You think you can handle the chloroform?"

Kate nodded.

Cliff found the small bottle in the bag and handed it to her. "Do you have a handkerchief?"

Kate looked up, and Nick nodded, starting at a run for the wagon and returning in minutes with a white, lacy piece of cloth.

Cliff Edwards looked at her. "I don't know how much we'll need. But if he starts moving at all, pour a little more on the cloth. We can't afford him moving when I'm taking out the arrows."

"I understand," Kate said.

"You sure you want to do this? Dallas could do it."

"I'm sure," she said softly, her hand resting gently on Seth's shoulder. She owed him this, at least.

At Edwards's nod, she placed the handkerchief over Seth's nose and slowly poured chloroform on it. Cliff waited several moments, and then put his hands on the remaining shaft of the arrow, tugging it as gently as possible from Seth's shoulder. His face tightened with the effort as he tried to maneuver the arrow and the wound widened, pouring more blood across Seth's skin. If only the damned thing had gone through, then he could cut off the shaft and pull it out the back, but it hadn't, and he was afraid to push it through. God help him, he just didn't know enough to risk it.

Kate felt herself tense all over, and she struggled to keep her hand steady on his face, to keep from trembling and being banished from his side. For some reason, she thought Seth might want her there. She hoped so.

The arrow finally came out, along with a new rush of blood, and Cliff called for the knife. Clutching the hot handle in a piece of cloth, Dallas handed it to him.

Cliff looked at Kate. "Don't go soft on me now."

"I won't," she said. She steeled herself as Cliff touched the white-hot blade to the wound and she heard the sizzle of skin and smelled the sickening odor of burning flesh. The patient flinched without opening his eyes, and moaned.

"More chloroform."

Kate obeyed, pouring more of the precious liquid onto the cloth, hoping it wasn't too much. Her other hand was balled in a fist so tight she felt her short nails drawing blood as they dug into skin. She welcomed it. She wanted to hurt.

Cliff's hands were now moving to the arrow embedded in Seth's side. The wagon master's fingers were again carefully trying to withdraw the arrow head. Kate saw the worry on his face, and the care.

"Damn," Cliff muttered. "It doesn't want to come." He handed the knife he'd used to cauterize the wound to Dallas. "Try to hold the wound open," he ordered as he continued to twist and pull the shaft from Seth's body.

Kate was not even breathing now, as if by holding her breath she could pass on life to the man lying beneath her hands.

Cliff pulled again, the time roughly, and the arrow finally came out, accompanied by a river of blood.

Another knife was ready now, and Kate stiffened against the repeat of such an ugly sound and such a devastating smell. She poured another drop of chloroform on the cloth and found herself holding her breath again, her heart caught in her throat. "Please, please, please," she heard herself saying in a soft, crooning voice. She didn't know who she was saying it to.

The blood finally slowed. Her hands dropped from the chloroform and grabbed the towel, soaking it in the bucket still beside her and washing the blood away again. The skin around both wounds was black and raw and blistered, but the bleeding had stopped.

She looked at Cliff. His hands were trembling slightly now as he dropped the knife. He looked up, directly at her. "That, Miss Kate, is why I wanted a doctor along. Christ, I hate this. The doc could have done this so much better."

He stood. "We'll have to wait here a couple of days, anyway. We can't move him on one of those wagons, and I'm not going to leave him, not with those Indians around."

Everyone standing around knew what that meant. Cliff Edwards had said repeatedly they couldn't stop for any one person, yet that was exactly what he was saying now. And there was not a word of disagreement.

"I'll take care of him," Kate said. "Put him in our wagon."

"You'll need respite, Miss Kate. I'll help." Kate looked up at a woman she'd spoken to only briefly. "He helped my man when he broke his arm. Anything you need, you call, hear?"

"You send your brothers over to our tent to eat. We'll take good care of them," another woman said.

"You don't worry none 'bout fixing meals, Miss Kate. We'll bring them over," a third chimed in.

The offers kept coming, even as Dallas and several other men picked Seth up and carried him to the wagon, laying him down on the bed that Jeremy had occupied. She suddenly thought of Jeremy and looked up. He was standing there, nodding his approval.

"I'll sleep under the wagon."

"Me too," Nick said.

If Kate wasn't so preoccupied with Seth, she knew, she

would question Nick's sudden generosity. He had been wanting to sleep under the wagon with Seth almost from the first day the Reb had joined them. But now she just nodded. "Get me some water, Nick," she said.

Kate spent the remainder of the day next to Seth, washing away the sweat that beaded on his forehead, her hands calming him when he started thrashing against what must be excruciating pain. Cliff had said to leave the wounds exposed, but every time she looked at the raw, ugly wounds she wanted to cry. It was evening before he really woke. She had been watching for any movement, and there was the slightest flutter of eyelashes, and then his eyes, his beautiful green-blue eyes, opened slowly, their depths fogged with pain.

She leaned down. "Seth," she whispered. "Can you hear me?"

His eyes opened slowly, fixing on her. "Kate?"

"Yes."

"Pretty Kate," he whispered, and closed his eyes again. A muscle throbbed in his cheek, and Kate saw his fists clench against the side of the bed.

She wanted to do something for him, something more than she had, but all she could think of was taking his hand and holding it, letting his fingers press against hers until she thought the bones would break. Just when she thought she could no longer bear it, his fingers relaxed and his breathing softened.

As it grew dark, she lit a lantern. Cliff came by occasionally and spoke softly, taking a brief look at the patient. So did Dallas, his hat in hand. "Damned good man," he muttered as he stared at the patient, who was now turning restlessly in his sleep. "But a damn fool," he said, echoing his earlier words.

Kate felt something poignant surge through her. "He'll always be a damned fool," she said, cussing for the second time in her life, but in a voice that was almost a caress.

Jeremy brought her a plate of food and asked if she

needed to leave for a few moments to stretch her legs or something, but she couldn't even bear to do that. Not now. Not when he might wake again.

She leaned back against the barrels, as she had seen Seth do when he looked after Jeremy, and she thought of the hours he had spent with her brother, asking for nothing in return. How patiently he had borne her hostility.

She replenished her cloth with water and brushed it along his face, tracing the fine crinkles along his eyes, and laugh lines around his face, the tiniest suggestion of a dimple in one cheek. Now that she thought about it, she knew she hadn't seen him laugh, not really, in all the weeks she had known him. Yet she instinctively knew that that mouth had once laughed often and richly. She wanted to hear it now. She wanted it more than she'd ever wanted anything in her life.

She brushed the blond hair back, remembering how rich it looked in the sun. Now it was damp and darkened by dirt and sweat. The usual sheen, the usual life, was gone from it.

Kate suddenly realized she didn't even know how to reach his family if anything happened. Someplace in Virginia. A brother. No one else. She remembered the terrible sense of aloneness she'd felt in him.

If anything happened? It couldn't happen. She wouldn't let it. She entwined her fingers with his, entwining her life with his. He might not want that. He probably wouldn't. Not now. But she would give him what she could. She didn't realize she was crying until she felt the wetness on her arm.

"Live, Rebel mine. Live." She heard her own harsh, insistent whisper. She heard it, and she felt the painful tightness behind her eyes, that denseness of immense grief as tears welled at a greater speed than could be released.

She heard herself whisper the same litany again, and the tears fell unrelieved. She had cried for her family and for herself the other night; he had helped her wash away so much of the loss and guilt. But now she was crying for him, for his losses, for everything he had borne so steadfastly, for the loneliness she had seen in him and ignored. She cried for all of it. But now there was no comfort. None at all.

Chapter Seven

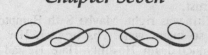

The night passed agonizingly slowly. Kate left Seth's side for only a few minutes to relieve herself. By dawn, he was alternately clammy and burning up with fever. She frantically searched his two bags for books on what to do. She finally found one that suggested, in the event of inflammation, the use of warm water or wet dressings "to encourage suppuration."

But she didn't know whether those treatments were right for a case like Seth's. Any touch resulted in his body reacting violently, even when he was unconscious. And he didn't regain consciousness for her to ask.

She sent Nick for Cliff Edwards, and together she and the wagon master huddled over the patient. The immediate area around the shoulder wound was reddish-purple, surrounded by a wider ring of red than earlier.

Seth was muttering, thrashing, much as he had during his nightmare weeks ago, and Kate knew that once more he was reliving horrors she could only imagine. But this time she wasn't able to wake him. She told Cliff about that night and watched as his eyes clouded.

"He drove himself too hard. These wounds shouldn't ordinarily kill someone, but I suspect he's worn out. Damn, he has to fight, and from what you told me, maybe he won't—maybe he doesn't want to.''

"He does," Kate argued fiercely. "He never gives up. He told me that." But he had, she knew. He had given up on her. She knew that was why he'd kept disappearing, why he'd gone with Dallas, why he had planned on leaving the wagon train, because he had never received anything from her but distrust.

Maybe Cliff was right. Maybe Seth Hampton was tired of fighting so many wars. His brother. Her. How many others? So much death. Hostility. Hate. He had fought them all with that same determinedly decent stubbornness of his. She had seen it that night he'd had the nightmare, had glimpsed the hell he was still carrying with him. And he had done nothing to help him, to even try to understand. She'd been too concerned with her own ghosts.

"Anyway," she said, "I'm not going to let him give up." She shook him gently, calling to him insistently. "Seth. Seth, you have to wake up. Seth."

She washed his face, then started calling him again. "Seth." The name sounded fine on her lips, as if it belonged there. Why hadn't she realized it earlier?

"Seth…"

He quieted, then opened his eyes. Their usual deep green-blue was hazy with pain. His gaze moved around, obviously trying to focus. He moved slightly, groaning as the pain struck him with renewed fury. Then his gaze found Kate.

"You're…still here?"

"Seth, listen to me. I have to know what to do. You have to help us, Cliff and I."

"Cliff…"

"He took the arrows out, cauterized the wounds—"

"That's why—" He didn't finish the sentence, and the words disintegrated into a sound that was almost a whistle, a sound that would have been a moan coming from anyone else. His eyes closed.

"Seth, there seems to be infection. Tell us what to do. Don't go away again. Don't go away."

His eyes opened again. He gave her a twisted effort at a smile. It nearly broke her heart, or what was left of it.

"Take more than an arrow to...kill me. Poultices. Warm water with tannic acid."

"Acid?"

He nodded.

"But—"

"But it will hurt like hell," he said in answer to her unspoken question, before he closed his eyes against the pain again. "Opium. Hypodermic syringe. In small bag...marked. Better than chloroform. I'll stay awake."

"How much?"

He tried a weak grin again, but it came out as more of a grimace. His eyes found Cliff. "We're not moving?"

"We've stopped overnight."

Seth looked around at the light flooding the wagon. "You're a liar, Cliff."

Cliff looked uncomfortable. "We took a vote."

"Damn, you need...to keep moving. Winter. Snow." He tried to move. "Oh, Christ," he muttered hoarsely, his eyes closing again. It was obvious that even that small effort had renewed the agony.

Kate had already moved away, peering into the bag and finding what he'd described. She had to keep him awake long enough to help her.

"Seth? Seth?" She knew the will it must have taken for him to surface again. His eyes opened.

"How much of the acid...and the opium? Where do I use the—" she looked at the needle "—this?" How could she ever do it, knowing so little?

"In arm...muscle," he whispered. "Just fill until I... shake my head."

She did as he ordered, looking doubtfully at the needle when he nodded. And then his body started shivering, almost convulsing, and his eyes closed as he slipped back into unconsciousness. She looked at Cliff.

"I don't think we have any choice, Miss Kate. You want me to do it?"

She did. She did with all her heart. Yet Seth had showed her, had trusted her. She owed him this. Hadn't she just told herself she would keep him alive? She shook her head and stuck the needle in a muscle in his elbow, concentrating with all her might.

In minutes, his breathing seemed to come easier, more regular. Cliff had ordered some hot water, and together they prepared the solution and dabbed it on the cloth, making a poultice and applying it to the shoulder wound. She winced as she did so, afraid, so afraid, that she would deepen his pain. If not now, then later.

But she wouldn't let him die.

Aided by the opium, Seth slept during the early hours of the day, while Jeremy kept watch, demanding that Kate get some rest. She wouldn't be good for anyone if she didn't, he argued, and he would wake her if there was any change.

The horses and oxen were fed. Scouts roamed the area, but there was no sign of the Indians. Cliff Edwards used the time to require everyone, including women, to do some practice shooting. They could replenish their ammunition at Fort Walker. It was already August now, and they needed to get through the mountains by the first of October.

But he wasn't going to leave a man who had saved the life of one of his scouts.

If he wasn't feeling so damnably pushed, he would have been bemused by Miss Kate and the doc. He should have known from the beginning that part of her hostility was due to her attraction to the Southerner. She had visibly softened during the trip, had dropped some of the reserve that distinguished her in the beginning. And yet, when everyone else had succumbed to the Southerner, she had seemed to cling to her prejudices.

But he knew love when he saw it, even if he personally had never suffered from that particular disease. And he had certainly witnessed it in the past several hours in the way Kate MacAllister had touched the patient, the way she had looked at him. If the doc survived these wounds...

He had seen enough of Kate MacAllister to know not to underestimate her unbending determination.

He grinned. The doc wouldn't dare die. He just wouldn't. And Cliff Edwards would bet his last bag of beans that Dr. Seth Hampton would accompany them all the way to the Sacramento Valley.

The path to that decision should be most interesting. He would also bet his last pouch of tobacco on that.

Seth woke to a sea of pain. He felt as if he were drowning in it. It was all he remembered—the pain. Pain and shadows. So many shadows. His head felt full of oatmeal, or something else much less benign. Like the devil's pitchforks.

He tried to move, but pain racked him. His shoulder was on fire, and another kind of pain, a sharp thrust that seemed to go through him, tormented the whole left side of his body. His mouth felt as if it were stuffed with cotton. His general condition, he thought, diagnosing himself, was something less than miserable.

He barely remembered an insistent voice calling his name when all he wanted was blackness. Sweet oblivion. Oblivion from the agonizing pain that burned through him, from the nightmares, from the certainty that there was no such thing as peace for him.

And then he had felt her hands, gentle yet unsure. He recalled the look in her eyes as she demanded from him his own cure, the intensity of her expression as she insisted he get well. Or was it his own imagination, the lunatic delusion of a sick man?

He tried to focus his eyes. Kate MacAllister was slumped beside him, her eyes closed, her face exhausted, her dress wrinkled. Her cheeks were smudged, as if a child's fist had rubbed tears away. But if there had been tears, they couldn't have been for him. She wouldn't cry for a man she called a Rebel, for a man she partly blamed for the destruction of her family.

She was so pretty, even with that smudged face. Maybe even prettier than when her hair was so neatly tied at her neck and her face was scrubbed clean. Tenderness crept into his soul, pushing away some of the pain. She looked this way because of him, because she must...care, or she would have given him over to someone else.

If anyone else had wanted him.

Maybe that was it. Maybe no one else would take the Rebel, and she felt responsible. That infernal responsibility of hers, that core of strength that kept her going, that had kept what was left of her family going. Jeremy! How was Jeremy? He was in Jeremy's bed.

But he couldn't wake her to ask. She looked so exhausted. How long had it been? Opium. He remembered that. He remembered the acid. That was why he burned the way he did, while the pain in his side was more like scissors slicing through him. Jeremy. Where was Jeremy? And Nick? He moved, and waves of new agony swept over him as he tried fruitlessly to reason.

Indians. Dallas. What had happened to Dallas? But Dallas was alive. He remembered seeing him, far away through a haze. Or was that a dream? The Indians were coming at them. The wagon was swirling again, just as it had before. And he was hot. So hot. But the Indians were still coming. "Kate," he cried out frantically. And then, "I'm sorry," he said through clenched teeth as he was slung back into the maelstrom of his nightmares.

"*I'm sorry.*" The low words woke Kate, pierced her consciousness with their anguish. She wasn't even sure she'd heard the words, or understood. She just had the impression of infinite sadness. How long had she been asleep? He had moved. She saw that much. He was still hot—

but not as hot, perhaps, as this morning, though she wasn't sure—and the splash of red on his shoulder had not spread.

She pushed back some ringlets of hair that had escaped the convenient braid and glanced down at her dress. It was stained with blood and the tannic-acid solution. But she didn't dare stir for fear of waking him. Twenty-four hours. It had been more than twenty-four hours.

A knock came at the back of the wagon, and she said softly, "Yes?"

It was Nick, a pot in his hand. He glanced down at Seth. "Still asleep?" He was whispering now as he handed the pot to Kate. "Some broth Mrs. Cochran sent over. How is he?"

"I don't know," she said softly, hearing her own desperation and wanting to control it. God knew Nick had enough heartaches in his young life. He didn't need another.

But her own desperation was impossible to control. She had feared she couldn't bear loss again, so she had built a shell of iron around herself. But it had split open. Seth Hampton had split it open, and she no longer had any protection.

She reached out and touched him, the heat of his body flowing into hers, and she suddenly realized she was glad that shell had split open. Whatever happened now, she had been awakened. It was like the story of Snow White. She was feeling again, just as deeply as she knew Seth Hampton had felt. She had known it from the evening he'd had that nightmare, and again that evening he'd comforted her when she had cried. She'd even known it before that, the way he cared for Jeremy and saved Nick's life. He cared about everyone. Not about the color of their uniforms or their politics or their prejudices, but about the person inside.

And she was learning to do the same, as he had forced her to do. She swallowed, cherishing the simple connection of her skin to his.

He moved slightly, as if, in some way, he felt that connection, too. His eyes opened, focused slowly and settled on her, a slow smile appearing that went straight to the core of her heart. It was so tentative, so strained, as if he were forcing it for her sake rather than his own.

"You...look tired," he said. "Have you been here—"

"Since you were wounded," Nick broke in, and he grinned as Seth's gaze moved to him. "I brought you some soup. Mrs. Cochran made it."

Seth had never felt less like eating—less able to eat—but he forced his smile to widen. "Thank you." And then he remembered his last thoughts, which were still wandering disjointedly in his head. "Jeremy?"

Kate frowned. "Jeremy is much better than you."

A small particle of light came into his eyes. "I don't think that's...much of a recommendation for my doctoring skills."

"Or mine," Kate said wryly. "How do you feel, or is that a ridiculous question?"

He moved again, and she saw him wince, his smile disappearing. She picked up the cloth and wet it, then wiped his face. When she finished, her hand fell naturally to his and he took it, his fingers almost crushing hers as he seemed to fight a wave of pain. Then his fingers slowly relaxed.

"Dallas?"

"He escaped without any injury—except guilt."

His brow furrowed in an unspoken question.

"He feels responsible. Says 'nobody ain't never died for me before,'" she said with a smile as she tried to imitate the scout. "'Don't want it on my ledger.'" *Or mine, either.*

"I'll try not to be the first," Seth said.

"He'll appreciate that." She hesitated. "So will I."

He moved his left hand—the one unhampered by injury—up to her face, and trailed a smudge where a tear had fallen. "Tears?"

"I was worried about you."

"I'm indestructible. My brother told me that once."

"I wish he, or you, had told *me*." She allowed his fingers to continue their path before his hand fell to his side. "Do you think you can eat? Everyone in the wagon train wants to cook something for you."

Seth looked surprised.

"You've made a lot of friends," she said, a little shyly. "I had to fight to keep you."

Seth raised an eyebrow. At least that answered one question, and the answer was a surprise. "A Rebel?"

"A Rebel," she confirmed. "Now, about that food..."

He didn't eat much, just a few mouthfuls of broth, before he sank back, exhausted. He closed his eyes, and she started to back away. "Don't go," he said.

She didn't. Instead, she gave him her hand and held it until once more he fell asleep, this time peacefully.

Chapter Eight

The wagon train resumed its pace the next afternoon. Seth insisted, claiming he knew how much his body could stand. His face had regained some color, and the swelling and redness were receding. The wounds, which he said should remain open to the air, looked ugly and raw, and Kate knew he was still in a great deal of pain and would suffer even more in the jolting wagon.

Their wagon took the lead again so that dust wouldn't get into his wounds. Kate stayed next to him, feeling every jolt, hurting herself as she watched him trying to hide the pain she knew he felt. To try to take his mind from it, she asked him questions, about Virginia and his family.

He gave her a weak grin when he said he came from "a long line of divided families." He and his brother had been nothing new.

"My grandmother's father was a Tory," he said, "and my grandfather a patriot. Her father killed his father's brother and burned his home and sent him to a prison ship. My grandmother didn't approve, and ran off to join Francis Marion, the Swamp Fox, in protest." He grinned. "I hear there were some fiery times.

"And then her daughter, my mother, who was a fervent

American, fell in love with a British raider who captured her brother's ship during the War of 1812.''

"But..."

He looked at her, that wry, twisted smile on his face. "You don't understand how that can happen, do you? How hearts have loyalties all of their own?" There was no question in his tone, only a resigned statement.

Seth continued slowly. "They each had a very strong love for each other, a stronger commitment than most. And fierce loyalty to each other. Perhaps because they went through so much together—and apart. I envied them that commitment, that love, that loyalty that surpassed everything else."

But as he spoke, the light seem to fade from his vivid sea-colored eyes, and Kate felt as if it had gone from her soul, too. She knew what he wanted, what he demanded: unreserved, unqualified acceptance.

She had thought she was giving it, yet he'd obviously sensed something in her that she hadn't even realized. How do you suddenly give up five years of anger? Of hate? It was like his wound, it took time to heal, and though she'd thought she had healed, he knew she hadn't. Not completely. And that total healing, she knew, was the only thing he would, could, accept.

They arrived at Fort Walker six days later. Seth was walking a little now. He had pulled on a shirt for their arrival, even though Kate knew it hurt him to feel anything close to his skin.

But nothing could hurt as much as the emptiness that filled her. He would be leaving now. He'd told her last night.

It had been after Nick so tentatively handed him the carving of Sundance, the horse's head held so proudly. Seth had taken it slowly, almost reverently. "It's beautiful, Nick," he said. "Thank you."

Nick had hesitated a moment, then said. "You are going on with us, aren't you?"

Seth had just shook his head. "I think I have a few days of recovery to go. It will be better accomplished at Fort Walker." Kate had known he was protecting her, just as he protected everyone. He hadn't wanted Nick to know she was the reason. But *she* knew.

There was a dance that night on the parade field, under a full moon, with lanterns providing additional light. It was the dance the young lieutenant had promised, and he was there. So was Seth, though he only watched. His arm was strapped to his body to keep it from pulling against the shoulder, and she'd offered to shave him, an act that could have been a disaster, since her hand shook so. Her whole body had gone weak at the intimacy of the act, at touching him, at being so close to him.

Seth looked relaxed as everyone from the wagon train stopped to tell him how much he would be missed, how they wished he would continue with them.

Kate noted the easy way he deflected the requests, even as his eyes warmed at their concern and their obvious affection. He smiled, and Kate knew a rare pleasure that sliced through her like a knife. She had never seen that smile before, and it was breathtaking, like the first sun in the morning.

She knew then that she had to have that sun, that she would do anything to hold on to those rays. And in that moment she felt them replace the last vestige of bitterness that remained in her.

She loved him! The knowledge was sure and shattering. She realized she had loved him for a long time, and now she wondered whether she hadn't fought it so hard not only because of her family, but also because she was afraid of another loss, another death.

Dear heaven, she had come so close to losing him to death, and now she realized how precious any time with him would be, so precious that she could no longer live in the shadows, afraid to love, to care, to live, when he was offering so much light.

She turned down the offer of a dance from the young lieutenant and walked over to Seth, holding out her hand.

"Will you take a walk with me?"

It was almost like the time midway through their journey, when he had asked her on a walk she hadn't wanted to take. And now she sensed *his* reluctance.

"Please," she said.

Seth looked at her searchingly and then took her hand. They walked away from the circle of merrymakers to the edge of the fort, where sentries stood watch. "Best not go beyond this," Seth said.

There simply was no place to be alone. And Kate knew she had to be alone with him. She looked around and finally spied a sign that read Chapel, and she knew that was what she'd been seeking.

The chapel was small and quiet and simple, with only a small cross on a podium. The glow from the moon and lanterns filtered in the windows, sending sprays of pale light dancing along the walls. The music from the dance was dim now, its gaiety a counterpoint to the silent dignity within.

Kate turned to him. "Please come with us to California, Seth."

"Why?" he asked simply.

Kate swallowed. So much was at stake. She had to find the right words. So she chose the only ones. "I love you."

He stilled, his gaze boring into hers. "Because of Jeremy? Nick? I don't want gratitude, Kate."

She bit her lip. "I'm not offering gratitude."

"I'm still a Southerner. I can't, won't, take back, or regret, anything I was or did."

"I know," she said softly. "And I don't want you to change. I want everything you are."

The green-blue of his eyes seemed to deepen, even as a glimmer of light shone there.

"Kate, you have to be sure. You have to be sure you will never look at me and see your brothers, or your father or...the man you almost married. I can't—I won't—live with reservations."

Kate stared into the strong face that she had grown to love so much. "I finally understand," she whispered, "what you meant when you said hearts have a loyalty of their own." And she did. His heart was the truest she'd ever known, so loyal to what he thought was good and right. It was hers that had failed.

"I need you," she said.

"I like want better," he said, a grin beginning to break the severe lines of his face.

"That, too," she said breathlessly.

"Ah, Kate," he said, "I didn't think you would ever say that. If I didn't think we would both go tumbling down, I would carry you away this minute."

She looked at him. Did he mean what she thought he meant? "Does that mean you'll go with us?"

"Only if you'll marry me," he said, his eyes creasing with a pleasure that gave his face even more depth, more distinction. Dear God, how she loved him! How could she have been so blind for so long?

"Yes," she said simply, with a joy that filled every ounce of her, that made her want to sing and dance and shout. How very good it felt. How magnificent. She didn't understand why he loved her, but she was ready now to accept it with every fiber of her being. With all the loyalty in the heart that she was learning to use better.

His smile widened, but there was still a certain hesitancy. "Will your brothers approve?"

"You've already won Nick's soul," she said.

"And Jeremy?"

Kate was honest. "I don't know. Jeremy doesn't say much."

Seth raised an eyebrow, and she knew he was thinking it was a trait that ran in the family.

"And if he doesn't?" He waited patiently.

"I'll be disappointed, but it won't make a difference."

Seth looked down and smiled again. "I love you, Miss MacAllister, my lovely Kathryn Mary," he said in that soft Southern drawl that seeped into her consciousness like warm honey. The same drawl she'd hated at first, and now wanted to hold on to forever. He didn't wait for an answer, but leaned down and kissed her. He had kissed her before. Tentatively. Searchingly. Even tenderly. But this was different.

She felt the difference to the core of her being, where the first tingling of her femininity started doing marvelous things to her whole body. His lips were gentle, but now there was assurance in them, a wonderful assurance, even though only one of his arms circled her body.

Kate was careful of his shoulder even if, for the moment, he seemed to have forgotten it. She thought how amazingly creative one could be when one had a mind to be so. She lifted up on her tiptoes, avoiding touching those raw parts of him, and yet passion made itself felt. It fairly strummed between them, like a telegraph wire strung tight between two poles.

It thrummed and reverberated and sang its own perfect song. Perfect except for the way she wanted all of him close to her, so close that she would never fear to lose him again. The barely restrained passion, out of necessity, turned instead to promise, a promise of things to come. Kate could scarcely wait.

Neither, apparently, could he. With a lightness she'd never seen in him before, he grabbed her hand, holding it tight. "Let's go find a minister," he said, with a grin that reached to his eyes. The dimple she had noticed during his illness deepened, and she wondered how she could ever have denied that face.

She knew only one thing. She would never do it again.

The wedding took place the next day, as final repairs were made on the wagons by the fort blacksmith. Everyone from the wagon train was present, beaming with approval. Several of the women had even provided quickly put-together wedding attire, one offering her own dress, another a veil. An army chaplain said the words, and Jeremy gave away the bride. With pleasure, he had told Seth. With a great deal of pleasure. And relief that Kate had finally come to her senses, he'd added with a grin that broke the usual solemnity of his face.

War, he'd said to her later, and in private, brought out the worst and the best in men. It ruined some. He'd seen that happen in Andersonville to men in both uniforms. He'd also seen the way some, again in both uniforms, rose to nobility. It wasn't the uniform that mattered, but the man inside it.

Nick stood as Seth's best man, and then he ran off to see his puppy, which had been born that morning. Seth had grinned at the abrupt departure, observing with a lustful gleam that he and Kate probably didn't have to worry about Nick being around much during their honeymoon.

As Kate repeated her wedding vows, she felt a peace she'd never known before, a wonderful sense of belonging and rightness. She knew then with certainty that her own wounds were completely healed—even the scars were nearly gone. What was left were good memories, the kind to keep and cherish.

Seth had taught her to cherish the good things. He had taught her so much. She looked at him, her heart swelling with love as he made his vows, his gaze intent on her. His face was relaxed in a way she hadn't seen before, his eyes alight in the way she knew they were meant to be. That craggy face, with its compassion, had always been attractive to her, but now he was incredibly handsome, with that smile that was no longer wistful, but wide and open and happy. His voice was so sure, so deep and rich as he said the words that made him hers forever. Her Rebel. Her stubborn Rebel, who would always go the way of his conscience, whether it was against the wind or not.

She loved him for that now. It had taken her a long time to understand how rare it was, how infinitely precious. She knew it would not always be easy. His conscience would not always coincide with hers, but she also knew how totally empty her life would be without him. She would learn to compromise, although not always to agree. And he, he'd said last night, would not want her to.

When the words were finished, he leaned over. "Mrs. Hampton," he said, "I love you." And then his lips touched hers with a gentleness that turned quickly, as it always did, into something much more violent, until the sound of titters finally penetrated. He gave her a "just wait" look, full of lechery, and she gave him a private but nonetheless promising smile in return.

Because of his wounds, the consummation of their marriage had to wait, although Kate thought she would die from wanting him so badly. They lay together at night, treasuring the closeness and the marvelous kisses as their bodies grew tense with anticipation.

Ten days after the ceremony, when they stopped for the night, Seth disappeared. He had been driving the wagon, while Jeremy had taken to riding Sundance and hanging out in Cliff Edwards's wagon to give them a little privacy. Nick slept quite happily under the wagon.

They had stopped earlier that night, coming to a halt before crossing another river. Seth had pulled their wagon off a little into the trees, where it stood alone, and then had disappeared on some errands after taking care of the oxen. Jeremy and Nick had also disappeared. She also noticed that everyone was looking at her a bit oddly—a smile here, a smirk there.

A summons came from Mrs. Cochran, and Kate hurried to the Cochrans' wagon, afraid that something had happened to Nick, but he was busy demonstrating his carving

skills to young Edie. Kate looked at the carving and smiled;
it was a puppy on its back, a bewildered look on its clown-
ish face. Obviously nothing was wrong with Nick. He
looked happier than he had in years.

She looked askance at Sally Cochran, who seemed in-
ordinately pleased with herself. "We were hoping Nick
could stay with us tonight."

Kate nodded, though she was puzzled. He had stayed
there before during the past few days, unwilling to leave
the pup. Or was it the little Cochran girl? Even at eleven?
Kate understood now.

"Here," Sally Cochran said, thrusting something into
her hands. "Something special for dinner tonight. Don't
look now," she admonished as Kate started to do just that.

When she returned, Seth was there. So was a table that
had mysteriously appeared, covered with a lace tablecloth
from someone's store of treasures, a bottle of wine from
someone else's, and a number of other delicacies. With a
sweep of his arm, Seth seated her as if she were royalty,
and from the distance came a lovely, romantic tune from a
fiddle.

Except for Seth, everyone had disappeared—almost by
magic, she thought with a smile. Or a conspiracy of wonderfully tender proportions.

Seth looked a little embarrassed, his eyes crinkling in the
most delightful way. "I asked the Cochrans to invite Nick
tonight, and Mrs. Cochran said something to someone, and
it seemed everyone thought…well, it might be a special
occasion or something." He didn't have to say any more.
Gossip always passed up and down the wagons like wild-
fire.

Kate knew she, too, should feel embarrassed, but she
didn't. There was so much affection in the offerings, so
much thoughtfulness. She loved the pleasure that shone in
his eyes even as he apparently worried about her reaction.

"It's almost like those medieval days—" she giggled

"—when they carried the groom up to the bride and tossed him in her bed."

"Hmm... I like that picture," he said.

"But without an audience," she chided.

"Just us." His eyes twinkled as Seth and Kate closed out everyone else and wrapped themselves in a world all their own.

Serenaded by an unseen fiddle joined occasionally by a harmonica, they ate slowly, their eyes feasting on another kind of delicacy altogether. Each other. Hands touched, lips smiled, eyes made promises. When they were through, Seth took her hand, and she knew it was finally time. Their time. He had declared himself well, and the entire wagon train population was signaling their approval of this odd match in their own separate, giving ways.

Kate knew that the old Kate would have been embarrassed. Obviously everyone knew what was going to happen this night. But she wasn't. She was profoundly moved that so many people cared so much. She guessed she would get used to it—with Seth as her husband.

Once in the wagon, they undressed slowly. The faint light of a part moon filtered through the canvas, but their silhouettes were visible only to them, thanks to the privacy of the surrounding trees. He helped her first and then she him, her hands touching his scars with tenderness.

But then those memories left as he kissed her, and there was only this moment, this wonderful, glorious moment. He was so beautiful in his lean masculinity. She gave him her hand, and smiled as he looked at her slowly, and very approvingly. And then they came together. They were still standing, each one's form felt and admired and loved by the other. Her hands ran up and down his side, and then he pulled one hand around to his back and drew her snugly against him, giving her a chance to get used to him, to the now-hard man part of him.

Kate had thought she'd known desire before, especially during those special times with him, but that had been nothing like the hunger rising in her now—the wanting, demanding tingling of every nerve and every sense in her body. She fitted herself closer to him, and their kiss deepened into a maelstrom of yearning.

Seth felt her body tremble with response and it fueled a hunger so strong he couldn't wait any longer. He picked her up and laid her down on the bed, running his hands over her body, memorizing it even though he knew it was his, now and always. So slender. So fragile and yet so strong. His hands met hers once more, and he felt her wondering longing in them, so shyly eager, so unafraid. This was the Kate he'd loved almost from the beginning, the Kate he'd always known existed. He moved his lips down to the hollow of her neck, caressing, exciting, and then farther down, to her breasts. He nuzzled them, licking until the nipples stood stiffly in their own need.

She held both hands out to him, drawing him to her. He felt her trembling turn to a kind of quivering, and he knew it was time. Seth controlled himself as much as possible. Slowly, go slowly. Gently. He was rigid now with his own need, and it took all his will to control it as he lowered himself, teasing her until her whole body arched toward him in instinctive, needy response. He entered her, feeling that fragile barrier, yet holding her tight against the pain he knew would come. But she wouldn't have his hesitancy, he sensed. With the same will and determination that she brought to everything, she arched against him once more, and he lost control, plunging into her with a need he now knew she shared.

There was the smallest cry on her part, and then no more. "Oh, Seth," she whispered in awe as little explosions of ecstasy followed each other like waves in a stormy sea, each tossing her up and then plunging her into depths of emotions and sensations she had never known existed. Her body caught his rhythm and she instinctively moved with him, then against him, as they hurried toward some irresistible beckoning peak, and then *it* happened, the indescribable, unexplainable zenith that exploded the world into spectacular pieces of floating sunbeams and star bursts. Shock waves of rapture rocked her very being as she opened her eyes and met his, eyes that were so bright and warm and loving. "I love you," she whispered. "Dear God, how I love you."

And then neither of them could speak as the sensations continued, their bodies quivering with the incredibly sweet joy of joining, of loving—of sharing the same rumblings of pleasure that kept alive and simmering the past few glorious moments.

He held her then, and she remembered what he had said days ago about his parents and grandparents. *Because they went through so much...they had a very strong love for each other. Hearts have a loyalty of their own.*

She had thought she understood before, but not as much as she did now. And when she looked up at him, she knew he saw everything she was thinking.

His kiss, no longer wistful, but very, very possessive, told her so. Her Rebel would probably always keep going against the wind, but she would always be there with him, fighting it. Joining him in their own mighty storm.

Wind and storm. Sunsets and sunrises. He was all of those. And because of him, she was, too.

*   *   *   *   *

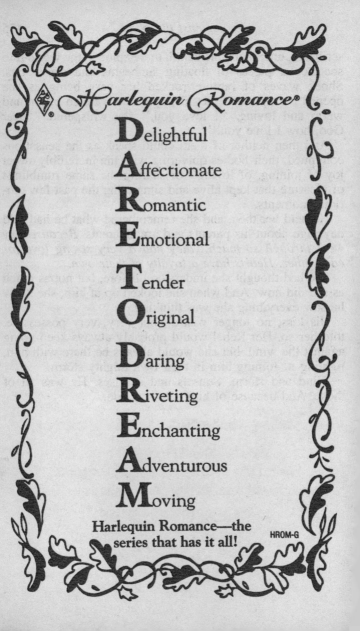

HARLEQUIN PRESENTS®

The world's bestselling romance series...
The series that brings you your favorite authors,
month after month:

Helen Bianchin...Emma Darcy
Lynne Graham...Penny Jordan
Miranda Lee...Sandra Morton
Anne Mather...Carole Mortimer
Susan Napier...Michelle Reid

and many more uniquely talented authors!

Wealthy, powerful, gorgeous men...
Women who have feelings just like your own...
The stories you love, set in exotic, glamorous locations...

HARLEQUIN PRESENTS,
Seduction and passion guaranteed!

Visit us at www.eHarlequin.com

HPGEN00

...there's more to the story!

Superromance.
A *big* satisfying read about unforgettable
characters. Each month we offer *six* very different
stories that range from family drama to adventure
and mystery, from highly emotional stories to
romantic comedies—and much more! Stories
about people you'llbelieve in and care about.
Stories too compelling to put down....

Our authors are among today's *best* romance
writers. You'll find familiar names and talented
newcomers. Many of them are award winners—
and you'll see why!

If you want the biggest and best
in romance fiction, you'll get it
from Superromance!

Available wherever Harlequin books are sold.

Visit us at www.eHarlequin.com